Evil Agreement

by

Richard L. Hatin

To Chantal
Enjoy!
Richard L. Hatin

Publisher Page
an imprint of Headline Books, Inc.
Terra Alta, WV

Evil Agreement

by Richard L. Hatin

copyright ©2012 Richard L. Hatin

To order additional copies of the book, or to contact the author:

Headline Books, Inc.
P O Box 52
Terra Alta, WV 26764

www.HeadlineBooks.com

ISBN-13: 978-0-938467-33-5

Library of Congress Control Number: 2012939308

Hatin, Richard L.
Evil Agreement
    p. cm.
    ISBN 978-0-938467-33-5
1. Thriller-Fiction 2. Mystery-Fiction 3. Religion-Fiction 4. Satanic Ritual-Fiction

To my best friend and wife Anne,
with whom all things are possible!

1

A large number of cars and small pick up trucks began to converge from several directions. They slowly merged into a procession of over seventy vehicles traveling east along the dirt road that paralleled the south bank of the Winooski River here in north central Vermont.

It was just after 1:00 a.m. in the morning. After traveling eastward for a little over three miles, the line of vehicles turned southward onto another dirt road. At the intersection two men armed with shotguns stood guard. Once the last vehicle had driven by, they pulled a wooden gate closed. They next padlocked it to prevent anyone from following. They went to their truck and soon joined up with all the other vehicles.

This narrow and winding dirt road would last for nearly a mile. The vehicles kicked up a dusty cloud that nearly obscured the driver's view of the road. Everyone was driving with only their parking lights on. No one was using their headlights.

Suddenly several young men with flashlights waved the vehicles to pull over and park. They began to park in the field next to the Game Warden's house while other vehicles pulled to the side of the road and came to a stop. Everyone exited their vehicles. Entire families stood together in the road. The ages ranged from eight months old to ninety-one. There was very little conversation between the assembled, only an occasional muffled greeting.

Many of the people had brought along flashlights or lanterns. A few had homemade torches. Soon the flashlights and lanterns were turned on with the torches saved for later.

The crowd, numbering close to two hundred, began to slowly move further southward along the dirt road. The sound of a bubbling small brook once known as the Sutton River could be heard as it passed the left side of the road. After traveling for another few hundred yards the crowd turned to their left and crossed over the brook by way of a wooden bridge. Now there was no longer a dirt road to follow. There were only two rutted tire tracks worn into the side of the mountain. This pathway was suddenly a much steeper climb.

No one complains about the hiking conditions, or the lateness of the hour. They are all familiar with what is to be expected.

A few of the travelers steal a glance at one another as they silently climb the mountain.

Tonight there will be a sacrifice. There is always a sacrifice. It has been this way since the 1840's.

Blood will be spilled. This is a necessary part of their "Malum Pactum," Evil Agreement. The ritual will be kept alive by a dark offering. A promise made long ago is still a promise to be kept.

Their ancestors had once been part of a coven that made a pact with Moloch, one of Satan's lieutenants. The coven, originally formed in 1843, made a solemn promise to Moloch to perform a special one-time ritual and sacrifice to invite Satan to life on earth, to rule over them.

Something went horribly wrong and the coven failed in keeping its Evil Agreement.

Ever since, the coven and their descendants have repeatedly journeyed back up this mountain to offer human sacrifice to Moloch and Satan, and to renew their vows to keep their promise, and complete the demanded invitation ceremony to Satan.

The large group of people finally arrived at their destination. They were nearly at the summit of the mountain that overlooks Camel's Hump, Vermont's second tallest peak.

The torches are lit and the promise keeping ceremony will soon begin.

Moloch, dark and evil will soon make his appearance and stand over them, at the blood stained stone altar, and demand the required offering.

However, unknown to all, their procession and gathering is seen from across the valley. From high atop Camel's Hump Mountain, a single pair of eyes has been watching. The one who is watching is soon joined by another.

The coven's secret existence is now at risk.

2

They had been hiking on the scenic Long Trail, which feeds into the Appalachian Trail, for fifteen days. They were planning to hike the entire length of Vermont's Long Trail. Fresh out of college the month before, Michael Delvecchio and Julia Brodsky had planned this hike as their graduation present to one another.

Julia was leading the hike this morning. It was Monday, July 21, 1997. The weather was overcast and cool. They were hiking the southeastern ridge leading to the summit of Camel's Hump. They had at least another hour's hike remaining before they would reach the summit.

They were at an elevation of around three thousand feet. The air was only slightly thinner at this elevation. They were in peak physical form. Even so, they felt the strain of hiking at this altitude. Julia stopped along the trail and looked back at Michael. He was a typical tourist hiker. His head seemed to be attached to a swivel as he turned in one direction after another taking in all the sights. Julia on the other hand was a point to point hiker. She moved resolutely from one point on the map towards her intended target location. Only something unusual could distract her from her primary focus, which was to reach her destination by the shortest route possible.

"Michael, I think this is a good place for a break."

Looking around for a moment Michael gestured to a large flat rock about fifty yards further up the trail "How about over by that rock? It looks like it opens up to a nice vista."

"Okay by me," she said, shrugging.

They soon arrived at the rock. It did indeed open up to a splendid vista overlooking several other mountains to the south and the valleys in between. The summer sun was beginning to burn through the cloud cover, bringing warmth to the chilled summer air.

They unbuckled and removed their backpacks and sat down on the rock. From a side pouch on his backpack Michael removed a plastic container half filled with his own custom blended trail mix of assorted nuts, dried fruit and cereal. He offered some to Julia who took a handful. He did likewise.

"Great view, huh?" said Michael.

"Uh-huh!"

Julia pulled out her trail map and began to examine it closely.

"According to the trial guide back at the AMC hut yesterday, the northern trail on the north face is closed because of erosion. Do you remember, she said this spring and summer have been unusually wet and they have had to temporarily close that trail? So, to continue north after we reach the summit this afternoon we are going to have to double back down this trail to that fork we came across a couple of hours ago. See, according to the map we can follow this lower trail around the middle elevation heading north and it will link back up with the main trail right here."

Julia is pointing to the map, while Michael is busy gazing at the panorama spread out below.

"Michael, you didn't hear a word I just said."

Looking at her holding out the map to him, he breaks into a smile.

"Julia, I heard you. I remember what the guide told us."

"Well, let's get going, Michael. It's your turn to take the point."

"Okay! Just give me a minute, will you?" said Michael as he lifted up his backpack and in one fluid motion he swung it up onto his back.

In a couple of minutes they were off to reach the summit.

The hike to the summit was a good deal more difficult than the earlier part of the climb. This part of the trail was steeper, mostly a bare rock surface, sometimes covered in moss. It was also damp from the low misty cloud cover, which frequently smothered the summit. The summit was 4,083 feet above sea level and at that elevation should have had ample tree cover. Instead the last four hundred feet was barren of trees or even small bushes. It was generally believed that acid rain from the south and west, which usually drifted to the northeast, had destroyed the fragile ecosystem of Camel's Hump summit.

As Michael and Julia reached the summit, the sun broke through the cloud cover once again. There was a stiff breeze blowing from the west. The entire summit was now awash in bright sunlight. There were broken clouds all around the summit, drifting away quickly to the northeast. Michael danced around with his arms raised in the air striking a familiar pose from the motion picture, "Rocky" while trying to sing the theme song even though he didn't know the words.

"Ta, Ta ta ta, Ta ta ta ta ta."

"Michael, you're something else."

"Yo, Adrienne, Adrienne, come here."

Even though they still had their backpacks on, Michael embraced Julia and gave her a hearty kiss.

They had lunch on the summit.

They started back down the trail around one o'clock. By two o'clock in the afternoon they had reached the area of the large flat rock where they had begun today's hike.

"Julia, let's pitch our tent here for the night."

"Why here, it's still early?"

"Because, I want to stop and smell the roses."

"I don't get it."

"We seem to be always moving along just to get to the next spot on the map. For once, I'd like to stop and enjoy the area."

"Okay, fine with me, Michael, but remember we need to reach Jay Peak within the next twelve days. Sally, Carey and Tommy will be waiting for us."

"I know," said Michael, "we'll make it in time, trust me."

"Michael, I wouldn't trust you as far as I could throw you."

"Julia, that really hurts," said a playfully pouting Michael.

They spent the rest of the afternoon exploring the area. Late in the afternoon they picked a spot to pitch their tent, a pine needle covered dry and flat spot about a hundred feet due west of the large flat rock.

After supper they listened to the portable radio that Julia had brought and read from the paperback books that each had stuffed into their backpacks. Julia enjoyed reading Anne Rice's books while Michael enjoyed reading action adventure books by Tom Clancy.

The chill of the night quickly embraced the eastern side of the mountain. The setting sun couldn't be seen from their location. However, the sky was free of clouds and soon the darkening sky began to twinkle with a vast display of celestial splendor. Far from the distraction of man-made light, the night sky revealed a wondrous galaxy of "billions and billions of stars," as Carl Sagan was often quoted as saying. Michael had read Sagan's book *Cosmos* and ever since found that he was drawn to look up into the night sky with renewed wonder.

The two settled in for the night around nine thirty and soon went to sleep.

3

"Julia, Julia, wake up, you've got to come and see this."

Sitting up in her sleeping bag, she rubbed her eyes and tried to focus on Michael, who was knelling beside her.

"What is it?"

"C'mon, hurry, before they're gone."

"Who's gone?" she said as Michael quickly exited from the tent.

Knowing him, he would just pester her until she went along with whatever was consuming him. She reached inside her sleeping bag and pulled out her hiking boots. She crawled from the tent and was greeted by the chilly night air. She suddenly had an urge to pee.

"Hurry up, Julia."

Because of the light from the nearly full moon she could see him moving over to the large flat rock. She stood up to follow him.

This had better be quick, she thought, *I've got to go.*

In a moment she was standing beside Michael who was about halfway across the large flat rock. Even with the moonlight, they had to be careful to not get too close to the edge. Distance can be deceiving in the woods at night.

"Look down there and tell me what you see."

Julia tried to focus her eyes upon the black void below. Directly below and to her left, which would make it about two miles northeast of their position, there seemed to a string of twinkling lights moving slowly in unison.

"Well?"

"I don't know Michael, it looks like a road or something and a line of cars in succession. Big Deal!"

"Wrong, now look at it again through these," he said handing her his binoculars. He was excited.

She took the binoculars and looked through them. It took her a moment to locate the lights and to steady her gaze. She slowly turned the lens into focus. It was unmistakable, even from this distance. The lights were coming from a long line of people climbing a path through the woods. Many of them were carrying lanterns or powerful flashlights. She thought she could even see children mixed in. There had to be over a hundred people making this curious trek. The trees shielded many of the people from view.

"What do you think?"

"I don't know."

"People climbing in a sort of procession right?"

"I suppose so, I'm going to go and pee."

"Uh-huh," said Michael who had reclaimed the binoculars from Julia and was now using them to examine the curiosity once again.

She went back into the woods and was relieving herself when Michael called out to her.

"Julia, you have got to see this!"

She soon returned and he handed her the binoculars again.

This time she had no trouble locating the moving lights. They weren't moving in a line any more. Instead they were formed into a circle around what clearly appeared to be a bonfire.

"Neat, huh?" he seemed to ask.

"What time is it?" asked Julia.

"Oh, it's uh...nearly two o'clock in morning."

"Curious, what would kids be doing on the side of a mountain in the middle of the night watching some bonfire?"

"That's what I was wondering," said Michael.

Even without the binoculars, one could make out the crowd around a now fully engaged bonfire.

"I'm going back to bed Michael."

"Yeah, me, too."

"Say, Julia, would you be interested in ..."

"Don't you dare ask me what I think you're going to ask me Michael Delvecchio."

"But..."

"The answer is no and I mean it."

Later that morning, after breakfast, they resumed their hike. Michael was persistent in pestering Julia to accompany him on a minor detour. He desperately wanted to explore the area where they had seen the bonfire earlier that morning. His intense curiosity combined with his ability to get his way soon prevailed upon Julia. They would pursue this little sidebar adventure, which Julia estimated would take the better part of the day provided that Michael agreed to let her chart their course for the rest of the hike. He quickly agreed to her terms. His hiking pace quickened once they had struck a deal.

By ten thirty that morning, they had reached the valley below. In this valley was a swiftly moving stream which was seemingly impossible to cross. Alongside the stream, on their side, was a hard packed dusty, dirt road. Michael moved along the road heading south by southeast. After a couple hundred yards the road curved to the left across the stream by the means of a professionally built wooden bridge. They were soon across the bridge following the road, which was now fading into a well-worn logging road.

A pair of unfriendly eyes watched as they crossed over the wooden bridge and moved along the fading road. The eyes belonged to a young boy who was no more than thirteen. He was wearing coveralls over a white t-shirt. He also wore an old camouflaged colored army surplus hat. He was carrying a 30-30 caliber Winchester lever action open sighted rifle. Once the couple disappeared along the road, the boy took off at a full run back down the road. He needed to tell the warden there were strangers lurking along the sacred path. The warden would know what to do. Maybe this time the elders would let him participate in the cleansing.

Michael was moving along at a faster pace. He kept looking to his right and left searching for signs of what the two of them had witnessed earlier this morning. The road, or what was left of it, was reduced to two ruts in the ground, which kept winding its way ever higher. Michael stopped and looked back towards Camel's Hump.

"What do you think, Julia?"

Julia was the better orienteer between the two.

She consulted her compass and shook her head.

"We're still too far south and we're not high up enough. I really can't be certain of the elevation."

"Okay, let's go then."

They pressed forward. After about a half an hour of climbing and following the path, Julia stopped and pulled Michael to a stop as well.

"Do you smell that?" she said.

"What?"

"I think it's coming from in there. It smells like burned wood."

Julia left the path and headed directly up the side of the mountain from their position. Michael followed close behind.

"Look, Michael, the branches are broken, and see the scuffed up pine needles. Lots of people went through here recently."

"God, Julia, you're good."

"Save your gratitude for later. I'm just trying to get this detour adventure over with as quickly as possible."

About a hundred yards from the path they came into a clearing. The grass was all matted down. In the center of the clearing they spied the charred remains of a huge bonfire. The bonfire had been set up inside a ring of huge boulders. To the high ground side of the fire ring sat an altar made of weathered stone. Michael carefully approached the stone altar. The surface was smooth and measured about three feet by eight feet. The surface seemed heavily stained. Julia bent down and retrieved a swatch of white cloth, which was trampled into the grass next to the altar. The piece of cloth was a strip about one inch wide and ten or so inches long. One end was jagged as if it had been torn.

"Julia, what is that?" asked Michael as he left the altar structure and headed over to the nearby woods, on the upper slope.

"What do you see?"

"I don't know."

"Wait for me," said Julia.

When the two of them reached the edge of the woods they stood before a wrought iron gate. Beyond the gate was a small graveyard. There were several headstones visible from where they stood.

Michael opened the gate and stepped inside the graveyard. The gate opened silently.

What, no creak or screeching sound? thought Julia.

Michael went silently from headstone to headstone. He seemed to be reading the engravings on each.

Julia walked quietly behind. The place gave her the creeps.

Tapping Michael on the shoulder she said, "Can we go now?"

"Julia, did you notice what these headstones have in common?"

"Besides marking someone's grave?"

"Yeah. Look it seems that everyone buried here comes from one family, and according to the engravings, they all died on the same day, October 31, 1843. Humph! That's All Saints Eve you know, Halloween. Isn't that fascinating?"

"Michael, please, I want to get going."

"Okay, okay"

Michael stood up and they headed out of the graveyard. Michael closed the gate's latch. They walked past the altar and the site of the bonfire and headed down the slope, to the woods and the path that lay beyond.

Since the graveyard, Michael suddenly couldn't seem to take his eyes off Julia. Now walking behind her, he couldn't help but notice her tight-fitting jeans. He felt an erection coming on.

A guy can't be expected to hike up and down mountains with a boner, thought Michael.

"Hey, Julia. Let's stop for a while and grab a snack and a drink."

"Okay, Michael. But only for five minutes, then we have got to move on. I want to put some distance between us and this place."

Once she removed her backpack Michael moved in on her. He felt a keen sense of arousal at just the sight of her. Kneeling behind her he began to rub her neck with his powerful hands. Before she could resist he had his right hand inside her shirt groping her breasts. She looked up at him and he bent over and embraced her in a passionate kiss. She could feel his erection pressing against her back. He began to unbutton her shirt.

"Michael, not here, not now, please!"

"Julia, where's your sense of adventure?" he said with a leering grin.

"But..." Julia felt herself exploding with a sense of her own sexuality. She had never felt this way before.

Before there could be any more conversation they fell into each other's arms and were soon engaged in removing their clothes, everything except for their hiking boots.

Michael sat down and pulled her on top of him. He pushed up against her while she pushed down upon him. They could feel each other's heat. The experience was dizzying.

In the nearby woods stood three pairs of eyes, two men and a thirteen-year old boy watched the young couple with growing anger. The young boy felt another urge as well. He noticed he was becoming aroused. He didn't want the elders to notice so he closed his eyes and struggled with his condition. He didn't want them to think he was weak.

Meanwhile, Julia had been placed on her back against the gentle slope of the ground. Michael spread her legs and slowly entered her. His rhythm was slow and deliberate. Julia was looking up directly into the sun. It was blinding in its intensity. Despite her own rhythmic passion Julia was developing a feeling that someone was watching.

She turned her head to look to the woods, nothing!

Michael pressed against her with increasing energy. He leaned over and began a long, tongue-probing kiss.

Julia responded to him, but couldn't escape the rushing feeling that someone was watching them. She opened her eyes and was startled to see, standing behind Michael, the large figure of a man silhouetted by the bright summer sun. She immediately saw this figure was swinging something at them. Before she could warn Michael, she felt a heavy blow to Michael's head, and the force caused their heads to knock. Michael's entire body suddenly went stiff.

Pushing with all her might she rolled Michael off of her. She sprang to her feet and found herself facing two men. One appeared to be a game warden while the other was dressed in coveralls and a sweat stained gray shirt. She glanced down at Michael.

Why doesn't he get up? Michael is lying on his back fully naked, still erect, with his boots on and with his eyes closed and his tongue sticking out.

"Michael!" she screams.

She tries to cover her nakedness by quickly picking up Michael's shirt and holding it up against herself.

The man in coveralls used his right boot to turn Michael over. Sticking out of the back of his head is a garden hoe blade buried half way into his skull. At the end of the blade is a small broken wooden shank, which was once part of the hoe's handle. There is blood pouring out of the wound along with gray matter that could only be one thing, Michael's brain.

"Michael," she screams again.

"He's dead, Walter," said the man in coveralls who is holding the now broken remainder of the hoe's wooden handle.

"Well, Bob, you know what you've got to do."

From the look on their faces Julia knew exactly what they had in mind. They were now going to kill her. She turned and ran back up the hill across the clearing where the bonfire had been. The two men ran off after her.

She stumbled once and as she got back to her feet she could feel a hand touching her shoulder. She twisted away and scrambled to her feet. She sprinted to the altar. Soon the three of them were circling the altar. She had to duck underneath the altar once to escape their grasp. She desperately wanted to talk to them, to perhaps talk her way out of this nightmare. During the pursuit, they never spoke a word.

Her body was glistening with sweat. Her heart beat thundered inside her chest. She was very near to a full panic. The men were also getting out of breath. They were slowing down. She saw her chance. She broke back down the hill. Running downhill could be tricky, especially when one was as tired as the two men were. She glanced back over her shoulder. They were at least fifteen yards behind. They were splitting up, as if to flank her. She now felt she could increase that distance easily.

As she turned to look downhill once again, a gunshot rang out. A single bullet pierced her throat. The shot came from the boy's 30-30 rifle. The bullet's path continued upward before exiting out the back of her skull. In the brief moment before she collapsed and died, her eyes caught sight of this young boy standing about twenty yards in front of her with his rifle pointed straight at her.

Julia's naked body collapsed to the ground.

"Nice shot, Sammy," said the Game Warden.

4

It was Tuesday July 28, 1997 a humid overcast day in Boston. Aaron Bailey had arrived early for his one thirty appointment with the attorney. He had driven up from his condominium in Middleborough, Massachusetts, down near the Cape, where the weather was a good deal more bearable. He still couldn't believe his maiden aunt, Laura, had passed away. He learned from her attorney that she had died from breast cancer just about a month ago. She had been living on Matinicus Island off the coast of Maine for the past fifteen years. A neighbor had discovered her body when she had stopped by to look in on her. She had died a couple of days before, according to the sketchy details Aaron had been able to gleam from the attorney. The attorney, sounding pompous and without emotion had informed him, in an all too brief telephone conversation that he had been named in her will.

He held the small piece of paper in his right hand on which he had written down the appointment details. Folding it up, he slipped it back into his sport coat's right side pocket. He stepped towards the brass-trimmed revolving door and pushed it open to the lobby of Two International Place, a large ornate building, adjacent to Boston's Rowe's Wharf. He walked across the polished imported marbled floor to check the wall mounted registry. He was to meet Attorney Michael Lowenstein at the law offices of Phinney, Cohen, Rudledge and Shearer at one thirty. The building's registry confirmed that the law offices he was seeking were located in suites 1604 through

1624. He moved towards the bank of elevators located on the opposite side of the lobby.

Aaron pushed the up button for the elevator and in a moment a soft "ding" could be heard as the number six elevator's doors swished open. The elevator car was already occupied by three extraordinarily attractive women. They were quietly talking to themselves. He stepped inside the elevator, moved against the right side as the elevator doors glided to a close. The women stole sideways glances at Aaron.

His eyes were mesmerized by the women's short business skirts and their all too obvious attractive legs. Their perfume blended into a new aroma that drifted all about the confined space of the elevator car. The women knew he was looking at them even though he was trying to be careful to not let on that he was. The elevator bell rang twice more, which noted the arrival on the requested floor. The doors opened and the women stepped off the elevator. Aaron was about to follow when he noted from the control panel that the elevator had stopped at the thirty-second floor. Aaron had forgotten to push the button to select the sixteenth floor. One of the three women, a brunette, was looking back at him and smiling. As the elevator doors closed he felt himself blushing. He now selected the correct floor and the ride resumed. He straightened his tie and for the first time since he had entered the building he noticed how cool it was. His clamminess from the humid outside temperatures had evaporated in the cool dry air of this office building.

An hour later he found himself signing some papers while sitting at the longest mahogany desk he had ever seen. It seemed his maiden Aunt Laura was quite wealthy having invested wisely over the years. The lawyer explained something about a revocable trust and that her estate would not require going through probate. There were a few details about taxes and some charitable gifts his aunt had favored in her estate. The bottom line was that she had left him as the principle benefactor of her assets. Her assets included over two hundred forty thousand dollars in cash, another four hundred thousand in stocks and bonds and several pieces of property located in Maine and Vermont, which were valued at over $1.1 million dollars.

Aaron asked about her and about the funeral arrangements, but the lawyer did not answer his questions with much detail. At the end of signing the papers the lawyer pulled a large brown envelope out of a manila folder.

"Mr. Bailey, I've been instructed to give this to you," he said as he slowly slid the envelope across the desk to Aaron.

"After you have read it through I have been instructed to meet with you once again regarding a property in Vermont."

"What is it?" asked Aaron.

"As you can see, it is sealed under the signature of your deceased aunt. We were given explicit instructions to deliver it to you at this time. We were also directed to advise you to not open it in our presence but to do so in private."

"Oh, I see."

"Now, Mr. Bailey, we have completed all that we can today. I will have my staff arrange to file the necessary papers to transfer your name to all of the stocks, bonds and deeds with the one exception of that Vermont property, which we will resolve at a later time. The transfers will take about a month. As we noted earlier, we have prepared to transfer her cash assets to your account at the Fleet Bank. We do recommend that you secure the services of a qualified financial advisor to guide you in setting up appropriate accounts. If you wish, we could recommend a couple of highly regarded firms who specialize in such matters."

Aaron nodded his agreement. With that, the lawyer slid a sheet of paper across the desk.

"Very well, here they are. You'll find their telephone numbers and the names of key staff who would welcome a call from you."

Aaron pulled the envelope and the sheet of paper off the desk. The envelope seemed thick with papers and it felt like there was a key of some sort inside.

Standing, the lawyer extended his hand to Aaron.

"My secretary will forward a transcript of our meeting to you today. It should reach you in a few days. We like to provide this service so our clients, who may be unduly stressed from their recent loss, can take their time in reviewing some of the matters we covered in our reading of the will or in executing the transfer of a trust."

"That is a good idea!" said Aaron.

"Please feel free to contact my staff or me once you are ready to meet on the matter of the Vermont property."

Aaron felt himself being rushed out the door although he willingly went along. His head was swimming with the magnitude of information that had just come his way.

He soon found himself standing alone in the elevator—the envelope was stuffed into his left coat pocket and the numerous business cards the lawyer insisted he take were stuffed into the right backside pockets of his "Bugle Boy" jeans. His face was stretched tight from the smile he was now wearing. When the elevator doors opened, he stepped into the lobby with a spring in his gait and he headed straight outside.

A warm blast of humid air slapped at him. The too bright afternoon sunshine caught him by surprise. He raised his hands to shield his eyes. In a moment he removed his tie and tossed it into a curbside trash basket. He strode off at a brisk pace to retrieve his car, a 1990 Volvo sedan, from the parking garage located three blocks south of North Station. He wanted to quickly exit the city and head back home. He was dying with curiosity to read what his aunt had wanted him to read in private. Within thirty minutes he was back onto the southeast expressway heading back home to the Town of Middleborough.

The ride back home passed quickly, notwithstanding the usual heavy flow of traffic. Driving into and out of Boston was complicated and arduous enough. The recent added construction caused by the "Big Dig," a massive construction project designed to put the interstate highway underground that up to now had divided the City, caused commuting to become daily torture for the thousands that had to travel into, around or through Boston. Aaron was grateful that he lived and worked on the "Cape" which is how the locals refer to Cape Cod.

He was a bachelor and a science teacher at the Town of Plymouth's John F. Kennedy Middle School. Aaron liked to take long walks—his favorite authors were Tom Clancy and Ian Fleming. His love life was uneventful. He had dated several women but was unattached at the moment. The one thing he was passionate about was playing bass guitar in a blues band made up of teachers from schools in the area. His band was called, what else, "Detention Time Blues Band."

He checked his watch, and decided that instead of heading straight back to his condo he would have dinner at the most upscale restaurant he could think of. He exited the highway and headed directly for the coastal route. Moments later he pulled his Volvo into the parking lot of "The Royals," Plymouth's most elegant ocean side restaurant.

It was just barely five o'clock, yet the restaurant's lobby already held a small crowd waiting to be seated. Even though he didn't have a reservation, he decided to try that age-old trick of slipping the host a twenty. He was surprised to find that it worked as he was seated immediately.

After he was seated at a small table next to the one of the floor to ceiling windows, he pulled out a small vial of eye drops and applied a couple of rewetting drops to each eye. He had taken to wearing soft contacts just three months ago. The woman he was dating at that time, Karen, the school nurse, had told him he looked sexy without his customary glasses. That did it. No more glasses for him. He later found that he enjoyed wearing contacts and wished he had tried them long ago. As he applied the drops a beautiful young waitress stood patiently next to his table. After blinking his eyes a couple of times he turned to his left and was startled to see her standing there. He immediately noticed her captivating smile, long slender fingers and finely sculptured nails.

"Oh, I'm sorry, I startled you," she said.

Her voice was soft, almost a whisper.

"That's okay, really. I was just in a hurry to put in the eye drops."

She glanced down at him and favored him with a pleasant smile. She reached across his table and picked up his water glass and poured it full with ice cold water.

"May I get you something from the bar?"

"Yes, I, uh, would like a martini, with a twist. Shaken—not stirred, you know, like James Bond."

He felt foolish for trying so obviously hard to be dashing and debonair. He was sure that his faint effort to play off the famous James Bond line was so badly bungled that this woman would think he was, at best clumsy, or at worst a clown.

"I think we can arrange that, Mr. Bond. I will be back in a moment with your martini."

Just then he took notice of her nametag. Her name was Korie. He watched Korie turn and walk through the maze of tables in search of his requested martini. He found her very attractive and part of him wanted to ask her for a date. The other part of him said, *Slow down Aaron*.

He pulled the envelope out of his left coat pocket and opened it up. He removed a hand written document that he immediately recognized had been written by his late Aunt Laura.

At the bottom of the envelope was a smaller envelope. He opened this smaller envelope and found it contained a long slender key, stamped with the number 4497.

His waitress, Korie, arrived with his martini just as he was about to begin to read the documents.

"Would you like to order dinner now, or would you like more time?"

"No, that's okay. I'm ready to order," he said as he handed her back the menu without having so much as glanced at it.

"Very well then, what shall it be?" she said with a slight smile.

"Let's see, I want your soup of the day for an appetizer. I also want a large spinach salad—hold the onions and the dressing. I want a baked potato with sour cream, summer squash and the large cut of prime rib cooked medium well. Oh, and I would like a bottle of your most exclusive red wine."

"Very good, Mr. Bond," she said continuing the small game that they had begun earlier. "And is there a particular wine that you wish, vintage Beaujolais perhaps?"

"I will leave that to you, surprise me! I like surprises."

"I was under the impression that nothing ever surprised 007," she said with a twinkle in her eyes. Before he could offer a witty come back, she had turned and moved away.

He noticed that she didn't write anything down.

This ought to be interesting, he thought.

He took a sip from his martini. It was glorious, simply the finest martini he had ever had, even though it was also the first one he had ever had. He decided to put aside the papers from his aunt and to settle in to enjoy his dinner. He would read them after dinner. He had plenty of time on his hands and he had money to spend. He sort of liked the money part, after all, for the past nine years he had lived off his teacher's salary which, though adequate, would never allow him much in the way of extravagance.

He took another sip and let his attention turn to the silent and expansive gray blue waters that filled his window side view. He could see several sea gulls holding fast in the sky as they caught thermal winds blowing towards the ocean. In the far distance, at the horizon, a sailboat's profile was barely noticeable. Down below, the harbor was still. Not one boat was coming or going. Dozens however, gently rose and declined at their moorings with each gentle ocean swell.

5

The Game Warden, Walter Yandow, pulled his four-wheel drive pickup truck, with the State of Vermont seal on the side doors, along side the body of the dead woman. The young boy and the other man had dragged the dead man's body down the hillside and now placed it next to the woman's body. The two were sweating profusely from the strain.

"Go git their clothes and stuff," said the Warden to the young boy.

The other man lowered the tailgate of the pickup truck. He climbed up into the truck bed and unfolded a large tarpaulin across the floor of the truck bed. He jumped down from the truck and stood next to the Game Warden. He took out his handkerchief and wiped the beads of sweat from his brow.

"Let's put her in first," said Yandow. He bent over and lifted her body by her shoulders. His big muscular hands, with their powerful fingers, dug deep into her now lifeless body.

The other man picked her up by her knees placing her lower legs under his arms. They swung her body back and forth a couple of times and then tossed her body onto the tailgate. Yandow climbed into the truck's bed.

"Bob, hold on to the tarp while I pull her in."

Bob held onto the tarp as her body was dragged to the front of the truck bed. The process was repeated for the dead man's body.

Sammy had made three trips to recover the belongings of the two dead hikers.

"Sammy, toss their stuff up in there on the side of the bodies," said Yandow.

"Yes, sir."

Bob climbed up into the truck. After the dead hikers belongings were placed next to their bodies, he pulled the oversized tarp over the entire collection. He lifted a cement building block from the rear corner of the truck bed and tossed it on top of the tarp to hold it in place. He jumped over the side of the truck onto the ground while Yandow closed the tailgate.

For just a moment the three of them just stood there in the summer sun. Overhead a couple of swallows fluttered about and the intermittent buzzing sound of cicadas could be heard emanating from several different directions. There was a slight breeze blowing from the southwest.

The young boy wiped the sweat from his brow with the sleeve of his tee shirt. He bent over and picked up his rifle.

"Sammy, did you pick up the bullet casing?"

"Yes, sir. Like I was taught."

"Now, Sammy, you've got to clean your rifle as soon as you get home. Okay? I'm sure Reverend Mitchell will want to personally speak to you about your part today."

Sammy nodded that he understood. He was grinning from ear to ear.

"You're heading straight into town?" inquired Bob.

"Yup. I'm going to take them to Foley's. Reverend Mitchell will want to see them before we decide what to do with them."

"Okay, I'll take Sammy with me."

With that, Yandow climbed into the cab of his truck and started it up. He put it into gear and pulled away slowly as he turned left to head back to the trail and down the mountain. Sammy and Bob walked over to the woods where Bob had parked his U.S. Army surplus jeep. The two of them climbed inside the jeep and were soon following the Game Warden back down the mountain. Several minutes later, the two vehicles crossed over the small, single lane wooden bridge that spanned the swiftly moving Sutton River.

Yandow's truck turned to the right onto a narrow dirt road to head into town with Bob and Sammy following close behind. In this area there are only a handful of year around homes. The front and side yards are filled with abandoned appliances, cars and snowmobiles. The narrow dirt road twists and turns gently downward for a couple of miles, where it suddenly meets another dirt road. Here the two vehicles turn to the left, paralleling the westward flowing Winooski River. This road is wider and more heavily traveled and as a result, its surface resembles a washboard's roughness. This road has more homes, but the surrounding landscape is the same. While people notice the vehicles as they drive by, no one waves or acknowledges the two vehicles. They move along this road for a couple of miles before it intersects with another road. This new road is paved. The two vehicles now separate. The Game Warden heads to the right, towards the center of Sutton. Bob and Sammy turn left and head toward the southern end of town. The two vehicles blend in with the normal everyday traffic.

Several minutes later, Yandow pulls his pickup truck around to the back of Ed Foley's Washington County Animal Shelter. The truck's tires make a crunching sound as it crosses the graveled back driveway. Yandow, a big man, steps out of the truck. He stands six feet four and weighs at least two hundred and seventy pounds. His belly hangs prominently over his wide black leather belt. His matching forest green uniform pants and shirt are stretched to their limits. His shirt sleeves display the traditional slashes indicating the rank of sergeant. He carries a sidearm holstered on his wide leather belt. It is a State of Vermont issued nine-millimeter Glock Police Special. He leaves his hat on the truck's front seat. He seldom wears his hat.

The underarm of his uniform shirt is heavily stained with perspiration. His pants are also stained with blood from the two victims.

Without knocking, he bounds up the back steps to the rear, enclosed porch, pulls open the door and lets himself in.

In the faraway distance there is a rumble of thunder as a summer storm is building in the heat of the afternoon. The storm will move through the Winooski River Valley cutting west to east through the Green Mountains of Vermont.

Yandow walks across the porch as the floor creaks and groans from his weight. He steps inside the open back door into an examination room, where he finds Ed Foley working on a sedated German shepherd. Ed's daughter Lisa is assisting him. The two are finishing up work on repairing the dog's broken right front leg. Ed looks up and nods to Walter who nods back.

Lisa smiles at the Game Warden, "Hello, Mr. Yandow. It sure is a sticky one, isn't it?"

He proffers a smile in return. "It sure is Lisa. I sure could use a cold drink. Ed, do you mind?"

"Nope, go on and help yourself."

Yandow moves towards the white enamel colored refrigerator tucked into the corner and pulls open the large door. Inside, mixed in alongside various temperature sensitive drugs, is half a case of diet cola. He takes out a can and closes the door. Leaning against the wall, he pops the can's lift tab and in a couple of seconds drinks down the entire twelve ounces. He holds back a belch and burps silently to himself.

Ed Foley looks over at Yandow and asks, "What have you got for me?"

"We bagged two in season."

Lisa blushed when she heard the expression "in season." She knew it meant they had caught a young couple having sex.

"Where are they?"

"They're in the back of my truck."

"Dead?"

"Yup, old Bob Senecal and I took out the man and young Sammy Porter shot the woman right in the throat. That Sammy is a good one, he is."

Lisa looked over at Yandow and said "I dated his older brother for awhile a couple of year's ago. They're such a nice family. His older brother had his share of silencings. It sure was a loss when he died in that car crash. Anyway, I'm glad Sammy got his first. It is his first, isn't it?

"Yeah, it's his first all right," said Yandow.

"Lisa, give me a hand with the dog," said her father.

They carried the dog into an adjoining room, where it was put into a large cage. There were several other animals in cages in this room. They each began to make loud, almost frantic noises as if they were pleading to be freed. After the dog was placed into the cage, Ed took a needle out of a small tray that was sitting on top of a cage that had a black and white short-haired tuxedo colored cat inside. He also picked up a vial from the same tray. He carefully stuck the needle into the end of the vial and withdrew a measured amount of medicine. He put the vial back into the tray. Next he bent over and stuck the needle into the dog's side, near the now splinted left front paw.

"Lisa, could you stay with Mrs. Kenard's dog until I get back?"

"Sure, Dad."

Yandow and the Vet headed out to the backyard to examine the dead bodies.

"Oh, and Lisa, please call the Reverend and tell him what we have!" said her father from over his shoulder as he led the way to the back yard.

"I will, Daddy."

The two men climbed down the back porch steps and headed over to the back of the pickup. There was a cluster of flies buzzing about over the side of the tarpaulin nearest to the front of the truck bed.

"Damn flies, they're on to the blood," said Ed Foley.

"I hate flies, Walter. I sure hate flies," said Ed as he pulled down the truck's tailgate.

6

His waitress placed a very large plate directly in front of him. The aroma of the prime rib drifted up from the delicious looking plate of food. The vegetables were attractively presented alongside the steak. Earlier the bottle of wine he had ordered had been opened and presented by a young man from the bar. Aaron sampled the wine and pronounced it superb. He had already consumed half a glass when his dinner's main course arrived. Korie, his waitress, removed the empty salad dish and refilled his glass of water.

"Please be careful, the plate is quite warm, you wouldn't want to burn yourself."

"Thanks, I'll be careful."

"Can I get you anything else?" asked the waitress.

"No, everything is fine, thank you."

"Do you approve of the wine?"

"Oh, yes. It's just perfect."

"Very well. I'll check back later. If you need me for anything, just glance my way and nod."

"Thank you, I will."

"Enjoy your dinner!"

With that she turned quickly and went over to another table, three tables away, and began to take their dinner order.

Aaron picked up his steak knife and fork and cut out a morsel from the prime rib. He sampled this piece and found the steak flavor to just burst into his mouth.

What could account for this wonderful taste? he thought. *Was it the cut, the preparation, or could it be the wine? Perhaps it was the combination of all three.*

He proceeded to cut several more pieces from the steak. He cut open his baked potato and filled it with sour cream. After consuming a couple of bites of the savory steak and a second glass of wine, he decided to read the papers from his Aunt Laura. He unfolded the sheets of paper and began to read.

September 14, 1993

My Dearest Aaron,

These words I write to you are the hardest thing I have ever had to do. You are reading these words after my death, because I haven't the courage to speak of these matters to you in person. I regret my weakness, please forgive me.

I have tried to provide you with a generous inheritance with which to build your life. Some of the inheritance came from my mother and before her, her mother and so on. This wealth began in our family many years ago and it is only proper that it remain for the benefit of a family member.

Now I must reveal to you some deep, and yes, dark secrets that I have kept from you since your birth.

Aaron, I am not your Aunt Laura, my real name is Elizabeth Corbin Powell. I am your mother. Your birth name is Aaron Corbin Powell. You were born at St. Elizabeth's Hospital in Boston, Massachusetts, on November 11, 1966. With these papers is a copy of your birth certificate and baptism papers. I legally changed your name with the help of some friends to

Aaron Bailey. I did this to protect the both of us. If I hadn't, your very life would have been in mortal danger.

I beg your forgiveness, Aaron. I wish that our family had never been caught up in this horrific nightmare, but we were. I raised you as a son, but under the guise of being your Aunt. It was a weak attempt on my part to protect you. I know I should have spoken to you directly, but I kept hoping that what my own mother had revealed to me was wrong. Unfortunately, she was not wrong, Aaron. Our family has been hunted for the past seven generations. With this letter, I shall try to give you a glimpse into your heritage.

My dearest son, Aaron, you are the first and only male born in our family since 1843. In 1804, the Powell family settled in Sutton, Vermont, where they took up farming in the Winooski River Valley. The family was modestly prosperous and bought more land, until they owned hundreds of acres of fertile valley land. They also began an orchard, a gristmill and a general store. They belonged to the Church of Everlasting Faith. In 1841, a new pastor arrived to head this church, since the older pastor had died during the winter of 1840 from small pox. Soon everything changed in Sutton. This new pastor was a dark and evil person. It was widely known that he promoted fear and paranoia in that small community.

This pastor, who called himself Elisa Porter Cummings, began a secret cult. This cult became a church within his church. The cult grew powerful and was very secretive about its affairs. The Reverend Cummings tried several times to get our ancestors to join his inner flock. They resisted at first, but after a while they began to reconsider.

Aaron, I can't possibly speak of all that went on back in 1843, except to say that eventually this cult took to worshipping Satan. They offered sacrifice to him, including human sacrifice. They referred to themselves as "Keepers." Reverend Cummings had convinced his followers that Satan wished to take on human form. He said that Satan had made a covenant with everyone who would participate in this transformation, that they would enjoy untold wealth and power, and even immortality. The ritual of raising Satan was set to occur on October 31, 1843. Our ancestors, led by Sarah Powell, our great grand mother, seven times removed, turned down this Reverend and his evil followers. As matriarch, her decision swayed the entire family who now refused to participate. The ritual failed because the coven was incomplete, and everyone blamed our ancestors. These coven members went to the family home and proceeded to curse and threaten everyone. Then they nailed boards across the doors and windows, and following that they set the house on fire. Everyone in our family died that night, everyone, except a tiny baby girl. A faithful servant by the name of Cora Jackson hid out in the root cellar. She dug at the side of the cellar's dirt walls and piled the damp clay up against the door. While the house burned down *that night,* Cora and the baby girl miraculously survived in that cellar.

At the first sign of light, Cora managed to climb out of that cellar with the baby in her arms. She escaped into the woods and managed to keep moving until she had traveled several communities away. She later was taken in by a widowed lady, a Mrs. Marcoux, who lived in Shelburne, Vermont. This lady let Cora and the baby live with her. The baby's name was Irene Powell. After hearing of the horrors of that dark and evil night, Mrs. Marcoux proceeded to adopt Cora and raise her as her own. Cora, Mrs. Marcoux, and the baby moved away to Philadelphia. Later, as she grew up, she went to a fine school for young women, thanks to the generosity of that widowed lady.

How do I know these things, you might ask? It is all answered for you in a diary of sorts kept by our family. This diary is for your eyes only. It is located in a bank safe deposit box at the main offices of the Bank of Boston. The key to that box is with these papers.

Get this diary and read it well. Believe its words, for they are the truth. As you will see the Keepers are still active, and they have been hunting for the descendants of the Powell family since 1843. These descendants of the "Keepers," as they are still called continue to be in league with the devil. Please believe me, Aaron. Take extra care when you read this diary. The Keepers would love to get their hands on it as well.

There is one other thing I must tell you. Our family still owns that land in Sutton, Vermont. We have not sold or given it up, because the land itself holds the key to Satan's efforts to take on human form. As long as it remains with our family and we remain hidden from the Keepers, then they can not complete the transformation. If we relinquish that land to someone' else, then it would be used to complete the coven and evil would win. You mustn't ever let this land fall into the hands of an outsider, and you must never, ever, go back to Sutton.

Lastly, Aaron, you must one day find a good woman and have a child with her. We must keep our bloodline going, or seven generations of our family, and the many who have died for this cause, will have suffered in vain.

I know this all must be overwhelming to you and I truly wish I could have revealed this to you in person, but please believe me, Aaron, this way is best.

Aaron, be strong and watchful, be brave and be wise, and keep faith with all of those who went before you.

I loved you with all my heart and I hope you still love me as well. My pain at not being able to hold you, as your mother, has been tempered by my joy in watching you grow up into a fine, handsome, caring man. You were always in my prayers. Please keep me in yours.

Love Forever,
Your Mother, Elizabeth

Aaron felt himself choking up with emotion. He was overwhelmed with so many confusing feelings. Tides of anger, love, abandonment, and bewilderment swept over him.

Laura was my mother, my very own mother, he thought.

He let out a soft sigh, "Oh," as he buried his face into his hands. Tears began to flow. He wiped at the tears with the end of the linen napkin. He had a large lump in his throat.

From across the room Aaron's waitress, Korie noticed that the customer she had played "James Bond" with seemed suddenly saddened and stressed. With that she moved across the dining room and approached his table.

"How is your dinner, Mr. Bond?" she asked in her most cheerful voice.

He heard her voice, and for a moment he snapped out of his sudden sadness. He couldn't face anyone right now. He needed time to think through the complex revelations that his mother had just revealed in her letter to him. With a wave of his left hand, he gestured for her to leave him alone.

As an experienced waitress, she recognized that her customer was distressed and wanted her to leave, but the personal side to her kicked in. She knew this previously happy, witty and yesm, charming man didn't really want to be alone. He just hadn't realized it yet.

"Why don't you let me have the chef heat up your dinner for you? You haven't taken more than a few bites."

"Yes, Yes," he whispered anything to get her to leave him alone with his thoughts.

She reached across his table and removed his dinner plate. At that moment, the faint but noticeable scent of her perfume reached him. In a moment's flash, his mind recorded the memory of this scent, along with his reaction. He had found it to be "flirty and sensual." As she turned and walked away, he again picked up his mother's letter and read it for the second time. As he did, he finished off his third glass of wine and poured himself a fourth glass. This one he poured to the brim.

After reading the letter for the second time, Aaron now turned his attention to the attached birth and church baptism papers. These too he read, word for word. He soon felt another rush of sadness rolling over him. For the second time tonight, tears began to flow. This time he made no effort to wipe them away. He turned his gaze to the window, and while he could see the nearby harbor just beyond the tinted glass, he could also discern his own tearful reflection staring back at him.

Aaron was transfixed, deep in thought, when his dinner plate was set before him once again. He turned slowly, not wanting to make eye contact.

"Thanks," he said.

"Don't mention it."

Korie turned away and went over to a nearby table to see how they were enjoying their meal. The table she chose to check on would allow her the chance to get a look at this somber young man. As her customers complimented the quality of their dinner, she stole a sideways glance in Aaron's direction.

Their eyes met for just a moment.

Aaron saw her glance at him. Embarrassed, he looked quickly down at his reheated dinner. He quickly picked up his knife and fork and took a bite of the prime rib he had previously cut.

In the brief moment that their eyes met, she saw the telltale signs of red swollen eyes and traces of tears glistening in the restaurant's subdued light. Most of all she saw sadness that almost seemed to her to be childlike, a sadness born out of innocence. Her heart was touched by what she saw, and more by what she felt.

Aaron sat there slowly chewing the piece of prime rib. He decided to return the papers and two envelopes to his left coat pocket. Time seemed to pass ever so slowly for Aaron. He felt a buzz building from the wine he had consumed. He also felt warm. After a few moments, he began to pick at what remained of his dinner. He had lost his appetite, so he pushed his dinner plate away. He hadn't touched his salad or fresh bread. He drew the half-empty glass of wine closer.

Reaching for the wine bottle, he poured the remaining wine into his glass. His glass was filled once again, but the bottle was now empty. As he placed the bottle back onto the table, he almost dropped it. The bottled settled on the table after teetering back and forth a couple of times.

Aaron had managed to get himself quite drunk.

7

A shiny, black, 1994 Mercury Grand Marquis drove slowly down the gravel driveway of the Washington County Animal Shelter. At the bottom of the driveway, the car turned to the right and pulled to a stop behind a forest green pickup truck. The side and back windows were darkly tinted. Only the windshield was not tinted.

From the back porch came Ed, who was closely followed by Walter. Ed Foley opened an umbrella. The warm summer rain had begun to fall just moments before. As with most summer storms here in the Winooski River Valley area of Vermont, this storm was sudden and the rain was heavy.

The two men stood silently next to the black Mercury. They huddled under the umbrella. The only sound that was heard came from the splatter of rain on the vehicles and the *tat, tat, tat* sound of the rain striking the tarp in the back of Yandow's truck. The men shifted their feet. Not a word was spoken between them nor did they look at one another. Instead their eyes were fixed upon the driver's side front door window.

Over five minutes passed since the car had arrived, and yet there was no sign from within. The rain was now beginning to puddle around their feet. A bright burst of light exploded behind them, which momentarily cast an eerie frame to the backyard scene. It was a lightning strike, which hit an old elm tree in the woods behind the Animal Shelter. The lightning exploded upon the tree, blowing away a large limb from the upper third of the tree. The loud *crack* from the exploding tree was almost immediately followed by a huge concussion, which shook the ground. The earth-shaking thunderclap would have caused almost anyone to jump. They continued to wait in silence.

A whirring sound softly emanated from the car as the driver's side window was powered down halfway. From inside the car's darkened burgundy leather interior spoke a raspy voice.

"I want to see them."

"They're in the back of the pickup truck under a tarp," said the veterinarian.

With a click followed by a louder click, the driver's side door was unlocked and now it began to open. Ed, who was holding the umbrella, now held it over the open car door. Walter stood almost at attention. No longer protected by the umbrella, he was quickly drenched by the heavy downpour. A distant boom of thunder echoed about as a short balding man emerged from the car. It was Reverend Simon B. Mitchell, pastor to the faithful of the town of Sutton's Church of Everlasting Faith. He wore a neatly ironed black suit, beneath which he wore a minister's dark gray shirt with a white collar. This man, with short gray hair at the temples, also sported a mustache and beard, neatly trimmed and shaved so that they outlined his mouth and the edges of his jaw. He had dark piercing eyes with crows feet age lines radiating from the corners. His shoes were polished to a mirror like shine. He closed the door of the car and then he too stood silently beside Ed Foley. As he stood there, he clasped his hands behind his back, military style.

Walter, now completely soaked, stepped aside to allow Ed and Reverend Mitchell to walk to the back of his truck. As they approached the back of the truck, Walter stepped in front of the two other men and pulled the handle of the tailgate. Walter hoisted himself up onto the tailgate by grabbing the rear corner of the sidewall and pulling himself up. The front of the truck was parked on a slight incline so the pickup truck bed tilted toward Ed and the Reverend.

Tiny whitish gray flecks of brain tissue floated down the truck bed upon the rivulets of rainwater. The channels in the truck bed funneled the rainwater into a series of tiny rainfalls. As the rainwater fell off the truck it struck the rear bumper, before cascading to the gravel covered, rain soaked ground.

"The tarp, Mr. Yandow, the tarp if you please," said the Reverend in his usual demanding tone.

Walter always wanted to milk the moment. He was, at times, almost theatrical in his manner around the Reverend. This Reverend suffered his eccentric behavior with little patience. He would frequently scold "Mr. Yandow" as he was about to now.

"Mr. Yandow, have you not noticed that it is raining? I don't wish to stand out here all day, so let's be done with it."

"Sure, Reverend, here they are," said Walter as he pulled back the tarp in one long powerful stroke.

The water, which covered the tarp, now flew at Ed and the Reverend, soaking them both. Neither man flinched.

"Sorry, Reverend, Ed," said Walter as he looked away as if to avoid eye contact.

"I didn't mean to..."

"Silence," said the Reverend in a commanding voice.

The Reverend now moved to the right side of the truck to get a closer look. He placed his hands on the truck's sidewall and stood on his tiptoes. Ed Foley stood next to him, holding the umbrella and not saying a word.

"Turn her over," said the Reverend.

Walter bent over and with his large powerful hands he grabbed her by the legs and twisted them, causing her stiffening body to roll over. Her backside was already turning a dark purple color from her shoulders down to her buttocks as her body's blood was settling and congealing inside her cold lifeless body.

The Reverend stared at her naked body for a moment as the rain splattered against her skin. Her eyes were wide open, frozen at that moment the bullet entered her upper throat, the very same frozen moment that she saw Sammy pointing a rifle at her.

"Now turn him over."

The Game Warden repeated the process with the dead man. Again the Reverend took a moment to examine the entire body of this victim as well.

"Have you gone through their things?"

"No, I haven't had time yet."

"All right, I've seen enough. Cover them up."

Walter did as he was told, only this time with less flair.

The Reverend turned to Ed and looked up at him said, "You know what to do. We're counting on you, Ed. We are doing His work and through His work we shall inherit the earth."

Ed nodded his understanding.

"Mr. Yandow, I will expect a full report on my desk by eight o'clock tomorrow morning. Leave nothing out, do you understand, and bring along their personal effects?"

"Yes, Reverend."

Ed spoke up for the first time since the Reverend's arrival. "What about an alibi, should we need one?"

"These were young hikers it seems. Their absence may not become a concern for a few days. After I see Mr. Yandow's report, I will set into motion a suitable cover story."

The three men walked back to the car.

From the back porch, a soft voice addressed Reverend Mitchell.

"Hello, Reverend Mitchell," said Lisa Foley. She smiled at the Reverend. She also offered a half wave with her right hand.

"Hello, Lisa and how are you today?"

"I'm fine Reverend, just fine."

"That's good, well I must be going now," said the Reverend in a softer tone as he smiled at Lisa and returned her wave.

With that, Ed opened the Reverend's door and held the umbrella over the Reverend as he slid into the front seat of the car.

Ed turned to Walter and nodded in the direction of the two small buildings set off from the house and the driveway. These particular wood shake buildings stood alone. One served as a shelter for hard to handle creatures that came into the possession of the Foley's from time to time. The other building was where the vet conducted his disposal of dead and unwanted animals.

"I'll get the bodies and bring them in, and then I've got to leave," said the game warden.

"I understand. Bring the guy in first, okay?"

"Sure."

Ed folded up the umbrella and walked over to the porch. He handed the umbrella to his daughter. The rain had lightened up.

"I'll finish feeding the animals and cleaning out the cages that need it. I know you've got work to do out back," said Lisa.

"Thanks. It shouldn't take more than an hour to an hour and a half."

"All right, I'll have supper waiting."

Ed turned and moved off in the direction of the disposal building. Meanwhile, Walter climbed up into the back of the pickup truck. He pulled back the tarp once again, uncovering the two bodies. Lisa remained on the back porch just long enough to catch a glance of the two dead hiker's bodies.

Lisa headed back inside the back porch door of the clinic into the operating room. Ed fumbled in his pants pocket for his keys. Finally locating them, he unlocked the door of the disposal building and flipped on a light switch. He quickly went over to a large stainless steel vat. Working the controls, he flipped a couple of switches and turned a knob on the top of the vat. The sound of a gas burner kicking into full operation filled the silence of the room with a "swoosh" like sound.

At the disposal door stood Walter. He was carrying the body of Michael Delvecchio over his shoulders.

"Put him on the table, right here," said Ed pointing to a stainless steel table. The table was six and one half feet long and thirty inches wide. Its edges were rounded and raised. The entire table was sloped to its center where a drain hole was located. Attached to the right end of this table was a deep stainless steel work sink, industrial grade. Suspended over the sink was an overhead radial saw.

Delvecchio's body was laid face up on the table.

Ed began to remove the man's hiking boots and socks. He handed these to Walter, who turned and headed out the door.

From over his shoulder Walter said, "I'll go and get the girl. Be right back."

"Okay, Walt."

Ed reached under the table and pulled out a pair of rubber gloves from a box marked "Large, For Surgical Use Only."

He reached to the back wall of the table and flipped a switch. The overhead radial saw's small red power light blinked on. He reached up and pulled the saw down until it was but inches from the corpse of Michael Delvecchio. He pulled on the saw's trigger and the radial blade began to spin at 3,000 rpm. Its high pitched sound filled the room. The blade was centered over the right leg of the corpse, just above the knee. He lowered the saw.

Outside, Walter pulled the lifeless body of Julia Brodsky from the truck and laid her across his powerful left shoulder. With his right hand free he closed the tailgate. As he turned towards the disposal building, he could clearly hear the unmistakable sound of the radial saw. By the time he reentered the building, both lower legs had been removed and Ed was busy moving the body into a better position for the rest of the carving. Without saying a word, Walter put Julia's body on a wooden side table next to the door.

Walter closed the door as he left the disposal building. Outside the door to the right, under a small overhead roof, stood several wooden kegs stacked on top of wooden pallets. The kegs were labeled in heavy black letters, **Bone Meal Fertilizer**.

8

Korie stood next to the bar. It was nearly midnight. The restaurant was closing down for the night. The customer that had attracted her sympathy, "Mr. Bond," was now quite drunk. She had brought him some coffee earlier in an effort to sober him up. He accepted the coffee and asked for the check. She brought him his check, which he paid after fumbling around in his wallet. He gave her a generous tip of thirty dollars. He had remained at his table for the past hour staring out the window. He seemed so very sad.

"Hey, Korie, what's with that guy?" said Danny, the bartender. He also doubled as the shift leader for the waitresses.

"I don't really know."

"Well, we're closing. See if you can move him along. If he's too drunk to drive, we'll call him a cab, but he's got to go."

"Okay, okay, I'll see what I can do."

Korie walked over to Aaron's table and sat down. She tapped Aaron on the arm to get his attention and received no response.

"Mr. Bond, please, we're getting ready to close. Would you like me to get you a cab?"

Aaron slowly turned towards her. He looked her straight in the eye and whispered, "I'm not Mr. Bond. My name is Aaron."

"Pleased to meet you, Aaron."

Korie's heart began to pump a bit faster now that she was speaking to him, face to face. She found him to be quite handsome. Whatever was making him sad also made him seem so vulnerable.

She placed her left hand over his left hand. He didn't pull away at her touch. Their eyes were now locked upon one another.

"Is there something wrong, Aaron?"

"Yes," he whispered as his eyes began to water up again.

"Uh, listen, why don't I give you a lift home in my car and you can take a cab back tomorrow to get your car? I really don't think you should be driving tonight."

"Your name is Korie, that's a pretty name," he said as he tried to force a smile.

"You wait here, I'll be right back," she said as she stood up.

She headed to the bar and whispered something to the bartender. He shook his head in obvious disagreement to whatever Korie was saying. Nevertheless, she quickly went into the employee's locker room and retrieved her coat and purse.

As she exited the locker room, she handed an envelope to the bartender. "There's the last of my tips for tonight. I'll check back for my share tomorrow, when I come in."

"You be careful."

"Thanks, you know I will. He just needs a lift home."

"Uh-huh."

Korie slipped into her coat and headed over to Aaron's table. She helped him to his feet and guided him to the front door. She had to struggle just to keep him up as he staggered between tables and chairs. Soon the two of them were outside standing next to her seven year old Honda Accord. She unlocked the passenger side door and helped him to sit in the front seat. He made a most ungraceful effort at this otherwise ordinary task. She had to lift his two legs and set them inside the car. She got into the driver's side and soon she was pulling out of the restaurant parking lot. She never gave it a second thought. This Aaron just seemed like he needed more from her than a ride home. It seemed to her that he needed a friend. She had decided to take Aaron to her apartment and let him sleep on the couch for the night. If he wanted to talk, that would be okay If he didn't, that would be fine too.

They drove silently to her apartment, which was just a couple of miles from the restaurant. It was a small cottage that she rented from an elderly couple who were both retired physicians. The cottage was set behind their house, but it shared a view of the ocean. The rent was unusually cheap. The elderly couple liked her a lot, and she appreciated their generosity. She ran errands for them on her days off from the restaurant. But most of all, she appreciated the fact that they didn't try to pry into her private life. They simply accepted her into their lives, and she would never do anything to hurt their trust and affection for her. She worried that bringing this man to her cottage apartment would upset them. She decided she would speak to them in the morning and explain that she just couldn't let this man go home alone. She felt they would understand.

Korie pulled her car to a stop alongside her cottage. She pulled the emergency brake on and turned the engine off. Aaron had fallen asleep during the short drive from the restaurant. He would have never made it safely home alone. She got out of the car and went to the passenger's side of the car and opened the car door. She reached in and unbuckled Aaron's seat belt. He was breathing heavily.

She took his head in her hands and shook it back and forth.

"Aaron, Aaron, please wake up, you're home." He slowly opened his eyes and looked at her and smiled a silly half-drunk smile.

"Home?"

"Yes, now let me help you get inside."

With that, she pulled his right arm and his whole body slowly followed along. He pulled his own legs out of car. She tugged at his arm. He grabbed on to the car door as he helped himself to his feet. After closing the car door, she led him to her front door.

"Hey, I don't recognize this. This, this can't be my place."

"I know you are too drunk to drive, so I decided to bring you to my place to spend the night. I hope you don't think I'm out of line."

"Naw," said Aaron as he leaned against the front outside wall of the house. His head was spinning. He tried to hold his head with his hands, but as he tried to lift them they felt like they weighed a hundred pounds each.

Korie put her house key into the front door deadbolt lock and unlocked the door. She opened the door and then reached around the left inside of the door and flipped an inside wall switch, turning on the foyer's overhead light. Aaron squeezed his eyes shut in reaction to the sudden brightness of the light.

"C'mon inside."

Korie took Aaron by the hand and led him inside. With her right foot, she managed to softly kick the front door shut. She led him into the kitchen first, where she had him sit at the table. She turned the overhead light on for the stove, which was the softest light in the kitchen. With his elbows on the table, Aaron buried his head into his hands.

"Coffee?"

"Sure," said Aaron.

Korie proceeded to make a carafe of coffee with her Mr. Coffee machine. She sat down at the table across from Aaron as the coffee began to drip into the carafe. The aroma of freshly brewing coffee filled the small kitchen. Nearly everything in this kitchen was white with sunflower yellow accents. Korie stared at this man she had brought home. As a young girl, she was always bringing home some hurt or abandoned animal. She would take care of them with a level of attention and affection that was uncompromising.

Korie reached across the table and pulled Aaron's hands apart. Their eyes met once more. They looked at one another for a short while.

"Aaron, what's wrong? Is there anything I can do to help you?"

Aaron, without saying a word reached into his coat pocket, and pulled the papers out and placed them upon the white table top.

"My aunt, who raised me all my life, died this summer. I didn't know she had died."

"I'm so sorry."

"Yeah, thanks. Well, anyway, she named me in her will. So today I went up to Boston and met with her attorney, who is handling her estate," said Aaron as he began to sniffle. Korie handed him a napkin.

"Pheeeze," as he blows his nose.

"Go on," said Korie.

"Well, it seems that she left me a lot of money. In fact, she left me everything."

"She must have cared for you a lot?"

"You don't know the half of it. I decided to come down to the Cape and celebrate. That's how I ended up at your restaurant. This is some celebration, huh?

"Nothing wrong with that. Do you miss her, is that why you've been so sad tonight?"

"Yes and no. It's because of these papers the attorney gave me," he said as he poked his right index finger down on the papers.

"Go on, read them," he said.

"Oh no, I shouldn't, they're yours, I mean they're private, meant just for you."

"I want you to read them."

"The coffee's ready. Why don't we have some coffee first?" she said as she rose from the table. She really didn't want to read these personal papers from this man's dead aunt.

She poured them both a large cup of coffee. She set his cup down in front of him. She went to the refrigerator and came back to the table with a carton of coffee creamer. She put that on the table and sat back down.

"There's sugar and sweet and low in that bowl."

He took two packets of sugar and tried to pour them into his coffee. He spilled sugar all around the cup. He waved away the creamer when she offered it to him. She mixed her own coffee.

"She wasn't my aunt after all. She was my mother."

"What?"

"Yeah, my mother. It's all in here," he said as he again pointed to the papers lying on the table.

"Korie, right?"

"Yeah."

"Please read them. It's a letter from my mother and a copy of my birth and baptism certificates. I want you to read them. Go on."

He pushed the folded papers towards her. Reluctantly, she picked them up. Her curiosity had been piqued. She unfolded the letter and began to read.

The night was passing quickly. She finished reading the letter and she and Aaron got into a discussion about what it might have meant or what it really meant. They drank more coffee. She made a second carafe. Aaron told stories about his aunt. He still had a hard time referring to her as his mother. He and Korie laughed and cried at these tales. As the night passed, Aaron eventually began to speak of her as his mother.

"Hey, thanks," said Aaron.

"Thanks?"

"Yeah, for looking after me tonight, and for listening to me."

"Hey, it's okay."

"What time is it anyway?"

Looking over Aaron's shoulder, she glanced at the kitchen wall clock. It pointed to three forty in the morning.

"Well, it's almost a quarter to four."

"That late?"

"Yeah, look, I'll make up the couch for you. It's big and comfortable."

"That's fine, I'll help, if you don't mind."

"Not at all."

Soon the couch was set up with a blanket to serve as a bed sheet, and another to cover up with. Korie brought Aaron a pillow from her bedroom.

Aaron was still a little wobbly, but he managed to organize the couch into a suitable bed. He felt dryness in his mouth that he wanted to get rid of. Too much wine followed by too much coffee had left his breath ten ways past raunchy. After Korie used the bathroom, she said goodnight to Aaron and headed straight to her own bedroom. Aaron went into the bathroom and took some of her toothpaste and applied a generous amount to his right index finger. He than applied the toothpaste vigorously to his teeth. He then rinsed a couple of times. His mouth felt better. As he was about to exit the bathroom, he noticed a small bottle of perfume sitting on the counter. He picked it up. He didn't recognize the name, but his nose quickly identified the perfume as the same one he had noticed Korie wearing at the restaurant earlier. He took a deep sniff and let the fragrance fill his sense of smell. The odor was one which aroused a deeply sensuous reaction in Aaron. His memory kicked in. He could see her standing over him, that first moment, when she had approached his table.

Aaron left the bathroom and took a step towards Korie's bedroom. He stopped and glanced down at the soft light emanating from the bottom of her bedroom door.

Don't be a jerk, he thought. *She's just a nice person who helped you out.*

He shook his head slowly as he headed back over to the couch. He took off his sports jacket, folded it and laid it across the back of a wooden rocker, which shared the room with the couch. He then took off his shoes, leaving his socks on. He next took off his sports shirt and pants and carefully folded them as well, laying them over his sports coat. He climbed onto the couch and in a few moments he had fallen deep asleep.

Meanwhile in Korie's bedroom, she was lying in bed and couldn't fall asleep.

Had he approached her bedroom door earlier? Was he thinking of her? Did he find her attractive? What would she have done if he had come into her bedroom? These thoughts swirled inside her mind.

Finally, *how do you feel about him Korie?* she thought.

There was no clear answer. With that she reached over to the small nightstand light and turned it off. Sleep came moments later.

Aaron dreamed of his mother Laura. She seemed to speak to him in his dreams.

"Aaron, please stay away from Vermont. Go far away. Change your name. Hide, they're coming," said his mother as she looked over her shoulder. She was obviously frightened.

"Who's coming?" said Aaron.

"The Keepers."

Aaron seemed to reach out for his mother in his dream, but the image soon faded away. Aaron drifted off to a deeper, dreamless sleep.

Korie dreamed about Aaron's mother as well that night.

She also spoke to Korie from the dream world.

"Please help keep Aaron away from them."

"From who?"

"The Keepers."

"What do they want Aaron for?"

"He's the missing link they need to bring him across."

"Bring who across, I don't understand."

"Him, the Prince of Darkness, the Lord of Sin, the Evil One, he goes by many names."

"Why me?"

"Because you are special, chosen."

"What do you mean, chosen?"

"Please, help him."

"I still don't understand."

The specter of Aaron's mother that appeared to Korie in this dream looked over her shoulder and when she looked back at Korie a look of total terror had overtaken her. She opened her mouth to let loose a scream. Korie in her dream state braced herself for the sound of the scream. Instead the specter's mouth was silent. The image broke up into wispy traces that seemed to collapse into the silent open mouth of the fading image. Korie's mind froze that image in place. But something was happening to the traces of the image that filled the blackness of her mind. A new image was taking shape.

It was soon apparent to Korie who or what this new image was. The sinewy muscular outline of a face filled her entire mind. The face was that of a Halloween Devil's mask that she must have remembered from her childhood. It was a bright red. It glistened from out of the darkness it seemed to be suspended in. The plastic like mask began to evolve into a lifelike face, still bright red.

"Korie, he's mine," it spoke.

"No, no. No!" she shouted.

Korie woke to find herself sitting straight up in her bed. She was drenched in a cold night sweat.

From beyond the bedroom door, she could hear Aaron snoring.

9

The blinds were fully drawn in the windows that were on three sides of the large conference room. On the remaining wall of the large rectangular room was a large white board with some half-erased words scrawled across its face. To its left was a large bulletin board, layered with various papers and photos of houses from all around the greater Washington County. Next to the bulletin board were three small wooden plaques proclaiming Sutton Realty as the Real Estate Company of the Year for 1992, 1994 and 1995. Next to these smaller plaques was a larger one, which had a picture attached showing a women receiving the plaque from another woman. The caption inscribed in the brass plate below read "Vermont's Woman Entrepreneur of the Year-1997, Phyllis Atkins, President, Sutton Realty, Presented by the Governor of the State of Vermont, Margaret C. Caron."

The door to the conference room opened and in walked several people who were engaged in conversation. They moved about the room, locating chairs at what appeared to be a prearranged seating arrangement. The conference table seats twelve, but at the moment only ten seats are occupied. A silence settles over the room as the people seated fidget in their seats, all but one person that is. Reverend Simon B. Mitchell is seated at the farthest end of the table from the door. His hands are folded in front of him on the table in a prayerful pose. To his left and going around the conference table is Bob Senecal, owner of Bob's Garage. Next is Judge Arthur W. Fairchild and then Mrs. Lawless, office manager for the Governor of the State of Vermont. Next to her sits Charles Trainor, a popular local radio station disk jockey. To his left, sits Ed Foley, the veterinarian. To Ed's left is a vacant chair. This chair is at the opposite end of the conference table from the Reverend. To the left of that chair is another empty chair. Continuing around the table is Phyllis Atkins, President of the Sutton Real Estate Agency, whose conference room they are now using. To her left is Judy Perillo, who owns a successful motel next to Interstate 89. Next is Ed Townsend, a retired FBI agent. Finally there is Shirley Carter, who owns Sutton's one and only beauty shop.

"Brother Foley, did you bring the ingredients?" asked the Reverend.

Not wanting to challenge the obvious question, he answers, "Yes, yes, I brought everything."

"Good."

With that the conference door opens slowly and standing in its open space is young Sammy Porter. He is quiet and obviously nervous. His eyes dart about the room. He recognizes everyone in the room. He is wearing a clean white short sleeve dress shirt, clean pressed slacks. His hair is combed straight back. He is nudged into the room from behind. Following him into the room is Walter Yandow. Walter ushers him to the lone seat at the opposite end of the conference table. Walter then moves to the last empty chair and sits down. Sammy, not sure what to do with his hands, places them onto the table and mimics the pose of the Reverend. The Reverend looks at Sammy from across the table and breaks into a small smile.

"Welcome to our humble gathering, Mr. Porter," said the Reverend Mitchell.

"Uh, thank you, sir."

"We are in your debt this day, Mr. Porter. Indeed, HE is in your debt as well. HE is most grateful and desires to reward you for your faithfulness. Are you prepared to accept HIS most generous gift?"

Sammy had been coached on the way over to this meeting of what was about to take place and what to say by his escort, Walter.

"Yes, Reverend, I am prepared to accept His gift and to take my place among His faithful." He managed a sideways glance in the direction of Walter, who was revealing a slight smile.

"Very well. Before we proceed, will Judge Fairchild administer the oath?"

Judge Fairchild, an old man who wore his reading glasses at all times, while looking over them most of the time, pushed himself back from the conference table. He was wheezing as he stood up. His allergies had been bothering him. He was carrying a large book, which was black leather bound and resembled a large ledger book that an accountant might use. Its cover was embossed in gold leaf with the shape of a pentagram.

At the very sight of the book, Sammy's heart began racing even more rapidly than it had already. He had only heard about the book from others in whispered conversations. Sammy stood up.

The Judge held the book in front of Sammy and then he reached down and took Sammy's left hand with his own right hand and placed it on the book. The Judge's hand was cold to the touch.

"Repeat after me, Mr. Porter."

"Yes, sir!"

"I pledge my life on this earth, my soul for all eternity, to faithfully protect and serve."

Sammy Porter repeated the oath, beaming with pride.

"I renounce the faiths of mankind, the words of the prophets, and I reject the works of the Son of God."

Sammy spoke in a firm voice, without hesitation.

"Be seated," said the Judge.

The boy did as he was told.

The Reverend now stood up before the group. He opened his arms as he spoke.

"Seated in this room, Mr. Porter, are the chosen Keepers of HIS word. We are all descendants of the original coven, hand picked for the important task of being the assembled ones, to serve our leader, the Monarch of Hell, in this life and for all eternity. Our ancestors once agreed to serve as we now serve. A sacred final covenant had been reached to bring HIM to this side, to once again walk the earth in human form. As you have been taught, Mr. Porter, that covenant was broken by an unfaithful one. We carry forward a sacred tradition that one day it will be fulfilled as it is written in the Book of Final Covenant, to which you have just laid your hand in a solemn pledge."

As the Reverend spoke, each one in the room sat straight backed in their chairs as if they were hearing these words for the first time.

"Mr. Porter, you have been chosen not by us but by HIM who seeks you. Yes, you have smitten the enemy in HIS name with the two silencings that you participated in. But HE calls you because of a greater part that you can play in serving HIM. You, Mr. Porter, have a gift, the ability to listen to the thoughts of others. A gift that "HE who we all made a promise to," revealed to us. Are you aware of this great gift?"

The truth was all that was required at this moment.

"Yes, Reverend, I…I sort of knew I could hear the thoughts of others. I didn't…"

The Reverend held up his right hand to silence Sammy.

"We will work with you to develop this gift which you will use to serve HIM. Now, before we proceed with your receiving HIS gifts for eternal life, I want you to look at this and focus all of your attention on this symbol of our loyalty."

The Reverend pulls from his waistcoat a shiny object at the end of a long gold chain. It is a crucifix hanging from the chain in an upside down position. The Reverend begins to slowly twirl the crucifix. It sparkles, reflecting the overhead lights.

Slowly it rotates.

Sammy stares at the distant object. After a few moments, the crucifix seems to be coming through the air towards him. It is getting larger and larger. The Reverend seems to be fading into the background. The whole room begins to fade to black, except for the golden sparkle of the upside down crucifix, suspended in the midst of a blacker than black void.

The voice of the Reverend drifts away. Sammy hears a whispered voice calling to him.

The others in the room sit forward in their seats, knowing t they will only hear one half of the conversation to come. Each remembers, in their own way, their own first direct encounter with HIM.

"Sammy, it is I."

"Yes, Master," he responds.

"Sammy Porter, since the beginnings of creation, the Creator has made each of us in his likeness and image. Do you believe?"

"Yes, I believe."

"In the beginning, we were promised eternal life, to stand beside the Creator, to share in his gifts. Do you believe?"

"Yes, I believe."

"We were cast out, thrown down, sent away. Condemned and unloved, to be feared by mankind. Do you believe?"

"Yes, feared by mankind. I believe."

"I am Moloch, Lucifer's most loyal lieutenant, on his behalf I offer you eternal life, power over all. I will make you Master over Mankind. We will not break our covenant to you. You will one day sit at HIS right hand along with all the other faithful. Do you believe?"

"Yes, Moloch, I believe."

Just hearing HIS name caused a mild gasp from some in the room.

"Samuel Porter, will you serve me loyally, will you strive to find the unfaithful one, are you willing to reach into this blackness and bring me forth so that I may pave the way for Lucifer's arrival to rule over the earth?"

"Yes, I will be a faithful servant, I will be a keeper, ever loyal."

With his eyes in a trance like state, Sammy extends his slender arms onto the table, palms facing upward.

"I want to serve," says Sammy Porter.

With that, Ed Foley rises from his seat and unfolds a small white cloth onto the table. Inside the cloth is a small vial attached to a needle, a small piece of gauze and a band aid. He is seated to Sammy's right. Standing next to the boy, he removes elastic from his own coat pocket and ties the upper left arm of the boy with it. Next, he searches for a suitable vein which he soon locates in the crook of the boys inner arm at the elbow. He takes the needle with the vial attached and plunges it indelicately into the boy's arm. In a moment, the vial fills up with rich, dark blood. Ed now pulls the needle and vial out of the boy's arm, while he places the piece of gauze over the puncture wound and applies modest pressure. The gauze is soon replaced by the band aid.

"Mrs. Lawless, will you please retrieve the sacred goblet."

She pushes herself from the table and goes over to the bulletin board. She removes a small device from her suit coat that resembles a garage door opener and points it at the bulletin board. Her thumb presses down on the device. At that instant, a soft click is heard as the bulletin board pushes away from the wall. She puts the device back into her coat pocket as she steps forward to the bulletin board. She reaches out and pulls it open to the left, revealing a hidden safe. She nimbly turns the dial a couple of times, then pulls down on the small black handle. She reaches inside the safe and removes a small earthen cup, etched with several markings. Protruding from inside the cup is a small yellowish brown bone of some sort. Mrs. Lawless walks to the front of the room and places the cup on the table in front of the Reverend. She continues around the table and returns to her seat.

"Mr. Foley, if you please," said the Reverend.

Ed moves from his seat to the head of the table. He pours the contents of the vial of blood that he had just extracted from Sammy Porter into the cup before the Reverend. From his coat pocket he removes a small folding case. The case glitters in the room's light. It is obviously made of gold. He opens the case and inside of it is a small vial of blood just like the one he just emptied into the cup. Ed empties this vial of blood into the cup as well. Also inside this gold case is a small gold compact. Ed delicately removes this compact and opens it over the cup. He pinches a small amount of gray ashen dust from inside and drops it into the cup. Ed replaces the compact and vial inside the case and places them back into his pocket. Ed returns to his seat next to Sammy Porter.

The Reverend pulls the cup directly in front of him and proceeds to gently stir the contents inside of the cup. He whispers an ancient incantation taught to him by Moloch. He passes the cup to his left and Shirley Carter, Sutton's one and only beautician, takes the cup with both hands. She removes the bone and licks at the dark red liquid that drips from it. She passes the cup around the table and each one present repeats this ritual. Finally after the cup has returned to the Reverend and he too has tasted its contents by licking the small bone, he rises and walks down to where Sammy Porter is seated and places the cup in front of Sammy.

"Moloch commands all to drink and share in the promise of the blood."

Sammy opens his eyes and looks down at the cup set before him. He picks it up with both hands and slowly drinks from it while closing his eyes.

Everyone else in the room rises from their chairs and applauds Sammy Porter. Joy engulfs them all. Sammy, finished drinking the contents of the cup, removes the bone and licks it clean. He puts the cup with the bone placed inside back down onto the table.

Sammy opens his eyes. They have changed to a deep, lifeless black. They resemble the eyes of a shark—haunting, menacing, cold and totally evil. Sammy responds to everyone's applause by rising and nodding to the room. Sammy raises his hands and gestures for all to be seated. The room falls silent.

Sammy now speaks in a raspy guttural voice that is clearly not his own "I am pleased you have chosen this one for our coven, our circle of Keepers. You and your ancestors have all served me faithfully for these many years and as I have promised to each of you before, I repeat once again. I, Moloch, on behalf of the Great Satan, solemnly pledge that you shall have all the riches of this earth, all the power known to mankind, all that there is shall be yours and your successors forevermore, once you have fulfilled our pact. Once I take up human form, and walk again upon this earth to prepare the way, you, each of you, shall rule beside us over all that is created."

Sammy now closes his eyes and sits limply back into his chair. He rolls his head once and then his eyes flutter open. His eyes are once again the eyes of Sammy Porter.

The Reverend speaks to Sammy.

"Mr. Porter, tonight you mingled your blood with the blood and ashes of the late John Farnum, Sutton's Fire Chief who had served each of us and the Prince of Darkness well since he became a Keeper over forty years ago. We all have shared in that blood union tonight. We have joined you as you have joined us. That blood and ashes potion was mixed with a bone from the family of the one who deceived the first Keepers that night long ago. Mr. Porter, now and forevermore you are one of us, a Keeper. Welcome."

They all rise and proceed to approach young Sammy Porter and shake his hand. He blushes from all of the attention.

Reverend Mitchell hands the cup and bone to Mrs. Lawless and she carefully returns it to the security of the wall safe. Soon the safe is closed, locked and the bulletin board is returned to its usual place.

Reverend Mitchell raps his knuckles upon the table to get everyone's attention.

"Please, if everyone could be seated we can go on to the rest of our affairs."

The room returns to a complete silence as they each await direction from Reverend Simon B. Mitchell. The Reverend serves as the current leader of the coven. He became the coven's new leader when he succeeded the late Cornelius Schenk who had been one of the Town's most successful businessmen. Long ago, Schenk founded a business manufacturing wooden screen doors and windows. His company, Schenk Screens Incorporated, at one time employed 360 people. After the Korean War, he sold his business to a large national company for what some say was several millions of dollars. He died in 1960, at the age of fifty-one, from syphilis. He had gone stark raving mad at the end. There had even been rumors that he had taken his own life.

The truth was neither. The Reverend Simon B. Mitchell, then a young twenty five-year old assistant pastor of the local church, had strangled Cornelius Schenk to death.

Moloch had told the Reverend it must be done. The Reverend was an obedient servant. Indeed, he was a most obedient servant.

10

Aaron woke up with a huge headache. His temples were throbbing with a pounding that seemed to increase with any movement. His eyes ached from a different sort of pain. They seemed to burn from within. He could only manage to open his eyes after a huge effort, and then only just a mere slit of an opening. He looked about the room and realized that it wasn't his own place. He sat on the couch for a few minutes trying to get a grip on his battling senses. He spotted his pants draped across the back of chair. He reached over and grabbed his pants and slipped them on. Aaron now seemed to remember talking to the beautiful waitress that had served him last night.

What was her name? he thought.

His morning after mental fog began to lift as he tried to focus upon his whereabouts. He stood up with the aid of holding on to the arm of the couch. As he looked about, he began to remember the layout of the place and more.

Korie, that's her name, he recalled speaking it in a whisper. He looked at his wristwatch. The digital display told him it was a quarter to twelve or nearly noon. Aaron headed to the bathroom, tiptoeing as he went. He remembered that her bedroom was just off the hall, which leads to the bathroom. He used the bathroom to relieve himself. Aaron also borrowed some toothpaste to swish around in his mouth. His mouth had tasted like worn out carpet. Now it felt almost normal.

After exiting the bathroom, he tiptoed to the door which led to Korie's bedroom. It was open slightly. As he tried to sneak a peak inside, he noticed a note taped to the door. Aaron pulled the taped note from the door and headed to the kitchen. In the kitchen, he read the note.

Good morning, Aaron.

I had to leave to go to work. Today I have a double shift at the restaurant. I'll try to call you this afternoon when I get a break. If you're still there, that is. Please help yourself to anything you want. If you want some fresh coffee, just turn on the coffee maker. It's all ready filled and ready to go.

If you have to go, I left the number of the local cab company on the note pad next to the phone. Don't worry about locking up, because my landlord keeps a close eye on the place.

I want you to know I enjoyed talking with you last night. I hope your head doesn't hurt too much.

Hugs, Korie

Aaron put the note into his pants pocket. Later after he had a cup of coffee, he called the cab company, whose number Korie had left for him. The bright summer light hurt his eyes when he first stepped outside. He held his right hand up to block the direct effect of the afternoon's light from his eyes.

"Where to?"

"Take me to The Royals."

The cab backed slowly down the narrow driveway. The cabbie had all the windows of his cab fully open.

"If you don't want the windows open, I'll close them," said the young driver.

"No, it's fine. I'm enjoying the fresh air."

Moments later, the cab pulled into the half filled parking lot of The Royals Restaurant. Aaron got out of the cab and paid the driver. The driver gave him a friendly wave as he drove off. For a moment, Aaron thought he would go inside the restaurant and see Korie. After a moment, he decided against going inside. He had made a spectacle of himself last night. She had been a Good Samaritan and helped him out. He would leave it at that.

Aaron fished around his pants pocket and came up with his car keys. He went over to his car and unlocked it. As he opened the driver's door, a blast of hot air pushed at him from the car's overheated interior. He went around the car to all four doors and rolled each window completely down. Aaron drove off, heading to his own place. From his apartment, he would call a local florist and have a bouquet of flowers sent to Korie at the restaurant, as an expression of his gratitude for her having befriended him the night before.

From the moment the cab arrived in the parking lot of the restaurant, Korie watched Aaron's movements from behind the tinted windows of the restaurant. As she served her lunch crowd customers, she kept an eye on the parking lot.

Would he come inside and thank her? she wondered.

Her thoughts were quickly answered when he headed towards his car. When the car pulled out of the parking lot, her heart sank.

There you go again Korie, helping some stray, she thought to herself. For a moment she indulged herself with some self pity. She had liked Aaron. There was a quiet but sensitive quality about him that she was attracted to. Her defenses took over now. She closed her mental drawer on Aaron, as she focused her attention entirely upon her job.

After entering his condominium, Aaron immediately called a local florist and ordered a huge bouquet to be delivered to Korie by three o'clock that afternoon. He dictated a note to be delivered along with the flowers. The florist took down Aaron's charge card number and assured him that the delivery would be on time as requested.

Aaron headed to his bathroom to take a long shower. Half an hour later, he emerged from his bathroom freshly shaved and showered. He went to the kitchen and poured himself a tall glass of milk. Aaron then opened the cupboard and pulled out a bag of chocolate chip cookies.

Milk and cookies for lunch. What would my Aunt, check that, my Mother, say about that? he thought.

He could feel the "blues" coming on, so he pushed the thought back deep into his mind.

With a fresh change of clothes, Aaron headed out the door on a mission. He was going to the bank to retrieve the diary that his mother's letter spoke about. The safety deposit box key was safely tucked away inside its envelope. He still carried the letter from his late mother. The jacket was sitting on the passenger side seat of his car. His mind was swirling with questions as he drove north along the highway back to Boston. He had a growing urge to follow this mystery to its conclusion, wherever it would take him.

Meanwhile, back at The Royals Restaurant a florist's delivery car pulled up in front and the young driver got out of the car. He opened the hatch back and removed a large bouquet of colorful flowers. He took the front steps to the restaurant two at a time. In a moment, he is speaking to the young female hostess. The hostess tells him to wait at her station for a moment. She enters the restaurant's large dining area and searches out Korie.

After whispering to Korie, the two of them returned to the Hostess's station.

"This is Korie," said the young hostess.

"I've been instructed to give these to you personally. Oh, and this card, too," said the young delivery boy as he placed the bouquet into Korie's outstretched arms. He tucked the note into the bouquet.

"Have a nice day," said the delivery boy as he turned and hurried out the front door.

The two women just stood there giggling over the surprise bouquet and admiring its beauty and fragrance.

"I'll find something to put them in," said the hostess.

"That would be great," said Korie. The hostess disappeared and in a few moments returned with a large, open mouthed wine carafe, half filled with water.

"I rinsed it out first," said the hostess as the two women opened the bouquet and arranged the flowers inside. As they finished with that task, Korie's eyes went wide.

"My customers," she said as she turned away and hurried towards the dining area. She slipped the note into her waitress's skirt pocket without opening it.

"Please put them in a safe place will you, Heather?" said Korie from over her shoulder as she hurried back to work.

"Don't worry, I will," said Heather.

Later that afternoon, Aaron walked out of the Bank of Boston with an old tattered leather bound book under his arm. He reclaimed his car from the bank parking garage and after several more minutes, he was once again on the Southeast Expressway heading south towards his condominium back in Middleborough.

Later, instead of heading to his condo he found himself heading back to The Royals Restaurant. He decided he needed to see Korie. Over the last few miles he practiced several versions of an apology. He took the leather bound diary with him into the restaurant. The hostess was new—at least Aaron didn't recognize her from the night before. He requested a table in Korie's section of the restaurant and at the window if at all possible.

The hostess said he could have such a table in a few minutes. As he stood in the waiting area he looked inside the dining area and could see Korie moving from table to table. Aaron enjoyed looking at her. She had a graceful way about her. Her face carried a natural smile that made her look radiant.

"Sir, sir...Your table's ready. Sir, I said your table's ready," said the hostess.

"Oh, yes, thanks."

"Follow me, please."

As Aaron entered the dining area, Korie immediately noticed him. She gave him a warm smile.

"Here you are, sir. A window table just as you requested. Enjoy your dinner. Your waitress will be with you in a moment."

"Thanks."

Aaron sat at the table. He placed the leather bound diary to the side of the table. Korie came to his table with a pitcher of water. She filled his water glass.

"Look, I want to apologize to you for my drunken condition last night. And I want to thank you for your kindness in seeing to it that I had a safe place to sleep it off."

"Hey, it's okay. It is not a problem, really." Korie standing before Aaron shifted her feet. Their eyes met. He wanted to say more but felt uncomfortable. She wanted to tell him she really liked him but she was unsure of his feelings.

"Well, anyway, tonight's special is ..."

"Wait, why don't you surprise me? You order for me."

"I can't, I..."

"Please. Oh, and no alcohol tonight. I need a clear head. Look, I picked up the diary that my mother wrote about," said Aaron as he placed his right hand on the old tattered book.

Korie looked over at the diary. Then she looked back at Aaron.

"All right. I'll be right back."

She turned and left. As she walked away he admired her legs. They were slender and seemed to him to project the delicateness of a ballet dancer.

Aaron pulled the diary over and carefully opened it up. The inside cover had faded inscriptions in several different hand writings, which read:

> The words of this journal are the true and honest account of my life, Irene Powell, formally of Sutton, Vermont. Born March 11, 1842. Died May 1, 1870.
>
> This journal holds the account of my life as well, Constance Morgan Powell, Born December 1, 1862. Died Approximately June 1892.
>
> Colleen Day Powell, Born June 22, 1877 and died December 30, 1911.
>
> My life and accounts by Sarah Miller Powell, Born July 7, 1900. Died February 10, 1931.
>
> Mary Fulton Powell, Born August 2, 1920. Died June 1, 1941.
>
> Elizabeth Corbin Powell, Born September 17, 1940.
>
> Aaron Corbin Powell, Born November 11, 1966.

Aaron took out a pen from his inside jacket pocket and added next to the entry for Elizabeth Corbin Powell the inscription that she died on May 14, 1997.

At that moment, Korie returned with a bowl of steaming hot clam chowder with a small bowl of oyster crackers.

"You're going to love the chowder. We're sort of known for our chowders. It's made from scratch."

"Thanks."

"Well, anyway, I'll be back later, enjoy."

Aaron took a small handful of oyster crackers and dropped them into the soup. He picked up his soup spoon and carefully took a taste, after blowing upon the steaming soup settled in his spoon. Its taste was delightful. Aaron now returned his attention to the diary, as he slowly ate the clam chowder. He was soon deeply engrossed in the accounts of this, his family journal. Starting at the beginning, he slowly turned the delicate pages. They were well worn with the edges creased and slightly torn in several places.

Time seemed to fly by as he studied the accounts of Irene Powell, his great grandmother several times removed. He learned more about this coven, devil worshipping cult. He read about the several attempts to locate her and how she eluded their efforts.

"Shit, I just can't believe this," he thought. His mind was swimming with all sorts of images.

He skipped ahead several pages into the diary to an entry by Colleen Day Powell. It was dated August 4, 1907.

> There was a strange man who visited the house today. Mrs. Cullity spoke to me about this gentleman, who came calling and asking about me. She said, she told him nothing. He said he was a long lost relative from Vermont. He told her I had come into some property and he was sure I would want to be informed about my good fortune. He insisted he had traced me to this house through correspondence with relatives back in Vermont. He left his card and directed Mrs. Cullity to be sure I received it. He said I could reach him at the Mayflower Hotel.
>
> Mrs. Cullity said the man seemed to her to be untrustworthy. She inquired at the Mayflower with her good friend Mrs. Hobbs, as to the circumstances of the man who called himself Mr. Harper. It seems

there was no one registered at the Hotel with that name. There was a gentleman there who resembled Mr. Harper but he had given his name as Mr. Carpenter. Mrs. Hobbs says all of her girls, that she is responsible for, are afraid of this man.

I've not written to anyone in Vermont, ever. How did they find me? What circumstance has led them to me?

The next entry read August 5, 1907.

I went to the Mayflower Hotel today. I had to see this man for myself. Mrs. Hobbs let me wear a maid's uniform and I worked with her daughter, Cynthia, cleaning and fixing rooms. When we knocked at Mr. Carpenter's (or Mr. Harper's) room, there was no answer. Cynthia used her passkey and we entered the room. It looked as if no one was staying in that room. The bed was proper. The room was as fit as could be. However, as we were taking our leave this Mr. Carpenter walks into the room. His eyes fix upon both of us. We excused ourselves and moved past him to the door. As I left the room, I looked back at this man who is now facing the mirror over the dresser against the far wall. His face is knotted with anger, but the reflections of his eyes were unmistakable. They were like two black coals set into the place where a persons eyes should normally be. His eyes were just as mother said they would be, black and lifeless. It is the Keepers of the Evil Agreement, they've come for me.

Korie had returned to his table and removed his soup dish. She brought him a salad. It was covered in a dressing that gave off a light bouquet of deliciously blended spices with olive oil.

"Is the diary interesting?"

"Yeah, very."

"Well, anyway, your entrée will be ready in a few minutes, Mr. Bond."

He smiled at this playful reference to their first meeting last night.

"Great, I can't wait. Can you tell me what it will be?"

"That would spoil it for you."

"Fine, I do like surprises," said Aaron as he flashed his usual smile.

Korie turned and left, but as she walked away she thought, *I can't believe I used that corny Mr. Bond line again. He must think I'm so duh...fake.*

Little did Korie know that Aaron really liked her playful reference to James Bond.

He returned his attention to the diary and read on.

The entry was dated August 7, 1907

.

I packed my things and left the house today. It was so nice living there these past four years. Mrs. Cullity has been like a mother to me. I had no choice. I couldn't put the others in danger. These coven people, who seek me, killed my mother and I know they would do the same to me. I will not be their handmaiden in bringing Satan to walk upon this earth. That evil man came around again last evening. He was insistent. Mrs. Cullity said if he didn't leave she would call for the police to dispatch him. He said he didn't want any trouble. We all could see him standing outside the house, across the street, under a gaslight, until late in the evening when he disappeared. At six o'clock in the morning, I packed what I could carry in one carpetbag and hurried to the train station. I left Chicago with very little. Mrs. Cullity said she would send the rest of my things when I get settled. The train ride is making me sleepy, but I dare not fall asleep during the nighttime. I am looking forward to meeting Mrs. Cullity's younger sister, Miss Whitehouse. New Orleans sounds like a magical place. I pray I shall never see those cold black eyes ever again.

Aaron began to carefully turn the pages in search for an entry that would detail how Colleen Day Powell's mother, Constance Morgan Powell, died.

Korie returned to his table with his entrée. She had brought him a thick cut of swordfish broiled in garlic and butter. It was presented on a plate with a generous helping of baked red gourmet potatoes accented with a sprig of parsley. She had also brought him a side dish of summer squash.

"It looks just great, Korie."

"Thanks. I hope you enjoy it."

"Do you have any herbal tea?"

"Yes, we do. I'll go and check on the flavors."

"That won't be necessary. Just surprise me again."

"So, you like surprises, do you?"

"It would seem so from what my life has been like lately."

"Any surprises in the diary?"

"Plenty. I sure would like to talk to you about them. What time do you get off tonight?"

"Well, tonight I don't have to work until close, I get off at ten."

"Great, would you join me for a late dinner or coffee or whatever?"

Shrugging her shoulders, she smiles, and says, "Sure I guess so. Oh, listen, thanks for the flowers, they're great."

"I'm glad you liked them," he said as he reached over to her and softly touched her right hand.

His touch felt like an electric shock without the electricity. Sweeping her hair back behind her ears with left hand, she smiled and looked away. She felt a blush coming on.

"Ten o'clock."

"What?"

"I get off at ten o'clock!"

Korie quickly turned and left to attend to the other tables in her area. All she could think about was Aaron. He was special, she just knew it.

Aaron returned to reading the dairy and enjoying his meal.

Later Korie stopped by briefly with his tea. The tea was a red zinger, strong, but without a biting aftertaste.

"Got to run, I'm behind with a couple of my tables," said Korie as she dashed off to attend to a table of six, just two tables away.

Aaron filled his time by sampling excerpts from the diary. The stories seemed to be woven from a common thread, tales of how his ancestors were pursued from one end of the country to the other. There were words of fear, hatred and anger and there were words of strength, courage and hope.

The night seemed to just melt away.

Just as Aaron was finishing his second cup of tea, Korie sat down across from him. He looked up and smiled at her arrival.

"So, Korie, are you done for the evening?"

"Yeah, and not a moment too soon. My feet are killing me," she answered with a tired exhale of air.

"Can I order you something to eat? Perhaps a cup of coffee?"

"Not really. The kitchen is starting to close down anyway.

Look, I've got an idea. About a mile and a half north of here, along Ocean Boulevard, is an ice cream stand that stays open until eleven o'clock. It's got the best homemade ice cream on the Cape. I sure could go for a large scoop of double fudge chocolate ice cream."

"Sounds perfect," said Aaron.

He picked up the check and the diary. He began to head for the cashier when he remembered he hadn't left a tip. It was an awkward moment to say the least. He started to turn back to leave a tip when Korie caught him by the arm.

"Hey, I don't want you to leave a tip for me. If you want to leave something for the busboy, that would be fine. Were friends, remember? If you'll buy me that ice cream we'll be even, okay?"

Aaron smiled at Korie and took her arm in his as they headed to the cashier. Moments later they were in his car driving up to the ice cream restaurant. The flowers he had ordered for her earlier in the day were wrapped and lying on the backseat.

"Over there, see it, Otto's Ice Cream Parlor."

"That's the place?"

"Yeah, you can park right in front."

He pulled his car to a stop almost directly in front. They both got out of the car and walked across the sidewalk to the takeout window. A large lady was sitting on a stool behind a sliding window screen. She was wearing a red and white checkered uniform that seemed way too tight for her. She was chewing gum at a furious pace. Her hair was dyed blond and she wore far too much eye makeup. She was reading a heavily thumbed copy of Cosmopolitan.

"Hi, Ginger," said Korie.

"Well, look it here, it's Korie. Where have you been keeping yourself, honey?"

"I've been putting in some long hours at the restaurant."

"I know the feeling, believe me. But the money sure is good, ain't it?" she said as she slid off of her stool.

"Ginger, let me introduce you to my friend. This is Aaron. Aaron...Ginger."

"Nice to meet you, Ginger," he nodded.

Ginger slid open the window screen and reached out for one of Aaron's hands. He was caught somewhat off guard. She snatched his right hand with her right and immediately turned his hand over, palm side facing up. She began to trace the lines in his hands with the index finger of her left hand. She wore an eclectic collection of rings on each finger of both of her hands. Korie laughed at her friend's antics.

"Ginger is a palm reader. She says that by reading the lines in the palm of your hands, she can predict your future. Well, Ginger, what do you see?"

Ginger's mind flashes with a burst of images. The images are of a child tied to a large flat rock. A huge knife is poised directly over the child's torso. There is chanting coming from dozens of people surrounding the flat rock. Their eyes are solid black, glassy, cold, and evil.

Ginger feels a chill grip her and her entire body quivers from the chill. The images have now faded away.

"Well, Ginger? Is Aaron going to become President of the United States? Is he about to take a long trip? Is he going to meet someone beautiful?"

Regaining her composure, Ginger releases Aaron's hand. She wipes her own hands on her apron.

"Uh, he's going to be famous, real famous," she answers with a less than hearty smile. She doesn't want to look either one of them in the face right now. If she does, she believes she would just burst out what she had just seen in her mind's eye.

"So, Korie, the usual?"

"Yeah. Aaron, what about you?"

"I'll have a scoop of maple walnut."

Ginger turned her back on the two as she prepared their order.

"Isn't she something?"

"Yeah, something," said Aaron.

He had also experienced the same mental images, only his version was a good deal fainter. One thing is for sure. He felt her fear. For the time being, he decided he would keep his thoughts to himself.

In a moment their order was ready. Aaron paid for the ice cream while Korie took their ice cream, along with a couple of paper napkins.

As they were about to leave for Aaron's car, Ginger called to Korie.

"Korie!"

Korie leaned over the counter. Ginger leaned forward as well.

"Korie, you be careful honey." Her eyes conveyed a sense of concern.

"What do you mean? Is it Aaron?"

"No, no, it's ...well...it's just that. Oh, I don't know. Just be careful, for me...okay."

"I will. Look, he's a nice guy...he just lost his mother. Anyway, we're just friends."

Korie's look of reassurance didn't deliver the intended effect. Nevertheless Ginger squeezed Korie's arm and managed a smile for her.

Ginger shouted to Aaron, who had just about reached his car, "You take care, Aaron. It was a pleasure meeting you, honey."

"Thanks, I will. It was nice meeting you, too."

When Korie got back into Aaron's car, she handed him his ice cream along with a napkin.

"What was that all about?"

"Just girl talk. Nothing important."

11

The Game Warden's car pulled to a stop in front of Sammy Porter's house on Weston Street. There were lights on in every room on the first floor of the small cape.

"Want me to come in with you?" said Walter.

"No," said Sammy with a tone of resoluteness the Game Warden had not noticed before. Sammy was riding shotgun.

"Leave him be," said Judy Perillo from the back seat. "He'll be just fine. She reached up to the front seat with her right hand and ran her fingers through Sammy's hair.

"Thank you for all of your help. I'm sure I can handle this," said Sammy as he exited the car.

He didn't hesitate but strode boldly to the front door of his house. The front door swung open and Sammy's mother stood in the doorway. She wrapped Sammy in her arms. She then looked out to the Game Warden's car and gave a wave.

"Your place or mine?" asked Walter as he looked into the back seat at Judy Perillo by glancing up into the rearview mirror.

"My place. I've got a new waterbed that I'm just dying to try out," she said as she put her right index finger up to her lower lip and managed a pouty look for the benefit of Walter.

The car surged forward as Walter Yandow pressed his foot down on the accelerator.

Sheeee...it...a waterbed, he thought.

Judy, on the other hand, was thinking about the newest member of the coven. This young boy was going to need some special help. Just the kind of help Judy enjoyed providing. She smiled her widest smile while she squeezed her thighs together. She shuddered from the effects of a mild climax.

Meanwhile, Sammy pushed past his mother and walked to the kitchen. His father, Steve, and older sister, Kelley, were both sitting at the table in the kitchen. Sammy's older brother, Jeff, had died the year before in a car accident. The table and chairs were circa 1950s with chrome legs and a Formica table top. Without saying a word, Sammy opened the refrigerator and removed a plastic gallon half filled with milk. He removed the plastic cap and stood in front of the open refrigerator door while he drank directly from the milk container.

His father stood up and wiped his hands on his khaki pants. He nudged Sammy's sister to stand as well. She was a year older and had been developing into a beautiful young woman. She had been working on a dried flower arrangement. His father, a twenty-two year counter man at the local lumberyard, was prematurely bald. Sammy's mother, Connie, sold Avon cosmetics at house parties to help with the family's expenses. She always wore a too generous amount of her products. She was a pleasant looking woman whose taste in clothes was too old for her age.

Sammy finished the milk and closed the refrigerator door. He wiped the slight traces of milk from his upper lip with the back of his right hand. He placed the empty container on the well worn kitchen counter.

Clearing her throat, his mother spoke first, "Sammy we're all so proud of you."

"Real proud, son," said his father as he extended his hand in a handshake gesture.

Sammy's sister just stood there silently staring at her brother.

"There are going to be some changes around here," said Sammy with a stern voice. His voice was deeper than the voice he had left with earlier that evening.

"First of all, no one is to call me Sammy anymore. My name is Samuel. Is that clear?"

Everyone nodded their agreement.

"Mother, I want you to stop wearing any perfume while in this house. I have always found the odors offensive. Father, when you go to work tomorrow, you are to speak to Mr. Steadman the owner, about your new job."

"My what?"

"You heard me. And as for you, my sweet little sister, you are to stop seeing Paul Lacosse. Moloch has revealed to me you have been unfaithful with someone who is not of our faith. He's is unclean, and an outsider. This must end, now! Moloch demands it, as do I."

His sister raised her left hand as if to slap her brother in the face when she noticed his totally black eyes. She froze in the middle of her swing. Her arms then went limp as she slowly sat down in her kitchen chair.

Samuel's father and mother stood silent, as they also noticed his cold, all black eyes.

Finally, his mother spoke "Samuel, uh, would you care for some supper. I could, uh, warm up something for you if you'd like."

"Yes, mother, that would please me."

Samuel sat down at the kitchen table, as did his father.

"Samuel, about this job, is there anything else you can tell me?"

"Everything is arranged. We will soon be moving to our new home. Moloch will take care of our needs as he always does!"

Kelley sat at the table with her brother and father. Her mother was busy fixing dinner for Samuel. Kelley, however, was in a deep trance. Her mind was now being taken on a mental journey by Moloch. It would be a journey guaranteed to return her as a fearful but obedient servant.

Samuel's mother served him a plate filled with his favorite, spaghetti and meatballs from a can. As he ate his supper, the rest of the family sat around the table in silence. Kelley's mind was busy serving up a kaleidoscope of horrors courtesy of Moloch.

Samuel stood up from the table and placed his plate in the kitchen sink.

"I'm tired. I'm going to go to bed now."

As Samuel left the room his mother quickly reached across the table and held her husband's hands in her own.

"Steve, we're so lucky," she beamed.

"I hope you're right Connie, I just hope you're right."

"Our Sammy, I mean Samuel is a Keeper, a chosen member of the coven. I just knew that he would make it someday. Yes, I just knew," she repeated.

"Yes, honey, a Keeper of the Agreement. I wonder what this job thing is that he spoke about."

"Oh, it will be wonderful, I am sure of it!"

Kelley can hear her parents speaking, but she is unable to speak herself. Moloch now begins to lessen his grip of terror. Deep inside she is terrified of her own brother, and now her father and mother as well. This deeply held terror was not generated by the efforts of Moloch. These were fears she had shared with her friend, Paul Lacosse, one day when they were riding home on the school bus. He too felt the same fear.

"I sometimes think I'm being watched. Even when I'm in my bed at night, it feels like I'm being watched. You know, kinda like someone's looking in my room from the bedroom window," confided Paul one day while sitting on the school bus next to Kelley.

"Yeah, I know what you mean. It's real creepy, like just this morning, as I looked in the bathroom mirror—I thought that I could see someone watching me from over my shoulder. I swear I could almost feel their breath on my neck."

Paul shivered a bit, which caused Kelley to do likewise. She then looked over her shoulder and around the school bus at the other kids.

"Do you think anyone is watching us now?" asked Paul.

"I don't know. I just feel weird like, you know."

Sitting at the kitchen table, Kelley felt herself coming back from the dark fugue she had been in.

"Honey, are you okay?" asked her mother as she wiped Kelley's forehead with a kitchen towel.

Kelley had been perspiring heavily for the past couple of minutes. She had also begun to shiver and her teeth were rattling as well. She still could not speak.

"Kelley, speak to us dear," said her mother.

Kelley's lips trembled. Her eyes swept from her father back to her mother several times.

"I...I...I...just want to go to bbbbb...bed," she managed in a stammer.

"Of course dear, you'll be alright. Learning that Samuel is now a Keeper is a shock to your father and me, too," said her mother in her usual condescending tone. She stroked her daughter's hair.

Her father reached out and touched her hand for a brief moment. Their eyes met and in that instant Kelley could see her father wasn't as enthusiastic about Samuel's ascension as her mother was. There was something else. Her father was afraid. Just as afraid as she was, only he was better at hiding it. In this moment, he had let his guard down, and she had detected his fear.

Kelley pushed herself up weakly and shuffled out of the kitchen. She climbed the stairs and headed to the upstairs bathroom. Before she entered the bathroom, she noticed the door to her brother's room was closed but there was a small strip of light coming from under his door.

He's still awake, she thought. Slipping into the bathroom she flipped on the overhead light switch and then closed the door behind her. As softly and as quietly as she could Kelly locked the door. Now in the locked room, she relaxed just a bit. She begins to remove her clothes to take a shower. Meanwhile, downstairs her parents are still talking about Samuel's new status.

Across from the bathroom in Samuel's bedroom he lies on his bed. He hasn't removed his clothes. He is staring up at the shadows on his bedroom ceiling cast by the small cut glass lamp, which sits upon his dresser. His mind is on a journey. He has been practicing his "technique"—an ability to listen in on the thoughts of others for some time now. Tonight he was going to try something entirely new. Instead of just listening in on someone's thoughts, tonight he wanted to see if he could change someone's thoughts, to control their mind and more. He felt confident he could. But whom would he "choose?"

Kelley turned on the shower and adjusted the water's temperature. She stepped into the shower and pulled the shower curtain closed. The spray of the water against her body seems to awaken her. Kelley now steps directly under the water's spray as she also reaches for a bar of soap. Kelley lathers herself up and begins to relax in the shower.

Meanwhile, Samuel sends his mind on a journey to find Walter Yandow. It doesn't take long. Samuel is careful when entering the thoughts of others. He doesn't want to give away his own presence. Tonight wouldn't matter. Walter's mind is filled with lustful, sinful thoughts. Perversions of every sort are playing out in Walter's mind. Samuel slips inside and begins to get acquainted with what Walter is up to.

"Oh, Walter, you're so goo...ood," whispers Judy Perrillo as Walter and she are entwined in each others arms having sex. They were moving as one on the rolling waterbed in her bedroom. After dropping Samuel off, Walter had driven straight to Judy's house, located on the small hill overlooking her hotel. A trail of their clothes traced from the bedroom out to the hallway down to the living room and then to the foyer.

Inside Walter's mind, he was trying to control his own climax. His hands were all over her ample breasts as his mind was overloaded with messages arriving from all of his senses.

Judy was lying on her back. She was clearly enjoying herself. She could feel the rocking motion of her own body, which was moving in unison with the rolling motion of the water bed. She closed her eyes. In her own mind, the body of Walter was now replaced by the young virile movie star she had nightly fantasies about, especially on those nights when she was alone.

She was beginning her own journey.

Samuel made his move. His mind took over the mind of Walter Yandow. Walter's subconscious mind knew who it was and it obeyed. Such was this new found power of Samuel's. Samuel now drove Walter's body into high gear. Every muscle in Walter's body was at Samuel's command.

Walter's body began to push against Judy with more force. His pace quickened. Judy noticing the change adjusted her own tempo. Walter's body began to function as if he were a large piston working with precision.

The force of their lovemaking had now exceeded anything Judy had ever experienced with Walter before. She opened her eyes and could see that Walter's eyes were closed, his teeth clinched and his brow was furrowed from the strain. He had released her breast moments before. His hands were now tightly gripping the bed sheets.

***

Kelley had been in the shower for several minutes. A sense that someone was in the bathroom with her suddenly seized her. She quickly pulled back the shower curtain. The steam filled room was silent. Her eyes scanned the room and then settled on the fogged vanity mirror. There was a trace of movement behind the sweaty glass surface. She could see a shadow lurking behind the steamed, wet surface of the glass.

Kelley turned off the shower and stepped from the tub. She wrapped a towel around herself and used another to quickly wrap her hair. The sense that someone was watching her was even stronger now. She picked up a small face cloth from the vanity, reached up and wiped the mirror's surface.

With one swipe, she cleared a streak of the mirror's surface. In that moment, her fear was convincingly confirmed by the evil image that was now staring at her. The face was muscular, ashen gray in color. The mouth was opened into a leering grin, which revealed deeply yellowing teeth. The eyes were black as coal. The overhead light reflected in those eyes.

Kelley put her right hand up to her mouth. She wanted to scream, but couldn't.

The face in the mirror now began to move. Its lips began to purse up. The evil one was sending her a kiss. Kelley, repulsed at this gesture, took a half step back into the wall next to the shower adjacent to the locked bathroom door. Her right hand reached out for the door handle and its lock.

The face now appeared to be three dimensional. It was projecting into the room itself. The face, now fully into the room, was still grinning at her. She frantically tried to unlock the door. It wouldn't unlock.

She turned to see that a hand was now extending out from the mirror. It was reaching for her. She pulled on the door handle, desperately trying to escape.

"Kelley." The voice was deep.

She couldn't bring herself to turn around. All of her energy was fixed upon escaping.

"Kelley, I will have you," said this deep voice from what seemed to be inches from her. She gave the door handle a last desperate twist. The door unlocked.

She flew from the bathroom with all the speed she could manage. She closed the door behind her. She held the door handle tightly. Her heart was pounding inside her heaving chest. She expected this monster to try and follow her. At her feet she noticed the bathroom light had turned off. She listened as best she could even though the pounding of her heart boomed in her ears.

Silence.

***

Samuel enjoyed being in control. He was enjoying the sensual experience Walter's body was providing. He had no trouble restraining Walter's body from climaxing. He simply willed it so.

Judy had climaxed twice. She wanted Walter to climax now, so the two could just relax together and enjoy the afterglow. Walter was not slowing down—in fact he was picking up speed. Their lovemaking was beginning to hurt.

"Walter, you animal. What's gotten into you?"

No answer.

Walter's face was twisted as he grimaced from the effort his body was putting out.

"Walter, please, can't we stop. It hurts. Please?"

At that moment Walter knells upright, as his arms shoot straight up. He lets out a roar as if he were some sort of primeval animal. He looks down at Judy.

Judy looks up at Walter. From the dim light of her nightlight, she can see his eyes. The eyes are radiating red, like burning embers.

Kelley hears a sound coming from her brother's room. It is a moan. She steps back from the bathroom door and runs to her own room. She quickly closes the door. Next she moves to her dresser and pushes it along the wall until it blocks the door. Kelley goes over to the bedroom window and pulls the drapes closed. She turns on the nightstand lamp and the overhead light. The only sound she hears is the low rumble coming from the small air conditioner in the lower half of her bedroom window. Kelley quickly removes her towels and slips into a fresh pair of jeans and a short sleeve, light green blouse. She puts on half socks and a pair of old sneakers. She removes a small hunting knife and a flashlight from under her mattress. She sits on the bedroom floor in the corner. She intends to try and stay awake through the night.

***

Walter's eyes blink and in that instant Samuel releases his grip on Walter. His eyes are now normal. They're Walter's eyes once again.

"Oh, Walter!"

Walter falls over onto his side. The waterbed's rocking motion recoils from his tumble. Walter's heart is pounding inside his chest with such force Walter is short of breath. For a moment he thinks he might be well on the way to a heart attack. Judy rolls over one her side and begins to stoke his chest with her right hand.

"Walter, do you know what I want to do now?"

***

Samuel's mother and father have decided to head to bed for the night. Steve and Connie silently climb the stairs to their upstairs bedroom.

Steve Porter goes to the bedroom while his wife heads to the bathroom. She opens the bathroom door and turns on the overhead light. She immediately notices her daughter's clothes heaped into a pile. After using the toilet, she picks up her daughter's clothes and tosses them into the hamper under the sink. Connie turns off the light and heads to her own bedroom.

Samuel is fast asleep.

Elsewhere Kelley sits in the corner of her room with a knife in one hand and a flashlight in the other. She is fighting going to sleep.

12

Aaron and Korie headed over to her place after they finished the ice cream. They sat together on her couch, reading from the Powell family diary.

"This is fascinating, Aaron," said Korie.

"I know. I'm still in shock about all this."

"So, what are you going to do?"

"What do you mean?"

"Oh, come on, Aaron. You must have given it some thought by now. If this is all true, then it stands to reason that this coven, or whatever they are, will come after you."

"I don't know. Part of me wants to believe this stuff, but part of me doesn't. I guess the part that believes also feels that my mother must have done a good job of shaking them off, because I don't think I've ever experienced anyone following me around. I've never even felt threatened by anyone. Maybe they've given up or died off somehow."

"You don't believe that, do you?"

"I don't know, honest," he said as he raised his right hand in a mock Boy Scout salute.

"But look at what the diary says. Your mother had to move several times. She says that during the last five years she felt her phone was tapped. Someone was reading her mail. Her house was broken into twice. She writes about someone following her around during a holiday in Miami that she took last year. Her words are filled with fear, Aaron."

"Yeah, I can see it, but some of that could have been her imagination too."

"You've got to be on your guard."

"I will, I promise."

Korie leans over to Aaron and gives him a big hug.

Aaron whispers in her ear "but what about the land in Vermont?"

Korie pushes him back.

"I don't believe you," she says with exasperation in her voice.

"Look, Korie, what if I go to Vermont and just check this property out? I need to know more about it if I'm to be faithful to my ancestors, right? Several of them died on that land. Six generations have been running from it ever since. I need...I don't know how to say it—I guess I want to see it, to feel it. I have to do this!"

Korie rolls her eyes back. She can't believe this man. He's so stubborn and maybe too naive for his own good.

"All right, go ahead and run yourself smack dab into trouble, if that's what you want."

Korie folded her arms in mock protest.

"Don't be angry with me. Listen, I was wondering if you'd go with me. Sort of watch my back, you know, keep me out of trouble. What do you say?"

"When were you planning this little adventure?"

"As soon as I could, tomorrow, the day after, whatever."

"But what about my job?"

She was hooked.

"Look, I'll pay you for whatever wages you lose by going with me. I've got plenty of money. It'll only be for a few days anyway. I'm sure they can find someone to cover for you for a short while."

"I don't know, Aaron."

He had to play his best card.

"I've got to go and soon, with or without you."

Korie had fallen in love with this mysterious man. Common sense was about to be tossed out the proverbial window.

"Shit, I guess I'm going."

Aaron was thrilled with her answer. He pulled her to him and kissed her with a renewed passion. She too felt a new urge. She responded to his advances with her own. She reached up with her two hands and held his head in her hands. She ran her fingers through his hair. Gently she stroked his ears, lightly tracing them with her fingers. Korie's lips pressed against Aaron's. Their breathing began to rise.

"Aaron, stay the night?"

"If you insist," he said playfully.

She rose from the couch and took him by the hand and led him to her bedroom.

That night they made love.

Later the next morning, Korie awoke to the smell of fresh coffee.

Aaron had been up for the past couple of hours. Her mind drifted back to last night. Their lovemaking was good, not great, just good. They were both a little tense with each other. She began to drift off into a dream recollection when a message flashed into her head, "*Vermont Trip!*"

"Shit!" she exclaimed as she tossed off the covers and pulled a robe from of the bedpost. She hurried to the bathroom. Before stepping inside the bathroom she spotted Aaron and gave him a friendly wave. He responded with a smile that could melt any woman's heart.

She didn't want to look in the mirror. She had this thing about mirrors and mornings. She used the toilet and then took a shower. Next she brushed her teeth. She took a brush to her hair as she blow-dried her hair only half way to dry. After this semi-morning ritual she dashed down to her room to dress. She chose a comfortable pair of Gitano's, a white tee shirt with an outline of Cape Cod traced across the front. The shirt's message, read "Cape Cod, Where Summer Begins and Ends." She also put on white canvas dock shoes. She pulled a brush through her hair once again. She also applied perfume to her wrists and a small dab behind each ear. She decided not to wear any earrings.

Korie now headed to the kitchen. When she arrived in the kitchen, Aaron was on the telephone talking sternly to someone.

"Yes, I understand you have a busy schedule. Look, I already told you that I need to see him today. It can't take too long to review the matter of the land in Vermont. How about if I agree to pay twice the firm's hourly rate? Yes, I'll hold." He held his hand over the receiver, "I'm on the phone with my mother's law firm. The coffee's in the carafe on the counter. I sort of helped myself. Oh, and I've charged the call to my home phone."

Korie kissed him on the cheek.

"Yes. Hello, look, I was hoping … Oh, I see, she already explained it to you. Uh huh...yes, Okay fine then, three o'clock it is. Thanks, I appreciate your squeezing me in on short notice. Sure, all right. Thanks again, good-bye."

Aaron hung up the phone.

"They're willing to squeeze me in. How accommodating! Did you hear? It took an offer to pay twice the hourly rate to get any attention. Well anyway, it's all set."

"The coffee's great," said Korie.

"Uh, Korie, about last night, I was a little nervous, I uh..."

She stopped him from continuing by placing her right index finger to his lips. He kissed her finger.

"I'll make breakfast. Omelet okay?"

"Sounds just right. Can I help?"

"No, just have a seat and read the newspaper or something," she said playfully.

Aaron left the kitchen and went to retrieve the morning newspaper.

They were soon eating breakfast.

After breakfast, she called a co-worker of hers. They talked for a while. Korie explained that she had a family emergency and would need to be away for a couple of weeks.

"Could you take my hours?" she asked.

They talked some more and soon struck a deal. It appears that her friend Liz owed her a big favor and would take her hours.

After breakfast, they headed to town and took a walk on the beach. They held hands. Long periods passed without either one saying a word. At lunchtime, they sampled some hot dogs and cold soft drinks from Buddy's Steamed Dogs push cart.

After lunch, they climbed into Aaron's car and headed to Boston to meet with his mother's lawyer about this mysterious property in Vermont.

Later that afternoon, they both were sitting in the same office that Aaron had visited earlier that week. They sat alongside the same long mahogany desk he had sat at during his previous visit. The lawyer was a half an hour late for their meeting. After the customary exchange of pleasantries, they got down to business.

"Mr. Powell, the property in Vermont has been in your family's possession for over a hundred and fifty years. The arrangement that my firm had with your family for say, the past seventy years, is that we are to transfer the deed to the property every couple of years to a straw corporation that we create. The purpose is to make it as difficult as possible for someone to trace the exact ownership of this piece of Vermont property. We pay all the property taxes and handle all inquiries concerning said property through this firm. We bill for our out of pocket expenses and we are paid a retainer of three thousand dollars a year to represent the Powell family."

"Where exactly is this property and what's it like?"

"It is located in Sutton, Vermont. While I've never seen it myself, it would appear from the description in the file that it is located in a rather inaccessible place on top of a mountain. Here, see for yourself. I believe this is the file, ah yes, here it is."

Aaron took the file from the attorney. He opened it on the table in front of him. Korie and he quickly looked through the few papers in the file folder.

"The description of the land on this appraisal card describes it as a parcel of one hundred and ninety-two acres," said Aaron.

"Yes, that is correct," responded the lawyer.

"It also says there are three buildings—a large barn, a smaller barn and a house."

"Yes."

"I wonder what condition the buildings are in?" asked Aaron.

"Probably really run down," said Korie.

"Oh, I quite agree. The property has been unoccupied for over a hundred years. However I believe there's someone here at the firm who is familiar with the area. Perhaps she could tell you what Sutton is like. Why don't I ask her to step in?"

"Sure," said Aaron, "as long as we don't mention this particular property."

"Of course."

Using the conference room telephone intercom, the lawyer buzzed the outer office. A young woman responded to his call.

"Miss Houle, doesn't that new paralegal who works for Edmund, come from Vermont?"

"Yes, sir."

"Could you ask her to stop in for a moment?"

"Yes, I will."

After a moment, there was a soft knock at the conference room door.

"Come in."

"I understand you asked for me?" said the tall slender woman. She wore a dark black knee high skirt. She also wore comfortable flat black patent leather shoes. Her blouse was of a conservative business style. It was off white. She also wore a black business blazer that fit her perfectly. She seemed nervous as she held her hands in front of her.

"I understand you're from Vermont, Ms. Shearer?"

"Yes, I am."

"Are you familiar with Sutton?"

"Why yes, I am. I'm originally from Waterbury which isn't very far from Sutton."

"It seems my clients are interested in some property in Sutton."

"Oh, I'm sure they'll love it in Sutton. It's a lovely place nestled in a river valley and surrounded by several beautiful mountains."

"Wonderful. Well, thank you for your time, Ms. Shearer."

"Yes, thanks," said Aaron as he extended his hand to her.

Instinctively she took his hand and shook it. Her hand felt blazing hot to his touch. Her eyes locked onto his.

Aaron could feel the heat radiating from their touch. His mind was suddenly slammed with two words.

"STAY AWAY."

His eyes met hers and he could see a flash of fear in her eyes. Korie watched the two shake hands, but her attention was drawn to the look on their faces. It was a look that suggested these two knew each other, or did they?

"Well, I've got to go," said the woman as she turned and quickly left the room.

Aaron turned to Korie. She hid her reaction and feelings from him.

Aaron pulled a pen from his inside coat pocket and took a page from the top of a small note pad the lawyer had placed near the middle of the table. Aaron copied down the details of the property. He also wrote down the property's tax card number.

"I'm satisfied with the way you're handling the property issue. Just keep doing what you've been doing. Now look, I've been thinking about all the other assets you described to me the other day. You know the need to try and professionally manage them. I don't think I'm a financial wizard, but this is what I have in mind. You continue to manage my family's affairs exactly as you have before. However, I want you to place everything I own outside of this Vermont property into a living trust. I want you to hire the best asset managers you can. I want to have my trust earn five percent net per year after taxes and expenses. Your fee, if you'll agree, can be for expenses and everything over the yearly net—oh, and one more thing."

"Yes, Mr. Powell."

He clearly had the attorney's attention.

"I want this done right now, while I'm here."

"Now?"

"Do we have the makings of a deal, or do I have to shop around for another firm?"

"No, indeed, Mr. Powell, there will be no need for that. Give me a few moments to make some arrangements."

This time, the lawyer pushed on a button which was recessed into the top of the table in front of the lawyer.

A young woman pushed open the conference room door.

"Miss Houle, will you find Mr. Hanauer and ask him to join us. And Miss Houle, please come in as soon as you can."

Moments later there were three other lawyers and a couple of legal clerks as well as three secretaries seated around the oversized table. Everyone had laptop computers. Questions and answers flew between everyone. Dinner was ordered out for some. The choice was Chinese takeout. Aaron was as animated as anyone as he responded to questions and tossed out a few of his own. By 7:15

p.m. that night, everything Aaron had asked for was in place. Handshakes were exchanged all around. Korie had even offered a few suggestions along the way, but generally remained in the background. One of the lawyers, had at one time during the session, referred to her as Mrs. Powell. Aaron politely explained that she was not Mrs. Powell, but that she was a very close and dear friend.

"I see," said Miss Houle, "and I don't believe I caught your last name?"

"Oh, it's uh..." stumbled Aaron.

"It's Catalano. My family is originally from northern Italy," said Korie as she slipped an arm under Aaron's.

Now that everything had been taken care of Aaron and Korie headed for the elevators. On their way they noticed several meeting rooms with their lights on, doors slightly ajar for air circulation and small groups of people engaged in animated discussions.

They waved a friendly goodbye to a law clerk who had accompanied them to the elevator. When the elevator doors closed, Aaron slumped back against the wall of the elevator car. He seemed exhausted. Korie put her arms around him and gave him a kiss.

"I didn't expect we'd be here for this long. You sure got a lot accomplished here this afternoon."

"I know. I didn't want to tell my mother's lawyer what I had in mind over the phone."

"Because someone might have been listening?"

"No, because he would have never agreed to meet with me on such short notice. I wanted everything taken care of in one meeting, not over several meetings taking months."

"So, what do we do now?"

"Now, we take in the 'Blues' at the House of Blues over in Cambridge."

The elevator door opened on the ground floor. They stepped out and exited the building from the front door with the help of a security guard.

"I thought you were tired."

"Korie, I am never too tired when it comes to the blues. Tonight they're doing a dedication to the great blues man, John Lee Hooker?"

"Oh, really."

"Let's go," he said as he took her by the hand.

Korie made a mental note to talk to Aaron about that paralegal from Vermont they had spoken to earlier. He, too, made a mental note of his own. He wanted to ask Korie if she thought there was anything peculiar about her.

High above the street, in the building they had just exited, someone watched their movements from a window, behind parted blinds of a darkened office. As Aaron and Korie ran across the street on their way to the parking garage, the watcher at the window dialed a cell phone.

"Hello. Yes. I know it has been a long time. Uh-huh. Yes, I understand. I haven't had anything to report since she died. Listen, I think she had a son. Yes, you heard right, a son. He's been here. My source came through. She called and tipped me off this afternoon. I haven't checked it all out yet, but it's got to be legit. Okay. Yes, I will. What about her? Yes, I see what you mean. Sure, I can find a replacement." The call ended.

The caller closed his flip phone and released the curtains when he noticed Aaron's car pull out of the parking garage.

He had work to do.

13

Ed Townsend hung up the telephone. Sitting in his small office, in the back of the first floor of his house, he leaned back in his well worn office chair. The chair creaked and squeaked from the strain. He folded his hands behind his head as he turned his gaze up to the stamped tin ceiling. The ceiling fan he had installed last year was turning at its slowest speed. A gentle cooling movement of air descended from above as the few papers on his desk moved only slightly from the fan's downward current. It was getting dark outside. Evening came early here in valley of the Winooski River, nestled at the base of the mountains of north central Vermont.

The old coat rack hanging by the door had a slightly soiled fedora hanging on it that he had worn for nearly twenty years during his time with the FBI. He had spent most of his life hunting spies and their Communist handlers during the Cold War. He had served with the G3 unit. Their assignment was to try and catch spies who worked their craft in and around Washington, D.C. In his spare time, he clandestinely hunted the last known descendant of the Powell family. He had personally hunted for Aaron Powell's mother for all of his thirty-one years in law enforcement.

Ms. Powell was equal to his challenge. She was cunning. She would leave false trails. She even laid traps to try and catch him, so she could identify the mysterious person hunting her. He had grown to respect her. So much of him was a highly trained law enforcement officer. But part of him, the part that controlled him, that drove him, was evil. He was a member of Moloch's coven. He had been inducted when he was twenty-nine years old. His being had melded with another from the evil world. On this earth he was Ed Townsend. In another place he was Briga, Lucifer's ancient ally, a ruthless hunter of souls. Murder and mayhem was Briga's trademark. Briga and Ed Townsend were as one when it came to the pursuit of Ms. Powell.

Hanging on the same coat rack was a nylon and leather holster, which carried a flat black Colt 44 Magnum loaded with Black Tallon ammunition. Sitting in a small holster strapped to the back of his loosely fitted pants was another pistol. He had another strapped to the upper calf of his left leg.

"A man can't be too prepared," was his motto. He was a deadly shot. He could place five shots in a tight grouping of less than an inch, at seventy-five feet, and in less than four seconds.

Ed Townsend's wife, Emma, had died eleven years ago from complications following surgery to correct a heart defect. Ed never remarried. Emma and he were close. They had grown up together in Sutton. She had reluctantly left Sutton and joined Ed during his years with the FBI. She would journey back to Sutton whenever she could. They never had any children together. Ed had never revealed his role with the coven to Emma. She never saw his evil side. Not everyone in Sutton was associated with the coven or even knew about it. It was a carefully guarded secret, whose oath, when broken, resulted in the certain death.

Ed had come to a decision. He was not going to reveal what he knew just yet. He would have to check this lead out personally. He leaned forward in his chair and stood up, placed his hands on his lower back and gently pushed to relieve the back strain he had been experiencing over the last few years. He took his hat and holster, turned off the ceiling fan, and headed out of his office. He was going upstairs to pack. He was going to Boston tonight. He would follow up this lead while the trail was still warm.

Ed packed light. He had developed an ability over his years with the FBI, of reducing his travel packing needs to the necessary bare essentials. After he closed his suitcase, he went outside and tossed the small bag into the trunk of his car. He checked his travel wallet, especially prepared for clandestine missions. It contained several false identifications, from driver licenses to credit cards. He had over three thousand dollars in small bills with him. Four hundred dollars was in the wallet, with the rest tucked inside the two false pockets of his well worn and heavily wrinkled suit coat. On the front seat was a copy of the latest Steven King novel, with a compartment carved out to carry essential lock picking tools. He always chose a Steven King book because they were usually large, and since he was a popular author, they didn't draw any suspicion. He was going to have to change cars several times to make sure he would be untraceable. He would visit airports and pick up a car from the car rental agencies, renting them for a week at a time. He would leave the cars in parking garages along his route. These cars would not draw suspicion if he left them for a couple of days.

Before he left the house, he placed one telephone call. It was to the Reverend Simon B. Mitchell.

"Hello, Simon, Ed here. Yes, I'm doing fine. Yeah, I've got a new lead. I don't know yet. I'm leaving right now to check it out for myself. I'll call you in a couple of days. Sure, I understand. I expect to be back by Saturday night. I'll try to make it back for Sammy's, I mean Samuel's, welcoming ceremony. If I do, I'll see you there. No, there isn't anything solid to report yet. I know the others would want to know! I don't think I need to remind you that we've had false leads before. Okay. Yes, I will. Later."

He hung the phone up and patted his shoulder holster to remind himself that he was packing his piece. The familiar shape was reassuring to the touch. He climbed into his car and backed out of his driveway onto Walnut Lane. Next he headed south to pick up Interstate 89.

Reverend Mitchell tried to contain his exuberance. In his heart, he just knew the all powerful coven would be completely restored on his watch. This new lead could turn out to be the long awaited missing link.

He went over to his fireplace. It was summertime and the fireplace was dark, heavily covered in soot and undisturbed. Reverend Mitchell knelt down in front of the open hearth and reached up inside the top of the fireplace. There was a scraping sound of stone against stone as three bricks that met at the upper left corner, moved away from the rest of the brick face to reveal a sort of drawer. The top of this drawer was metal. He pulled up on a small black metal ring, which lifted the metal lid open. Out of habit, he looked around the room even though he was completely alone.

He carefully removed a sheaf of old yellowed papers. These papers were tied together with a black ribbon. He carried the small bundle over to his desk, where he laid it carefully in the center. Moving around the desk, he sat down. He turned on the small brass desk lamp. He untied the black ribbon and began to pour through the papers. Selecting one in particular, he pulled it closer to him. He began to read the words inscribed on the yellowed dog eared paper. He moved his lips much like someone in silent prayer.

Stopping at a particular point in his reading, he stood up in a bolt. He slammed his right fist into his left palm with a smacking sound.

"Yes! I knew it. I knew it," he exclaimed to the empty room.

"It was foretold by Elisa Porter Cummings," he knew somehow, he knew. "Moloch must have told him," he said as he paced back and forth in his office.

He turned and headed for his telephone, but before he could reach it, it rang. The sound of the ringing phone startled him for a moment. He hesitated, but before the second ring was over he picked up the receiver.

"Reverend, John here. We've got a problem. There are some boys in town from Barre looking for some trouble. They've been pestering some of our girls down on Route 2, next to Frida's."

"Anyone go with them?"

"No, not yet, but these boys are pretty persistent from what I hear."

"Keep an eye on them for me. Call me if any one from our Church falls in with these outsiders."

"I will, Reverend."

Reverend Mitchell hung up the phone. He had changed his mind and would speak to the entire Church about what he had read in Reverend Cummings prophetic writings at Samuel's welcoming ceremony. With Moloch's help, Ed Townsend will return Saturday night with joyous news that they have located a male Powell descendant. The coming of Moloch could be soon, very soon and then they all will rule this earth as Moloch had promised that first time long ago.

He carefully put all the old papers into a neat stack and retied them with the black ribbon. He carried them over to the metal drawer and placed them back in the box. He closed the lid and pushed the bricks back into place. It only took a gentle nudge for the bricks to slide back into place. Once again, his fireplace looked as ordinary as it was supposed to.

Each member of Moloch's coven was imbued with a unique power or force. Reverend's power was special indeed. He had the ability to find that one weakness even the righteous had and to use it to break them down, to destroy them and to deliver their soul to Moloch. It was so because he, himself, had no scruples, no moral compass. He was as nearly and completely evil as Moloch himself.

His telephone rang again.

"Yes, I see. Okay, call Trainor, Fairchild and Yandow. That should be enough. I'll meet you behind the recycling center in ten minutes."

He hung up the phone and hurried to the hallway where he retrieved his hat from the old oak hat rack next to the door. Soon he was in his car hurrying to the rendezvous point. As his car pulled to a stop in the backyard behind Sutton's recycling center, two other vehicles pulled to a stop next to his car. He walked over to greet the others. As they were shaking hands another car pulled up and stopped. The driver of this latest vehicle got out of his car. It was Walter Yandow. He headed straight for the others.

"Hello, Walter. How's it running?" asked "Chucky" Trainor, a local radio personality.

"You know Bob, if he works on a car it's gonna run right. The man's a genius."

"I wouldn't go quite that far, Walter," laughed Judge Fairchild.

"Where does this car come from?" asked Reverend Mitchell.

"Rochester, New Hampshire. It's a big old Ford Crown Victoria with a 351 cubic inch Police pursuit package. Bob picked it up at a place called Seacoast Salvage. The car had an electrical fire and was totaled by the insurance company before it could be delivered to New Hampshire State Police. Right now, she runs like a deer. Even with the extra weight from the roll cage and other reinforcements, it hauls ass," said Yandow.

"The usual black, I see," said Trainor.

"Does a bear shit in the woods?" responded Yandow.

"Enough, let's go," said the Reverend.

They all piled into the car. The Reverend sat in the back with the Judge while Trainor rode "shotgun" with Yandow behind the wheel. They all immediately buckled their shoulder safety harnesses that Bob Senecal had installed for their safety. Yandow placed the key in the ignition and turned the key. The car roared in response. In a hail of sprayed gravel, he spun the car around and exited the recycling center backyard. They drove off in the direction of Frida's Famous Fries, a popular summer hang out for area teenagers out on US Route 2.

In just a few short minutes, the Crown Victoria pulled to a stop at the gas station across from the fast food restaurant. An old man came out of the station and pulled a rag from the back pocket of his work coveralls. He was carrying a bottle of windshield washer, which he proceeded to spray on the windshield. As he began to slowly clean the driver's side, the Reverend poked his head out from the backseat window.

"Hank, can you point out the interlopers?"

"Sure can, Reverend. They're the ones standing next to the dark blue pickup with the light bar on its roof. See it on the left, the Toyota."

"I see it now, thank you."

"I do what I can."

Hank continued to wash the windows of the car while keeping an eye on the activity across the street. His passengers likewise watched the activity with keen interest.

Frida's Famous Fries was once an A&W car hop restaurant. It took on its new name when an interloper from down country (shorthand for southern New England), bought the place in 1991. The middle aged husband and wife kept to themselves. They were not church going people, and certainly weren't candidates for the Reverend's closely held congregation. The followers of Moloch left them alone even though they recognized this new business would bring outsiders, interlopers, to their community. They had to accept this risk. Being able to hide among others was an accepted way of life for Moloch's Church and its coven.

Every once and a while they had to move to protect themselves from discovery. This was such a time. A young girl, age fourteen and daughter of a Church member, was being tempted to go for a joy ride with two boys from Barre, a community about twenty-five miles southeast of Sutton. This girl, named Brittany, knew a great deal about Moloch's Church. If she, through any means, revealed what she knew it could threaten their life's work.

They watched and waited.

Brittany was obviously flirting with these boys and they clearly enjoyed her attention. She was wearing a halter top, cut-off blue shorts and sandals. The boys were wearing dark colored tee shirts and blue jeans with dirty white sneakers. One of the boys was smoking a cigarette.

Brittany opened the driver side door and was looking inside.

"We could give her mom or dad a call and they'll come and get her," said Chucky.

"And what would that accomplish, Mr. Trainor?" said the Reverend in an icy tone.

"I don't know, I..."

"Moloch demands our obedience. He has kept his word and we must keep ours as our ancestors did, or have you forgotten, Mr. Trainor?

"No, Reverend, I haven't, I'm sorry."

"Look, she got into the truck," said Judge Fairchild.

"Yeah, and it looks like the boys are following her lead," said Walter.

"Our mission is clear, our purpose is for the greater good, let us do Moloch's work," said the Reverend.

The pickup truck with the girl sitting in the middle pulled out of Frida's parking lot and drove off in a southerly direction down US Route 2.

The black Ford left the gas station and followed the truck from a distance, tracking its taillights.

After a couple of miles the truck slowed down and took a left turn onto Middlesex Road. The Ford Crown Victoria followed along.

After three miles or so, the truck turned right onto an unmarked dirt road. Once again the Ford followed. After a half mile, the truck suddenly turned around in the narrow dirt road. It bounced in and out of the ditch. Yandow stopped the car.

"What are they doing?" asked the Judge.

"They've figured out they're being followed," said Yandow.

The truck lurched forward. A cloud of dust kicked up behind the truck as it shot straight at the black Ford Crown Victoria. The truck's light bar was turned on and the high beams were on as well. In a moment, the truck slammed to a stop directly in front of the car. A cloud of dust blew across the eerily lit scene. The truck engine gunned a couple of times and roared as it rocked in place.

Yandow gunned the police engine of the Ford Crown Victoria and it roared its response.

Suddenly, the truck surged backwards for nearly a hundred feet and suddenly spun around. Now, its tail lights once again faced the former police car. The rear wheels of the truck spun furiously as they kicked up a plume of white gray dust in the direction of the car. The truck pulled away quickly, disappearing down the dirt road.

"They're running," said Yandow.

"They must not be allowed to get away," said the Judge.

"I know," said Yandow as he stepped firmly on the gas pedal and the car shot forward.

In a moment, they could see the truck taillights flickering in the dust filled haze. Several seconds later their car was within ten feet of the truck's back bumper. Both vehicles were traveling over seventy miles an hour along the narrow, windy, sometimes rolling road. At times, their speed slowed to forty miles an hour and at others it exceeded a hundred. Houses and mailboxes whizzed past. Tree branches wiped against the truck and car.

"Mr. Yandow, end it," demanded the Reverend.

With those words Yandow pushed the car faster. It slammed into the back of the truck. The truck fishtailed from the impact, but the driver managed to still hold the road. The truck's rear lights were smashed and no longer worked.

"What the hell?" said the boy sitting in the passenger seat.

"Those crazy bastards just hit my truck," said the driver, "they can't be cops."

"Please let me out, please. If they catch me, they'll kill me," screamed Brittany. She was sitting in the middle of the two boys.

"What the fuck are you talking about?" said the boy riding shotgun.

"They want me. I'm not supposed to be with interlopers," she cried.

"Bitch, you're talking crazy," said the driver.

Bamm.

The truck was slammed from behind again.

"Loose him man, loose him," screamed the boy passenger.

"I can't. I'm going as fast as I can on this shit ass road."

Bamm...Bamm, screech...

The truck tailgate was now pushed in.

"The crazy fuck's trying to pass me," said the driver.

"Moloch, I was wrong. I was wrong, please," she cried as she reached for the passenger's side door handle, trying to open it.

"Get her under control, Freddy...shit," said the driver.

The former police car slammed into the truck's left side as Yandow tried to force the truck off the road. The truck's right side smashed a mailbox into hundreds of pieces as the vehicles careened along. Another car's headlights loomed about three hundred yards ahead. Yandow saw it first. He slowed the car down so he could pull in behind the truck. The young boy driving the truck noticed the oncoming car and braced for what he thought was going to be certain impact between the three vehicles. He had not noticed the Ford pull back.

Swoosh.

The wind currents whipped the passing vehicles, rocking them as they speed by.

The incident lasted only a short while when once again Yandow had pulled the restored police car alongside of the truck.

This time, the truck's young driver responded by slamming his own truck into the car's now dented right side. The car held steady. The three people in the truck were screaming all at once. Nobody noticed the car had lurched back a few feet until its right front tire was pulled even with the truck's left rear tire. Now the car pulled quickly to the right.

There was a sudden impact that sent the truck into a spin. The tires bit into the road's heavily packed dirt surface as the truck went sideways. It began to flip itself along the road at over eighty miles an hour. Two bodies flew out of the truck as the doors flapped wildly. The headlights broadcast their bounding light into an empty field to the left side of the road. The truck came to rest on the roof, in the middle of the road, over three hundred feet from the last impact with the pursuing car.

Yandow managed to pull the Ford Crown Victoria to a stop immediately after its last contact with the truck. The occupants watched the tumbling truck until it came to a stop. The Ford's headlights covered the dust filled crash scene. The car now slowly moved forward towards the first body, which was lying in the ditch on the right side of the road. The car stopped and Chucky and Walter got out first.

"He's still alive, he's got a pulse," said Trainor who was bending over the twisted body of the boy passenger. The boy was unconscious.

The Reverend and the Judge got out of the car and slowly approached the boy.

"By the power granted to me by Moloch, the Prince of Darkness, the right hand to the all powerful Lucifer, I condemn you to death. Your soul will belong to Moloch, may you serve him well," said Judge Fairchild.

Chucky pulled the boy's head up from the ground. At the angle he held the head the boy was unable to breath. In a moment the boy stopped breathing.

The four men walked down to the second body. It was Brittany. She was lying on her right side with her back to the truck. She, too, was unconscious. She had an obviously broken arm. Her eyes were rolled back, her eyelids frozen open, so that only the white's of her eyes could be seen. Blood ran down the side of her face from her left ear. Her legs were badly scrapped and bloody.

"Should we take her or send her to Moloch?" asked Yandow.

"Let's see the other boy first," answered the Judge. His decision on these matters was final as ordained by the word of Moloch.

They moved along to the truck. The smell of gasoline was everywhere. The gas tank had ruptured during the tumbling and it was now leaking gas onto the ground underneath the truck. Pinned beneath the steering wheel, inside of the upside down truck, still strapped in with his seat and shoulder belt was the driver. He moaned softly as the four men approached. Glistening glass splinters offered multiple reflections from the Mercury's headlights. The long shadows of the men now stretched across the truck. The night was quiet except for the boy's moaning.

From his upside down position he could see, through one eye, the approach of shadowy figures. His other eye had been cut out of its socket by a shard of glass from the broken truck windshield. He had several broken bones. His right lung was punctured by a broken rib. His breathing was labored. He was well into shock so he didn't feel the full effects of the pain messages his body was generating. He could now only see the feet of the men standing next to his truck. The driver door was missing. It had flown off halfway along the several rollovers that the truck traveled in its solo crash.

"Please help me," said the young boy through a shortness of breath. Blood now dripped from his mouth.

"C'mon, somebody please."

"By the power given to me by Moloch..." said the Judge.

"Who in the fuck is Moloch?" demanded the boy.

"You will soon know him," said The Reverend.

"...and may you serve him well," finished the Judge.

Yandow knelt down and reached inside of the truck.

"You fuckers," cried the boy.

His neck snapped to the right as Yandow ended his pain and his life.

"Take her to Ed Foley," said the Reverend. "I want her alive for tomorrow's ceremony. He'll know what to do."

"Where do I put her?" asked Yandow.

"In the back seat. Trainor will ride in the back seat with her. The Judge and I will ride in the front with you."

"Okay with me, c'mon Chuck, give me a hand will yuh?" said Yandow.

The two headed over to Brittany and picked her up and headed back to the car.

The Judge stood next to the truck. He had a match box out. He struck a wooden match and tossed it under the truck. In a moment there was a *whoosh* sound as the dripping gasoline on the ground caught fire.

The Judge turned and walked away with the Reverend, they both headed to the car. Brittany, still unconscious, was now in the back of the car. When the Judge and the Reverend were about twenty feet from the car the truck's gas tank exploded. Since the truck was upside down, the brunt of the fiery explosion blew skyward. The explosion also caused the truck to completely catch fire. The concussion from the explosion nearly knocked the two older men over. They scampered to the car and climbed into the front seat. The car backed up a few feet and half turned around.

As the car pulled away from the crash scene, Yandow looked into his rearview mirror. He could see the burning truck, its light filling up the mirror. His eyes focused upon the burning body strapped inside of the cab.

The burning scene disappeared from view as the car moved away, around a small curve and over a short hill.

14

Aaron slipped the hostess an extra twenty. In a couple of minutes, Korie and he were led to a small table to the left of the stage. A local band was playing a mean rendition of *Dust My Blues* by Elmore James. The size of the crowd at Cambridge's House of Blues was above average. Even though the place was air conditioned, it still was hot due to the crowded conditions and the gyrating energetic pulse of a large group of people getting into the music.

Aaron began to nod his head in time with the music as soon as they were seated. The band was tight—their blend of blues riffs with a traditional brass overlay held sway over the mostly middle age crowd. Aaron and Korie were seated close enough to the stage that the sound of music emanating from the amplifiers drowned out any possibility of polite conversation. Korie pulled her chair around so she could look at the band. This placed her closer to Aaron. He smiled at her, leaned over and gave her a kiss on the cheek.

The band finished their song to a rousing applause from the appreciative audience.

The lead singer stepped up to the microphone and called out to a woman sitting over at the bar.

"Sylvia, hey, come work with us? What do you say we do *Koko's Mother Nature*? C'mon folks, help us to get Sylvia to come on down," said the singer as he encouraged the room to clap their hands as a form of encouragement.

The woman waved off the entreaties of the crowd. This just produced the opposite effect. The crowd made even more noise. Some began to whistle and hoot.

Aaron really got into this crowd exercise. He stood up and shouted, "Sylvia, who loves you?"

His effort seemed to elicit a response from the woman as she left her seat and began to work her way through the crowd.

Soon she was helped up onto the stage. She nodded to the crowd and favored them with a friendly grin. Sylvia looked over to where Aaron was seating.

She took the microphone in hand, removing it from its upright stand. Now looking at Aaron she said, "This one's for you, lover."

The crowd broke up with laughter and applause.

Now Sylvia looked directly at Korie and said with a wink, "Honey, he's a keeper, if you know what I mean."

The music started with a soulful guitar riff pulling in a solid bass line and drum riff. Sylvia followed with a powerful throaty voice that called out to the room, "don't mess with Mother Nature, cause you'll be sorry if you do."

The song was one of those great blues number's with a traditional slow back beat that just called to your soul. Soon everyone in the room was swaying to the rhythm of the music.

Korie even got into the spirit of the moment.

As the song ended, everyone stood up and gave Sylvia a rousing ovation. She blew everyone a kiss and stepped from the stage.

As she headed back to her seat, Korie leaned over and through the noise managed to playfully ask, "She seems to know you rather well."

"Yeah, she does."

"Oh, how so?"

"She used to sing with my band."

"Well, you sure are a man of mystery. You have a band?"

"Sort of, some teacher friends and I have this blues band and well, we just like the music, you know, like the music is good for the soul kind of thing."

"And Sylvia?"

"Yeah, she's got a great voice. She used to teach math at the middle school in town."

"Use to? What happened?"

"Breast cancer. Last year she had a double mastectomy, chemotherapy, and all that. She's doing okay She can't work right now because she's too weak. You see those three other women that she's with?"

"Uh-huh."

"They're all teachers, too. They're her support group. She can't sing with our band because she gets too tired. Over the years she has sung with several local blues bands that have performed here. She's known by a lot of people. Everyone just loves her. She's got a gift in that voice of hers. I'm glad she's well enough to get out for some fun."

"She sounds special."

"Yeah, she's special. Sylvia's a fighter."

Just then a waiter stopped at their table. They both ordered some beer and dinner.

A new band was just finishing setting up. They were another local band from the seacoast area of New Hampshire. The band consisted of a three-piece horn section, a lead guitarist, rhythm guitar, bass, drums, keyboard player and a female singer. She was somewhat tall with long blond hair. She wore a small black dress. The band wore black suits and white shirts. The bass player wore dark glasses. The average age of the band members was definitely under thirty.

They began to play with a passion and skill that caught the attention of the room. Halfway into their first song, the audience gave them a boost with approving applause. The room was into the music.

Their drinks were brought to their table. Some people in the room were dancing to the music in whatever space they could find. Korie and Aaron were thoroughly enjoying themselves. Soon their dinner was served. The night passed quickly.

***

Ed Townsend pulled off of Interstate 89. He drove under the highway and pulled into an all night gas station combination convenience store. He was about twenty miles north of Concord, New Hampshire. He topped off his gas tank. This was his second car of the night. He had rented this car at the Lebanon, New Hampshire Airport. He left his own vehicle parked at a Motel Six parking lot. He rented a room at the motel for three nights. He told the clerk he was going to leave his car in the lot for the duration because he was going to be picked up by a co-worker. He also left word that he didn't want his room disturbed because he would be working late hours and would need his rest. The counter clerk quietly agreed, especially when Ed handed her a couple of tens, to ensure her understanding of his request.

After he had paid for the gas, he started up his car and pulled to the side of the parking lot. He turned his overhead light on as he studied the map. He spotted what he was looking for. He was headed for the Manchester, New Hampshire Airport. There he would again rent a car as well as find a safe haven for his current vehicle. Before the sun would rise he will have traded cars at the Providence, Rhode Island Airport and Boston's Logan Airport too.

He drank his coffee black, one sugar. That night, he drank several cups to help him stay awake. At six thirty in the morning, he pulled his last rental car to a stop under the portico of the Comfort Inn in Cambridge, Massachusetts. He checked in and headed to his room. He unlocked the door and turned on the light from the wall switch. He dropped his small overnight bag onto the bed. Ed used his cell phone to make a phone call.

"Yeah, I'm in town. Never mind where. Yeah, uh-huh. Okay. Look I need to get some shut-eye. I'll meet you at Quincy Market under the rotunda at two, sharp. You'd better bring me an address and anything else you can get. And don't be late."

He closed his flip phone and placed it on the nightstand. He went back to the door and hung the "do not disturb" sign on the outside handle. He turned off the overhead light and proceeded to unpack his overnight bag in the semi-darkness. He untied his shoes, kicked them off and stretched out on the bed. In a few moments, he was sound asleep.

***

Aaron had driven Korie home and spent the night. He slipped out midmorning and drove to his place. He packed a suitcase. Aaron took a relaxing shower. After the shower, he took his suitcase and drove back to Korie's place. As he entered the unlocked front door he immediately noticed the aroma of pancakes and sausage coming from the kitchen. He headed for the kitchen.

"Smells great," he quipped.

Korie was standing at the stove with her back to him. She was wearing a short robe. Her long slender legs caught his eye.

Korie didn't turn around at hearing his voice. She just shrugged her shoulders.

Sensing that something was wrong Aaron went up to her and touched her shoulders. She didn't seem to respond to his touch. He turned her around. She had a spatula in her right hand. Korie hung her head down. She didn't want to look him in the eye right now. He lifted her chin and immediately saw that she had been crying.

"What's wrong?"

She dropped the spatula on the countertop and threw her arms around him. Her hug was powerful.

"I...thought you weren't coming back," she whispered.

"But Korie, I..."

"Never mind, just hold me."

After a long moment she pulled back from him and kissed his cheek.

"Stupid, huh?" she said as she pulled her hair behind her ears with her left hand.

"No, not at all," he smiled.

"Uh, sit down, breakfast is ready."

Aaron went to the table and sat down as Korie served breakfast. They ate and talked for the next hour.

Finally Aaron mentioned he had slipped out earlier and packed a suitcase full of clothes. He was eager to head to Vermont.

"C'mon, Korie, I'll help you pack."

"No thanks, I can handle that myself. Now, how long do you expect this adventure to take?" she said as she sipped her cup of coffee.

"Two or three days, tops. I just want to see it myself, maybe check out Vermont while we're there. I hear it's as pretty as a postcard. If it goes any longer than that, we'll buy clothes up there. See, problem solved."

"You're so smart."

"Thanks."

"Conceited, too!"

"Uh-huh."

They had a good laugh together.

Korie put their dishes on the counter and headed to her bedroom.

"It'll take a while, so why don't you relax in the living room."

"Sure."

When she entered the bedroom she could hear water running in the kitchen sink. Aaron was beginning to wash the breakfast dishes. This fact amused her and brought a smile to her face. She went to her walk-in closet and pulled a large suitcase out of the back. She heaved it onto her bed and proceeded to fill it to overflowing.

Before setting off for Vermont, they stopped at Korie's landlord's house. She told them that she was going to be away for few days and could they watch her cottage for her. They agreed and reminded her to lock the front door.

They immediately left Plymouth, Massachusetts, for Vermont at a few minutes past 1:00 p.m. Aaron planned to reach Montpelier, Vermont, by dinnertime.

***

Ed arrived early for his meeting with his informer. The crowds at Quincy Market were less congested at this time of day. Nevertheless, there was still a good crowd. He spotted her coming in from the Faneuil Hall entrance a few minutes before two o'clock.

Their eyes met. Ed was standing at a lunch counter eating some fish and chips that he had bought a moment ago. His contact went over to the N.Y. Deli and bought a sandwich. She headed over to Ed's lunch counter and stood opposite of him.

Unwrapping her sandwich she said, "He's for real. Yesterday he met with the Powell Family lawyer in our firm. He seemed quite interested in the Vermont property. He was with a young woman. I couldn't get her name."

"That's it?" scowled Ed.

"No, there's more, here, see for yourself," she said as she slipped him a small manila envelope.

He opened the envelope and pulled out several papers. He read them slowly. She ate her sandwich in small bites. She was afraid of Ed. She hoped she had performed well. That decision, however, was his alone to render.

"This is good. We now know where he lives, what he does for a living. Yes, this is good."

"Thanks."

"What about his accounts, his resources, assets, that sort of thing?"

"I don't think I can get to that stuff. That information is probably under lock and key in Lowenstein's office safe. I know I can't get access to that. The stuff I brought you I managed to get by buddying up with his legal secretary. She's a gossip. It was almost too easy, but it's all she knows. I swear."

"Okay, but keep working on it. Look, I've got to go now. I'll be in touch," he said as he wiped his mouth with a paper napkin. Ed put the papers back inside the envelope and stuffed the envelope in his suit coat pocket. The manila envelope stuck out of his pocket. He took his plate over to the trash can, tossed his garbage inside and walked out the same door she had entered just minutes before.

She finished her sandwich and felt more relaxed now that he was gone. She realized her work on behalf of the coven and Moloch was vital. Indeed, she believed what she had just handed him was the breakthrough they had all been waiting for.

Checking her watch, she realized she needed to hurry back to work. She tossed her nearly finished sandwich into the garbage and took her soft drink with her. She headed out the Faneuil Hall entrance and proceeded back towards her office. The summertime crowd in this part of Boston is always heavy. Pedestrians seldom wait for the crosswalk signals before hurrying across traffic filled streets. She moved with the flow and now found herself standing at a curb. A young courier on roller blades rushed past.

She had no idea she was being stalked. Ed was just a few feet behind her. The crowd stepped from the curb and rushed across the street. Cars trying to speed through honked their horns in anger at the pedestrians who had darted in front of them, causing the drivers to come to a sudden stop. She had hesitated and hadn't followed the first rush of people across the street.

Perfect, he thought.

A tourist trolley was coming down the street closely followed by a large truck bearing the advertising for a regional brewery. She saw these vehicles and held back from trying to cross the street. After these two, she noticed there was no traffic and there would be time to cross.

Just as the trolley passed by with its loudspeaker blaring, she felt a push from behind. She lost her balance and fell face first into the street. Her soft drink flew from her hand as she tried to stop her fall. She fell into the shadow of the oncoming truck. It would be the shadow of her death. The driver of the truck saw her tumble forward directly in front of his left front wheel. He hit his brakes but it was too late. He felt the bump of her body as his truck rolled over her. The driver felt sick to his stomach. He felt another bump as the twin rear tires rolled over her body as well. He had been going only twenty five miles an hour. The truck came to a stop in a few feet. He jumped from his truck to help the woman.

A couple of woman screamed and held each other. A man jogging down the street stopped a few feet from her body. The truck had rolled over her upper body. Her head was crushed. Her arms, sprawled in front of her, were broken too. Her purse lay at her side. A spilled soft drink container rolled along the street. The jogger pulled a cell phone from his fanny pack and dialed 911.

"She fell into the street. I couldn't stop, I couldn't stop," said the truck driver. A police officer on horseback followed by another officer on a bicycle arrived on the scene. The officer on horseback radioed for a police car and an ambulance. He was told that both were already on route. The officer on the bicycle dropped his bicycle and knelt next to the victim. He checked her pulse. Nothing.

Ed watched and waited for the arrival of the ambulance. No one had noticed his pushing her in front of the truck. Everybody was too busy and distracted with their own lives to notice much. The ambulance arrived in a few minutes. The EMTs checked her over just in case there was a chance to save her life. The results were the same, she was dead. A police officer took photos of the scene after which the EMTs covered her body with a white sheet. An officer picked up her purse and began to look through it for identification. Two other officers began to speak to the crowd to see if anyone had noticed anything. People's heads just shook no to the questions. Before the police could question Ed, he decided to move along.

He pushed his way through the growing crowd.

Some tourists even snapped pictures of the dead woman's shroud covered body.

A souvenir is a souvenir, thought Ed as he put distance between himself and the death that he had orchestrated.

He pulled his cell phone from his pocket, flipped it open and dialed a number.

"Ed, here. Good news, it's a Powell all right. I'll bet anything he's the one she raised as a nephew. Yeah, yeah, I know. Uh-huh. Sure. Yeah, I took care of that, too. Listen, there's more. He's coming to Vermont. Yes, you heard right. When? Now, I think. I know, I know. Okay. I'm heading back now. I should be there tonight. I'll meet you at Samuel's welcoming."

He powered off his cell phone and put it back in his pocket. He had much to do. He would abandon the rental cars along his return route. A simple call to the local police to report an abandoned or possibly stolen car would ensure the cars were returned to the rental companies. He needed to clean up all loose ends. After taking the "T" back to Cambridge, he checked out of the Comfort Inn and picked up Interstate 93 heading north back to Vermont. It was 3:40 in the afternoon. The traffic, while heavy, moved along without interruption. He pushed the accelerator down to get his speed up to seventy-five miles per hour. Even at that speed, he was passed quite frequently. He kept it at that speed. He didn't need to draw any attention from the patrolling State Police. He could easily talk his way out of any ticket—after all he was a "brother" law enforcement officer, even though he was retired. The professional courtesy was good for life.

This revelation of a male Powell and that he was heading to Vermont almost seemed too good to be true. His lifetime in law enforcement made him skeptical of most things.

This is almost too easy, he thought.

15

Reverend Simon B. Mitchell hung up the phone. He was filled with emotion. He most certainly would share this good news with the entire Church membership, but first, the coven itself. He called Josephine Lawless.

"Hello, this is Jo."

"Josephine, this is Simon." He could never quite bring himself to call her Jo.

"I've got some special news. We have located a male Powell. He's a direct descendant."

The news was greeted with silence.

"Josephine, did you hear what I said?"

"Simon, don't you play around like that." She was the only one who could speak so boldly to him.

"It's the truth. I just took a call from Ed. He's confirmed that Elizabeth Powell had a son. He's located him. Our time could soon be at hand."

"Where is this Powell now?"

Josephine was always one who could cut to the chase.

"That's the best part. He's coming to Vermont. Ed's tracking him even as we speak."

"Reverend, this is the most joyous news our faithful have yet heard."

"Yes, I agree. I expect to tell them tonight at Samuel's welcoming ceremony. I do think the coven needs to meet this afternoon, the sooner the better."

"I agree completely. Is Samuel to join us at this meeting?"

"Yes, of course. I was hoping you would call the others and set up the meeting for around four o'clock at the Judge's house."

"I'll do that. See you then."

The Reverend hung up the telephone. There was a soft knock at thedoor of his study. He opened it. Standing in the outer office were the parents of Brittany. It was Clement and Anne Coolidge. Mrs. Coolidge's eyes were red and swollen from crying. Mr. Coolidge's eyes were puffy as well.

"Come in, please," said the Reverend as he gestured to the two leather chairs set before his desk.

They both headed to the chairs and sat down.

The Reverend went around his desk and sat down as well.

The father spoke up first, "Our daughter is a foolish girl, but she meant no harm. We've raised her the best that we can, and we just know she would never tell—she just wouldn't."

"I'm sure you have done the best by her," said the Reverend, "but you both know the law."

"Isn't there anything we can do?" sobbed the mother.

"No, I'm afraid not. If there is anything that binds us together, it is the law."

In an uncharacteristic effort to soften the blow, Reverend Mitchell decided to share the good news. "Listen, I shouldn't tell you this now. It's supposed to be a surprise. I guess it wouldn't do any harm to tell the two of you, knowing how faithful you both are, that is."

"What?"

"We have located a male Powell," he said.

He let the words sink in. The Coolidge's sat forward in their chairs. The expressions on their faces rapidly shifted from deep sadness to soft smiles.

"Can it be?" said Anne Coolidge, wiping away a tear.

"Yes, I believe so. Now your daughter, Brittany, will serve Moloch and all of us in a very special way. You should both feel honored."

"Anne, just think, our Brittany and the finding of a male Powell. It's an omen—a powerful omen," said Clement Coolidge.

"You must keep this a secret until tonight's ceremony."

They both nodded their agreement.

After a bit more conversation, Brittany's parents left the Reverend's office. They had come to him, hoping to plead for their daughter's life. Now they were leaving rejoicing in the role their daughter would play on this historic day. They were beaming with new found pride. They hugged one another as they headed to their car.

The Reverend watched them leave from the slender window next to the front door.

He turned and headed to his office. He had much to prepare for and he couldn't waste a moment.

Josephine Lawless had wasted no time in contacting the others. The calls were brief and to the point. She did not mention the good news the Reverend had revealed to her. Her years as the Office Manager to the past five Governors had taught her the value of keeping executive secrets. The Reverend should be the one to reveal this news to the others. This is how it should be, of that, she was certain.

Everyone was at the Judge's house except for the Reverend. Samuel was driven to this meeting by his father, in their new truck. No one asked Josephine why a meeting had to be called. It was routine for everyone to obey whenever a call was put out for a meeting of the coven. Judy Perrillo went around the living room drawing all the drapes. Shirley Carter, the self employed beautician, was still wearing her work clothes as was Bob Senecal and Walter Yandow.

"I hear the State Police have been contacted about a couple of hikers who failed to arrive at their destination!" said John Farnum, Sutton's Volunteer Fire Chief.

"The woods are a dangerous place sometimes, especially for a couple of flatlanders," answered Walter with a smile.

Before the conversation could continue, the Reverend walked in the door.

He smiled at the fellow coven members and nodded an acknowledgement to a couple. It had been getting hot and humid the past couple of days and today was the worst. In the short distance from his air conditioned car to the Judge's house, he had broken into a powerful sweat. He removed his handkerchief and wiped at his brow.

The Judge poured him a glass of ice tea from a carafe sitting on the side table next to a bookcase filled with musty old law books.

The Reverend turned around and spoke to the assembled members of the coven.

"Let us join hands," he said.

With that, Ed Foley and John Farnum rolled back the antique rug in the center of the room uncovering a pentagram carved into the old wide pine floor. Everyone now stood in a circle around this symbol and held hands. The room was lit by a couple of small lamps sitting on end tables next to the sofa. A room size air conditioner hummed from the side window.

As they clasped hands, each of them seem to fall into a trance like state. Their eyes now closed, they rolled their heads from side to side. In a few moments, they each opened their eyes and for each, their look was the same. Their eyes were now entirely a glistening black. Their faces became muscular and distorted and their bodies seem to swell to the point they seemed in danger of bursting out of their now tight fitting clothes. The Reverend spoke in a voice that was his, but slightly distorted.

"Faithful servants of Moloch, I bring you THE ONE MESSAGE we have been waiting for, as our ancestors have, from long ago. We will share this news with Him. Now join me in calling to our Prince of Darkness."

The entire coven except for Samuel, who had not yet been taught all of the ways of the coven, now chanted in unison as they swayed to the chant.

"We call to you all powerful Moloch, Certe Ne Diaza Orce Pru, Giasha Morte Lee Xintra Moloch," they repeated three times.

In the low light of the room, a shape began to take form in the center of the circle. The shape seemed to be struggling to untangle itself. This shape, shrouded in a haze of eerie spinning light, now stood erect before them. The shape was well over six feet tall. The shape was a human form was at the same time not human. The head was misshapen. There were two knobs on the top of its head just above each eye, protruding nearly three inches. The arms were unusually long. The hands had long fingernails that made the hands seem bigger than they already were. Its unclothed torso was dark, muscular and scaly. It stood upon two powerful legs, which had cloven hooves instead of feet. This shape also had a tail that seemed to have the characteristics of a snake. The eyes were dark, sunken and radiating red. They glowed as if they were on fire.

"Welcome Great and Powerful Moloch," spoke the Reverend.

The shape was none other than Moloch himself. He had been summoned from the nether world. Hearing his name called, he turned silently and faced the Reverend. Moloch thrust his face directly in front of Simon.

"Yes," he hissed.

"We have found a male Powell."

The words brought great pleasure to Moloch as he pulled back from Simon and raised his long arms up, fist clenched. The news also surprised everyone else except for Josephine who had heard earlier. They reacted with smiles and shouts for joy. Their tongues, now serpent like, darted from their mouths and licked across their lips.

"Tell me more," demanded Moloch.

"One of our coven is tracking him now. It seems that this male is coming to Vermont. He may even be coming here to Sutton."

Without turning around, Moloch twisted his body and immediately placed his face within inches of Samuel.

"And what can you tell me, Samuel?" said Moloch. He pronounced Samuel's name almost one letter at a time.

Samuel closed his eyes. His face grew contorted in an almost painful way. And then he spoke.

"I can see Ed. He is driving back here. He has some papers that confirm what Reverend Mitchell has spoken. His heart is full of joy for you."

Moloch now spoke to everyone. As he did, he twisted his body so that he could place his face directly before each.

"I renew my vow to each of you, your ancestors and your descendants, too. I will walk this earth. With your help I shall prepare the way for Lucifer to rule over all. You shall rule by our sides and shall share in the power, the glory and all the riches that earth promises and you shall have life everlasting for your loyalty. Now go and do what must be done. I return to Lucifer with your news." His shape began to lose itself as it vaporized and blended with the swirling lights.

When the last of his presence had faded away, the coven members returned to a trance-like state. Moments later they opened their eyes, now normal, and began to hug one another. Samuel got a few hearty slaps on his back. After a while they settled down and organized into action groups.

***

It was a little past six o'clock when Aaron pulled into the parking lot of the Ethan Allen Inn. The motel was situated on a hillside in Berlin, Vermont just three quarters of a mile from Interstate 89. Berlin was less than three miles south of Montpelier. It was very humid. Aaron exited the car and stretched his legs which had become stiff from all the driving. Korie also got out of the car and stretched her legs. The two weary travelers walked into the motel's lobby. It was small but well appointed with several Vermont type artifacts and photos. They approached the desk. A young man exited a side office and approached the desk.

"Yes, may I help you?"

"Why yes, I believe you can. I would like a room for three nights for the two of us."

Korie poked him in the ribs, which prompted him to poke her back.

The desk clerk raised his eyebrow to their behavior as he placed a check-in register card and a motel labeled pen on the counter.

"Very well, please fill this out while I check on room availability."

Korie spoke up, "Non-smoking please."

"All of our rooms are non-smoking. We were one of the first motels in Vermont to practice a non-smoking policy," he said proudly, "I see we do have a room available. The rate for double occupancy is seventy-four dollars and sixty cents a night. That includes tax and a free continental breakfast. Now, let's see," said the clerk as he examined the register card.

Korie and Aaron were both road weary.

"Mr. Powell, I see here you'll be paying by charge, may I have your card to take an impression?"

Korie pulled Aaron on the arm.

"Excuse us for a moment," she said to the clerk.

"We can't use your real name, not here in Vermont, especially when we're this close to that town.

"You're right. What do we do now?"

"I've got an idea. I'll pay for the room. I'll put it on my charge card. You can pay me back later."

"Better yet, I'll pay with cash when we check out. We'll use your card just to hold the room."

They turned back to the clerk, who seemed mildly amused by their behavior.

"Listen, we're going to put the room on my card, okay?" said Korie.

"It makes no difference to me, plastic is plastic."

In a moment, the clerk processed the charge card and then gave them room keys. The keys were plastic cards with a magnetic strip coded to unlock only their room.

"Your room number is 245. It is located around to the left, fourth entrance down. It's a poolside room. Please enjoy your stay with us and should you need any assistance please feel free to call the front desk. My name is Victor and I'll do my best to make your stay is a pleasant one."

"Thanks, Victor. One question, if I may? How's the motel restaurant?"

"It's not bad. We have a new chef. He's developed some nice entrees. I think you'll enjoy the food. Service is good, too."

"Thanks."

Korie and Aaron headed back to their car and pulled it around back. Before they entered the motel they both took a moment to notice that from the parking lot overlooking the valley below, they could see at least thirty miles to the east, the same to the north and west.

"That mountain over there must be Camel's Hump," said Aaron pointing to a tall mountain to the west.

"Yeah, and look at that huge storm cloud just to the west of the mountain," said Korie.

"Swimming pool," said Aaron as he gave Korie a playful poke.

"Sounds wonderful, let's take a dip before dinner," said Korie.

"Perfect."

They raced for the entrance door.

***

Ed Townsend's butt hurt from all the driving he had done over the past couple of days. It was six thirty and he had just passed mile marker 10 on Interstate 89 in Vermont. He was heading north. The heat and humidity of this summer day was oppressive. His windshield was stained from the hundreds of bugs that had met their end against its streaked surface. The Interstate Highway in Vermont wound around hills and mountains just as often as it climbed up and then down again. Ed was tired, but also anxious to get back to Sutton.

He looked in his rearview mirror and spotted a State Police cruiser bearing down on him with its blue swag lights flashing.

"Shit."

There was a sudden wail from the police siren. Ed pulled his car over to the right side breakdown lane. His car came to a stop. He waited for the officer to approach his car. The State Police cruiser had stopped behind Ed's car. The officer positioned his car so the driver side was set slightly closer to the driving lane of the highway. Ed could see the officer using his radio to check out the description of his car, as well as the car's license plate number.

Standard procedure, thought Ed.

The officer opened the door and slowly approached Ed's car. He kept his eye on Ed for any sign of sudden or unusual movement. The early evening winds were picking up. As a car speed past the stopped cars, the rush of air caused the officer to hold on to his hat.

Both of his armpits were heavily stained with perspiration. He wore dark aviator glasses.

Ed had rolled down the driver's side window when he first pulled over. The officer was now standing next to the driver's door.

He bent over slightly and asked, "Do you have any idea how fast you were traveling, sir?" His face bore no expression.

"Yes, I do, officer, I was doing seventy."

"I followed you for a couple of miles and you were doing over eighty, sir. May I see your license and registration please?"

Ed pulled his identification wallet from his back pocket. As he sat forward, he could feel the lump in the middle of his back from the gun he wore strapped to his belt. At the last rest stop he had removed his shoulder holster and laid it on the passenger car seat, over which he had placed his suit coat.

Ed opened his wallet. His license was on the left side window and his U.S. Government F.B.I. identification and badge were on the right. He handed the I.D. wallet to the officer. According to official policy, he should have turned in his badge and Government I.D. when he retired. However, according to tradition in his unit, he took it with him. So far no one had asked for it back. If they had, he would have said that he had turned it in. The system does make mistakes.

Ed gambled this officer would not check on his "official status." Ed's gamble paid off.

"F.B.I. huh? Well, Mr. Townsend, please try to keep your speed under control. Wouldn't want to have an accident and hurt a citizen."

"You're quite right, officer. Thanks."

"Have a nice day, see you down the road."

The State Police officer handed the wallet back and returned to his cruiser. Ed returned his I.D. to his back pocket. The State Police cruiser pulled out and passed him. The young officer gave Ed a friendly wave, which Ed returned.

Ed put his car in gear, checked his mirror and pulled back onto the highway. The stop had delayed him further. He had kept his cool. He knew the unofficial code of the law enforcement brotherhood would protect him from most minor matters. Why not, he had given others in the brotherhood a pass or two in his day? Professional courtesy is almost always extended to a member of the law enforcement family.

Meanwhile, in Sutton, people were getting ready for the ceremony they would attend later that night. Clothes were washed and pressed. Lanterns were checked and rechecked. People called others for a ride. Others sat down to dinner while others read from the secret book, the Book of Covenants.

Ed Foley and his daughter, Lisa, prepared the unconscious Brittany. They combed her hair. They washed her wounds. They reset her broken arm but had not put it into a cast. Lisa had skillfully applied makeup to Brittany's bruises. The last thing was the dress they put on Brittany. It was a white dress that resembled a smock in its simplicity. Brittany's right arm was hooked up to an I.V. bottle. The bottle dripped slowly as it silently carried a narcotic into her damaged body. Her breathing and pulse were as normal as possible under the circumstances.

Ed wanted to tell his daughter about the good news, but he refrained from doing so. He was a loyal member of the coven. He was adept at keeping secrets. He knew many secrets and never betrayed the trust placed in him.

"She should be fine," said Ed.

"When do we leave?" asked Lisa.

"We'll leave around ten thirty or so. We need to be early so we can park as close as possible. I'll get the stretcher and leave it on the porch until we need it."

Lisa left Brittany alone as she went upstairs to shower and change. She wanted to look her best for the welcoming ceremony.

16

Aaron and Korie unpacked quickly and headed to the pool with towels in tow. After taking a brief dip in the motel swimming pool, Aaron and Korie towel dry themselves in their room.

From behind, Aaron strokes Korie's shoulders. She had just put her panties on and was taking a bra out of her side of the dresser. Aaron reaches around Korie and envelopes her in his arms. He is wearing only his boxer shorts. Korie twists herself around until she was face to face with him. Her arms were restrained by his. He leans towards her and invites a kiss. She resists his offer.

"Hey, come on," he pleads.

"Look, I don't want to start something, not now." She smiles for him, not wanting to injure his fragile male ego.

"Just one kiss?"

"Okay, lover boy. One kiss, but then you're buying me dinner, right?"

"That depends on how good a kisser you are."

He released her arms. Taking him by his arms, she pulls him to her with such force their bodies collide. She reaches up and takes his head in her gentle hands. She looks him in the eyes and then slowly moves closer. Their lips meet and make the slightest contact. She holds this position for a moment longer, when suddenly she pulls him to her and she presses her lips, indeed her entire body, against him. The force of the kiss takes him by surprise. He staggers backwards a bit, yet she presses on with their kiss. Korie twists her mouth from side to side, kissing his. Now she takes his lips between her teeth and bites down gently. She can tell by his breathing that she is getting his attention. He is quickly becoming aroused. Korie now pushes him backwards, and Aaron falls down on the bed in a mock swoon.

"How's that?"

"Incredible!"

She reached into one of dresser drawers and tosses him a polo shirt.

"You owe me dinner."

"You bet I do."

They finished getting dressed and headed down to dinner in the motel restaurant. The place wasn't very crowded. Aaron asked for a window seat so they could enjoy the view of the mountains. It was quarter past seven. They ordered cocktails. Korie noticed the building storm clouds to the west. The vista from this hilltop location was spectacular. The evening sky was filled with dark slate blues and grays, set off by vibrant streaks of yellow sunrays, accented with tinges of red and orange. The approaching storm clouds climbed higher and higher into the sky.

***

All around Sutton, people were sitting down after their own dinner. Farmers were tired from a long day's work in this humid summer weather. The season's first hay crop had been above average and the second crop was looking like it was going to top the first cut. Joggers were out taking advantage of the evenings long shadows to cool down their runs, at least as cool as could be expected under the circumstances.

This small Vermont town with its Jekyll and Hyde dual personality moved about its business so the normal everyday people never noticed the town's dark side, a side of pure evil. Neighbors, co-workers, bosses, spouses, teachers, doctors, young people and the elderly were as divided as could be, good amongst evil. The town hosted a cabal of devil worshippers practicing their craft without detection. Tonight was to be a night of celebration. A new Keeper had been chosen. He would be welcomed by his fellow practitioners into this dark cult.

They began traveling the back roads that all converged at the same location. The roads, washboard worn, gave up trails of choking dust. Cars were carefully parked in a field next to the Game Warden's house. They parked like they were going to a county fair. Young boys with flashlights pointed each newly arriving car to an assigned parking spot.

Brittany's battered body is carefully lifted out of a car. She is unconscious, in a drug induced stupor. She is placed on a stretcher which had been brought along. The stretcher is now moved out ahead of the crowd handled by two willing volunteers. They walk slowly.

There was s steady stream of people moving up the heavily worn path to the outdoor altar. The evening air was filled with the aroma of pine and sumac. Wild flowers, from black eyed susans to miniature marigolds, skirted the path. Once an old logging road, the path was wide and smooth underfoot. To the left was the small stream that bore the name of the Sutton River.

This is the same path that Michael Delvecchio and Julia Brodsky had traveled along just a couple of weeks before.

Many of the faithful, both young and old alike, were happily talking together. Several kerosene lanterns, and battery powered ones as well, were evident. A few of these assorted lanterns were already lit. A couple of young boys picked up stones and tossed them into the stream. The animals of the forest pulled back from this sight or gave it the usual wide berth.

Among the faithful were members of the coven. Whenever noticed by the other faithful, the members of the coven were given an enthusiastic wave, a friendly nod or a warm handshake. A few would even venture to speak in private with a coven member, in search of their counsel or to seek a special favor.

The faithful in attendance this evening numbered close to three hundred.

After walking along this path for nearly a half mile, it turned to the left across an old wooden bridge. Now the path grew narrower and was angled much steeper. To the left of the path, nearly at its very edge, was a steep drop off that grew higher and higher as the path climbed upward along the mountainside. The chirping sounds of crickets could be heard everywhere.

An old woman, a former kindergarten teacher, was busy preparing the altar site along with a couple of middle aged men. One of the men is the president of the local bank, while the other owns a car wash along U.S. Route 2, south of the town. The woman unfolds a black shroud that she carefully uses to cover the entire altar. Her next step is to attach to the altar's downhill side a red silk banner with a gold embroidered pentagram. She also places certain artifacts under the altar. Meanwhile, the two men are busy building two large pyres to be used as bonfires later during the ceremony. These pyres are located twenty feet to left and right of the altar. They are careful to ensure that the base of these two stacks of oil soaked timbers are surrounded by the usual large fieldstones. The timbers are stacked into a teepee style shape.

Just as they are finishing their work, the first of the faithful begin arriving. People move to their usual locations in front of the altar, more out of habit than any design or plan. No one has brought a chair to sit upon. A chair would be taken as a sign of weakness.

The stretcher carrying Brittany is deposited to the uphill side of the altar. Ed Foley checks Brittany's pulse and it is weak. She is bleeding internally from injuries she sustained in the truck crash last night. Her stomach, distended from the bleeding, makes her seem to be mildly bloated. A middle-aged woman, who by day works in a nursing home as director of the nursing staff, approaches Lisa. The woman hands her a neatly pressed red robe. Thanking her, Lisa takes the robe.

Lisa, with some help from her father, removes Brittany's clothes. They cover her naked, bruised and broken body with this robe. Brittany's parents have arrived and are being warmly greeted by the other members of the faithful for their good fortune.

Each coven member is carrying a small bag. As they reach the altar area, they head up the mountainside to the woods beyond. It is in these woods they enter a small tent that has been erected for their use. Taking turns, they enter the tent, remove their clothes and don black robes. Exiting the tent, now barefoot, they return to the altar area. It is getting dark now and most, if not all, of the lanterns people have brought have been lit. There is a slight breeze this evening. The wind is picking up due to a summer storm that has been building in the west. The storm is now moving into the area.

Samuel Porter and his family have arrived. Hand shakes and expressions of congratulations are extended to the Porter family, especially Samuel Porter.

The last to arrive is Reverend Simon B. Mitchell. He takes Samuel by the arm and leads him to the uphill side of the altar.

"Samuel, you must wait here while I go and change. I shall be back in a moment and then we can begin."

"Fine."

"Are you nervous?" asked the Reverend.

"Not at all."

"Good, remember, wait here."

The Reverend turned and headed off to the tent to change.

Judy walked over to Samuel.

Smiling she takes his hand and strokes it with her other hand.

"Samuel, I'm so happy for you."

"Thanks."

"Samuel, if you ever need anything, anything at all, I want you to know you can come to me," she said with a smile that sent an entirely different message.

"How very generous of you," said Samuel with a smile.

Her intentions were lust. His was barely controlled rage.

She pulled back from him, letting go of his hand. He instead held her hand in his. His grip was painful to her. Her eyes caught his. She felt an overwhelming sense of power coming from his look. It was a look she had seen before. His demon spirit was more powerful, higher ranking than hers.

He released her hand. She bowed her head to him in a slight nod. Judy turned away from him and took her place with the other members of the coven.

The coven members are arranged into two groups, one to either side of the altar.

Stepping from out of the uphill darkness is the Reverend. Now that he had arrived, the ceremony could begin.

The Reverend stood at the center and behind the altar. Raising his hands above his head, he spread them apart, which was taken by the faithful as a sign for silence. Samuel Porter's welcoming ceremony was now underway.

"On behalf of Moloch, Beelzebub and Lucifer, the Demon of all Demons, allow me to greet you as brothers and sisters. Tonight we are gathered, as we have times before, and as even our ancestors did so many times before, to welcome a new member of the coven. Our new chosen member has preserved our sacred place with his own silencing. He has proven his loyalty. He has taken of the blood. Moloch, himself, has blessed him. He has received a most important gift from Lucifer as well, the gift of a mind seer."

The Reverend pauses for effect. As he surveys the faithful, he sees their eagerness, their yearning.

"I give you Samuel Porter."

The crowd breaks into applause. Samuel is waved forward by the Reverend. Samuel steps up to the altar. Despite his earlier comments, he is now showing signs of nervousness. Shirley Carter and Walter Yandow approach Samuel and begin to remove all of his clothes. After his clothes have been removed, he is given his own black robe by Phyllis Atkins. He pulls the robe over his head and faces the crowd once again. They press forward to hear him.

He bows his head.

Now looking up, there is a clear transformation that has taken place in Samuel. His eyes are now totally black, piercing, shiny black, like a child's marble. His hands are much larger and muscular. His fingernails are much longer and twisted in form. His head and especially his face are bulging with muscles that distort his countenance. Samuel also seems taller. He fills his robe with a more powerful presence than what he had just moments before. He smiles upon the gathering. His teeth are yellowed and somewhat misshapen. His tongue, snakelike in shape, slithers from inside his mouth and flickers in the night air. Finally, beneath his robe, his feet have changed into cloven hooves.

Reaching into cooling night air, above the altar, he raises his own arms. His robe's sleeves slide down to reveal hairy powerful arms.

"I take the name of Upuaut, for I am the one who comes before."

The crowd begins to chant "Upuaut, Upuaut, Upuaut..."

The entire coven itself begins to change. One by one, they too transform into hideous demons just like Samuel, as their human bodies manifest the presence of the evil spirits that have possessed their bodies. These are the spirits they are bonded with, their partners from Hell.

"Bring to this altar our sacrifice," hissed Samuel.

Ed Foley and Chucky Trainor lift and place Brittany upon the altar. She is wearing the red silk robe that was especially prepared for her.

"I offer this sacrifice to Moloch, to Beelzebub, to Lucifer, and to all who inhabit the other world. Join me in calling him forth," commanded Samuel. His power and presence was greater than had ever been seen before. Even the other coven members could see this.

Samuel began the familiar chant, "Certe Ne Diaza Orce Pru, Giasha Morte Lee Xintra, Moloch..."

Samuel's voice, deep and inhuman, could be heard above all others.

Suddenly the wooden pyres ignited with a "swoosh" like sound. The two were completely engulfed in fire within less than a couple of seconds. The fires bathed the scene in an eerie yellow light. Rising from the ground in front of the altar is a faint specter figure that begins to take shape and soon appears as solid as anyone or anything. It is Moloch, scaly, horned, cloven hoofed, powerful tail, red burning eyes—the whole package.

He stands in front of the altar, appearing at least nine feet tall. He smiles at the assembled faithful. He seems to be absorbing their expressions of awe.

Moloch speaks in his unearthly voice, "Tonight I bring you a message from Lucifer himself. As you know, long ago your ancestors and Lucifer's Legions, and the pact we had agreed to, was broken. Broken by a cowardly, God fearing, Powell. On that night long ago, we had our revenge, but that, too, was stolen from all with the escape of a Powell family member. We were twice denied."

The crowd reacts as if it's at a revival with chants of "Yes Denied...Denied."

Bending forward as if to better connect with his audience he presses his point, "Yes, denied, by a Powell."

"And who have you and your ancestors been searching for?"

"A Powell," shouts someone from the audience.

"A male Powell," shouted several others.

"Yessssss...," says Moloch with his snakelike tongue.

Moloch leans back and now walks along the left side of the altar. He stops and places his powerful right hand upon the shoulder of Reverend Mitchell.

"Speak," commands Moloch.

"We have located a male Powell."

There are gasps in the crowd, shouts of joy and fists pumping in the air.

The Moloch specter now moves to stand behind the altar and along side of Samuel.

"Upuaut, I thank you for this offering. Beelzebub, Lucifer and all from the other world welcome you. Upuaut is now the leader of this coven, for Lucifer has spoken through me. Let all obey or forever live amongst the land of the undead."

The Reverend is taken aback by this unexpected event. He believed he would be shepherding his flock during this important time, and now he is usurped by a new member of the coven, fourteen year old Samuel Porter. He strains to control himself.

"Take this sign from the King of the other world. In two days, there will be an earthquake that destroys only one thing. It will destroy a place of worship in a place called Budapest. A thousand lives will be lost. Know of it and know from whom it comes," said Moloch.

He turns to Samuel and gestures for him to proceed.

Samuel now takes a dagger from the altar top. He holds it skyward. The night sky bursts with a bright flash of lightning and then another and another.

There is no thunder. This lightning is what old timers call heat lightning. It arrives without the usual rumble of thunder.

Samuel takes the dagger and traces a cut across Brittany's left wrist. Blood spurts from the cut. Samuel holds a large cup beneath the cut to gather the blood. It soon is filled almost to the brim.

Moloch, having temporally taken on physical presence, raises his arms up over the altar, palms side up. He takes the dagger from Samuel and cuts his own scaly wrist. His own blood begins to drip from this cut. Samuel holds the cup underneath Moloch's wrist and collects this new blood into the cup, which was nearly filled with Brittany's blood. Once the cup is filled Samuel carefully places it back upon the altar. Moloch next lays his hands palms side down, above the body of Brittany, not quite touching her. He begins to lift his hands higher into the air. The now dying body of Brittany rises into the air, like some sort of grand illusion. Her body next turns right side up, facing the crowd. Blood still runs down from her cut wrist, dripping from the ends of her fingers. She is nearly drained of blood and life. Her complexion is ashen gray. Slowly her body begins to fade from view. In its place is a specter of her body. This specter now appears to move towards Moloch. Lightning flashes in the sky overhead. In a flash of bright white light, Brittany's specter and Moloch's disappear. Her red silk, blood stained robe falls from the sky and lands upon the altar.

Samuel, now called Upuaut, picks up the large cup from the altar. The blood within is still warm. He takes a small drink. He next passes it among his fellow coven members, who also drink from the cup. Soon the cup is passed to the crowd, who continue this unholy ritual.

The lightning is exploding all around the mountaintop.

As the cup is returned to the altar, Samuel, still Upuaut, leads the gathered in a closing chant.

"Hec uq nim olo braq, sy ter sca hur."

With the repeating of this chant three times, the ceremony comes to an end. During the chanting, the coven members evolve back to their human form. The crowd applauds one last time.

148

The coven members now approach Samuel, one by one. They nod as they pass him by. The last to approach is the Reverend. He nods like the others and passes by. Samuel, however, can see into his heart and he sees a boiling tempest of anger and hatred.

Samuel is not in the least alarmed by what he sees in the Reverend. Anger and hatred can be good, especially if channeled the right way.

Samuel smiles to himself with the thought, *what is bad can be good, could it be that what is good can be bad?*

The faithful are lined up to meet and greet the newest leader of their coven.

A new coven leader, along with news of a male Powell about to be in their midst has generated a powerful and urgent sense of optimism. The people are excited, almost giddy in their glee over these two events. Together, they were taken as powerful omens, signs that their day of triumph was drawing near.

After a while, the crowd began to disperse and trail back down the mountain.

Another series of heat lightning flashed about. The night sky was exploding with lightning bursts as if it were a Fourth of July fireworks grand finale.

The last to leave is Samuel.

17

Aaron and Korie stayed late in the restaurant. By the time they finished their dinner, desert and then after dinner drinks, it was nearly eleven o'clock. They were the last two customers in the restaurant.

"It's late, Aaron, why don't we head back to our room? I'm sure the wait staff would like to close up."

"I guess you're right. Their vacuuming is sort of a signal, huh?"

"I am quite sure it is."

They rose from their table. Aaron left a generous tip on the table. They stopped at the register. No one was around. Aaron looked into the kitchen's round windows and got the attention of someone. In a moment a young woman, their waitress, stepped through the kitchen doors and headed to the register.

"Did you enjoy your dinner tonight?" asked the young woman.

"We did, thanks," said Korie.

"I left your tip on the table," said Aaron.

"Thank you, sir."

Taking his change, Aaron stuffs it into his pocket. Taking Korie by the arm, they head back to their motel room.

"Want to go for a swim?" asked Korie.

"Again?"

"Sure," she responds as she pulls his arm and him closer.

"Okay."

Moments later they are swimming in the pool. It is nearly midnight. Northwest of their location, the night sky explodes with brilliant flashes of lightning. There is no sound of thunder. Korie swims over to Aaron, puts her arms around him and kisses him passionately. She presses her body against his. He responds to her initiative with his own. He pulls her closer to him, lifting her partly out of the water. His face becomes buried between the swells of her breasts. She plays with his hair, running her fingers through his wet clinging hair. Her own hair dangles across his forehead. She kisses the top of his head. He slowly allows her body to slide back down. She begins to kiss him all over. He does likewise.

Their passion is approaching a point of no return. The lightning storm is moving slowly towards their location.

Aaron tries to unhook her top.

"No, Aaron, not here, please."

With those words they release one another, exit the pool, grab their towels and break into a half run back to the privacy of the motel room. Aaron closes and locks the door to their room. When he turns around, Korie is standing directly behind him, naked.

Before words could be spoken she helps him out of his swimming trucks. They both tumble onto the bed.

Earlier, Aaron had left the window to their room wide open, with the air conditioner off. He had pulled back the curtains to let the summer breeze blow in through the open window.

The open window now framed the arriving lightning storm. Brilliant flashes of light streaked across the night sky. With each burst of lightning, the dark purple clouds of the storm were outlined in several dark shades of red, gray, yellow, pink and purple.

Korie and Aaron's lovemaking was the most intense they had ever experienced as they alternated positions. The rhythm of their passion was feverish and powerful.

Outside their window, the storm was now directly overhead. Lightning bolts traced their irregular web across the sky. The lover's room was frequently illuminated by these pyrotechnics.

One earthshaking explosion of thunder shook the motel.

***

Ed Townsend had arrived too late for Samuel's welcoming ceremony. The faithful were already coming down the old logging road.

"Ed, have you heard the news? There's a male Powell," said one of the overjoyed faithful.

"Yeah, I know."

"Isn't that exciting?" said another.

Bob Senecal spotted Ed up ahead. He walked over to him and took him by the arm over to Ed's car.

"Ed, have you heard yet?" asked Bob.

"What is it that I'm supposed to hear?" asked Ed.

"Moloch has replaced Reverend Mitchell with a new leader."

Surprised, Ed asks, "With Who?"

"Samuel Porter."

The name sinks is.

"I wonder why?"

"Beats me," said Bob.

"Where's the Reverend now?"

"Back there, somewhere," nods Bob over his shoulder.

Heat lightning flashes overhead.

"And Porter?"

"Still up there, I believe."

"Interesting."

"You could say that again. Well, I've got to be going," said Bob as he heads toward his tow truck.

The crowd moved past Ed as he stood in the road waiting for the Reverend. Spotting him, Ed walks over.

"Simon, I just heard," said Ed.

"It is the will of Lucifer. I shall continue to serve," said a stoic Simon.

"What about the Powell male?" asked Ed?

The Reverend looks up at the newest burst of heat lightning.

"See Samuel for directions. He is now the chosen one. He speaks for Moloch and for all of us now."

His eyes are moist as if he is about to shed a tear. He turns his head down and silently moves off to his car.

Ed watches him leave.

This sudden change in leaders for the coven has unsettled Ed. He is a man who is accustomed to strong decisive leadership.

Shit, the boy is only fourteen, maybe fifteen, thought Ed.

"I am almost fifteen Mr. Townsend, but why should that matter?" said a voice from behind him.

Ed turns around and sees no one on the path coming down the mountain. He looks to his left, his right and now behind him, still no one.

"Mr. Townsend, we still serve the same master. Our mission is unchanged," said the voice.

Another flash of heat lightning, and then another. The logging road leading up the mountain is lit up like daytime. There, standing alone in the middle of the road, is Samuel Porter. He is about fifty feet from Ed. He silently walks towards Ed.

Now they are standing an arms length apart.

"Take me home," said Samuel Porter.

Without question, Ed obeys his new leader.

Neither spoke another word all the way back to Samuel Porter's house.

***

Korie has fallen asleep. Aaron carefully rolls himself out of bed. He walks over to the open window and stares out at the last traces of the heat lightning storm. There are now breaks in the cloud cover.

After a few minutes the night clouds are gone and the night sky sparkles with millions of stars. The three-quarter moon is now visible, high in the southwest sky. Aaron reached down and picked up the wet swimsuit and heads into the bathroom to hang it up. Along the way he picks up Korie's as well and hangs her suit up on the shower bar alongside his. Naked, he heads back into the room and pulls a pair of boxer shorts out of the dresser drawer. From his luggage bag, he removes the Powell family diary.

Aaron turns on the desk lamp and sits down at the small desk and begins to read the diary, this time cover to cover. The stories within are compelling. He finds time just flies by. Reading the dairy, he begins to understand the sense of mission his ancestors have felt and lived all of their lives.

What is ahead for me? he thought.

Aaron is beginning to appreciate his heritage. His great grandmother several times removed and her family showed unbelievable courage in standing up to the coven and its evil leaders. Their courageous stand prevented the devil from taking on human form.

Why did the devil want to take on human form? What was the rush anyway? Why then? Why was his family still hunted? Why doesn't this coven just move on and find someone else? Will it ever end? Is it over now? Was his mother clever enough to have thrown them off of his trail? What risk was he taking coming to Vermont? Would he be able to recognize these people? Would they recognize him? These questions and hundreds more swirled around in his head.

Gradually, a sense of purpose was forming for Aaron. His ancestors had suffered and were hounded for over a hundred years. Somehow he felt he could bring this to some sort of end. He felt a wave of confidence sweep through him. He began to form the outline of a plan. But first, he needed more information. As he thought about his possible plan, he experienced a temporary fugue. Deep from within, his mind's eye sent him a message.

Aaron could see an altar sitting in a field along side a hill. Next to this altar are two huge burning bonfires. There were several people standing behind this altar. He couldn't see their faces because they were wearing robes with hoods pulled up over their heads. Each of them gestured to him to come forward. He could feel his body gliding up the hillside. As he came closer, he could see a woman's shroud covered body lying upon this altar. The shroud was pulled over her face. Robe covered people now surrounded him. They were placing their hands all over his body. A couple of the hoods were tossed back to reveal that the person within was a woman. These women began to caress his body with sensual strokes. They removed their robes and began to rub themselves against his body. A couple of other hooded people tossed their hoods off. These were men who were smiling. These men were speaking to him, but he could not hear any spoken words. Standing to the back of this group of people was a hooded, cloaked one who was much larger then the others. This one now reached towards Aaron to hand him a large shiny dagger. He could feel himself take the instrument in his hand. He looked at the handle of this dagger—it seemed to be embossed with tiny figures.

As he looked closer, he could see that these tiny figures were moving, they were alive. Somehow these figures were bound to the dagger's handle.

The naked women had managed to arouse him to a sensual pitch. As he looked at them, they smiled at him with a sinister look that both frightened him and aroused him as well. Suddenly, he noticed their eyes. Their eyes were shiny, cold black. He now turned to face the altar. The large hooded person pulled back the shroud uncovering the woman. She was naked. He looked down at her. Something was familiar. He forced himself to look at her face. It was Korie.

The large hooded person now pulled his hood back to reveal himself to Aaron. This was no human. It was a scaly, fearsome creature. Its head had two horns jutting from its forehead. Its eyes were a smoldering red. This creature smiled at Aaron. Its smile revealed yellowed misshapen teeth. The creature took Aaron's hand that held the dagger into its own. The creature was raising Aaron's hand with the dagger pointed down at the body of Korie. The tiny, but alive figures on the daggers handle squirmed inside Aaron's hand. One such creature managed to push herself through. She had squeezed between Aaron's second and third fingers. Aaron was struggling against the grip on his hand. He glanced at this tiny human figure between his fingers. It was his mother. She shouted at him.

The only sound his dream experience allowed was her shout. "No..."

Aaron was resisting with all of his strength.

"Mom, help me," he responded.

His hand holding the dagger began to descend. He struggled mightily. The other hooded people were clapping their approval. The naked women that had been seducing him just moments before were pressing against him. Their arms had joined the hideous creature in pushing Aaron's hand downward.

With all of his might he let loose a scream, "No..."

Korie was now knelling beside him.

"What's wrong?" she asked.

He turned to his left and looked at her and for a moment he wasn't quite sure whether he was still dreaming or whether he was awake. Korie was wearing a white terry cloth robe loosely tied at the waist.

She stood up, pulled Aaron to his feet, and held him in her arms.

"You must have been having a nightmare."

He couldn't answer her, not yet.

"Why don't you come back to bed? It's nearly five o'clock in the morning. Have you been reading the dairy all night long? It's no wonder you had a bad dream?"

Aaron stared at her in disbelief. His dream had been so vivid, so real to him.

He suddenly broke fully free from the fugue that he had been in. He grabbed Korie by the arms and looked deep into her eyes.

"Korie, I could have..."

She pulled herself free and took hold of his head. She kissed him before he could continue.

"You need to get some rest, we'll talk later," she said.

"You're probably right," he said slumping down onto the bed.

Korie pushed him back onto the bed and tucked him in with the bed sheet. Korie now turned and headed towards the bathroom. As she walked towards the bedroom the light shining from under their motel room caught her attention. Something or someone moved just on the other side of their room's door. The light was broken by a shadow, which moved across the light.

Someone has been listening at our door, she thought.

Korie ran to the door. She stood on her tiptoes and looked through the door's peephole. She couldn't see anyone outside the door. She unlatched the door chain, unbolted the door lock and pulled the door open. She looked to her left, no one. She quickly looked to her right and she noticed someone turn around the corner of the hallway.

"Hey, wait up," she shouted.

She ran after the mysterious person.

When she rounded the corner, she didn't see anyone. There was a sound below her. The person had taken the stairway to the floor below and had exited the motel. She ran back to her room and tiptoed past the now sleeping Aaron to the open window. Korie surveyed the parking lot for any sign of the person who had been listening at their door.

Across the parking lot, in the dawn of the soon to be rising sun, she spotted someone sitting in a pickup truck. The truck started up and pulled quickly away. She couldn't see the license plate. All she could note was that it was an old truck, dark green or black in color. She thought the person driving the truck was a man, but even to that she couldn't be sure.

What the hell was that person up to? she wondered.

Her mind began to fill with all sorts of possibilities. Meanwhile, she still had to use the bathroom. Before she did, she locked their motel's room deadbolt lock, the chain latch and the sash lock. She wasn't going to take any chances.

When he gets up later, we're going to have a little talk and settle up on a plan, that's for sure. No more free wheeling, she thought as she closed the bathroom door behind her and flipped on the light switch.

18

Ed Townsend couldn't wait to consult with the other coven members. He had cultivated sources, spies and informants, all over the greater Sutton area. Many were fellow church members. Others, mercenary by nature, provided tips to Ed for a fee or a favor. One of his paid informers had been driving around the area's motel parking lots. Ed had obtained Aaron Powell's license plate number from the State of Massachusetts Motor Vehicle Registry. He had a friend, whose daughter Ed had once saved from a life of crack and prostitution, who worked high up in the ranks of the Registry. He was only too happy to oblige Ed's need for information.

The informer, Teddy Hawkins, was a nervous sort. He had spent half his life as a patient of Vermont's State Mental Hospital, in Waterbury. With drugs he could generally keep his bad habits under control. His bad habits included torturing small animals and petty larceny. Ed would frequently settle Teddy's problems before they landed in court. During his drive back to Vermont, Ed had placed a call to Teddy and another couple of "scouts," as he often referred to them, to be on the look out for Powell's car. It was Teddy who had come through.

Teddy was quite excited about his having found the Powell car parked in the back of the Ethan Allen Motel. He was carried away with his find. Ed had offered one hundred dollars for anyone spotting the vehicle. Teddy had earned the reward, but went looking for more. He wanted to impress Ed. After Teddy had located the car he decided to go one step further. He would get a look at this Powell fella. If Ed wanted a description, then Teddy could step up to the plate, "Yessirree, and hit one out of the park."

Teddy had approached the motel's night clerk with a story that he had noticed that one of the guest's car had a flat tire. He just wanted to get word to the person, so they could get it taken care of bright and early in the morning.

"A traveling person doesn't need to be surprised by bad news," offered Teddy.

"I guess you're right," said the night clerk as he wrote down the number of the license plate and description of the car Teddy had offered moments before.

"I guess you'll let him know in the morning," said Teddy.

"Yeah, I'll leave a note in their box and I'll slip one under their door later, when I go off shift."

"Do you mind if I help myself to a coffee?" asked Teddy.

"No, go right ahead."

Teddy sauntered over to the continental breakfast table and poured himself a cup of coffee. While he was making himself the coffee, he watched the night clerk place a note in a numbered slot, Powell's room. He now had Powell's room number.

"Thanks for the coffee," said Teddy as he left the motel.

The night clerk waved his good-bye.

Teddy headed straight for his truck. He pulled it around back and parked it a couple of spaces down from Powell's car. He was planning to wait until morning to get a look at Powell, when the motel's back entrance door opened and was propped open by a man using a small box. Teddy quickly left his truck and headed straight for the now opened door. Motels usually lock their doors at night, so that only guests may enter or exit using their passkey.

A guest was apparently getting up extra early to head out on the road. Teddy passed him on the stairs. The two men avoided eye contact, each for their own reason.

The motel is usually quiet at this time of the morning. It was nearly five in the morning. Teddy slowly approached the room he believed Powell was staying in. He reached the room and stood still at the door. He put his ear to the door and listened for any sound.

He heard a man's voice. It was then followed by a woman's voice. He shuffled his feet at the door. He tried to appear like he was trying his room key for the benefit of the motel's security camera located at the far end of the hallway.

Teddy heard someone's feet padding across the floor heading towards the door. He broke to his left and ran for the stairs.

He heard a woman call out, "Hey, wait up," only he wasn't going to wait.

Once out in the parking lot, he ran for his truck. He had to get away before anyone could get a good look at him. If Ed knew what he had tried, Ed would be furious. If he could make a clean getaway, Ed would never have to know.

Teddy pulled his truck out of the motel's parking lot and headed straight for Ed Townsend's house.

Ed was pleased with Teddy's information. He pressed a couple of fifty dollar bills into Teddy's sweaty palm.

"Ain't you going to check it out first?" asked Teddy.

"No need, Teddy. I have a good idea what he's up to. Besides, he's probably still sleeping. He doesn't know we're on to him, does he Teddy?"

"No...No he doesn't, Ed. I mean, how could he, right?" answered a plainly nervous Teddy Hawkins.

"Now Teddy, make sure you take your medicine today. You're looking a little tight, so get some rest. Remember, I don't want to have to come and get your ass out of the slammer again anytime soon."

"I'll be okay, Ed, I promise."

Teddy left and climbed back into his pickup truck. He adjusted his Montreal Expo's baseball cap and then backed out of the driveway. His mind was now on the stray cat he had picked up at the Town's dump yesterday and what he was going to do to it.

Ed watched Teddy leave.

The scum that life serves up, thought Ed.

Ed went back inside. He had some planning to do. First up would be to contact Samuel and bring him up to speed on what Ed's uncovered so far. Ed knew he had no choice on this. Moloch had chosen a new leader and a new leader it was. It didn't matter to Ed who the leader was, only that they get the job done. Ed's years of police work had programmed him to respond to the pursuit in a matter of fact way. His altered state, Kratua the master torturer, was one impatient devil. However, even Kratua recognized the importance of landing the Powell male and therefore didn't push Ed to hard. They both would have their satisfaction before all of this was over, of that they were both certain.

Korie pulled the covers off of Aaron. She had opened the curtains to their widest position.

"C'mon, Aaron," she said as she shook him awake.

Aaron rubbed his eyes with both hands in that little boy way, thumbs tucked inside clenched fists.

"What time is it?"

"Never mind what time it is. I think that whoever was following your mother now knows we're here. We've got to move out of here, pronto."

"All right, just let me have a moment in the toilet, okay?"

"Sure, but hurry, I've already packed for both of us."

Aaron shuffled off to the toilet and closed the bathroom door.

Korie heard the toilet flush. In a moment Aaron emerged. He had splashed water on his face.

"Okay, I'm ready."

They picked up their bags and opened the door. Korie looked down the hall to the left and then the right. The hallway was empty.

"Hurry," she said.

They headed down the hallway, down the stairs and out the back entrance. They both headed to the car. Aaron started it up and pulled it around to the front of the motel.

"We've still got to check out," he said.

"I know. You wait here. I'll go," she said.

She took her purse and ran into the lobby of the motel. Aaron sat in the car with the motor running. The morning was foggy and cool. Aaron had to turn on the windshield wipers. Directly across the large parking lot sat an eighteen-wheeler. Its engine was also running. Aaron thought he could see the trace outline of the driver sitting in the cab.

Is he watching me?

Aaron couldn't be sure. *Who was Korie talking about this morning? Who was watching? When and from where?*

As his mind began to fill with nervous paranoia he spotted Korie running out of the motel's lobby. She quickly entered the car.

"We're all set."

"Good."

"Let's go."

"Fine, where?"

"I don't know."

"Me either."

"Well, we can't just sit here."

"You're right."

"I've got an idea," said Korie.

"Let's hear it."

"First, we've got to get rid of this car."

"Why?" asked Aaron.

"Because earlier this morning I think whoever was watching us also knows what we're driving. We need to dump this car today."

"Well, according to the Vermont map, we're only about thirty-five miles from Burlington. It's Vermont's biggest city. There must be a place we can get rid of the car. You know, maybe a car dealer or something."

"Sounds fine, let's go."

Aaron looked away from Korie and back across the motel parking lot. He put his car in gear and pulled out of the parking lot onto the street. He turned left at the light and headed back to Interstate 89. In his rearview mirror, he noticed that the truck had also pulled out of the parking lot. Smoke was pushing out of the truck's twin exhaust stacks.

Aaron took the entrance ramp heading north on the interstate highway. For a few moments the truck was no longer in view.

Korie started to tell him about the incident outside their motel room door.

Aaron was only half listening. He pushed the car's speed up to sixty-five. He was pulling away from the slower truck.

"You were having some kind of bad nightmare. You were sitting in that small straight back desk chair. I wasn't sure if I should try to wake you up. You know what they say about waking someone up who's having a nightmare? Anyway, when I touched you, it must have broken the spell that the nightmare had on you, because you sort of woke up. I helped you to bed and you were asleep as soon as your head hit the pillow."

Korie continued to relate the morning's event, but her voice began to trail off. Aaron could see in his rearview mirror that the truck had closed the distance between them. It was now less than a half mile away and closing. Aaron stepped on the accelerator and the car's speed shot up to seventy-five miles an hour. Aaron looked back up into the mirror. The truck wasn't closing anymore.

Aaron pulled to the left lane to pass a Volvo station wagon. He looked up to his mirror again and the truck was somehow now only a couple of hundred feet behind him. It was in the left lane and gaining.

Aaron griped the car's steering wheel so hard his knuckles were turning white.

Korie noticed that Aaron was not really focused in on her detailed narration. He was perspiring and seemed nervous.

"Aaron, what's wrong?"

"We're being followed. It's that big rig directly behind us."

Korie turned around and looked out the car's back window. All she could see was the massive grillwork of a Peterbilt Diesel, Roadway Special. The truck couldn't be more than five feet off their rear bumper.

"Step on it, Aaron."

"I am," he answered.

Aaron had his car doing ninety-five miles per hour. He passed a couple of cars in the right lane so fast that they seemed to be frozen in place.

"He's closing in again, Aaron."

Aaron looked in the mirror and all he could see is the truck's chrome grill.

One hundred miles an hour and the truck was still there. The two vehicles were flying along the left lane of the interstate. They were now in an area known locally as Bolton Flats.

"I've got an idea. Hurry, fasten your seat belt."

Korie sat back in her seat and buckled her seat belt.

"What are you going to do?"

The truck's horn blasted at them. It blasted several times.

Korie put her hands to her ears. The sound was both deafening and frightening.

When the horns stopped Aaron said, "I'm going to quickly pull into the right lane and put on my brakes. I'm going to just tap them hopefully enough so that the truck will shoot right past us. Ready?"

"Ready."

At Korie's ready Aaron smoothly pulled to his right and tapped his brakes. He was right. The truck driver couldn't attempt a similar maneuver at that speed without loosing control of his rig. The huge truck and trailer shoot right by. Aaron was now behind the truck. As he kept an eye on the truck in front of him, Korie looked back along the highway. She immediately spotted a police car with its blue lights flashing racing towards them.

"Looks like we have more company," said Korie.

Aaron glanced up into the rearview mirror and he too spotted the police car. He then returned his sights to the truck, which was directly ahead of him. The truck's speed and Aaron's by now had been reduced to sixty miles an hour.

"The truck driver spotted the police car, too," said Aaron.

The State of Vermont police car pulled along side of the truck in the left lane. A voice could be heard coming from the police car's loudspeaker.

"Please pull the truck over to the side," and as if for further emphasis, "now."

The truck put on its right turn signal and began to pull over to the right side breakdown lane. The police cruiser pulled to a stop directly behind the truck.

Aaron and Korie drove past the truck and cruiser as they continued north towards Burlington.

Several minutes later, they pulled off the highway and headed up Williston Road, into South Burlington. They stopped at a used car dealership named "Randy's Dandeezs." After some haggling, they sold Aaron's car for at least fifteen hundred below its book value. After signing over the title, they signed the papers for the used car they were buying to replace the car they had just sold. Soon they were headed to downtown Burlington. They asked Randy to recommend a good hotel. Without hesitation he recommended the Radisson Hotel. Twenty minutes later Korie had rented a room for the two of them.

This room was on the seventh floor and had a gorgeous view of Lake Champlain.

Korie let Aaron have first dibs on the bathroom.

She laid out their clothes in the twin dressers. Aaron came out of the bathroom.

"Your turn," he said.

"Thanks, I'm going to take a shower and then change clothes. Maybe we can grab some breakfast after."

"Sounds good to me. I'll take a shower after you. I worked up quite a sweat racing that asshole truck."

Korie headed into the bathroom and closed the door. She turned on the overhead heat lamp and room fan. She turned on the water and began to remove her clothes. In a moment she was standing in the shower and it felt good, real good.

She had been in the shower for several minutes. The warm water cascaded down her body. Her entire back muscles felt stiff from the tension of the morning escape and chase. She turned her back to the showerhead and let its warm spray caress her achy body.

Aaron sat on the edge of one of the two full size beds. He was channel surfing when he stopped on the local channel's morning news. He turned the volume up.

"This is Brian Detmer, a good friend of the two missing hikers. He's organized a volunteer search for the two young hikers that will begin to explore the Long Trail along Vermont Route 100 today. Tell me Brian, have the authorities given you any information that will help you in your search efforts?"

The young man with a couple days growth of beard wearing a tee shirt and carrying a backpack responded, "All we know is what has been already reported. They were last seen hiking on Camel's Hump. We think they headed north from there, so we're going to start at Camel's Hump and spread out heading north."

"Well, Brian, we wish you and the other searchers the best out there. This is Kathy Brown, reporting live from the base of Camel's Hump Mountain on efforts to locate the missing hikers. Now back to the studio, Mark and Leslie."

"Thanks, Kathy," said the young woman sitting behind the television studio desk as she shuffled her papers. She turned to the male announcer, which was his signal to speak next.

"As our viewers know, every year several hikers get injured or lost in Vermont's woods. We wish the searchers the best, and remind everyone watching to always let someone know your hiking route, and stick to it."

"That's a good tip, Mark. Well, now on the lighter side today at ..."

Aaron turned the volume down. He could hear the shower running in the bathroom. He reclined back onto the bed, closing his eyes for a moment.

After a while, he turned over on his side and looked towards the window and the rich blue sky beyond. The curtains on the floor to ceiling window had an intricate pattern to them. The pattern was a sort of pastoral scene. There were people picking flowers, hoeing in a garden and riding a wagon. His eyes focused upon a figure of a woman who was working inside of a white picket fenced in flower garden. She seemed to take on a three dimensional appearance. He looked closer, sitting up now on the edge of his bed.

The woman was wearing a long dress and a bonnet of the sort worn in the mid-1800s. She suddenly turned around and looked at Aaron. She was holding a flower basket filled with freshly cut flowers. This woman seemed to walk towards Aaron. She appeared to be able to step out of the drapery's pattern. She now seemed to be walking in the air. She came closer until she was standing in the middle of the bed next to the window. She couldn't be more than two inches tall. Yet her weight caused a small indention on the beds surface.

"Aaron, don't be afraid. I'm your great grandmother several times removed. I'm Sarah Powell."

"This can't be happening. It's some kind of dream. I have a bad habit lately of having weird dreams," protested Aaron.

"This is no dream, Aaron. We have been able to speak to you all along, but there was no need."

"Who is this, we?"

"All of your ancestors. Your mother, her mother and so on, up to and including me?"

"I don't understand," he offered.

"Oh, we think you do, Aaron. It's just that you've been blocking your powers. You will learn to use them as we have."

"But you're all dead," he said standing up and pacing in front of the television.

"Yes, we're dead."

"So if you're dead, then how are you here and where are you speaking to me from and don't say those drapes," he demanded.

"We Powells exist in a nether world. Our bodies have died, but our spirits live on in this in-between world. We are bound by our blood to fight on to victory over this Dark One who wishes to take on human form. We can not rest until we defeat him, no matter how many generations it takes."

"What does this Dark One want with our family, couldn't he find another?"

"Oh, Aaron, you have so much to learn. An evil agreement is a final covenant. This coven that has pursued our family is in a pact with Lucifer's lieutenant Moloch. It is Moloch who must come forth upon earth in human form to prepare the way for Lucifer."

"Why?" said Aaron, sitting on the bed once more.

"Because, Lucifer is in a race of sorts. He wants to steal away the earth and all who inhabit it before the Second Coming."

"But, but if my memory is right, then Lucifer and this Moloch's efforts to return to human form would mark the beginning of Armageddon."

The tiny figure bowed her tiny head for a moment, and then she raised it again. With her apron she dabbed at her left eye and then her right eye. She was crying.

"Yes, Aaron, Armageddon."

"But why our family? I mean, shit, that's a lot to put on us. Why can't this happen to some other family?"

"No one knows. We believe that throughout the ages this battle has been waged ceaselessly with other families. They have won their battles and now it is our turn."

"It's not fair," he protested.

"It is what it is, and we must accept our fate. We must not fail." The tiny figure of Sarah Powell turned and headed back towards the curtain.

"Wait, wait I need to know more."

Turning she said, "In time, Aaron, in time. Those missing hikers—they're dead. The coven killed them. Now this coven has a new leader, and he's the most powerful yet."

With those final words the figure now was standing in its place on the drapes. The tiny figure that revealed herself as Sarah Powell turned her back to Aaron and became part of the tapestry as before.

"Who were you talking to?" said Korie, who was now standing in the room with one towel wrapped around her head and another barely wrapped around her torso.

"You're not going to believe me."

19

Reverend Mitchell hasn't been able to sleep. He has spent the night and early morning hours pacing the floor in his office. He is bitter and angry that Moloch has deposed him for the novice, Samuel.

For the umpteenth time, he curses his fate.

"I have been loyal. I've sacrificed everything for him and this is the thanks I get. Son of a bitch."

He slams his right fist hard into his left palm, with a smacking sound.

"That Samuel had better not fuck up, no sireee."

The Reverend's dark side partner was the devil, Zeeka. Zeeka was a devil that had made a habit of partnering with some of human histories worst and most notorious. He rode with Attila the Hun, as his trusted advisor. He traveled with Rasputin, as a dim-witted companion. He also was a whispered confidant to Goebbels, whom history knows had great influence over Hitler. Zeeka, with a whisper, could do more damage than a sword, an arrow or a gun. Zeeka was furious as well.

The Reverend and Zeeka worked each other into a fury that each had never tasted before. Both had been slighted, seemingly cast aside, in favor of one who had not earned the right to play center stage at what was promising to be one of the greatest events in human history. Together they both yearned to regain their rightful place.

"I'll watch and wait. All I need is one fucking mistake on his part and I will claim my rightful place. Lucifer himself will give it to me. Fucking Samuel Porter, Fucking Moloch," said Reverend Mitchell (or was it Zeeka?).

The truck driver waited until the State Police car had pulled away before he used his cell phone. He dialed a number and waited.

"Hello Ed, this is the Road Warrior. I was just following that Massachusetts tag you told me to be on the lookout for."

"So, what's up, Road Warrior?"

"I was tracking him as he headed up I-89 towards Burlington. The son of bitch topped out at over a hundred miles per hour. I got pulled over by a State Smokey. Picked up a ticket for speeding, anyway, he's probably in Burlington or beyond by now. Oh, and Ed, he had a woman with him, riding shotgun."

"Thanks for your help, Road Warrior. Got the name of the Officer who ticketed you?"

"Sure do, his name is Ed Garrett."

"I'll fix your ticket."

"Thanks. Any word on my daughter?"

"Not yet, but I've got a friend of mine in the Atlanta Office who is working the case. I'll give him a call after we hang up. If there is any news, I'll get back to you."

"Thanks again, Ed."

"Don't mention it. Bye."

Before Ed called his FBI buddy in the Atlanta Office, he called his friend in the Burlington Police Department. They spoke for a couple of minutes. Ed was calling in a favor. He needed some help locating a certain car bearing Massachusetts tags and its occupants, a male and female. What he needed, he explained, was some quiet help. No heavy police presence, just a helpful tip on where to find the car and its passengers.

His Burlington Police contact agreed to put some manpower on it right away. Ed got the man his job and his ongoing recommendations had helped propel the man's career. He looked up to Ed as a mentor.

Next, Ed called his FBI Academy roommate, the current head of the Atlanta Office.

"Gary, Ed here. How's the low life?"

"You know same old, same old. Ed, I know you're calling about that Vermont kid who's a run away. Well, I've got some good news. We located her and her ATM robbing boyfriend. I was just about to give you a call. It seems that her alleged boy friend has managed to pile up a heap of charges in a short time. Anyway, my men got a tip that he was planning to rob a drive in bank on Mohammed Ali Boulevard. We put some of our people inside and outside. We nabbed him yesterday afternoon. Unfortunately, he put up a struggle resisting arrest and managed to get both arms broken."

"My heart bleeds."

"Yeah, mine too. Well the girl was sitting in the getaway car, parked around the corner from the bank. She's okay except for one thing, Ed."

"What's that?"

"She's pregnant. She keeps crying. Says she wants an abortion."

"Gary, could you fix her up with a plane ticket? If you can, please fly her to Burlington, Vermont. Her dad and I will meet her at the airport. I'll break the news to him before she gets in. Just call me with the flight time. Now, let me give you my charge card number for her ticket, and thanks for all the assistance too."

"Forget it Ed, this one's on me. I'll be back to you in a few minutes with that flight info. Take care of yourself."

"You know that I do, so long."

With that, he hung up his phone. He had to meet with Samuel soon and he wasn't looking forward to the experience. He would give his Burlington source a couple of hours, after which he would set up a meeting with Samuel to brief him on his progress or lack of it, whatever the case may be.

* * *

"You were talking to who?" said Korie.

"I just told you, I believe I just had contact with someone from the other side. Like I said, I was talking with my great grandmother several generations back. It was Sarah Powell."

Korie sat down on the bed, still clutching the bath towel wrapped around her torso.

"Is this the first time this has happened?" asked Korie.

"I'm not really sure. I've had dreams before where I thought I was having a conversation. But these dreams always seemed to occur at night. They seemed to be ordinary, that's all. This one just happened during the daytime."

"You're going to have to tell me more. Start by telling me about the first dream you had that was connected to this Powell legend."

The only dream Aaron could recall in any detail was the dream he had about the altar and the young girl, the coven members, and of course the knife, which seemed to be alive with the tiny bodies of his ancestors. He described the dream as best as he could recall. Korie had several questions, some of which he could answer, others he could not.

He next described his most recent encounter where Sarah Powell seemed to come alive and walk right off the fabric of the hotel room drape. Since this daydream had just taken place, Aaron's account was more detailed. Korie asked no questions this time, she just listened.

"That's some dream. I'm no expert on this sort of thing, I mean, who is, right? It sure sounds like your ancestors are trying to help you somehow. I wonder if you can control these conversations. You know, like call them up and have a discussion."

"I never thought about that. Maybe!"

"Why don't you try?"

"Right now?"

"Sure, now, while I'm right here."

"I don't know."

"What do you mean, you don't know? Aaron, for crying out loud, if they are trying to speak to you, maybe they can help somehow. It's worth the try, isn't it?"

"But what if it doesn't work? Maybe my dreams are some sort of psychotic event. They lock people up for that sort of thing."

"Aaron, they don't lock people up for that sort of thing anymore. At least I don't think they do."

"Well, that's reassuring."

"I was just kidding. Now come over here and sit on this bed. It will take me a minute to slip on some clothes, and then we can give it a try."

Aaron came over and sat on the bed nearest to the window.

Korie meanwhile put on some cutoff shorts and a tee shirt decorated with the slogan "Don't Ask Me, I Just Work Here."

"Okay, let's start," said Korie.

"How?"

"Well, I'd say just look again at that drapery and let your mind go."

"All right, here goes," said Aaron with a sigh.

Korie knelt up on the bed and began to massage his neck and shoulders. Her fingers pressed down against his muscles as she worked to try and get Aaron to fully relax.

Aaron stared at the drapery for several minutes. Nothing seemed to happen. He scanned the pattern over and over again, nothing. Aaron felt very tired and closed his eyes for what seemed was just a moment. When he opened his eyes again, he was no longer sitting on the bed, but was instead sitting in one of his aunt's overstuffed chairs. He was back in time when he was only ten years old. His mother, who at that time he believed her to be his aunt, was massaging his neck and shoulders. She was humming a song that

175

Aaron recognized as familiar even though he could not name the tune itself.

"Hmm, Hmm, hmm......hmm. Now doesn't that feel better Aaron?"

"Yes, it does," he answered.

"You took a nasty fall out of that cherry tree over at Mrs. Kopecke's house. Now Aaron, you know better than to go and climb trees and steal cherries from our neighbor."

"But I asked permission first."

"Aaron, Mrs. Kopecke told me she had agreed that you could pick all the cherries that you could reach from the ground, not from up in her tree."

"I'm sorry."

Aaron paused and turned around and looked at his Aunt and said, "You're really my mother, aren't you?"

With a smile, she answered, "Yes, but you already knew that."

"I don't seem to understand everything that's going on. A while ago I dreamed that I had talked to Sarah Powell. I suppose you know about that?"

"Yes, as a matter of fact, I do."

"Then why am I having these dreams?"

"Think, Aaron."

Aaron paused and reflected on this turn around gambit.

"Is it because you've come to help me?"

"We can't stop Moloch. Only you can do that."

"But you can help me somehow, is that it?"

"We can only share our knowledge. Our powers are no longer of your world."

"Powers, what powers?"

"Aaron, please!"

"I get it. I must have powers like this ability to talk to you and Sarah Powell. Am I right?" he asked eagerly.

"Aaron you have much, much more."

"Like what?"

"You must find this out for yourself. Now I must go."

"Wait, give me a hint."

"I'm sorry," she said as her image began to fade.

"Can you give me a sign so that my friend Korie will believe me?"

The faint image seemed to nod as it disappeared altogether. Aaron opened his eyes and he was lying on his back on the bed nearest to the window. Korie was sitting on the adjacent bed.

"What happened?" asked Aaron.

"Well, from my vantage point, I'd say you had a dream about your mother, because you were talking to her."

"Did you hear her talk to me?"

"Of course not, all I heard was your side of what was obviously a two way conversation."

"She agreed to give us a sign that my contacts are real."

"What sign?"

"She didn't tell me that part."

"Okay. Well, I didn't see anything move in here. Maybe this sign will show up later."

"No, it's already here, I'm certain of that."

Aaron got up from the bed and walked around the room and the bathroom looking for an unknown sign. Korie did likewise. After several minutes, they both gave up and sat back down on the bed farthest from the window.

"It's here, I just know it," said a determined Aaron.

Glancing at the bed nearest to the window, he noticed there was something under the bed covers in the center of the bed.

"That's it," he said as he sprang up from the bed and began to pull the bed's covers back.

There, in the center of the bed, was a small wallet of the sort that children have made for generations. It was a small child-size, hand stitched, brown leather wallet. Aaron picked up the wallet.

"It's mine," he murmured.

Korie watched as he opened the wallet. Inside of the wallet was a standard printed identification card with Aaron's name and address written in a child like handwriting.

"Look, I wrote my name inside."

Aaron lifted the identification card and peered behind it. He noticed something and began to carefully remove a small photograph.

Aaron looked at the photo and a tear welled up in his eye, and ran down his left cheek.

"It's me and my mother."

He showed the photo to Korie who by now was absolutely dumbfounded by the appearance of what seemed certain to be Aaron's childhood wallet.

Korie could only respond, "She's beautiful."

Korie kissed his cheek on the spot that the tear had just traveled. His skin was hot, as if he had a fever.

"I have powers. My mother said I have special powers."

"Well, what do we do now?" asked Korie.

"I have to read my family's diary cover to cover. There has to be something, some kind of message hidden in those old stories."

The two of them began to read the Powell Family diary out loud to one another, each taking turns when the other grew tired.

***

Samuel's sister Kelly, nearly fifteen years old, had been living in absolute terror since that first night when her brother returned home from his initiation with the coven.

She had nightmares every night. The same evil creature threatened her in her dreams, night after night. Kelley was not getting much sleep. Her nerves were worn threadbare by the nightly terrors that were visited upon her. She avoided the bathroom at night. She showered only during the daytime. Her closet seemed to have become the home for another creature from hell. She was sure that another hellish creature had recently taken up residency under her bed. She could not, dare not, speak of these fears with her parents. They had become her brother's cheerleaders.

Kelley was desperate. She remembered her brother's admonition to not have any contact with her boyfriend, Paul Lacosse. She had to speak with someone before she went completely mad. She decided in her well-worn state of mind to contact Paul.

Kelley announced to her mother, "Mom I've run out of my shampoo. I'm going to go down to the grocery store and pick some up. I'll be back in a few minutes."

Kelley was half way out of the front door when her mother called out to her.

"Kelley, you can use some of mine dear."

"Oh, Mom," protested Kelley.

"All right then. But be back in half an hour. I'll need some help changing the bed sheets. I want to put fresh linen on the beds today and rotate the mattresses."

"Okay, I'll be back in half an hour."

With that Kelley sprang from the doorway and bounded down the front porch. She sprinted around the side of the house and headed into the garage and pulled out her bicycle. She hadn't used it since last summer. She was at an age where she had become too old for a bicycle and yet too young to drive a car. She was in luck. The bicycle's tires still held a respectful amount of air pressure. She quickly hopped on and pedaled for all she was worth.

In less than five minutes, she had reached the grocery store. It was an independent store set in the middle of a small plaza. On one side was a hardware store, and on the other side was a branch bank. The only other storefront in the plaza was vacant. Kelley leaned her bicycle up against the brick wall outside the grocery store next to the pay phone. Kelley fished in her pant pockets and quickly removed a handful of small change. She selected a quarter. Kelley picked up the receiver and deposited the coin. She quickly pounded out Paul's telephone number from memory. It began to ring.

"Please be home, Please...," she whispered to herself.

Halfway into the sixth ring there was a click on the line.

"Hello."

"Hello, Mrs. Lacosse."

"Yes."

"May I speak with Paul?"

"Who's calling?"

For a moment, Kelley thought of giving a fake name. However she was fairly sure Mrs. Lacosse recognized her voice and so giving a fake name would only arouse suspicion.

"It's Kelley...Kelley Porter."

"I see, well Kelley, he's outside mowing the lawn right now. Can he call you back?"

"Uh...no, not really, I mean, I really need to talk to him. I'm not at home right now...I'm uh, baby-sitting and I don't want the phone to ring and wake the baby."

Kelley knew her excuse was lame, but it the best she could come up with on the spur of the moment. She crossed her fingers.

"Well, I suppose it would be all right. He could use a break. I'll go and get him, just hold on..."

Kelley held the receiver to her left ear. As she waited for her boyfriend, she turned and scanned the plaza's parking lot. Everything seemed normal.

"Kelley, say Kelley, is that you?" said a slightly out of breath Paul Lacosse.

"Yes, Paul."

"How are you doing?"

"Fine, I guess." She couldn't find the right words.

"I haven't heard from you for a while. I was kind of thinking that maybe you had ...maybe you know, found someone else."

"Oh, Paul, I'm so sorry. I just haven't been able to get away to call you. I have to be careful. Paul, I need your help. I need to talk to you, in person. Do you think you can get away tonight and meet me somewhere?"

"Sure!"

"Good, how about meeting behind the town library, say around eleven o'clock."

"Okay. Can you tell me what it's about?"

"Not now, Paul, but I promise I'll tell you everything when we meet tonight."

"All right, see you then, bye."

"Sure, bye."

Kelley hung up the phone, turned around and bumped into Mrs. Lawless.

"Oh, excuse me…I didn't see," said Kelley. Her words hung in the air as she recognized whom she had bumped into. As a fellow member of her brother's coven, Mrs. Lawless was someone Kelley knew and feared. Each and every member of the coven would be aligned with her brother.

"Well, Miss Porter, what brings you to the plaza today?" she asked in a tone of voice that suggested power and dripped with intimidation.

Kelley wasn't sure if Mrs. Lawless had heard any part of her conversation with Paul.

"I have to get some shampoo. I, um, called home to see if my mom needed anything for supper while I was here."

Kelley hoped Mrs. Lawless hadn't heard her telephone conversation with Paul. If she had, her lying now would just compound the trouble she was in. If she hadn't, maybe this little lie would allow Kelley to slip away.

"I see. Well, Miss Porter, it's Kelley isn't it?"

"Yes."

"It was a pleasure to meet you, Kelley Porter!" she said with a touch of sarcasm.

"Well, I've got to go. It was nice meeting you, too," said Kelley as she ducked around Mrs. Lawless and headed into the grocery store.

Once inside the store, Kelley looked out the large windows at the front of the store. She noticed Mrs. Lawless was still standing on the walkway in front of the store. She was facing the window and speaking on a cell phone while she seemed to be looking inside the store. The store's front windows were heavily tinted, still Kelley felt as if Mrs. Lawless was looking right at her.

Kelley turned away from the windows and headed over to the cosmetics and sundries aisle, looking for shampoo. She glanced over her shoulder back towards the front windows before she turned down the aisle. Mrs. Lawless was gone.

Not everyone in Sutton was a member of the church. The people of Sutton mingled everyday. One half of the community had no idea their co-workers, spouses, neighbors or friends were devil worshippers. It had always been that way. The devil worshippers needed Sutton to appear as normal as possible. They didn't tolerate intruders—they called them "interlopers." While they accepted living amongst non-believers, they had to be constantly on their guard to not reveal who or what they were. The secret has been well kept for over a hundred years.

Occasionally, the non-believers treaded on dangerous ground.

Samuel Porter was shooting baskets alone in his driveway. He was still a young boy and knew he needed to keep up that appearance for the benefit of the non-believers. He could hear the sound of someone running in his direction even before he turned around. He tossed the basketball up towards the rim, which was fifteen feet away. The ball hit the front of the rim and skipped straight up in the air over the rim. He stared intensely at the ball and with his mind he nudged it forward. The ball came back down straight thought the net.

Nice, thought Samuel.

"Sammy, Sammy, help me!"

Samuel Porter turned around and spotted young Bobby Warfield running towards him. Bobby Warfield was ten years old and a nearby neighbor. He lived down the street, only three houses away. He was an only child, small for his age, and wore wire rimmed glasses. His family belonged to Samuel's Church.

"What's wrong, Bobby?"

Bobby stopped in front of Samuel. He had a couple of cuts and scraps on his face. He wasn't wearing his glasses. He had a streak of blood running down his nose. He was crying.

"Those Dulac brothers beat me up and stole my new bicycle," he said through a series of sniffles. He held his hand out and showed Samuel his broken glasses.

"They broke my glasses, too."

"You'll be okay."

"But..."

Putting his hand on Bobby's shoulder, he said, "Come with me."

The two of them walked down the street towards the Dulac's house. Bobby Warfield walked a half-step behind. The Dulac boys were fourteen and fifteen years old. The oldest was Tim. He had stayed back three times in grammar school. He would be returning to the seventh grade next fall. His younger brother was named Kenny, and like Tim, he, too, had a penchant for pausing in his educational advancement. This coming fall, he was going back to the fifth grade. Their father had visited the State Mental Hospital in Waterbury on several occasions. He was also an alcoholic. The Dulac boy's mother had died eight years ago.

The Dulac boys were just your basic bullies.

Samuel stopped at the entrance to the Dulac driveway. Bobby stopped too and stood next to Samuel.

"What are you going to do?"

"Me, I'm going to do nothing."

"But why did we come here?"

"To get your bike back."

"They ain't going to give it back without a fight, that's for sure."

"That's what I'm counting on."

"Huh?"

"Hey Porter, who's that with you, your fag friend?" shouted Kenny Dulac. He was standing at the opposite end of the driveway in front of the ramshackle old garage with his hands defiantly set on his hips.

"Say, Tim, look who's here. It's that hot shit Sammy Porter and he's brought along that puke, Bobby."

From out of the garage's darkness stepped Timmy. He wiped his hands on an old rag and then tossed it back inside the garage.

Timmy stood there staring at Samuel and Bobby.

Samuel started down the driveway with Bobby keeping a safer distance, at least four steps behind.

Seeing Samuel coming towards him, Timmy pulled a screwdriver from his back pocket. He tossed it up into the air much like someone juggling a knife. It slapped back into his hand.

Samuel stopped about five feet away and looked from one boy to the other.

"Give him back his bicycle, now!" demanded Samuel.

"What bicycle?" sneered Kenny.

"Yeah, what bicycle?" joined Timmy.

"Timmy, that little snot-faced Bobby has been spreading lies about us," said Kenny looking at an obviously nervous Bobby.

"We don't like people telling lies about us, do we Kenny?"

Kenny nodded his agreement.

"And we don't like some smart ass telling us what to do."

"Yeah, smart ass."

Fixing his eyes on Kenny, Samuel spoke directly to Kenny.

"Did you know Timmy killed your cat, Buster, three years ago, by snapping its neck with his bare hands?"

Kenny shot a glance at Timmy.

"Don't listen to him, he's lying."

"Timmy I've got some news for you, too."

"Oh, yeah, what?"

"Kenny left those porno magazines on your bureau on purpose, so your father would find them and give you a whipping."

"You did that?" said an instantly angry Timmy as he shot an accusatory look at his brother.

"No, I swear, I didn't...," said Kenny in protest.

Before Kenny could say anything else, Timmy threw the screwdriver on the ground and proceeded to smack his brother across the back of the head causing Kenny to stumble for a moment.

"Kenny, Timmy diddled your girl friend Connie in the back seat of your old man's car just two days ago."

"That's a fucking lie," shouted an angry Timmy.

"See for yourself Kenny. You can find her panties under the front seat, where Timmy hid them," said Samuel with growing satisfaction.

Kenny ran inside of the garage and opened the back door of his father's beat up, rusted Ford Taurus. He began a search for the evidence.

Timmy wasn't so confident anymore. He in fact looked confused, so Samuel moved in closer.

In almost a whisper, Samuel spoke to Timmy.

"Kenny's taken the pictures of your mother from out of your secret place and he's keeping them with his baseball collection under his bed."

There was a moment of hesitation before Timmy bolted to the house and bounded up the back steps flinging open the screen door. Just as he disappeared inside of the house Kenny stepped out of the shadows of the garage holding a pair of girl's panties in his right hand. His face was twisted in rage. He walked towards Samuel.

Bobby could see a name embroidered on the panties now in Kenny's hand. The pink letters spelled out the girl's name, Connie.

"Where did he go?" demanded Kenny.

"He'll be right back, just you wait right here."

From inside of the house, through the opened but screened windows, came the sound of Timmy racing down the stairs. In an instant, he burst out of the back screen door flinging it open with such force that it strained against its spring and slapped against the side of the house. He jumped down to the ground. His face was filled with a red-hot rage.

Timmy had a small envelope in his left hand. He half ran towards his brother.

"You bastard!" screamed Timmy.

"You fucker!" shouted Kenny.

The Dulac boys dropped the envelope and the panties and flew at one another. In a flash, they were throwing punches at one another with incredible fury. They were soon rolling around in the sand and gravel of the driveway like two snarling dogs.

"Bobby, go and get your bike," commanded Samuel.

"But..." protested Bobby.

"Do as I say."

Moving as fast as his two nervous little legs could carry him, Bobby hurried inside of the garage and spotted his bicycle right away. They hadn't had anytime to dismantle it. Bobby grabbed it by the handlebars and wheeled it out of the garage. He stopped next to Samuel.

"Let's go," said Samuel as he turned to leave with Bobby.

Before he left, Samuel kicked the screwdriver over towards the two fighting boys.

"Who knows, we might get lucky," said Samuel with a grin.

Samuel and Bobby left the Dulac boys fighting in their own driveway.

20

Aaron and Korie had spent the better part of the day reading the Powell family diary, or "Chronicles," as Korie had nicknamed it.

"Shit, look at the time, it's nearly six o'clock," said Aaron.

Korie stood up from the edge of the bed and raised her arms over her head. She stretched herself for a moment.

"Well, we're nearly done. There are only about twenty more pages."

"I know," said Aaron. He put the diary down on the bed.

"I'm really hungry," said Korie.

"Me, too," said Aaron. "What sort of cuisine would you like for dinner?"

"Oh, I don't know. Look, here's one of those magazines that tell you all about the restaurants in the area," said Korie, as she picked up the glossy magazine from the small desk.

"Good idea. Let's see what there is to choose from," said Aaron.

They were both surprised to see the extensive listings of restaurants for such a small city. The cuisine selections ranged from Southeast Asian, Korean, and Indian, to Vegetarian and Greek. It seemed that there was as complete a dining range as one could normally find in America's largest cities. There were also a wide range of clubs offering comedy, rock and roll, DJ's, hypnotists, jazz and of course Aaron's favorite, blues.

"What about this place?" said Korie pointing to a particular advertisement for a blues bar and restaurant.

"We don't have to always go to blues bars just because of me, you know," protested Aaron.

"I know. But I enjoyed myself at the House of Blues. C'mon, let's check it out."

Aaron took the visitor's guide magazine from Korie and read the club's ad.

"Burlington's Choice for the Finest Blues Music in the Tradition of the Masters. Suds, and Other Spirits, Fine Food Delta and Chicago Cuisine at Mojo's, 176 College Street. Cover Charge Waived with this Ad."

"Okay, let's go for it," said Aaron as he tore the page with the ad out of the magazine.

"Don't you think that you ought to hide the diary?" asked Korie.

"Yeah, you're right, but where?"

They both surveyed their surroundings for a suitable hiding place.

"I've got it," said Korie. "Follow me, and take your key."

"What?"

She picked up the diary and headed out the door. Aaron followed right behind. Korie headed towards the end of the hall, and turned to the right down another hallway. Halfway down the hall, she turned to her right, into a small alcove where there were three vending machines, one for candy and sundries, another for soft drinks and another for ice. She looked behind the narrow space behind the ice machine and then slipped the diary behind the machine.

"There, snug as a bug."

"Are you sure it won't slip down, or get snagged by the ice machine's motor?"

"Sure, it's in there solid. See for yourself."

Aaron checked it out for himself. It seemed quite secure.

"I guess, we're all set then," said Aaron.

Korie and Aaron returned to their room. They freshened up and then headed down to the hotel lobby. Aaron checked with the front desk to obtain directions on how to get to Mojo's.

"According to the desk clerk it's just a three blocks from here, maybe a ten minute walk," said Aaron.

With that they headed out the front door of the hotel. They took a left down the street, and after a short distance they turned left again, onto College Street. Soon they were standing outside of Mojo's. The pulsating sound of a Junior Parker tune was rolling out the front door of the club.

They stepped inside and were greeted by a smiling face. The man had a smile that spread, it seemed, from ear to ear. He walked with a slight limp. He took a step towards Aaron and Korie.

"C'mon in folks. How many?"

"Two," said Aaron, "Oh, and we have this ad coupon."

"Keep the coupon. Let me fix you up with a table. Follow me!" said the man as he limped away.

They followed him to a table, along the wall, on the right side, past the bar. The man set a couple of menus down on the small table, and then stood back to let Aaron and Korie get to their seats. The place was nearly full. There was a small stage to the back of the club and the bar was located to the rear of the right side.

"First time here at Mojo's?" asked the man.

"Yes," said Aaron.

"You like the blues?" he said with a raised eyebrow.

"Like it, he plays in a blues band back home," bragged Korie. The man chuckled at that remark.

"Damn, I just knew it. I can tell a fellow blues man."

Wiping his right hand on his apron he extended his hand to Aaron.

"Ron's the name. I own the place. Play a little blues, too. A man's got to, you know," he said with a nod to Aaron.

"Yeah, I hear you," said Aaron.

"What do you play, if I might ask?" said Ron.

"I play a Bass!"

"No shit! Me, I play the guitar and some harp, too. I've got a 57 Fender Stratocaster and a Blues Master Tube amp.

"That's great."

"Say, tonight's amateur night you know. Feel free to jump on in."

"I don't have my gear."

"No problem, I've got enough gear back stage to outfit three bands. Take your pick. Anyway, I talk too much, ask anybody," he said waving his hand in a sweeping gesture.

"It sure was nice chatting with you," said Korie.

"Me, too, I've got to go and play hostess. Your waitress will be along in a minute." He turned and walked away.

"He sure is nice," said Korie.

"Yeah, I like him."

They then took a moment to look around the club. The place was once some kind of old factory. Overhead there were wide, rough, hewn beams. The floor was smooth, with well-worn, wide, wooden, darkly stained planks. The walls were covered with newspapers from Chicago, Memphis, New Orleans, Kansas City and Austin.

The tables were covered in some kind of plastic, which serve to seal onto the table tops assorted album covers of old time blues albums. Their table had covers from John Lee Hooker, Sonny Boy Williamson and Albert King.

A young woman approached their table with a large plate in hand. She placed it on their table. She had also brought a couple of smaller empty plates.

"What's this?" asked Aaron.

"Ron sent it over. Its chicken wings cooked with a special sauce, compliments of Mojo's."

"That's really nice. Tell him thanks."

"What's in this special sauce?" asked Aaron.

"Ron won't tell us, except to say, it's a secret recipe that he picked up from B.B. King."

"He knows B.B. King personally?" asked Aaron.

"Yup. He's played in several bands. A lot of these guys come here when they are in the area for the City's Blues Fest. They all know Ron. He's a good shit. Oops, sorry!"

"No, no, that's okay," said Aaron.

"By the way, I'd order a beer or something before you get too far into those chicken wings. They can be a bit much," said the young waitress.

"Okay, let's get a pitcher of beer," said Korie.

"Sure," echoed Aaron.

"Well, we've got..."

"Surprise us," said Aaron.

"You sure?"

"Yup."

"Okay."

They each took a wing and took a bite. Korie chewed slowly. Aaron finished off his first, and licked his fingers.

"Damn, these are good!"

"Uh um," said Korie.

The pitcher of beer was delivered to their table along with two chilled glasses. Aaron poured the beer for the two of them. He was enjoying himself and so was Korie.

The music of Junior Parker pounded throughout the place. The club was now filled up. Several people were seated at the bar sipping their drinks.

Later Aaron and Korie ordered their dinner. They decided to split a deep-dish pizza pie, Chicago style. It exceeded their expectations. They ordered a second pitcher of beer.

From the stage a small overhead light came on. It lit up a singular microphone. Stepping up to the microphone was the owner Ron.

"Evening folks. Welcome to Mojo's," he said.

A couple of young men moved about behind him setting up more microphones. One of them pulled the curtain back which revealed the rest of the stage. It was already equipped with a set of drums, a keyboard and several amplifiers.

"While the boys are setting things up, I just want to thank you all for your support. Tonight's our ninth anniversary, and we're damn proud of your helping to make Mojo's a success."

The entire place burst into applause.

Ron waved the applause down and continued while his staff set up some monitors in the front of the stage.

"Thanks, thanks. Now let's have some of you blues men and women wannabees down front. C'mon Slick, get your ass down here."

That elicited a loud laugh from the crowd.

"You, too, Randy and you, Boss Man, C'mon. And where's the brass police. Are you a Parker-man?"

"Hold your ass," shouted a voice from the back of the place.

This brought another round of laughter. Slowly several people moved to the stage. They carried guitars, basses, trumpets, and trombones. A guy moved to the set of drums and another to the keyboard. The keyboard player hit a few notes before he flicked a couple of switches, and found the sound he was looking for, a Leslie Organ.

Moments later the assembled began to selectively strike a note or a chord as they each warmed up. Three women joined the people on the stage.

Ron stood at the center of the stage. Someone handed him a guitar. He slipped the guitar's strap over his shoulder. He picked out a string and gave it a lick. The guitar was plugged in.

Ron stepped to the microphone, looked over his shoulders and said, "Are we ready?"

Several people nodded in the affirmative.

"Ladies and gentleman, this is a song Elmore James song called, *Dust My Blues*.

With that, he launched into a mean gritty blues riff that brought the crowd to their feet in applause.

Aaron and Korie joined in the applause with enthusiasm.

Soon the place was rolling with music, as the so-called amateurs played one standard after another. The owner, Ron joined in on the first few, and then he stepped off the stage. He received high five's from the tables as he passed by. He gestured with his thumb to Aaron to head up to the stage.

Aaron waved him off.

***

Meanwhile, back at their hotel room, a shadowy figure stood at their door. He took a plastic card from his suit coat and slipped it into the magnetic door lock. There was a single click and the door was unlocked. The intruder stepped inside. He turned on the wall light switch. He had an accomplice in the desk clerk who was slipped fifty dollars to keep a look out for Aaron and Korie, and to call their room if they should return while this man was searching their room. The clerk said he was sure that they had gone to Mojo's. They had left only an hour before so there should be plenty of time.

Ed Townsend had received excellent cooperation from his friend at the Burlington Police Department. The Police had located their car at Randy's Dandeezs. There they had learned that the woman and man had taken a cab into the City, presumably to a hotel. An officer had stopped by this hotel to check the guest list. He found what he was looking for. A woman with the first name of Korie had rented a room. She was traveling with a male companion. A short time later, Ed was given the same information. He quickly drove to Burlington.

Once inside their room, Ed turned on the light switch which turned on the floor lamp next to the credenza. Ed began a systematic search of their room looking for anything he could find that would help him to know these people better. With such knowledge, he was sure he could find a weakness he could exploit. The coven couldn't just snatch Aaron Powell and force him to join in their evil plan. That could backfire, just as it did for the first coven, back in 1843. This time they needed to willingly draw him into joining their coven. Failing this approach, Ed wanted to have a backup plan. One such plan he had already begun formulating. He was prepared to kidnap Korie and use her as bait.

Ed looked in the drawers and carefully examined their clothes. He opened their empty suitcases and searched them for false compartments. He lifted the mattresses, to see if there was anything hidden under them. He examined the bathroom. He looked through their assorted toiletries. He even stood on the toilet seat and pushed up the ceiling panels searching for anything they may have hidden.

Returning to the bedroom area, he stood in the center of the room. He could sense these two had access to information of some kind. This morning, they knew they were being followed and yet, they hadn't run away. They had chosen to come to Vermont. That indicated Aaron Powell was interested in the Powell property. When they ran from the other hotel this morning, they had to have picked up on the fact they were being watched.

What's their plan? thought Ed. *Something here can tell me, I can feel it.*

He sat down on the edge of the bed and looked slowly around the room. His eyes passed slowly over the pastoral designs of the floor length drapes. He stood up from the bed and went to the curtains and pulled them open. He looked behind them from the ceiling to the floor.

Nothing.

He was about to let go of the drapes, when his hands felt something moving along the drape's surface.

He was startled by this sensation and let go of the drapes. Standing back from the drapes he looked at them with renewed interest. He carefully examined the tableau of several human figures woven into the brightly patterned drapes. Some of these figures were walking, carrying baskets of vegetables or flowers. Others stood next to picket fences, seemingly engaged in conversation with passing figures. Others still worked in gardens or orchards. There were several children in these scenes as well. There was no mistaking the movement he had felt, but he couldn't locate the cause. The pastoral scenes were repeated many times across the fabric, as the pattern seemed to repeat itself every three feet.

Ed reached out and touched the edge of one of the drapes and waited for the sensation, to repeat itself. Several moments passed with no repeat of what he had experienced before.

He examined the fabric up close. It seemed to be normal, machine stitched, drapery material.

Maybe he had imagined it.

He dropped the drape and returned to his systematic search of the room. He began removing the bureau drawers and checking their undersides for anything hidden.

Still nothing.

Lastly he removed a Swiss army knife from his coat side pocket and pried open the screw head. He knelt down next to the room's combination heater and air conditioner and unscrewed the front panel. Nothing was hidden inside. He replaced the panel. He stood up, and again scanned the room for clues. He spotted the tour guide magazine on the coffee table. He picked it up and leafed through it.

Nothing.

He put the magazine down on the bed. He had searched everything and had come up empty handed. Unless something else turned up, it was looking more likely that snatching Korie was going to become the priority plan to leverage Aaron's cooperation.

Ed left and locked the room. Moments later he passed through the hotel's lobby. He nodded to the front desk clerk who nodded back. Ed headed out to take in some music at Mojo's.

***

Kelley Porter had headed to bed early tonight. She had announced to her parents that she felt really tired.

"That's okay, dear. You're a big girl now and you should know when you need some rest," said her mother.

"Remember when the kids were younger, we had to fight with them to get them to go to bed," said her father.

Her parents had a good laugh at her expense. It didn't matter. She just wanted to get away from them. Forcing a half smile, she kissed her mother and father and then headed upstairs to her bedroom.

Her brother had been picked up earlier in the evening by Walter. They were going to a meeting at the Reverend's house. She hoped they would be gone all night.

Kelley closed and locked her bedroom door. She turned on the night light on her bureau. Next she went to her closet, and pulled a backpack from out of the corner. She began to pack it with things she would need. Her plan was to get her friend Paul to run away with her. They would steal his father's car and drive south on the highway to White River Junction. From there, they could catch a bus to Boston. She had studied a highway map of New England she had slipped out of the glove compartment of the family car before supper. Her plan was simple. They had to get away, far away, before anyone knew they were gone.

She pulled the covers back on her bed and propped the pillows to form the rough shape of someone lying down. She pulled the covers over these pillows and was satisfied with the level of deception they offered. She turned on the small radio on her nightstand. The radio was dialed in to WGMT. The station was playing requests tonight. The DJ was Charles "Chucky" Trainor.

"All right now. It's your close and personal friend, Chuck waiting here for you to call in your requests for a song for someone special. It's hot and humid tonight in the Winooski River valley. It's a night made for lovers and loving so give me a call at 45..."

Kelley was very nearly done packing. She picked up a stuffed bear from the deacon's bench at the foot of her bed and placed it at the head of the pillow shape on her bed.

She took one last look around her room. She would miss her room but she knew she had to get away. Deep down inside, she felt her very life depended on her getting away.

"Hello, Chucky, this is Beverly."

"Well, Hello...Beverly," dripped Chucky.

Kelley unlocked the bedroom door. She knew if it were locked, it would arouse suspicion. Her parents might discover her plan before she had time to fully implement it.

She turned out the nightlight and crawled out the window.

From the radio came the sexy voice of Beverly, "Chucky, may I call you, Chuck?" she said with emphasis.

"Sure. Now Beverly, it sure is hot out there tonight, isn't it?"

"Chuck, you don't know how hot it is honey," she purred.

"Oh, I think I know, yes I do. So Beverly do you have someone special on your mind tonight?"

"Uh-huh."

"Is there a song you want us to play for you two lovers tonight?"

"Chuck, can you play...?"

The sound from the radio had now faded away as Kelley made her way along the porch roof, which was just under her bedroom window. She was now at the other end of the house. She put the backpack on and pushed herself off the edge of the roof. Her dangling legs felt the post of the porch and she wrapped her legs around it. Slowly, she slid off the roof and made her way down the post to the porch rail. She quietly jumped down onto the porch. She went down the side stairs and quickly broke into a half run. She took a moment to glance down at her watch. It was twenty minutes until eleven. She didn't want to be late, so she quickened her pace, to a jog. She would be at the back of the library in less than fifteen minutes.

Several streets away, Paul Lacosse, Kelley's boyfriend, slid out of his own first floor bedroom window. He quietly pulled his bicycle out of the garage. He walked it down the driveway before hoping aboard and pedaling off to the library to meet Kelley.

Paul arrived first. He laid his bicycle down onto the damp grass.

The night was turning cooler. The air was filled with the night sounds of crickets, frogs and the occasional flutter of bats that were scooping up summer insects, as they feasted in the dark.

Paul could her someone coming. He heard the slapping of someone's sneakers on the paved sidewalk. Then he heard the crunch sound of someone running down the gravel driveway of the library.

It was Kelley. She was nearly out of breath.

"Paul ...Paul...Thank you, for...coming," panted Kelley.

"Hey, you knew I would. I would do anything for you, Kelley."

He tried to put his arms around her but immediately noticed her backpack.

"What's this, Kelley? What's going on?"

"Listen, Paul. I need your help, like, in a big way."

"Help to do what, exactly?"

"I need to run away, Paul, and I want you to come with me."

"What?" he exclaimed, as he put his hands to his head in disbelief.

"I need to get away...tonight...or something bad is going to happen to me, I just know it."

"I don't understand."

"Listen, I'll tell you everything. But you've got to promise me that either you'll run away with me tonight, or at least, you'll help me get away, tonight! Do you promise?"

Paul was troubled by this sudden and unexpected situation. His love for Kelley was strong, but running away was another thing. His father could be mean, and violent, when he was pissed off, and Paul running away was sure to set his father off.

After a brief hesitation, Paul jumped in with two feet.

"Okay, I'm in. Now tell me what's happening here, and why you have to run away tonight? If I'm going to set off my old man, it had better be good."

Kelley proceeded to tell him about the menacing spirit that had threatened her in the bathroom and in her bedroom. She told Paul all about her brother and the coven, at least as much as she dared. She didn't want to tell Paul too much and then scare him off.

"Shit, that's incredible," was all he could say.

"So, you can see, that's why I've got to get away."

"Yeah, so what's your plan?"

She told him about their taking Paul's family car and trying to get to Boston.

"They'll follow us and try and catch us, and then my ass will belong to my old man," said Paul.

"Paul, I don't care. I'm not coming back!"

"But what if they find us?"

"I'm not coming back!" she said defiantly.

Somehow, he knew, just what she meant. She'd rather die than return to Sutton.

"Okay, but we're going to need some money," said Paul. "My mom's got an old cookie jar filled with money that she puts aside for school clothes. I think I can get it."

"Good, now let's..."

Suddenly, Paul put a finger to her lips, signaling her to be quiet. He gestured to the front of the library. He quickly picked up his bicycle and pointed towards the woods at the back of the library property. They moved as quickly and quietly as they could. When they were near the edge of the woods, they both looked back at the library. A car slowly came down the library's driveway with only the parking lights on. The silhouette outlined by the street light gave it away as a police car. Suddenly, the window mounted spotlight shown along the back of the library, and then began to sweep out to the grass and woods where Kelley and Paul were standing. They both dropped down into the tall grass and watched as the spotlight passed over them. After a moment, the car could be heard pulling out of the driveway, back towards the street. Paul stood up first and then gave a hand to Kelley. Paul picked up his bicycle and the two headed into the woods. After just a short distance they came to the railroad line that ran through the town along the eastside of the Winooski River. They turned left and walked along the tracks. The moon was out, it was three quarters full.

They walked perhaps a quarter of a mile, and then stopped at the back edge of the Town's graveyard.

"Let's cut through here," said Paul, "it'll bring us right out to my street."

"Why not ditch the bicycle here?" said Kelley, "since we can't bring it with us."

"I guess you're right," Paul said with a sigh. He was going to miss his bike. He was actually looking forward to running away by driving his family's car. His father had been giving him driving lessons. How ironic it would be, to run away, in the same car he was taking his driving lessons in.

They began to make their way through the cemetery.

"Hey, hold up, I've caught my foot on something," said Paul.

He pulled and pulled but couldn't free himself.

"Wait, I've got a flashlight," said Kelley as she dropped her backpack and fished around inside. In a moment she had found the flashlight, it on and pointed it down at Paul's trapped foot.

"Eieeeee," she shrieked as she dropped the flashlight.

"What is it?" asked Paul as he reached down for the flashlight. He picked it up and pointed it at his own foot. What he saw caused him to freeze with fear.

It was a bony hand gripping his sneaker, like some sort of rotted twisted root. He yanked his foot with all his might. The hand was incredibly strong. Paul's yanking had now pulled the hand further out of the ground. Its arm was now protruding out of the ground. It was heavily soiled with black earth. The arm jerked his foot back so that Paul fell to the ground and the flashlight rolled away from him, its light slapping at the darkness.

"Kelley, help me!" pleaded Paul.

She picked up the flashlight and pointed it again at the dark gray bones of the hand, which had her boyfriend's leg firmly in its grasp. To her horror, another hand broke through the grass in front of the tombstone, and grabbed Paul's other leg.

"Kelley, help!"

Kelley put the flashlight down and pulled at Paul's arms.

Suddenly he lurched out of her grasp. She fell down on her butt.

"Kelley, what's happening?" cried Paul.

She reached for the flashlight and shown it on his legs. They were now half way into the moist earth. He was buried up to his thighs.

Kelley scrambled to her feet, dropping the flashlight on the ground. Its light now pointed at Paul. She grabbed Paul by the shirt, and pulled as hard as she could.

"Kelley, I love you!"

"I'm going to get you out of this," she protested.

His body jerked again. This time there were snapping sounds like branches being broken. He was now buried in the ground up to the middle of his chest. He was sobbing.

"Kelley, Kelley," he kept repeating, "It hurts sooo...much."

Kelley was frightened and confused. She felt helpless.

"Kelley, come here," said a familiar voice.

Kelley turned around and saw the moon lit silhouette of three people, standing off about twenty feet from her location.

"Kelley, he's not for you," said the same voice. She recognized it as her brother Samuel.

She leaped to her feet and flew at her brother. The other two people stopped her before she could reach him.

"Stop this now, Sammy," she demanded.

"Why?" he demanded.

"Because he's not to blame. Running away was my idea."

"I'm sorry Kelley it's out of my hands."

"Kell...ey," screamed Paul one last time.

She turned just in time to see his body completely pulled beneath the surface. His arms flapped wildly, then his hands grabbed at the darken clumps of soil. His fingers stiffened and relaxed, as his hands disappeared into the ground. The flashlight on the ground highlighted the entire gruesome event.

The crickets had stopped their usual chirping. The night was absolutely silent.

Kelley turned towards her brother and tried to fly at him with her fists, in a blind hateful rage. She was restrained by the two people who accompanied her brother, Bruce and Scott Morton. They were in their early twenties, and owned their own business, Green Mountain Video's and Games.

"You bastard," she screamed at the top of her lungs.

"Now, Kelley, that's not nice. Mom and Dad would be hurt by your vulgarity. Kelley, I'm afraid you're going to have to pay a heavy price for breaking our covenant of silence with an outsider. Even I, can't save you, now."

She spit at Samuel and tried to kick him.

He held his right hand up, as if to hold her off, yet not touching her, when suddenly she went limp. She was conscious but was no longer in command of her body. She was dragged from the cemetery, her two sneakers digging twin trails in the moist earth. The two Morton brothers placed her in the back seat of a police car. Samuel climbed into the back seat of the Reverend's car. Bruce Morton got into the front seat of the police car while Scott got in the Reverend's car. The two cars moved away slowly.

In the cemetery, bats now flew in frantic but purposeful directions. The cemetery was always a good place for hunting.

21

"It was fortuitous that Mrs. Lawless spotted her this afternoon. Her hearing acuity is exceptional," said the Reverend.

Samuel did not acknowledge the Reverend's small talk. He had a great deal on his mind.

"Is there a way we can reach Ed Townsend?" asked Samuel.

"We've already called his house, and left a message on his answering machine," said Scott Morton.

"Does he carry a pager, a cell phone?" asked Samuel.

"I don't know!" answered the Reverend.

He was trying to hold back his anger. It seemed that Samuel was deliberately trying to ignore him.

"You should have inquired into it, long before now," scolded Samuel.

The Reverend's ears stung with the bite of the criticism just leveled at him. He couldn't afford to react—he had to remain in control.

"You're right!" answered the Reverend with as much control as he could command.

His hands gripped the steering wheel of the car with such force that his knuckles were turned white.

Meanwhile, sitting in the back seat of the Police car, Kelley was fully conscious, but still could not move a single muscle in her entire body. She could hear the two men in the front seat talking in hushed tones, so low she was unable to discern a word that was spoken. Her heart ached for her friend, Paul. She got him into this mess, and it had cost him his life. Tears ran down her cheeks. Her nose ran. She wanted to sob but couldn't move. She grieved in tortured frozen silence.

The two cars moved along the streets of Sutton in tandem. After several minutes, the cars pulled slowly into the driveway adjacent to the Church of Everlasting Faith. The white siding of the church seemed almost luminescent in the moonlight. Its stained windows were flat-black. They seemed to absorb the pale night light without giving back any reflection. The cars proceeded deep into the driveway alongside of the church. The Reverend got out of his car as did Samuel and Scott Morton. Police officer and Bruce Morton got out of the police car. Kelley was momentarily left in the back seat by herself.

The Reverend fumbled with his keys. After a moment he selected one and walked over to the bulkhead doors, which led to the church's furnace room. This was the only way into that part of the church basement. He unlocked the padlock and slipped it off of the latch panel. With a strain he pulled back the two heavy wooden doors. They creaked and cracked with sounds doors often make that aren't opened very often.

The Police officer shone his flashlight down the steps that led to the furnace room. Another door stood closed at the bottom of the wooden stairs. The Reverend was careful as he climbed down these stairs. He unbolted the cellar door and pushed it open. He reached along the door jam and flipped on a light switch. The light reached up the stairs and lit up the faces of the four people standing at the top.

"Go get her and bring her down here," said Samuel to the two Morton brothers. They turned and headed towards the Police car. Samuel and the Police officer descended the stairs into the furnace room.

"Over here," called the Reverend.

He was standing near the furnace. He reached overhead and pulled on a small chain. They heard a low rumble as the stone-faced cellar wall began to swing away giving way to another room. The Reverend reached for another light switch, and soon the secret room was dimly lit with a small overhead light bulb. Cobwebs were everywhere. Against the back wall were two pairs of metal clamps, set into the stone, at a height of five feet. Another similar set of clamps were set much lower, at a height of less than a foot off of the ground. In the middle of the wall were several protruding rings. The floor was nothing but trampled dirt. The ceiling was made of the same blocks of stone as the foundation and walls. What little air had managed to enter this room through the cracks in the stone foundation, was dank and stale. Several sets of chains hung from the ceiling, on hooks set near the left wall.

"No one will find her in here," said the Reverend.

"Fine," said Samuel as his eyes took in the starkness of this hidden chamber.

Kelley was dragged into the chamber. Her sneakers had worn away at the toes from her feet having been dragged. The Reverend took a key ring that hung on the backside of the stone door, and unlocked a pair of the highest clamps. The two strangers held Kelley up and placed her wrists in each of the clamps. The clamps were locked by the Reverend. The same was repeated with the clamps nearest to the floor, which soon held her ankles tight to the wall.

The Reverend took down a chain from its hanger and chained her waist, to the wall. Her body was held firmly against the cold stone wall. Her weight bore down against the manacles. The edges of the manacles cut into her wrists and ankles.

Kelley could see everything that was going on but couldn't move a muscle to resist. She looked at her brother, but could not detect any sign of compassion. He seemed cold, almost inhuman. Tears ran down her cheeks.

Her brother turned his back on her and left the chamber. The Morton Brothers and the Police officer also turned and left. The last to leave was the Reverend. He looked at Kelley and almost seemed concerned. Nevertheless, he reached for the light switch, and turned the light off. He then left the chamber. Soon, a low rumble signaled the closing of the heavy stone door. It was absolutely dark inside the chamber. Kelley's heart thundered inside of her chest.

How could my fucking brother do this to me? she thought.

Her lungs strained to catch a breath and took in the heavy air of the foul smelling chamber. She felt the need to wretch, but her stomach muscles wouldn't cooperate.

Did they leave me to die? thought Kelley. At least she still had control of her mind, but how long would that last in this chamber and the tortuous situation that she found herself in?

The four men and Samuel climbed up the cellar steps and into the night air. Everyone, except Samuel, drew in a deep breath. Without as much as another word, each returned to their respective vehicles. The Reverend, having already turned off the furnace room light, now padlocked the bulkhead doors once again. He, too, headed to his car, and after a moment the two cars pulled away slowly.

Across the street from the Church stood a silent figure. The person was standing in the deep dark shadows of an old maple tree, trying to not reflect any street or moonlight. The figure was an old woman. She had watched the arrival and departure of the two cars. She knew what was going on but also knew she could not interfere. The time wasn't right.

Poor child, thought the woman. She bowed her head in silent prayer.

The old woman carefully looked in several directions, before she dared to venture from out of the shadows of the old tree. She slowly turned and walked down the street back to her own place. She had much to do.

***

Aaron and Korie were thoroughly enjoying themselves. Aaron had even taken up the owner's offer and joined the assembled group of so-called amateurs on stage for a couple of numbers. He rejoined Korie. Sweat was pouring down his forehead. He was really into the music. The other informal band members had given him some polite applause when he elected to return to Korie.

A young man was now singing up on the stage. He was in his early twentys, but his voice possessed a gravely, timber quality that seemed born to sing the blues. The horn players, two saxophones, a trumpet and a trombone provided a solid foundation of brass. The assembled band played so tight it seemed they had been playing together for years.

Aaron signaled to their waitress to bring another pitcher of draft beer. He picked up his napkin and wiped his brow.

"Damn, that was fun!"

"Why did you quit then?" asked Korie.

"Because I didn't want to leave you alone."

"I'm okay."

"Well, there's another reason."

"What's that?"

"I'm really not up to their level."

"Is that right?" she said as she took the napkin and wiped his neck.

He smiled at Korie and then took her hand that held the napkin. She dropped the napkin on the table. Aaron opened her hand and pulled her hand to him. He slowly kissed her palm, not once but a couple of times. She smiled at him, with a smile that had love written all over it.

The waitress arrived with the pitcher of beer.

"Thanks," said Korie.

"Yeah, thanks," said Aaron. "Say, can I ask you a question?"

"Sure," said the young waitress as she leaned over the table to better hear the question.

"Are those all really amateurs? I mean, they're really good."

"They call themselves amateurs. But they've been coming here and playing together a couple of times a week, since before I started here, two years ago. Ron's got a lot of friends who play, and they like the laid back feel of the place."

"Thanks again."

"No problem."

The waitress turned and left.

"See, I told you they were good, too good."

"You're quite the sleuth," she said playfully. "I'm going to the ladies room. Don't drink all the beer while I'm gone and don't pick up any blues mommas either."

Korie stood up and meandered around the tightly packed tables to reach the ladies room.

Aaron poured himself half a glass of beer and took a sip.

Ed Townsend walked into Mojo's. The place was crowded, but as with most crowds, there was movement and gaps. Ed maneuvered himself to the bar where he located an empty stool a young woman had just vacated. He sat down.

"Jeez this seat is warm," he said almost without thinking.

"Just imagine," said the bartender who removed the half-empty glass from the bar in front of Ed, which the woman had left behind.

Ed smiled at the subtle humor.

"Give me a scotch and make it neat," said Ed.

"Sure," said the bartender.

In a moment the amber colored drink was placed in front of him.

"Tab?"

"No thanks. How much?"

"Four fifty."

Ed placed ten dollar bill on the bar and pushed the bill towards the bartender.

The bartender picked it up and left to retrieve some change. He returned with the change but Ed waved him off. The bartender nodded his thanks at Ed and turned to serve other customers.

Ed turned on his stool and began to search the crowd. In a couple of moments he spotted Aaron sitting all alone, at a small table. He knew it was Aaron because Ed's own inner evil spirit sensed the presence of Aaron's spirit, the proverbial Powell spirit.

At that very moment, Aaron felt a sudden and deep chill seize him. It felt as if he had been suddenly doused with a bucket of ice water. He shivered and his teeth began to chatter.

Aaron didn't understand what was happening. For just a moment, he thought he might be coming down with something.

Now the sounds in the room were getting quieter. It was as if someone was turning down the sound of the entire room, much like one does with a television remote control. He could see the band was still playing, the singer was still singing and people seated at tables were still talking. But now, there was absolutely no sound, whatsoever. Aaron's hands griped the edges of the table. He could feel the table. He reached for the glass of beer, and could feel the coolness of the lower half, of the partially filled glass.

What's happening? he thought not daring to speak out loud.

He needed Korie right now. She was always calm and levelheaded. Aaron was beginning to feel a rush of panic seizing him.

What's taking her so long? he thought.

A soothing voice spoke to him. Its sound seemed to be coming to him from where Korie had been sitting just moments before. His eyes noticed that the air across the table from him was now shivering, much like the air around a mirage.

"Aaron, you are in danger. One of Moloch's coven is near. He seeks you, yet he is not ready to take you, and you are not yet ready, for what is to come," said the female voice.

Aaron watched the agitated air waves. Soon, a shape began to form inside this effect. It was a woman. The woman was wearing clothes Aaron couldn't recognize. She had on a hat, with a large feather on one side, a neck broach, over a high-necked French lace blouse, with full lace cuffs that extended from beneath the deep blue, almost black, velvet jacket. She was stunningly beautiful. Her hair was black and shiny and tied up under her hat. Her hands were delicate, she wore no rings.

"Who are you?" whispered Aaron.

"I am Constance Morgan Powell, daughter of Irene Powell and mother to Colleen Day Powell."

Aaron sat there in stunned silence.

She looked over his shoulder and focused her green eyes in the direction of the bar.

"Don't turn around, Aaron. The evil one is seated on a stool, near the wall, next to a tall table. He is drinking from a small glass and is watching you."

"What, I mean how did, I mean...?"

She held her hand to his lips to silence him. He didn't feel her touch, but the gesture was clear.

"You must leave here tonight. The man who is after you has already searched through your possessions before he came here. Take Korie with you and leave quickly. The two of you must go to Sutton, tonight. The time is coming soon—there is no time to waste. When you arrive in Sutton look for a place called Mother Nature's You will be safe there. You must finish reading our diaries. Once you have finished reading them, call for us and we shall come."

"Will I be able to talk to my mother?"

The specter nodded affirmatively.

"What does the man who is after me look like?"

"You can see him with your mind's eye, without turning around. Just close your eyes and concentrate on the area near the high table behind you. You will see him."

Aaron closed his eyes, and concentrated with all his might.

In a moment, a picture was formed in his mind, as if he was now looking through a rearview mirror. He could see several people seated at the bar. All were engaged in conversation with someone, except for one man. This man was staring straight ahead. He was holding his glass up to his chest but it appeared he hadn't drunk much, if at all. The man's eyes caught Aaron's attention. Aaron began to focus in on the man's face, then his eyes.

His eyes were black as coal. They were as lifeless and menacing as those of a great white shark, killer's eyes.

"I can see him," said Aaron.

"See who?" said Korie.

Aaron opened his eyes and saw Korie seated across from him. His ears picked up the normal sounds of the activity in the room.

"You were sitting there with your eyes scrunched closed. What's happening Aaron?"

Aaron told her what had just taken place. From her vantage she could plainly see the man Aaron described to her.

"So, how do we get out of here without him following us, at least not right away, that is?" asked Aaron.

"Easy," said Korie. "When I went to the women's room I passed the men's room and on the opposite side of the hallway is a fire exit door."

"Okay. So we leave out that door. Won't he be suspicious if we both head out to the bathroom and don't come back in a couple of minutes? He'll guess we've run off, and head straight for the hotel."

"That's why you're going to stay here."

Aaron looked incredulous.

"Look, if we're both gone then he will be suspicious. But if we split up, then I think we have a chance to get away. I'll leave out that back door and head back to the hotel and get our things. I'll meet you out front with the car, thirty minutes from the time I leave. However, you've got to make him stay."

"Sounds like it might work but how do I make him stay?"

"I don't know. Since he's interested in you, give him what he wants. Play some music again. That ought to get his attention."

"Okay, so how do we start?"

"Easy," she said as she turned and signaled for the waitress.

In a moment the young waitress was standing at their table. Korie spoke to her for a moment—the waitress nodded a couple of times. She gave her the glass she had been using. Korie had slipped a ten-dollar bill inside the glass. The waitress turned and left.

Korie and Aaron turned and watched the band perform a B.B. King cover. She began to push Aaron on the arm and back to get up and head to the stage. Reluctantly he stood up, shrugged his shoulders, and then headed in the direction of the stage.

Moments later the waitress arrived with a clean glass and a small plate of Buffalo wings. She leaned over and spoke discreetly to Korie, and then left her alone.

Aaron meanwhile had made it back to the stage just as the band finished up the B.B. King number. The person who had been playing bass gestured to Aaron to take his place. Aaron stepped up onto the low stage and took the bass from the man. After shortening the strap he slipped it over his shoulder.

The lead guitar player leaned over and said "We're going to do another B.B. King piece called *Ain't Nobody's Business*. Can you handle it?"

"Just give me the key, and I'll follow right along."

He gave a little smile and wave to Korie who was still sitting back at their table.

The song began.

Korie half filled her glass and took a couple of sips from it. She sampled the Buffalo wings and found them to be delicious. However it was time to put her plan into action. She bent over a bit and held her stomach as if she was feeling a stomach cramp. She repeated this gesture again. Korie stood up and began to slowly make her way past several tables, while she held her left hand to her stomach.

Ed watched Korie head to the bathroom. He turned his attention to the band and more specifically Aaron.

He's not half bad, thought Ed. He turned around and asked the bartender for a refill. The drink was poured and Ed once again handed the bartender a ten dollar bill and told him to keep the change.

During that moment, Korie slipped out the emergency door next to the bathrooms. She went down the small alley way to the front of Mojo's. There was a cab waiting in front of the restaurant. She quickly got in the cab and gave the driver her instructions. The cab driver put the car into gear and pulled away. Moments later, Korie paid the cabbie and got out in front of the Radisson Hotel. She went to a side entrance to avoid going through the lobby. Just inside the entrance she located the emergency stairwell and pulled on the door handle. It wouldn't open.

That's right, shit. This is the first floor, hotels always lock the emergency stairways from entrance on the first floor, she thought. She hurried to the elevators, making sure she couldn't be seen directly from the lobby, she was careful to keep her back to the security camera. If what Aaron had been told was correct, then someone inside of this hotel had cooperated with that guy at Mojo's. She wasn't going to take any unnecessary chances. The elevator doors opened on her floor and she hurried down the hallway holding her hands to her temples as if to massage a headache. She reached her room, unlocked the door and quickly slipped inside. Everything looked in place. Nothing seemed to have been disturbed.

Could Aaron have the message wrong? she thought.

Then she noticed the tour magazine she and Aaron had read earlier when they had decided to go to Mojo's. She remembered specifically having left it on the table. She was sure of it. It was now lying on the bed.

That was all the confirmation she needed. Her efforts now kicked into high gear, as she opened the dresser drawers tossing their clothes onto one of the beds. She pulled their luggage out of the closet and in just a few minutes she had managed to cram all of their belongings into their luggage.

Korie took the television remote and turned on the television. She changed channels until she located the hotel's house channel. Using the remote control she selected a menu which allowed her to check out of the hotel electronically. With that task completed she left the room key card on top of the low dresser. She picked up their luggage and left the room. She went back down the hall and stopped at the icemaker machine and reached behind it to retrieve the diary. It was still where they had left it. She unzipped Aaron's large bag and stuffed it inside. Moments later, she was putting the luggage into the trunk of their car which was parked inside the Hotel's garage. She got inside of the car, started it up and pulled out of the parking slot.

"Shit!" she said. She had just remembered that she needed the room card key to exit the parking garage.

Damn, this means I'm going to have to go to the front desk and get an exit pass.

Just then she noticed another car drive by on its way out of the garage.

What the hell, she thought as she put the car into gear and followed the other car to the exit gate.

The other driver put his room key card into the exit gate slot. The gate slowly rose up. The other car pulled through the exit gate. Korie pulled up close behind the other car. There couldn't be more than a foot between the two cars.

I hope he doesn't stop, she thought.

The gate began to descend. It landed on the trunk of Korie's car and bounced up a foot in the air after it hit the trunk. It descended again. This time, there wasn't anything in its way, since Korie's car had now cleared the exit. Korie headed to Mojo's to get Aaron.

Meanwhile at Mojo's, Aaron and the other band members were in the middle of playing the *Texas Hop*, originally performed by Pee Wee Crayton.

Ed had finished his second drink.

The band was looking to take a break. Aaron looked at his watch and noted that it was too early for Korie to be out front.

He spoke up to the members of the band, "Say, how about one more just to close out the set? It will be my last one."

"What did you have in mind?" asked the keyboard player.

Aaron thought for a moment, when inspiration struck. He reached into the back pocket of his pants and pulled out his harmonica, which he had a habit of carrying around.

"If someone will take the bass, I'll be glad to play the harp on *C-Boy's Blues* by the Fabulous Thunderbirds, if you fellas know the tune."

"Cool," said one of the trumpet players. "We haven't played any T-bird covers in a month. I'm in."

In a moment, places were exchanged as the band slipped into *C-Boy's Blues*. Aaron's harmonica playing was the best he had ever done. The room was soon tight once again with the band, and the music. When the number was over, the room erupted into a standing ovation for the tired musicians.

The lead guitar player spoke into his microphone "Hey, you people are just great. Listen, we're going to take a fifteen minute break, okay? I know Ron would want you to take this opportunity to order some more suds, so he can pay his bills. So help the poor guy out."

There was a smattering of laughter from the room. People began to mill around as the band members came off the stage. Aaron headed for the door. He was stopped by Ron.

"Hey man, you've got a gift with that harp. You blew us away."

"Thanks," said Aaron. "I'm in a hurry right now. Listen could I pay you for our drinks and..." as he fumbled with his wallet he pulled out four twenties and handed them to Ron.

"That should more than cover it," said Aaron as he looked over Ron's shoulder. He could see Ed had left his seat at the bar and was now heading in Aaron's direction.

Ron was studying Aaron's eyes. He could see the nervousness and fear.

"Something wrong?" asked Ron.

"No, uh, not really, it's just that I've got to go."

"Uh-huh. Your waitress told me that your girl friend had to slip out the back earlier. You in trouble? Someone after you? Cause if they are I'll be glad to help. You just say the word. We blues men have got to stick together, you know."

Aaron took a chance "Sort of trouble, I guess, there's a guy who has been following my friend and I for a couple of days, and we don't know why. He scares the shit out of us, and he's here now. In fact, he's coming this way."

For a moment Aaron and Ron's eyes met. Ron's brow furrowed up as he tapped Aaron on the hip. "Go, I'll slow him down for you. Hurry!"

Aaron smiled at Ron, "Thanks."

Aaron turned and headed to the front door.

Ron turned around and he immediately spotted a tall man dressed in a well-worn business suit heading for the door after Aaron. The man's focus was entirely on Aaron. He didn't see Ron approaching him from a right angle. Even though Ron walked with a limp he could manage some speed when he needed to, especially in his own place. Ron managed to head the man off a few feet from the front door.

"Hey, what's your hurry?" asked Ron as he stepped in front of Ed.

"Out of my way."

"You don't look like a satisfied customer. As the owner, I'm interested in your feedback. Are you unhappy with the food, the service, what is it?"

Ed tried to step around Ron who managed to stay in front of him. Aaron had exited the front door and climbed into the car as Korie pulled away from Mojo's.

"Everything was fine—now get out of my way."

"Really..." said Ron.

Ed was getting exasperated by this man. He pulled out his old FBI badge. He flashed it in the face of Ron.

"FBI business, now move."

"Is that a real badge? Shit, it is," said Ron.

Ed's senses were on full alert. They told him this man had run interference for Aaron. By now Aaron had slipped away. From deep inside, a power was unleashed.

Ed's eyes met Ron's.

Ron didn't like what he saw in those eyes. His senses told him he was looking into the face of a monstrously evil person. Suddenly, Ron's two legs began to burn with a sensation that felt as if his legs had been tossed upon a bed of white-hot coals.

The pain was beyond anything Ron had ever felt before. He buckled from the searing sensations. He had to grab the back of a nearby chair to steady himself.

Ed easily stepped around Ron and he, too, left Mojo's. In the cool air of the summer's night, a slight breeze was blowing from the west across Lake Champlain. He knew he had lost Aaron and Korie. It didn't matter that much. He suspected that sooner or later, they would turn up in Sutton. He decided to head back home. He had a good look at the two and they both seemed ordinary enough. The two would not be a match for the combined power of Moloch's coven. The end was coming.

Moments later, Aaron and Korie entered the ramp to head south on Interstate 89. They were going to Sutton.

Aaron suddenly received a flash image of Ron. He could see Ron sitting on a chair massaging his legs and wincing with pain. Somehow Aaron could feel the same pain in his own legs. He began to rub his own legs. Korie was talking to him but her voice seemed faded and weak. Aaron was concentrating on the image of Ron and his suffering.

Aaron's mind began to focus on Ron's hands. His mind flashed a message to those hands that seemed to ignite a healing sensation.

Ron was also seeing Aaron in his mind. The two men were mentally joined as if they were one. Aaron wanted Ron to pass his hands over his legs but not to touch them. Ron did just that. As he did, the burning sensation was lifted away. Ron stood up. His legs felt as they did before his encounter with the "FBI" man. He slowly walked towards the stage. He felt a strong urge to play some music.

Aaron had fallen asleep.

Korie turned the car radio down as she headed along the dark highway.

***

Samuel was in his bedroom. He had closed the bedroom door and locked it. He now called for Moloch.

Samuel pulled back the braided rug that covered the center of the floor in his room. He had painted a pentagram inside of a circle on the well-worn wooden floor. He turned the light off in his room and drawn the shade closed. The room was totally dark. The darkness felt comfortable to Samuel. He awaited Moloch by standing and facing the pentagram, with his arms down to his side, with his hands held slightly forward, palm side up.

Inside the pentagram a small swirl of spinning light began rotating just above the floor. The spinning light swirled upward and grew in size until it reached the ceiling. The whirlwind of light filled the entire circle surrounding the pentagram. A shape, now familiar to Samuel, began to form inside of the pentagram. This shape became more solid in appearance in a matter of moments. The shape also emitted an eerie glow that seemed to ebb back and forth between green and yellow.

Samuel marveled at this apparition from the nether world which was now putting in a personal appearance in his bedroom. Samuel's face reflected back the pulsating light emitted by the form now standing before him.

"Upuaut, the time for our master to join you here on earth is rapidly approaching. Everything must be ready," said Moloch.

"We shall be ready," said Samuel.

"He will be pleased to learn of your efforts."

"Thank you."

"My sister was caught trying to run away with a non-believer."

"I know. The use of your powers to destroy the young non-believer was interesting. We have given you many powers and you will need them all to serve our Master."

"What do you want me to do with my unfaithful sister?"

"Save her for later. She is to be one of His concubines. She will learn to serve, for her body and soul will belong to Him."

Samuel smiled slightly.

"The male Powell and his girl friend are somewhere in the area. They are going to come here, soon. Should we seize him?"

"No. He must participate of his own free will. That is the way."

"He will join our coven, then?"

"Yes, as it was foretold."

"Does he have powers?" asked Samuel.

"Yes, he does. But your powers are greater. You have ten other coven members with special powers to call upon. His powers shall not be a problem."

"What about his girlfriend?"

"She is of no consequence in this. If she gets in your way, destroy her."

Moloch began to fade into a swirling mass of changing light. The swirl of light began to compress upon itself, until the light collapsed into the center of the pentagram with a snapping sound. Samuel's ears popped from the sudden change in air pressure in the room.

***

Kelley had regained control over the muscles in her body. For the past hour or so, she screamed at the top of her lungs. She had to stop, her throat ached and was dry.

She strained against the clamps and chains that held her, but they were still secure. Her wrists were sore from the chaffing caused by the edges of the clamps. Her hair was becoming mated from the perspiration she had worked up. She began to worry about dehydration. Then worst thoughts entered her mind.

Maybe they're not coming back at all. Maybe they're just going to wait for me to die here. No food, no water, just this fucking darkness, she thought.

Suddenly she could feel something moving down her right arm. Its touch was light but noticeable. It was an insect of some kind, she was sure. It stopped half way up her arm. Its tiny legs moved from side to side as if trying to decide which way to go. It resumed moving up her arm. Soon it was at her shoulder.

Kelley shook her body as much as she could to try and shake the insect off. It didn't work. She turned her head to the right and tried blowing against her shoulder to blow the insect off. The insect simply moved out of the way of her blowing.

It began to move again. This time she could feel it walking on her hair. It moved in a slow and probing fashion, slowly to the top right side of her head, and then slowly it stepped onto her forehead. Kelley screamed, and shook her head back and forth, to try and shake the insect off. By now she was sure it was some kind of spider. She stopped and stayed motionless for a few moments.

Was it gone? Did it fall off? she thought. *Please,* her mind pleaded. She was crying.

The spider wasn't dislodged at all. It had held on. It began to move again. It slowly crawled down the right side of her face. Kelley kept her eyes and mouth closed tight. The spider now moved down to her neck. Kelley felt this was her chance. She turned her head and chin down to the right, against her neck, in an effort to crush the spider.

She missed!

The spider moved down her neck until it reached the top of her tee shirt. Its tiny legs probed the edges of the shirt.

The spider moved to the center of her shirt where it found the shirt was slightly raised. The spider went under the fabric.

Moments later the spider bit Kelley. Its bite sent a new wave of fear into an already panicked mind.

What kind of spider is it? "Oh God...Please somebody help me," whimpered Kelley.

Other spiders, dozens of them, moved confidently about the darkened chamber. One by one, they each began a journey in search of food.

22

Korie pulled the car off the highway at the exit marked Town of Sutton. She pulled into an all night Sunoco gas station. Aaron got out of the car and began to pump gas into the car.

"Fill'er up, ma'am?" asked Aaron.

"Yes, and please wash the windows while you're at it. We seemed to have driven through a fog bank of bugs."

"I can handle that."

Korie climbed out of the car. She stretched her back by placing her hands on her lower back, and pushing her hips forward. The move was not missed by Aaron.

"I have got to use the bathroom. I'll pay for the gas and then, I'll see if I can get directions to this Mother Nature's we were told about."

"Fine, I'll just wait in the car."

Korie headed off to the gas station where a young woman sat behind a counter which allowed her a complete view of the entire array of fuel pumps.

Aaron could see the woman and Korie talking. Korie headed to the bathroom at the rear of the store. Aaron finished pumping the gas. He replaced the gas cap and got back inside of the car. He sat there in the dark for a couple of minutes. Only the overhead lights of the gas station provided illumination.

Aaron noticed headlights reflecting in the rearview mirror. The other car was leaving the interstate, coming down the road past the gas station. Aaron began to experience a feeling of fear—it was a sort of 'deja vu' for him. This sensation was exactly the same feeling he had experienced before, while he and Korie were at Mojo's.

The car slowed down as it approached the gas station but did not pull in. Instead, it slowed down and came to a stop alongside the gas station lot. This car was parallel to Aaron's car. Aaron saw the car was occupied by one, lone driver.

The son of a bitch is looking at me, thought Aaron.

Aaron could feel an icy cold sensation begin to seize him. He shuddered and unthinkingly felt the need to blow into his hands. It had to be nearly eighty degrees on this hot humid summer night, yet Aaron felt chills that made him feel as if it was thirty degrees with a strong northeast wind. He was now chilled to the bone.

A woman's voice spoke to him.

"You are much more powerful than he. He's just testing your powers. Go on and let him think you are terrified. You can do this. Give him back a message of fear and weakness. Just think back to your childhood of the time you were chased by that big dog. You remember it. He chased you up a tree, and you were terrified he would come up the tree to get you. That feeling is still with you. Find it again and send it to him."

Aaron didn't recognize the woman's voice, but she seemed to connect with Aaron. He closed his eyes and searched his memory banks and quickly pulled back into focus that long ago, seemingly lost terror she had directed him to. His mind replayed the moment from his youth. Aaron could feel the fear building up inside of him.

When the childhood fear peaked he commanded his mind to embrace the feeling, and then send it out to the man in the waiting car.

With that, his own mind sent a flash to the mind of the man sitting in the idling car.

Aaron opened his eyes and focused upon the silhouette in the car. The car was at least a hundred feet away, but somehow Aaron could see the man seemed to be moving inside of the car.

Did he just raise his hand to touch his temples? thought Aaron. He couldn't be sure. The car now began to move away. The taillights soon disappeared down the road.

Aaron was still staring intently at the car as it faded from his view, when the driver's door opened and Korie slid into the car.

"Did anything interesting happen while I was gone?"

"Uh no, why are you asking that?"

"Because, Aaron Powell. You have that same look on you face like you had back at Mojo's tonight. I figured something had to have happened. Am I right?"

"No, I don't think so," said Aaron. "I'm just very tired, that's all."

It was the first time he had ever lied to her. He didn't know why he did, *it just came out that way,* he thought.

Korie looked at him suspiciously, but that lasted for only the briefest of moments.

"Well, anyway. I've got directions to Mother Nature's."

"What is it, or who is it, I should ask?" said Aaron.

"You'll see when we get there. It's only about five miles down this road."

She put the car in gear and pulled out of the gas station. Aaron meanwhile looked out the open car window. Warm summer air blew inside the car bringing the sweet smell of cow manure, freshly spread in the farm fields that lined both sides of the road which paralleled the nearby Winooski River.

Aaron's eyes searched for signs of the mysterious car he had seen earlier. It was not to be found.

In less than twenty minutes they pulled into the darkened, gravel parking lot of a bed and breakfast inn. The neon roadside sign announced the place to be, is Mother Nature's Bed and Breakfast

Inn. In smaller, unlighted letters beneath the lit sign, one could make out an additional message. This message announced that the place was also the home of Mother Nature's Curiosity Shop. Further, beneath the large neon sign was a smaller neon sign that seemed to be malfunctioning. It flashed "Vacancy" at irregular intervals.

Korie got out of the car first and then Aaron. They both looked over the exterior of the place. It appeared to be a little long in the tooth. There were no lights in any of the windows. In fact there were no other cars in the parking lot.

"Not a good sign," whispered Aaron.

"I know!" whispered back Korie.

Just then, a woman's voice spoke to them from the shadows of the long front porch.

"She ain't much to look at but she's comfortable and the price is right."

Aaron recognized the voice as the one, which had spoken to him back at the gas station.

"Before you come on up, you may want to pull that car around back. Sutton folks are too curious, if you ask me. Go on now."

They still couldn't see the person.

"Help me with the bags," said Korie.

Korie and Aaron retrieved their bags from the trunk. Korie drove the car around to the back, locked the doors, and ran down the gravel driveway to the front. Aaron and their bags were nowhere to be seen.

"Up here, we're up here," said Aaron from the deep shadows of the porch.

He stepped to the spindled railing so Korie could see him with the help of the weak light reflecting from the roadside sign. There were no streetlights along the road. The Inn was located just north of the center of town. The closest streetlight was a couple hundred yards to the south.

Korie climbed up the front steps and stepped into the darkness of the porch. Aaron reached for her hand and led her to the far end of the porch.

As they neared the end of the porch, Korie could hear the faint sound of someone swinging on a porch swing. The swing creaked ever so slightly from its gentle motion. Korie's eyes began to adjust to the darkness. She could see the outline of someone sitting on the old porch swing.

"Sit next to me dear. I won't bite," said the old woman.

"Okay," said Korie.

"I was just telling your Aaron that I've been expecting you two for a couple of days now."

"Expecting us? I don't get it," said Korie as she sat down on the swing.

"Aaron, please bring Korie and me some of the ice tea I made. It's in the refrigerator in the kitchen. Just go in the front door and head straight down the hall, last door on your left. There are glasses in the cupboard, over the kitchen counter, to the left of the sink."

"Sure," said Aaron as he headed off in search of the kitchen and ice tea.

The old woman took Korie's hands in hers. The old woman's hands seemed cool to the touch. Her grip was surprisingly strong. The woman stopped swinging the porch swing. She turned slightly to look at Korie.

"Do you have any idea why you're here in Sutton?" asked the old woman.

"Well, everything's happened so fast. I guess I'm with Aaron, because I care about him."

"Caring about him won't do dear," interrupted the woman.

"If you mean, do I love him, I guess I ...I guess I do," said Korie.

"Good, because he will need your love if he is to survive. Now go on dear, you were going to tell me why you're here."

"It appears Aaron is a descendant of a family that's been persecuted by an evil group of people from this town. They're supposed to be devil worshippers or something. Anyway, Aaron wanted to come to Sutton, to see for himself if all this is true."

"And what about the diary?" asked the woman.

"How did you know about that?" asked Korie.

"I know a great deal."

Pausing, Korie said, "Just what did you mean when you said if he was to survive?"

"Aaron is in a great deal of danger. What he does, indeed what he freely chooses to do, will affect the fate of this world for generations to follow! The forces of evil are expecting him. They are going to use all of their powers to bring him into their ranks. He is the missing piece in their plan to bring Moloch to life, human form, so he can prepare the way for Lucifer."

"What you're talking about, it seems so ...unbelievable. It almost sounds like you're talking about the end of the world."

The old woman released Korie's hands and resumed swinging the porch swing.

Korie's mind was now racing with all sorts of questions.

Meanwhile, in the house, Aaron had located the pitcher of ice tea, and found drinking glasses in the cupboard, where the old woman said he would. He looked around the kitchen for a tray. He spotted a small tray sitting on top of the refrigerator and put the pitcher of ice tea and glasses on it. He picked the tray up, and was about to turn off the kitchen light, when he noticed a small picture hanging over the wall switch. The picture was only three inches by five inches and was set inside a dark, old, wooden frame. The picture was of a young woman, perhaps in her early twenties standing next to a young child. The child was a girl of no more than six or seven years old. Their clothes, although simple in design, suggested the picture was taken sometime during the nineteen twenties. Neither person was smiling.

Aaron felt a sense of familiarity with the women in the picture. He looked more closely at the photo. The people in the picture were standing in front of a large house of some kind. The bushes in front of the house were in bloom. They looked like forsythia bushes but Aaron couldn't be sure.

I know that woman, he thought to himself.

His eyes began to take in more of the picture's detail. Aaron could see a number on the house, but couldn't quite make it out. The front entrance, included wide stone steps leading up to a large porch, much like the one at this Inn. The entrance consisted of two large side-by-side doors with an arched window overhead.

Something in the bushes drew his attention.

It looks like there is someone hiding in the bushes, he thought.

It seemed to Aaron there was a faint, almost ghostly shape standing in the shadows of the bushes directly behind the two people.

As he tried to focus his eyes even more keenly on this image, it faded from sight.

Try as he might, Aaron could no longer see the mysterious shape in the bushes.

He decided to turn out the light and bring the ice tea outside to Korie and the old woman.

I didn't even ask her name, thought Aaron as he walked slowly down the hall toward the front porch.

***

Reverend Mitchell was not pleased with the way things had turned out. His anger had been festering ever since Moloch had removed him as coven leader, and replaced him with Samuel Porter.

The Reverend was a small man in stature. Envy and hatred swelled inside of him to the point he believed he would just about explode.

As he had every night since Samuel was placed in charge of the coven, he paced the floor in his bedroom. Back and forth he went. As was his habit when he was angry, he repeatedly smacked his right fist inside of his left hand, in a gesture of explosive anger.

"Damn that little fucker," he shouted.

Smack, was the sound, as he again slammed his fist into his open hand.

"I should be the leader, not him. I'm the one who has made the sacrifices for years, who has put up with the bullshit around here, who has protected the coven from those who would destroy it. What has that little, pimple-faced, son of a bitch done? He killed one interloper. Big fucking deal. I've killed over a dozen myself."

The Reverend kicked a small table over. The table had a small crystal bowl on top of it, which shattered into several pieces.

"It should be me who brings Moloch to human form, and who greets Lucifer when he returns in triumph. Damn!"

The Reverend was working himself into a serious sweat.

His devil spirit alter ego, Zeeka, was equally angered by the turn of events. Moloch had become Lucifer's favorite. Zeeka once served at the left hand of Lucifer, as his most trusted lieutenant. His position of prominence was a tribute to the misery he had been able to bring about on earth. Zeeka was deposed in favor of Moloch, who had gained favor with Lucifer when he presented him with plans for something called a Great War. This Great War idea was to help hasten the time when Lucifer would be invited to again walk the earth and rule over all that lived upon it. How ironic that his human alter ego was now likewise deposed by Zeeka's despised competitor. Zeeka was a devil wronged, and also a devil totally corrupted by jealousy and envy. He was the perfect match for the Reverend. Together they would find a way to regain their rightful position.

Throughout the night, the Reverend paced the floor nurturing his anger. He had averaged less than three hours sleep since Samuel's ascension. Likewise, Zeeka would share the pain with his human soul mate. This pain was good for the two of them.

Pain is something you can build on, thought Zeeka.

The Reverend simultaneously shared that thought. He couldn't agree more.

***

Kelley hung against the wall. The manacles around her wrists and ankles were cutting into her skin. Her wrists and ankles were swelling from the poisons, which were slowly entering her body from the spiders, which were feasting on her flesh. She was experiencing a building allergic reaction to the tiny doses of toxins. Her nose was running uncontrollably. Her eyes were swollen shut. Her ears ached with a pounding rhythm. Her lower back felt numb.

Her mind kept revisiting the moment when her close friend, Paul Lacosse, had been sucked into the black earth of the cemetery. His voice pleading with her for help, and her own voice was unheard in response. In her nightmare fugue she was speechless. The powerlessness she felt in not being able to save him from her evil brother, dragged her deeper and deeper into the bottomless pit of despair.

"Oh, Paul," she whispered in a scratchy strained voice. "I'm so sorry."

***

The ice tea was superb. The night air was still quite humid.

"So, I never got your name. It's not Mother Nature, is it?" asked Aaron.

"No! You may call me, Miss Beacon."

"Okay, Miss Beacon. You seem to know a lot about us. Will you please explain to us what is going on?" asked Aaron.

"There are some things I will tell you that will be beyond belief. Only your faith can accept what I will tell you. Everything that has happened to you two, and is yet to happen, has been foretold and is foreseen, except for one thing."

"You're talking in riddles. I don't get it," said Aaron.

"Will you just relax and let her tell it the way she wants," admonished Kelley.

"It is the way I must tell it," said Miss Beacon.

Aaron sat down on the porch and leaned against the house. He took a sip of ice tea.

"Okay, I'm sorry. Please continue," he said.

"High in the hills beyond," gestured Miss Beacon to the west, across the road and river, "there is an old graveyard."

Korie leaned back on the swing as it gently rocked back and forth.

"Buried in that graveyard are the bodies of Irene Powell's family. Also buried there, is her mother Sarah, two aunts, three uncles, a cousin, two sisters and three brothers. They were all burned to death."

Miss Beacon bowed her head for a moment, before she resumed telling her story.

"What is written in the diary you have been carrying with you is as true as can be. There is an evil presence here in Sutton. It's been here for well over 160 years now. This Moloch's Coven of Keepers, as they call themselves, is at their strongest since that night long ago. Their ancestors once came close to bringing Moloch to life, in human form. Your great grandmother, many times removed, stood in their way. The crossover failed because the coven was incomplete, thanks to her. When the coven learned that Sarah's daughter, Irene Powell got away they were furious. Moloch promised them if they could lure Irene, or one of her descendants into willingly joining the coven, then Moloch would still be able to crossover to human form."

"Then what?" asked Korie.

"Then Moloch paves the way for Lucifer to take on human form too, as the Antichrist. Finally, Lucifer begins Armageddon," said Aaron.

Miss Beacon nods in agreement.

"How did you know that?" asked Korie.

"I just know, that's all. I can't explain it."

"Then, Aaron being here in Sutton just heightens their chances to complete this coven and start Armageddon. Doesn't it?" asked an excited Korie.

"Not necessarily."

"What do you mean by that?" asked Korie.

"Aaron is the only one who can stop Moloch's plan."

"And how am I supposed to do that?" asked Aaron.

"You must destroy him," said Miss Beacon.

Aaron leaned forward, and in an obviously nervous voice asked, "And if I can't destroy him?"

"Then Lucifer will walk this earth, he will bring on Armageddon. He will destroy all life on earth. It will be the end of this world."

"That's, that's just too much, I can't ...believe that, me, I'm supposed to save the world. Where's God in all of this? Isn't he supposed to come again at the end of the world and save us somehow? I mean, he created the world. It's his world. How could he just watch it being destroyed by Lucifer? It doesn't make sense," said Aaron, as he shot to his feet.

"Yes, God created this world. It is also true, that he will come upon this earth to save the souls of the faithful. That is all. You see, you're not the first person in human history to face this challenge. I believe you already know this. Remember, I told you a moment ago that this has all been foretold except for one thing?"

"Yes," said Aaron.

"This battle has been waged several times already, and each time, human beings have prevailed in battle. The one thing that is unknown is, when in the course of time will someone chose not to try, choose not to fight, prove too weak to prevail?"

The words just hung in the air.

"I see. I could be the one to fail, to bring about the end of the world. That's some fucking burden," he said with a tension that was all too obvious.

"Easy, Aaron," said Korie as she rose from the swing and threw her arms around him.

"You will not be alone," said Miss Beacon.

Korie and Aaron both stopped hugging and turned and looked at Miss Beacon.

"This, we've got to hear," said Korie, as she sat down on the porch floor in front of the swing. Miss Beacon took Aaron by the hand and sat him down on the swing.

"Think, Aaron. Who could help you?" asked Miss Beacon.

"I don't know, I mean, I'm not really sure. My ancestors?" asked Aaron.

"Yes, they can and will help in their own way. But there are others."

"Korie?"

"I'll help, honey. You can count on me."

"And you, Miss Beacon."

"Of course, dear. I am here to assist in any way that I can."

"I can't think of anyone else."

"Oh, there will be others. You'll see."

They continued talking, until the first light of the morning sun began to brighten the southeast sky.

"It's getting late. Let me show you to your room. You can settle in while I start breakfast."

Aaron and Korie picked up their bags, which had been lying on the porch since last night. They followed Miss Beacon, in through the front door, into the foyer, and up the stairs to the second floor.

When they were alone in their room Korie said, "She sure is an incredible old woman."

"Yeah," said a subdued Aaron as he unpacked his things.

"What's wrong?"

Aaron's eyes were swelling up with tears. "I don't want to let them down. My ancestors, my mother, shit, the whole world," he said as he tossed a shirt into the open drawer.

She turned him around and hugged him. She searched her mind for something to say that could make him feel better, but nothing inspiring came to mind. All she could do was hold him. She softly shed her own tears, not wanting to add to his burden.

"All I can do is try, Korie, all I can do is try," he repeated.

"I know," she said.

Meanwhile, in the downstairs kitchen, Miss Beacon prepared a hearty breakfast, even though she half expected that neither Aaron nor Korie would have much of an appetite. Miss Beacon allowed her mind to travel to a place beyond her kitchen. Her mind's eye was now entering the dark place where Kelley was entombed beneath the church. She pushed hard to reach Kelley's own subconscious.

"You've got to hold on. Help will reach you soon. You will survive. You will have your revenge."

Kelley heard the voice inside of her mind.

"Where are you?"

"Near."

"Why can't you help me now?"

"Because it is not safe, it is not time. Soon it will be!"

"Who are you?"

"Think of me as your guardian angel. I will stay with you until tonight, and then I will come for you."

Kelley seemed to perk up slightly from the contact. She tried to stand as erect as she could, even on her swollen feet. She shook once to shed some of the spiders. It seemed to work. Several fell off and the others decided to retreat from her body. She was left alone for the time being.

Meanwhile, Korie and Aaron headed back downstairs to breakfast with Miss Beacon.

As they entered the kitchen Aaron asked "Miss Beacon, if I may, you know, you never explained how you know so much about my family. In fact, how did you know we were coming, and that we would end up staying here?"

Korie looked at Aaron disapprovingly.

Miss Beacon only smiled as she put two cups of coffee on the small dining table in the kitchen.

"There's sugar in that bowl and fresh cream in the refrigerator. I'm making some fresh strawberry pancakes for breakfast. It's a specialty of mine."

Aaron pressed his line of questioning.

"Look, I need to be able to trust you. I feel as if I do. But, I need to know the truth. You can understand that. So please, tell me! How are you connected to this Powell family thing? And how did you...?"

"All right, I will tell you. I was going to tell you soon anyway."

She placed dinner plates in front of Korie and Aaron. Each plate was filled with a stack of homemade pancakes, covered with fresh strawberries cut in half, which in turn were covered with a dollop of real whipped cream.

"You can pour some maple syrup over them if you want. It's in that small crock," she said gesturing to the delicately, hand painted crock sitting across the table.

Miss Beacon sat down with Korie and Aaron. She wiped her hands on her apron.

"Aren't you going to have some?" asked Korie.

"Dear, I don't need to eat," she said with a cherub-like smile.

Korie held a fork filled with whipped cream and a large piece of strawberry, in front of her mouth, which was wide open in disbelief.

Aaron was sipping some of the hot coffee, when he too froze in place. Aaron slowly put the cup back down on the table.

"You don't eat. You know all about my family history. You also know about this Moloch, and you knew we were coming here. Who or what are you?" he demanded.

"Aaron Powell, you will need to be much sharper than that. You saw me last night when you looked into that picture over there, on the wall, next to the light switch. Don't you remember?"

"Yes, I remember examining that picture. There was a woman and a little girl and ..." he said as he looked over towards the picture, and then back at Miss Beacon, who was sitting perfectly still.

Aaron looked back at the picture and again at Miss Beacon. He then ran his fingers through his hair while he tried to focus. His forehead became furrowed.

"What is it, Aaron?" asked Korie.

"I know, I know...you're a ..., a guardian angel. Am I right?" he exclaimed, as if he had just given the winning answer in Jeopardy.

"Indeed, I am."

"But, a guardian angel, I mean, don't they have wings and uh..., aren't they, well, a little younger?" asked Aaron.

"Oh, that. We can be any age we want. Most of my colleagues like that little naked child with wings look. It's sort of classical. As for me, I sort of like this matronly look."

"Just whose guardian angel are you?" asked Korie.

"I'm Aaron's angel. I have been his guardian since he was born," she said rather proudly.

"But I don't remember ever seeing you before. And haven't you owned this place for a long time?" said Aaron.

"Well, you see, I can travel about in the blink of an eye. I had to buy this place and run it for the past fifteen years, just to establish a cover for being here, and to give you a safe haven here in Sutton. I'll admit it hasn't been easy, what with traveling back and forth, between your life and here."

"My guardian angel?" said Aaron.

"Aaron, look at me," said Miss Beacon.

"Yes."

Before his very eyes she began to change her appearance. One moment, she was the neighbor down the street, when he was a little boy, the neighbor that he stole cherries from. Next, she was his third grade teacher, Miss Carson. She next changed to look like the girl he once had a crush on, when he was a sophomore in high school. She then changed into several other people, and ended with looking like his close friend, and onetime fellow teacher, and singer in his band, Sylvia.

At the end of the series of transformations Aaron and Korie were absolutely speechless, as Miss Beacon returned to look like Miss Beacon.

"Now, now, go on and eat those pancakes. I've made them special for you. We can talk some more after breakfast. I've much to teach you and very little time to do it in."

Meanwhile, Miss Beacon sent a mental message to Kelley Porter "Hold on dear. My friends and I will be coming to rescue you. I promise."

Korie and Aaron slowly began to eat the strawberry pancakes.

"Are you a guardian angel only for one person at a time?" asked Korie.

"Oh, no dear, we can be guardian angels for several people at a time. Right now, I am carrying a light load."

"So, besides Aaron, who else are you a guardian angel for?" asked Korie.

"I'm your guardian angel, too, dear. And I have one other that I guard, a young girl from right here in Sutton.

"Incredible," said Korie.

"Tell us about the young girl. Will we meet her?" said Korie.

"Indeed you will. We will be rescuing her tonight."

"Rescuing her?" asked Aaron.

"Yes. I'm afraid she is being held in a terrible place, by the leader of this evil coven. She is being punished for trying to run away. She is expected to become a concubine for Lucifer when he takes human form."

"But you're her guardian angel, can't you do something for her now?" asked Korie.

"Not alone. But now that you're here, together we can rescue her and protect her from the coven. More coffee?"

Korie and Aaron were amazed by this old woman who had chameleon like abilities. They both felt safe around her.

Aaron still was wrestling with the burden of his future. His mind kept returning to what Miss Beacon had said was his destiny, to wage a battle against the forces of evil, to prevent Armageddon.

His mother, and all of his ancestors had spent their lives, indeed had sacrificed their lives, so he would one day have the chance to wage this battle. He didn't want to let them down. He was a Powell and deep inside of him there existed a strong sense of right and wrong. There also existed, a strong sense of purpose. The two feelings were now merging into a new awareness of who he was and what he was meant to do. Miss Beacon was to become his teacher, his mentor. He would prove to be a fast and eager student.

Indeed, he would be as good a student as all the other Powell's that she had looked after, for the past one hundred and sixty plus years.

23

It was nearly seven o'clock in the morning. The summer sun had topped the ridge of the mountains to the east. Early morning light rays sliced through the opening in Samuel's bedroom window and painted a bright yellow swatch on the well worn, wooden floor.

In the middle of his bedroom floor, under the rug, was the pentagram he had previously drawn on the wide planked, pine floor. The rug began to slowly spin. Its rotation speeded up with each revolution. The center of the rug began to lift off of the floor. It moved as if someone, or something, was pushing against it from below. The rug was spinning without touching the floor. It slowly rose in the air spinning like a top.

Underneath the rug was a swirling motion of lights of several colors. It rose nearly to the ceiling when it suddenly flew across the room and landed against the bedroom door. The mass of lights began to form into a shape.

Samuel was still sleeping. He rolled over in his bed. He rolled from his back onto his stomach. One leg hung over the side of the bed. The bed covers barely covered him.

From the outside of his bedroom window came the sounds of chickadees chirping.

The shape continued to take on a more solid form. Scaly skin began to show first. The shape stretched itself. Two powerful arms with equally powerful hands extended upward and outward, a couple of times, as if the shape was trying on its solid form for fit.

It was Moloch, paying a call to his new protégé. Samuel had called to him from his sleep. Moloch didn't need much of an invitation. He had a need to confer with Samuel anyway. He was now nearly completely solid. His burning red eyes looked down upon the sleeping Samuel.

Once his transformation was complete, he stepped to the foot of Samuel's bed. He extended his arms and hands over the bed, slowly raising his hands. As he did so, Samuel's body also rose up off of the bed. Samuel was now suspended in the air, over his bed. Moloch turned his hands in a circle. Samuel turned over in the air. Now Moloch brought his hands and arms up towards his chest. Samuel's still sleeping body moved, so that Samuel was now hovering over his bed in a standing position facing Moloch. His feet were just a few inches off the surface of the bed.

"Samuel, awaken," commanded Moloch.

Samuel's eyes fluttered a couple of times and then opened. A smile filled Samuel's face.

"Welcome, Moloch. This is quite a surprise!" said Samuel.

Samuel didn't seem to notice or care that Moloch had control of his body or that his body was suspended in the air over his bed.

"The Powell male is now in Sutton. I have spoken with Townsend and it is confirmed by him."

"That's good news. I will immediately begin work to draw him in," said Samuel.

"There is more. This male Powell is a powerful spirit. We know he is receiving help from others. He must be made to see the way."

"We will destroy anyone who stands in our way, Moloch, anyone! That is our promise."

"We have given you powers over other humans. But his help is coming not just from humans, but from powerful spirits."

"Isn't that your responsibility?" asked an emboldened Samuel.

"Yes. I have legions of devils available and willing to join in this battle. However, these spirits are not just powerful, they are clever and formidable. Their powers will be used to try and block ours. It may come down to your powers and your own commitment to our Agreement. You cannot rely on the other coven members to be the decisive factor. In the end, not all coven members will fulfill their obligations. We picked you for this mission because of your unique strengths."

"Is there weakness in our coven? Tell me, and I will personally destroy them!" said an obviously agitated Samuel.

"Not a weakness, but a traitor."

"Tell me, I must know who it is."

"No, this traitor must be allowed to carry out his treachery. At the proper time you will deal with this weak and miserable human. We, in turn, will deal with the human traitor's devil mate."

"I see."

"I am also here to give you a special gift. **He** wants you to have this new power."

Moloch held his two hands together, as if he were cupping them to hold water. Instead his hands held a flame that rose up and flickered in the air. There was nothing visible inside of Moloch's hands that were now burning. The flame appeared to simply be.

Samuel held his own hands together in a similar fashion. Moloch turned his hands over, as if to pour something from them.

His hands were now directly over Samuel's hands.

The flame moved from Moloch's hands into Samuel's hands as if it were some sort of liquid.

Samuel stared down at his hands, which now held the burning flame. The flickering reflected in his eyes, which were now totally black, as if they were two highly polished marbles.

"Hellfire?" asked Samuel.

"Yes," answered Moloch.

Samuel pulled his hands to his chest. As he did so the flame seemed to travel into his chest in one seamless motion.

At that moment, a small chickadee landed on the bedroom windowsill outside the screened and open window. Samuel looked over at the tiny bird. The bird seemed to be looking back at Samuel. It tilted its tiny head back and forth a couple of times, then it froze.

Samuel slowly raised his left hand, palm side facing the window. In a split second, a small ball of fire burst from out of Samuel's hand and exploded towards the bird. The bird turned its head as if to take flight when the ball of flame enveloped it. The flame lasted for less than a second. Suddenly, the bird was no longer there. In its place was a small pile of ash on the windowsill. There was also a hole burned through the window screen about the size of a baseball.

A gentle breeze arose and the bird's ashes were soon blown off the windowsill.

"Awesome," said a pleased Samuel.

He turned to speak to Moloch, but the powerful devil spirit had disappeared.

Samuel now felt his body slowly settle onto the bed. He jumped off of the bed, and padded over to the window to get a closer look at his handiwork.

"Hellfire!" he exclaimed.

His eyes were still solid black. He pulled the curtain closed and crawled back into his bed. He laid there with his hands folded behind his head, wearing a huge smile, and sporting a budding erection.

***

Ed Townsend and Walter Yandow had breakfast together at Dee's Diner on U.S. Route 2. Sitting in another booth, two booths away, was Ed Foley and his daughter along with Phyllis Atkins. Sitting alone at the counter was Bob Senecal. Sutton was a small town, and this diner was a popular spot among local folks. It had a reputation for quality home cooked meals and a simple, but welcoming atmosphere. It also helped that the owner, Dinah Little, was a member of the Church of Everlasting Faith.

Ed and Walter were exchanging small talk about one of their past pursuits, the slaughter of interlopers.

Ed Foley, his daughter, and Phyllis were busily engaged in a discussion about Ed's daughter having a romantic interest in a fellow member of the Church.

Bob Senecal was busying himself by reading the day's edition of the *Burlington Free Press*. His attention was caught by a small story on page seven. The story was reporting on the status of the search for two missing college hikers, Michael Delvecchio, and Julia Brodsky.

Search Called Off, proclaimed the headline.

Members of the Vermont Chapter of the Appalachian Mountain Club, along with close friends of the two missing hikers have decided to suspend their search efforts. It has been three weeks since Michael Delvecchio, 24 of New Groton, Connecticut, and Julia Brodsky, 22 of New Rochelle, New York, disappeared while hiking along the central stretch of Vermont's Appalachian Trail.

The two hikers, with reported limited hiking experience, were last seen on the south trail leading to the summit of Camel's Hump Mountain, on July 2.

"Authorities have not ruled out foul play," said Corporal Gilpin, of the Vermont State Police, Barracks 3. *"We just don't have much to go on. We haven't yet turned up a piece of physical evidence which would give us some idea of what happened to them."*

The story went on to note that authorities were hoping that others hiking along the trail may yet turn up a lead.

Meanwhile Appalachian Mountain Club members and friends have decided to suspend their search efforts.

"The trail is pretty dense, and there are many valleys and switches. They could be anywhere. For now, some of us will

keep searching on weekends," said Dan Britto, friend of the missing hikers.*

Bob ordered a refill of his coffee.

***

The Reverend knocked on the door. There was no response. He knocked again. This time someone answered the door. It was Judge Fairchild. He had a small towel wrapped around his neck.

The Judge used a corner of the towel to wipe a bead of perspiration off of his forehead.

"Morning, Reverend. C'mon in."

"Thank you," said the Reverend.

"Still exercising, eh Judge?"

"You bet your ass, Reverend. It's the secret to a long life."

The two men walked to the rear of the house through the kitchen and out onto a screened patio. A tabletop radio was playing a classical piece by Mozart. Fresh cut flowers were artfully placed inside a crystal vase which sat in the center of the wicker coffee table. The patio floor was covered in Vermont slate. Flowers of several varieties hung from baskets along the top edge of the screen windows.

"Have a seat. Can I get you some coffee or juice?" asked the Judge.

"Why thank you, coffee would be nice!"

"How do you take it?"

"Black, please. Just black."

"Be right back."

The judge headed off to the kitchen.

Meanwhile the Reverend settled into a wicker chair which was padded with an overstuffed pillow, with a bright south sea print cover. Off in the corner of the patio wind chimes made soft tinkling sounds as a gentle early morning breeze passed through. The Reverend noticed a small tray on the underside of the wicker coffee table. It was filled with several bottles of herbal medicines. The tray also held a small dish which contained well over twenty different pills of assorted shapes and colors.

On a wicker end table there were several gardening and decorating magazines.

The Judge lived alone. He had never been married. He had developed quite a reputation as a young defense attorney. For a while, he practiced law in Connecticut. He returned to Vermont, over twenty years ago. Shortly thereafter, he was put up for a state judgeship. His reputation continued to grow on the strength of his brilliant legal mind, some would say. Fellow coven members knew the real truth. Over the years, and with considerable help, he had developed a dossier on nearly every public official in the State of Vermont. For those with something to hide, the good Judge was there to lend an ear and a hand. For the pure of heart, and the social do-gooders, Judge Fairchild always had something on a close relative, or a friend or business partner. It was no wonder he was appointed to the State Supreme Court in 1983. He retired in 1996, but his influence continued as strong as ever.

Judge Fairchild returned from the kitchen with a small tray. He put the tray on the coffee table. He handed the Reverend a cup of steaming coffee. The cup and saucer were obviously very expensive china.

"Thanks," said the Reverend. He put the cup and saucer on the coffee table in front of him. He selected a linen napkin from the tray and unfolded it onto his lap. He picked up the coffee cup and saucer and took a careful sip of the coffee.

"It's my own custom blend. I have it shipped here four times a year from Hawaii."

"It's exquisite," said the Reverend as he took a second sip.

The tray also had a small basket filled with dried fruit, bread sticks and a pitcher of chilled fruit juice. The wind chimes tinkled again.

"Would you care for a glass of juice? It's fresh. I made it just before you arrived. I always make fresh juice after my morning exercise."

"No thanks, the coffee is enough."

"Very well," said the Judge as he poured himself a tall glass of the sweet nectar.

"Mango, strawberries, banana and kiwi, it's really quite delicious."

"It does look good, but I'll pass."

"So Reverend, what is on your mind that you should decide to pay me a visit so early in the morning?" said the Judge, as he sat back in his chair and crossed his legs.

The Judge was wearing a dark blue cotton blend running suit with three white stripes down the sleeves of the jacket and the pants.

Reverend Mitchell put his coffee back on the table and slid forward in his chair. He folded his fingers together in a prayerful clasp out of habit.

"May I speak candidly?"

"Of course," said the Judge as he took a sip of his custom blended fruit juice.

"I am deeply concerned about the status of our coven."

"Go on."

The Reverend had to move slowly here. He was risking his life and his place in the post Armageddon hierarchy.

Swallowing hard he continued, "How can we be sure that Moloch is telling us the truth?"

Without taking his eyes off the Reverend, the Judge placed his left arm across the back of his chair and then took a long swallow of juice.

"And what truth are you referring to, good Reverend?"

Opening his hands he said, "That Lucifer wants Samuel to lead the coven during this time of fulfillment."

Smiling he responded "Why Reverend Mitchell, is it possible that you are envious of young Samuel?"

"Look, this isn't about envy, or jealousy. Our church members have been loyal for over one hundred and sixty years, to the tenets of our Malum Pactum, our Agreement. This could be the time that we finally triumph. I can surely feel it and I know you feel it, too. We are poised to be the coven that delivers Lucifer. But if we fail, how much longer must the faithful wait? Could failure strengthen the hand of the other side and lead to extinction for Lucifer, for all of us?'

The Reverend inched a bit forward.

"What if Moloch, not Lucifer, picked Samuel?"

"To what end?"

"Maybe, he is using this opportunity to depose Lucifer." He let this point sink in for a moment.

"Why would he risk his place in the dark side?" said the Judge, as he placed his half finished juice glass back on the tray.

"Think about it," said the Reverend.

"My spirit partner harbors no such fear. Does yours?"

Without hesitating, the Reverend said, "Yes."

"So you believe Moloch is deceiving all of us in a plot to depose Lucifer, and this plot will fail because he has chosen a child to lead, and that somehow Lucifer doesn't know about all of this? Incredible, Reverend, that's quite a tangled web."

"Look I am taking a big risk even talking about this. I...needed to get this off my chest. Maybe you're right. Perhaps it's my own paranoia."

"Perhaps it is," said the Judge. His keen mind was now running in overdrive.

The Judge sent out a mental message to his spirit partner, Pontris, who had been listening in on the entire conversation.

"Pontris, was an evil spirit who catered to nurturing the evil tendencies of powerful people from throughout history. He had instigated people to poison, torture, stab, and shoot lovers, spouses, family members, opponents and enemies. His very handiwork had inspired several of Shakespeare's plays.

Kings were murdered, lovers vanquished, rivals destroyed as kingdoms and empires rose and crumbled throughout history.

Can it be? thought the Judge.

Pontris' response was revealing and to the point.

"In my world we never speak directly to Lucifer or him to us. All of our conversations with Lucifer flow through but one demon, Moloch."

So Moloch is in a position to deceive not only your world, but ours as well, thought the Judge.

Pontris' answer was swift. "If it can happen in your world it can happen in mine."

"Reverend, let's suppose, for the sake of discussion, you are correct. How do you propose to prove your theory, without alerting Moloch and incurring his wrath?"

"That's where I'm stumped, Judge. I can't figure out how. I was hoping, that with your counsel, I could come up with a possible way to test my theory."

The Reverend was a clever man. His appeal for advice would allow the Judge to help, without becoming directly involved, at least, not yet.

The Judge stood up and walked over to a wicker stand of ivy that sat in the corner of the patio. He picked up a spray bottle and began to spray the plants.

"Perhaps a test isn't necessary. It is written in the Book of Covenants that Lucifer's predecessor, in this instance, Moloch and his faithful coven, shall destroy anyone that threatens the fulfillment of Lucifer's triumphant return. Am I not correct, Reverend?"

"Yes, that is correct," said the Reverend as he stood up from his seat and approached the Judge's side.

"Then, how is it that Samuel is allowing his sister to live? How is it, that Moloch is allowing Samuel this exemption from the covenant? How is keeping her, as a prospective concubine, fulfilling our Book of Final Covenants? What are we to make of this Reverend?"

Reverend Mitchell was inwardly smiling. He knew he now had an ally.

Just then the phone in the kitchen rang.

"Excuse me," said the Judge as he put the spray bottle down and headed into the kitchen.

He was gone for only a couple of minutes.

"Samuel is calling for a meeting. We are to meet at Phyllis' offices in one hour."

"Then I'd better be going. I'll see you at the meeting," said the Reverend.

The Judge, who is a least a foot and a half taller than the Reverend, put his hand on the Reverend's shoulder.

"What you came to me about shall remain between us. I believe you may be quite right about Samuel and Moloch. We are bound by our hearts and soul to uphold the Book of Covenants. For now let us see what is being planned. We will speak again, Reverend."

"Thank you, Judge. All I want is to do is what is right."

"I understand."

The judge showed the Reverend to the front door.

***

Miss Beacon pulled her Land Rover out of the garage. It looked terrible. It had dents and dings everywhere and the color was no longer uniform due to fading, scrapes and some rust. The tires were new, the engine sounded good and the windshield had a crack on the left side that traveled from top to bottom.

Aaron and Korie climbed into the back of the vehicle, and pulled a blanket over themselves as Miss Beacon had instructed them to do. They also slid as low in the seat as they could.

Miss Beacon put the Rover in gear and turned around in her back driveway. She pulled the vehicle out onto the road and headed south. A car passed her heading in the opposite direction, it was Shirley Carter. She was a beautician and a coven member. Miss Beacon and Mrs. Carter exchanged a brief wave with one another.

It was getting hot under the blanket.

"How much longer must we stay under the blanket?" asked Aaron.

"Not much. We'll be turning off this road in a couple of miles. You can come out then."

In a few minutes, Aaron and Korie were suddenly jolted by the bouncing of the Land Rover, as it pulled off the paved road onto a path through high grass. Miss Beacon's Rover drove straight over a piece of split-rail fence that long ago had been knocked over. She didn't slow down one bit. Still traveling about thirty miles per hour she reached over the seat and pulled back the blanket cover.

"You can come out now."

"Thanks," said Aaron as he tossed the rest of the blanket off him and Korie.

"Why don't you slow down a bit?" asked Korie as she and Aaron bounced around in the back seat.

"Not until I get to the tree line."

Miss Beacon was a small woman, and the steering wheel was oversized on the Land Rover. She could barely see over the steering wheel as it was.

Korie and Aaron looked out the windshield and saw the trees rapidly approaching. Neither could discern a road or even a path. They both looked at each other, while the same question popped into their heads.

She is going crash this thing! they thought.

"I am not going to do any such thing," said Miss Beacon.

Neither was surprised at her telepathic power.

"Climb into the front seat, Aaron," said Miss Beacon.

Aaron started to when the car suddenly veered sharply to the left. He fell back into the rear knocking Korie back at the same time.

Miss Beacon deftly pulled the Land Rover to the left, barely threading it between two large pine trees. She spun the steering wheel to the left and right with ease. Suddenly she stopped the Rover.

"Sorry about that little turn. You can get into the front now. Oh, and Korie, would you be a dear, and hand me that small pistol from the satchel under the tarp in the back? Take the other two pistols for you and Aaron and leave the shotgun alone. I don't think we'll be needing it today."

"Pistols?" asked Aaron.

"Yes. You may have powers but you sure can't stop a bullet, at least not yet anyway. We're dealing with some powerful and motivated people, Aaron. We can't take any chances. Too much is at stake."

"She's right, Aaron," said Korie as she turned around from having retrieved the weapons. She handed a small pistol to Miss Beacon, who slipped it into her dress pocket. Korie handed Aaron a pistol. It was larger and held a clip that loaded the bullets from the bottom. Korie's pistol was the same.

"Do either of you know how to use one of these?" asked Miss Beacon.

Aaron shook his head no. Korie, on the other hand, said, "Sure, I've had some experience with guns."

For the next several minutes Miss Beacon explained the features of the weapon to Aaron. She showed him the safety, how to choose single shot and how to select semi-automatic. She also showed him how to load the gun and the rudiments of aiming the weapon. Satisfied he understood the basics, she had Korie locate the extra clips of bullets, making sure they each had two extra clips. With the safeties now engaged, she put the Rover into gear and once again began to weave her way through the dense woods.

The Rover began to climb upward through the woods. The windows remained rolled halfway down. The scent of the forest drifted through the half open windows. The air was filled with the blended aromas of pine, hemlock, beech, birch, maple and sumac. Underneath this was another fragrance. It was the odor of decay. What lives in the forest also dies there! The dead or dying parts of the forest contributed their own smells.

It was dark and cooler here in the woods. The Land Rover bounced up and down and even sideways, as Miss Beacon followed an unrecognizable trail.

"Do you know where we're going? I don't see any signs of a road or trail," said Aaron.

"Yes, I do. We could just drive up the front walk and announce our arrival, but I don't think that would be a good idea."

Korie wasn't speaking. She didn't dare. She was sure the bouncing of the Rover would loosen her teeth, which kept clinking with each bounce. Korie could also feel her ears begin to pop from the change in elevation.

Miss Beacon slowed the Rover down as she maneuvered it in a tight turn so it was pointing downhill in the direction they had come from. She turned the vehicle off, opened her door and climbed out of the Rover, stepping on the step bar beneath the door before she set foot on the pine needle covered forest floor.

Aaron and Korie climbed out of the Rover as well. They joined her next to the drivers' door.

"We'll walk from here. We must be careful. Now take it real slow. We don't want to meet up with anyone. If we do, we'll have to be ready to eliminate them. No one must know we were here. Can you handle that?"

"You make it sound like we're a SWAT Team," said Aaron jokingly.

"This is life or death, Aaron, deal with it," said Miss Beacon in a stern tone of voice.

Aaron looked at Miss Beacon and then at Korie.

"Sorry," he said.

"Can you tell us more about what we're here to see? You were kind of vague back at the Inn," said Korie.

"Of course. About three hundred yards from here, further up the mountain, is an old barn. It holds some terrible secrets. I want Aaron to see it for himself. After that, further up the mountain is a clearing, with an altar where the coven comes to worship. It was built on the ground where the Powell family home once stood. Next to this clearing is the Powell family cemetery. We've come in, sort of the back way. We've climbed the mountain on its southeast side. The barn, clearing, altar and cemetery are all on the northwest side."

"Well, I'm ready. Let's go," said Aaron. The three of them began to head through the woods, up the mountain's steep slope.

They moved slowly and as quietly as possible. The woods were filled with the sounds of life. Birds chirped and squirrels scampered from branch to branch in the tall trees overhead. A steady breeze pushed against the taller trees causing them to sway and twist about. The breeze added a sort of "swooshing," sound to the noise of the forest. At ground level there was barely any air movement.

Pine needles softly crunched underfoot.

After a slow and careful advance that took over forty minutes, the outline of an old barn was noticeable. They continued moving from low scruff pine to low scruff sumac to camouflage their advance. In a few minutes, they were standing at the south side of the barn. Its old, wooden, weather worn side had sizable gaps between the planks. They looked inside through the planks, but were not able to see anything. Since the barn was closed up, the only light that managed to squeeze between the planks or through the dust clouded, small windows provided a sort of deep twilight effect.

"I don't see anyone," whispered Aaron to Miss Beacon.

She acknowledged his comment with a gesture to keep quiet. She moved cautiously along the side of the barn until she was next to the front corner. She looked carefully around the corner for a moment, and then motioned for Aaron and Korie to move up.

"I'm going to open the barn door. You two cover me from here. If you have to shoot don't hesitate. If I can't get away, you two will have to go to the car and get out of here. Here are the keys," she said as she handed the keys to Aaron.

"Be careful," said Korie.

Miss Beacon nodded her agreement and then slipped around the corner. She walked along as if she belonged, all the while her eyes and ears were on full alert. When she got to the front door she grasped the door lock with her right hand and it snapped open. She pulled the latch bar away, and slid the barn door open about four feet. In a moment, Aaron and Korie heard her voice near their corner.

"It looks clear, just hurry. I'll meet you at the door."

Aaron and Korie moved swiftly to the front of the barn and slipped inside. It was musty and very dark inside. Their eyes hadn't adjusted to the limited light. Behind them the barn door slid closed.

They turned around and nearly bumped into Miss Beacon.

Aaron immediately felt very uncomfortable inside the barn. He felt as if he couldn't breath. Korie didn't feel much better.

"Slowly, take a couple of deep breaths."

They both did, but it didn't seem to help that much.

The summer breeze slipped through the barn. The barn itself creaked and popped at regular intervals.

"Do you hear that?" said Korie.

"What do you hear?" asked Miss Beacon.

"I don't know, except that…wait, there it is again."

"How about you, Aaron? Do you hear anything?"

"Yeah, its weird, it's like voices—many, many voices. It seems they are coming from far away though."

"Aaron, listen real close, I think I can hear someone calling your name. Miss Beacon, what's going on?" said Korie.

"Yeah, I can hear that voice, too. Where is it coming from?"

Miss Beacon moved deeper into the shadows of the barn and shortly thereafter, she reappeared with an old fruit crate. It was filled with old clothes. She put the crate down on the ground and pulled a jacket from the crate. She handed it to Aaron.

The instant he touched the jacket he could feel the strong presence of the very person that once wore the jacket. The garment had belonged to a French Canadian. A young man named Edouard Larochelle. He was a woodsman who had come to Vermont from his home in Quebec, where he had left behind a young wife and three small children. He had come in search for work to help support his family. Instead of work, he had found death.

One day in 1879, he had taken his logging team along the northwest side of the mountain. He tied the horses to a downed tree and headed up the side of the mountain in search of quality hardwoods. It was the last time anyone saw him. He was beheaded with a sickle by a loyal member of the coven from the Church of Everlasting Faith.

His voice now pleaded with Aaron to avenge his death.

Another crate was sitting on the ground beneath Aaron's feet. Aaron was beginning to sweat as he handed the jacket back to Miss Beacon, who placed it back in the crate. Korie reached down and touched the jacket and immediately felt a wave of sadness wash over her.

"Here, hold this," said Miss Beacon, as she handed a child's dress to him that she had removed from the crate.

Upon touching the tiny dress, Aaron's mind was filled with the image of a little girl named Emily. She was only five years old. Her mother and father tried to leave the Church in 1902. They had come to fear for their lives and their immortal souls. They were killed in their beds by a coven member wielding a butcher's knife. Their throats were slit from ear to ear. Emily was suffocated.

"Mommy and Daddy said you are here to help us," said the voice of young Emily.

"Yes, I am," said Aaron.

"Thank you," she said.

Aaron dropped the tiny dress back into the crate.

Korie touched the side of Aaron's face with the back of her hand. She felt a trail of tears running down his cheek.

Meanwhile Miss Beacon had put the first crate back and returned with another.

This crate didn't have much inside of it. Miss Beacon pulled a couple of small things from the bottom and took Aaron's right hand. She opened his hand, palm up. She placed a couple of porcelain teeth and a badly bent pair of wire rim glasses in his hand.

This mental picture was as vivid as can be. The former owner of these items was a doctor from Burlington. He had died in a tragic campfire at a deer hunting camp, just about three quarters of a mile from the barn. He had unfortunately stumbled upon the clearing where the altar was located. He made the mistake of telling his hunting partners, one of whom was a member of the Church. He had died in 1957.

Next Miss Beacon placed two smaller and newer crates next to Aaron.

"How many of these does he have to experience?" asked a worried Korie.

"Just these last two."

Miss Beacon took the teeth and glasses from Aaron and returned them to their crate.

Now she pulled a plaid shirt from one crate, and a man's sleeveless T-shirt from the other. She handed these items to Aaron, who took them from her reluctantly.

In a flash he could sense Michael Delvecchio, and Julia Brodsky. He could sense their love for one another, their special bond. His mind was now propelled with fast moving images of torches in the night, an altar, a cemetery, love making and then the total panic Julia had experienced as she tried to escape. Aaron could see in his mind what she had seen just before she died. Aaron could see Samuel Porter standing in the clearing pointing his rifle directly at her. His mind now shifted to slow motion. Aaron could see Samuel lower his eyes to the rifle sights to take aim. He could vividly see his index finger pull on the rifle's trigger. Aaron could see the bullet leave the barrel of the rifle, on its way to the intended target. He next saw a flash from the gun barrel, and behind the flash he could plainly see Samuel smiling.

Suddenly Aaron felt a white-hot, searing pain in his throat passing through to the back of his head. The pain was savagely intense.

He clutched his throat.

Aaron was making gurgling sounds. He fell to his knees.

Korie immediately knelt down to help him.

"What's wrong with Aaron? Speak to me. Miss Beacon we've got to help him."

"He'll be fine. He's got to finish first."

Aaron could hear them speaking but he wasn't able to talk. His mind was now filled with the voices of Michael and Julia.

"Aaron, these people have to be stopped," said Michael.

"They watched us make love and then they killed us," said Julia to Aaron's mind.

"How many more will die, Aaron? Did you know there are over four hundred crates in this barn, and another one hundred and twenty in another barn behind the Game Warden's house?" said Michael.

"Women, children, old people, Aaron, we were all slaughtered like animals. If they are allowed to succeed just imagine what they will do?" said Julia.

Aaron was now getting his voice back, the pain in his neck and the back of his head began to subside.

"We're all sorry you had to experience this. But you had to know what you're up against. Our prayers go with you," said Julia as she and Michael faded from Aaron's mind.

Aaron stood up. His legs were a bit wobbly so he held onto Korie for stability.

Korie heard it first, and then Aaron and Miss Beacon heard it next. There was a chorus of voices, speaking as one hushed voice. The voices called out Aaron's name.

"Aaron Powell, go in God's name. Aaron Powell, go in God's name. Aaron Powell, God's warrior, go in God's name."

"It's time to leave. We still have to see the altar and the cemetery," said Miss Beacon.

24

"Where is he, Ed? You're our FBI man, our expert in detection and surveillance," demanded Samuel.

Ed could feel everyone looking at him.

"He's here in Sutton. I'm sure of it. I followed him to Sutton last night. I watched him get some gas at the station next to the highway exit," said Ed, in as calm a voice as he could muster.

"Where did he go after that, Ed?" said Samuel with a touch of sarcasm.

Ed began to feel uncomfortable. He didn't like being grilled like this in front of the other coven members, especially by young Samuel Porter.

"Ed, I asked you a question."

"Okay, okay! I don't know where he is at this exact moment. But..."

Interrupting him Samuel said, "Ed, you don't seem to appreciate the situation here. It is your job to know exactly where he is at all times. Now that we've located him we can't afford to let him slip through our fingers. Can we Ed?"

Who, in the fuck, does this little asshole think he is? thought Ed. *WE located him, WE, shit, I located him, not WE you little son of a bitch!*

"I will begin to search for him immediately after this meeting. I will find him. That's a promise," said Ed defiantly.

"No, Ed. You will go and look for him NOW!" insisted Samuel.

Ed pushed his chair back from the table and stood up. He noticed no one was willing to look at him now. Everyone's head was down, their eyes directed at the table in front of them. He headed for the door. He had to pass by Samuel on his way to the door. In a show of bravado, Ed made sure he walked as close as he could to Samuel, without touching him. Ed opened the door and stepped out into the hallway. As he pulled the door shut, he looked back into the room and noticed the Reverend had raised his head up. The two men's eyes met for a brief instant.

"Now that Ed's gone, we need to put our plan in motion to lure this Powell into joining the Church. Only after that, can we bring him into the coven. Once in the coven, we must waste no time. We will immediately, upon his initiation into the coven, begin the High Ceremony, to call forth Moloch into human form. Whose form he chooses is Moloch's to decide. It could be any one of us or some other. There can be no mistakes this time."

"And what is our plan if this Powell proves unwilling to join our church?" asked Reverend Mitchell.

"He will join. Why else would he have come here?" responded Samuel.

"I don't know why he's come here, but I think the Reverend is right. We need to consider the possibility, at least, that he can't be persuaded," said Josephine Lawless.

"We could threaten to hurt the woman he is traveling with," offered Chucky.

"Better yet, we kidnap her to ensure his complete cooperation," said Shirley.

"He must be put in a situation where his only choice is to cooperate," said Judge Fairchild.

"We don't need to resort to violence. That could scare him off. I tell you what, it would be my pleasure to seduce him," said Judy.

"And his too, I imagine," said Walter.

That remark brought about some light hearted laughter, which seemed to break the tension in the room. Even Samuel laughed a bit.

"Judy has made a good point," said Samuel.

Judy beamed with pride at Samuel's words. She sat up even straighter, pushing her breasts about as far forward as was humanly possible.

Everyone stopped their chuckling and looked in Samuel's direction.

"I believe that once we locate him, we should set Judy up with him. She can use her talents to learn more about this man. We need to know who is helping him besides the woman he is traveling with. There has to be others. She also might be able to learn if he has any weaknesses or special powers."

Several coven members snickered at the last remark. Samuel paused for them to settle down.

"Walter, I want you, Bob, and Chucky to go help Ed along. When Powell is found, I want you to come to me immediately, is that understood?"

"It sure is," said Walter.

Shirley and Phyllis acknowledged his order with a nod.

"I also need Ed Foley to go to the Church basement."

Speaking to Foley, Samuel continues, "We are holding my sister in the old root cellar. She tried to run away last night. I want you to check on her. Give her some food, drink, and drugs if you have to, you know, calm her down. She needs to be kept alive. She has been chosen to become a concubine for Lucifer upon his arrival. We can't have her dying on us."

"I'll do what I can," said Ed.

"Not good enough. You keep her alive, is that clear?" he said slapping the table for emphasis.

"Okay, I understand. Is that all?"

"Yeah, everyone can go now except for you, Judge and you, Reverend."

The other coven members got up from their seats and drifted out of the room. Samuel rose from his seat and turned his back on the Judge and the Reverend as he closed the door.

The Reverend took that moment to shoot a glance at the Judge, who then simply nodded his head.

"I don't want the others to hear this," said Samuel solemnly.

Neither man responded.

"I'm concerned about this coven. I have reason to believe there may be a traitor in our midst."

The Judge and the Reverend resisted the urge to look at one another. Neither was quite sure what to expect next.

"You two are our most senior members. I need your help. I know I have been rough on you Reverend. It's been difficult adjusting to my new responsibilities. However, let me get directly to the point. I need you two to keep an eye on the others for me. Anything suspicious, anything at all, I want you to bring it to me right away. This time our coven will not fail Moloch or Lucifer."

"Let me get this straight. It's your belief that a member of this coven is untrustworthy?" asked the Judge "and you want the two of us to spy on the others, to see if we can ferret out the traitor?"

"Yes!"

"And on what do you base your suspicions, may I ask?" inquired the Judge in a low voice.

Samuel looked the Judge straight in the eye, their eyes locked for a moment. The Reverend watched this exchange. His stomach was filled with a huge knot of absolute panic. He struggled to control himself.

"Moloch told me."

"I see," responded the Judge as he leaned back in his chair.

Samuel watched the Judge's every move. The Judge remained steely cool in his mannerisms.

"What do you think, Reverend?" asked the Judge.

"Yes, Reverend. What do you think?" echoed Samuel as he shifted his gaze over to the Reverend.

"Why I think Samuel's right. We can't be too careful," said the Reverend. He could feel perspiration running down his back.

"I'm glad you agree," said Samuel, "so I can count on the both of you?"

"Sure," said the Judge.

"You know you can count on me," blurted out the Reverend.

"That's what I was hoping for," answered Samuel. "Well, let's get going. We all have important work to do."

The two men stood up from the table and left the room.

Samuel finally stood up, went out the door, closing it behind him as he left the room.

***

Ed Foley pulled his car into the driveway of the Church. He drove down the driveway and parked his car in the back. He got out of the car carrying a small black bag. It was the sort of small bag family doctors used to carry with them when they made house calls. He went directly to the hatchway leading to the Church basement. He used his passkey to gain entry to the basement.

He opened the secret door leading to the hideaway room where Kelley was being held. He turned on the one light in this musty and dank room. There she was, hanging against the wall, held there by the rusty but true, forged steel manacles.

The room smelled of urine. Kelley had wet herself. There was no other choice.

There was a cluster of tiny gnat like flies buzzing in the dank air over the dirt floor she had soiled. Her head hung down, with her chin resting against her chest. Even in the dim light Ed could plainly see dozens of red welts covering every patch of her exposed skin.

Spiders, he thought.

"Kelley, it's just me, Ed Foley."

There was no reaction to his voice.

"Kelley, can you hear me?" he asked.

No reaction.

Ed moved in closer and touched her left arm, just above the rough edge of the manacle. Her skin felt cool and dry, like the feel of a potato that has been stored in a root cellar. He felt her neck to take her pulse. Her pulse was weak.

"Shit, this isn't such a good idea keeping her here like this," he said out loud.

Ed put his small bag down on the floor and opened it. He fumbled around for a moment before he found what he was looking for.

Ed removed a small bottle of medicine and a syringe in a cellophane plastic bag. He tore open the cellophane with his teeth. He put the medicine bottle, which was labeled epinephrine, in his left hand and gingerly removed the syringe with his right hand. He let the syringe wrapping fall to the ground. He stuck the syringe in the rubber cap of the medicine bottle. Turning both the bottle and the syringe upside down, he pulled on the needles' plunger and drew a dose of the medicine half way into the syringe.

Ed withdrew the needle from the medicine bottle. Bending over, he tossed the medicine bottle into the medical bag. He placed the syringe between his gingerly clasped teeth. Ed rummaged in the bag for a moment, and removed another small bottle with clear liquid contents. He also found a gauze package, and removed a piece of gauze. He stood up and poured some of the clear liquid onto the gauze. He recapped the bottle and tossed it back into the bag. Now he used the saturated piece of gauze to rub the liquid onto Kelley's right arm.

"I'm going to give you a shot to help you regain your strength. It's going to sting a little," he said, half thinking she was conscious enough to hear him.

He injected the small dose of epinephrine into her arm. He stood back and to watch her reaction. For a couple of minutes there was no perceptible reaction. Ed noticed her breathing was becoming more rapid. He could see her chest rise and fall, as she seemed to be trying to draw ever deeper breaths. Kelley began to moan. Her head rocked back and forth even though her chin still rested on her chest.

Suddenly, she lifted her head with such swiftness and force that she banged it against the stone wall behind her.

Her eyes were wide open in a strained sort of stare. Kelley's mouth was half-open and her nostrils were flared open as well.

"Kelley, it's me Ed Foley."

She jerked her head to the side to look at him. Kelley was struggling to hold her balance. Blood streaked down from her wrists and ankles because of the chaffing effect of the manacles.

"Unlock me!"

"I can't."

"I said, unlock me."

"You know I can't."

"You're nothing but one of my fucking brother's toadies."

"I'm a member of the coven," he said defensively.

"I can't wish you would all go to hell, because that's what you assholes want anyway," she said with clear anger in her voice.

"You shouldn't have tried to run away."

"Fuck you!"

Ed wanted to get this over with. She reminded him of his own daughter that he had treasured and raised with pride, ever since his wife had tried to run away back in 1981. As hard as it was, when called upon, he dismembered her body and disposed of it, after the coven had arranged for her demise with her own hand.

"I've brought you something to drink."

The mere mention of drink pierced her tough armor.

"You, you did?"

"I know it's not much. Here it is," he said after removing it from his medicine bag. He held up a bottle of an orange colored sport drink.

He uncapped it and held it to her swollen lips, as she gulped down a couple of swallows.

"Easy now. The first couple of swallows are going to hurt a little. Just go slow, okay? That's better. Good."

In a moment the bottle was empty. He put it back in his bag, and zipped the bag closed.

"Ed, please let me out of here. I promise I won't try and run away. I swear," she pleaded.

"I'm sorry. I can't do such a thing. It's in Samuel's hands. Maybe I'll check in on you later."

"How much longer am I supposed to be held here like this?" she said with her anger beginning to rise again.

"I don't know. Listen, just don't move around too much. Save your energy as much as you can," said Ed as he reached for the light switch.

"But Ed," said Kelley as the light went out "What about the spiders?"

He didn't answer her.

***

Ed Townsend sat in his car, which was parked outside the Jolley Roger Motel. It was one of over three dozen hotels, motels and bed and breakfast inns that he would visit today. They were scattered all over the valley. In the winter, during ski season, or during the fall foliage period, they would be booked solid. In the summer, it was different, slower and much, much less subscribed. Still, checking them all would take the better part of the day. He had sent the others Samuel had assigned to him on other duties. He directed them to check out the stores and restaurants in the area. Split up, they all could cover the valley before the day would be over. Ed was confident someone would turn up who had seen Powell and the woman.

He slammed his open palms on the car steering wheel as his temper exploded.

"That little son of a bitch. Damn!"

Ed was struggling to control his anger. His FBI training had taught him to control his emotions. Uncontrolled emotions in a FBI agent were not tolerated. Such displays would assuredly lead one to washing out of the Bureau.

He knew of his own lifelong loyalty to the coven. He recalled his many sacrifices, the countless risks taken, and his single mindedness of purpose in hunting down the Powell family over the years. He never asked for any accolades. He never sought any special treatment. All he expected was a little respect.

"Damn," he said as his current burst of anger was subsiding. Future eruptions were inevitable, but for now he had regained control.

He got out of his car and walked slowly up to the front door of the motel office. Ed pulled open the aluminum door and stepped into the air conditioned office. Sitting behind the small counter was Connie Gibbey. She was a very large woman who wore muumuus almost year around. She was wearing one today. It was lime green. She wore a matching lime green scrunchy in her hair. She had three chins. She was fanning herself with a small bamboo fan. Each finger on her hands was adorned with a gold colored ring. She also wore too much makeup and too much perfume. Today was no exception. Her attention was focused upon a small color television sitting on the end of the counter.

As the aluminum door hissed closed behind Ed, Connie turned her gaze away from the television just long enough to notice who had entered her office.

The room was cooled by a large window air conditioner. It was set on high. The temperature in the room was probably down to sixty-five degrees.

"Bitching hot, eh Ed?"

"Yeah, bitching," answered Ed.

Connie Gibbey was not a member of the Church of Everlasting Faith. Indeed she wasn't a member of any church.

"What you up to these days, Ed?"

"Not much Connie, you know a little of this and a little of that."

Connie chuckled at something she noticed on the television.

"Jerry's my man," she said.

"Say, Connie I'm sort of in a hurry. I've picked up a little private investigative job, you know, for an insurance company."

"Ed Townsend, dick for hire, heh heh heh…" as she launched herself into a hearty laugh at his expense.

She shook with laughter.

Ed was not amused.

"You sure are something, Connie. Listen, I'm looking for a fellow I think is staying somewhere in the area. His name is Powell, that's Aaron Powell and he is traveling with a young woman, last name of Cotalano."

"Check the register yourself," said Connie as she put the register binder on the counter.

He looked at the motel's register. The last entry was over a week ago, a man who stayed just one night. Probably a salesman just passing through. He also might have been scared off by one of Connie's amorous moods. She had been known to talk her way into a guest's room with a bottle of tequila in hand. Once inside, she would work to get the man drunk. Then she would force him onto the bed and have her way with him.

Ed folded the register closed and left it on the counter.

"Thanks, Connie," said Ed as he turned to leave.

"Say, Ed, what's your hurry? I could fix up a tequila sunrise. It would take the sting out of this heat wave."

"No thanks, I've got to go."

She watched the backside of his pants as he stepped through the doorway.

The aluminum door hissed closed behind him.

Ed felt a wash of heat and humidity once he stepped outside. The contrast between the cool air inside the motel office and outside was dramatic. Ed also had felt the predatory stare of Connie on his backside.

In his thoughts, he vowed, *when Moloch and the coven take over the world, he would personally come back and gut the bitch.*

He climbed back into his car and drove it around to the side of the long row of bungalows, which formed this low budget motel. He was looking for any sign of a car being hidden in the back.

He noticed nothing but Connie's beat up Dodge Caravan.

Ed pulled his car around and headed down the road to the next motel.

***

After putting the old wooden fruit baskets back where she had taken them, Miss Beacon motioned to Aaron and Korie to follow. They carefully walked out of the barn. Miss Beacon reattached the door lock.

With Miss Beacon leading the way, the three of them headed off toward the altar.

They moved slowly, stopping frequently to check for signs of anyone else being in the area.

After a few minutes, they stood on the edge of a large clearing. They were on the upper hillside to the altar. From where they stood they could plainly see the stone altar. All three of them searched the nearby woods for any sign of someone who might be lurking in the darkness, perhaps someone with a gun.

Satisfied that it appeared safe, Miss Beacon turned to Korie and Aaron and said, "We can't take too long here. We don't want to be out in the open for too long."

They both nodded their agreement.

"Okay, let's make a run for it," said Miss Beacon as she headed towards the altar in a sort of half jog.

Aaron and Korie ran faster and soon passed her. They arrived at the altar, stopping short by a good two paces.

Aaron looked at its rough surface. Korie knelt down and looked beneath it. In a moment Miss Beacon joined them as she stood to Aaron's left.

Aaron's eyes noticed dark brown stains on the altar's surface. Immediately, his mind attributed these stains to human blood. He held out his hands as if he was pushing against something. Aaron saw that the stains had turned to fresh puddles of blood. These puddles began to grow until they eventually began to drip from the altar onto the ground below.

Korie wasn't seeing any of what Aaron was seeing, however, her senses were on high alert. The altar almost felt alive to her. The air around it felt cold, like the chill one might feel in a butcher's meat locker. Korie began to rub her chilled arms.

Miss Beacon watched the two of them out of the corner of her eye. She kept glancing around in search of any possible threat.

"This is where dozens of people have been slaughtered in the name of Moloch. Yes, I am sure it's a devil with the name of Moloch," said Aaron.

"That's the name he uses," added Miss Beacon.

"Aaron, I don't feel right. This place scares me. Can we go?" asked Korie.

Aaron looked deeper into the stone surface of the altar. In a large puddle of blood his mind's eye was still seeing, he began to see the face of Moloch forming in the blood. The face rose up out of the blood puddle. Even Moloch's horns were plainly visible. The face began to speak to him.

"Aaron, welcome home," said the small face of Moloch.

"No, never, you bastard," answered Aaron.

"What is it?" asked Korie.

Without waiting for a response Miss Beacon pulled on Aaron's arm to take him away from the altar.

Korie joined in and pulled Aaron's other arm. He struggled against their combined efforts.

After a brief struggle, they managed to pull him several feet away from the altar. This seemed to have a calming effect on him.

Dropping his head, Aaron responded to them.

"Thanks," he said.

"Let's go to the cemetery now, and then we can leave," said Miss Beacon as she tried to hurry them along.

Korie was plainly worried for Aaron. So much was happening so quickly. He was already hurting from the discovery that his late aunt was really his mother, and now all this.

Will he be strong enough? she thought.

They arrived at a wrought iron gate to the cemetery. There were several small, obviously aged headstones sticking out of the ground. Aaron walked over to the first headstone. He knelt down on the grass in front of the tombstone.

The inscription read, "Here lies Jacob Powell, Husband and Father. His Love Of Family Was Only Exceeded By His Love Of God, May He Rest In Peace, Born, June 2, 1801, Died, October 31, 1843."

"How did all these headstones get placed here?" asked Korie in a whisper.

"In 1910, Colleen Powell sent two hired men to Sutton. They were instructed to come here, and set these headstones and install this fence. They announced their plans in town and even hired a couple local men to help. The coven members, back then, decided to let them carry out their plan. They hoped if a Powell wanted so desperately to honor their ancestors, maybe they might slip up and reveal their whereabouts. When the work was done, the men hired by Colleen Powell headed back into town and made a sizeable deposit in the local bank, leaving instructions it was to be used for the care and upkeep of this place. The night before the men were expected to leave town, the coven members planned a little party for them. Only when they went to grab them, they couldn't find them. They had up and disappeared. Not a trace," said Miss Beacon as she smiled.

Aaron had made his way through the cemetery, and was now kneeling before the tombstone of Sarah Powell. Miss Beacon and Korie walked over to Aaron and stood behind him.

The headstone's inscription read "Sarah Powell, Mother and Wife. God's Child, Her Life Served His Will. Born, September 11, 1806, Died October 31, 1843."

A tear trickled down Aaron's right cheek.

"I'm here now. I understand. I will do my best. I won't let you down. I love you," he said as he leaned forward and kissed the cold stone.

Aaron stood up and reached out to Korie, who took him into her arms. They stood there for a moment holding each other tightly.

"Where's Miss Beacon?" asked Aaron.

Korie pushed Aaron back. She looked to her left, and then to her right. Next, she spun completely around.

"She was right here. She was standing right next to us just a moment ago," said Korie.

"Well, she's probably waiting for us near the edge of the clearing. We'd better get going," said Aaron.

The two left the cemetery holding hands. Aaron closed and latched the gate. They headed back towards the clearing.

Suddenly, Korie put her hand up to Aaron, signaling to him to stop and listen.

There were voices up ahead.

One of the voices was clearly Miss Beacon's.

"I don't know what you think you're doing young man, but you had better put that gun down. Do you hear me?" demanded Miss Beacon in a loud voice.

Korie and Aaron crept closer to the edge of the woods, and could plainly see what was taking place in the middle of the clearing. There was a young man, no more than thirteen years old, pointing a rifle at Miss Beacon. The two were standing approximately twenty feet apart.

"I can't. Now just shut up, will ya? I know who you are and you're an interloper. I've been told to keep an eye out for your kind."

"I don't know what you are talking about. When I speak to your mother and father, I'm sure they will severely punish you for this little episode."

He laughed.

"You don't get it, do you? I'm going to kill you. I'm going to become famous like Samuel."

While the two were at a standoff, Aaron led Korie along the edge of the woods. He wanted to get as close to the backside of the young boy as possible.

"Kill me, oh dear. Why kill me? What have I done?" she pleaded, as she began to cry.

"Just shut up."

Miss Beacon put her hands to her face and began to sob heavily.

"Damn you," he said as he cocked the gun. It made an audible *click* as the hammer was poised to slam into the loaded chamber of his 30-30 caliber rifle.

Aaron quickly looked around for a weapon of some kind. Korie handed him a piece of hardwood that was lying at her feet. It was about four feet long. The diameter was similar to the thick end of a baseball bat.

Seizing the piece of wood, Aaron broke from cover and sprinted the forty feet through the worn grass towards the backside of the young boy. He raised the piece of wood and swung it with all of his might.

Just an instant before the wood hit the side of his head; the young boy sensed someone or something behind him coming in his direction. In that briefest of moments, he began to turn his head, but in doing so his finger jerked against the gun's hair trigger and the gun went off.

The piece of wood wielded by Aaron struck the boy's head with such force that it broke in two. The boy's head rocked violently to the left from the force of the hit. Blood exploded from the side of his face as his now lifeless body collapsed to the ground. The rifle, which had just discharged fell away.

Korie ran from the woods into the clearing.

Miss Beacon was lying on the ground.

25

Ed Townsend met up with Walter, Ed Foley and Chucky at the Town Common. The others had parked their cars in the shade of a hundred year old maple tree that stood at one end of the park. There was a soft breeze passing through the Common, which took the edge off the high humidity.

This summer heat wave had lasted longer than anyone could remember. Local meteorologists were blaming it on the lingering effects of last winter's El Nino. A cold front, descending from Canada in the nearby north, was expected to pass through the area later in the day. Severe thunderstorms were predicted and would be welcomed by most, since it would signal the end to this heat wave. Several days of clear, dry and cooler weather was expected to follow.

Ed stepped out of his car and strolled slowly over to the park bench that Ed Foley and Chuck Trainor were lounging on. Walter was standing near the end of the bench, with one foot up on the bench. He was leaning over with his arms folded, and resting on his knee. The guy's saw Ed Townsend coming. No one made a move to acknowledge his arrival. These guys tolerated Ed Townsend, but none of them considered him a friend.

"Walter, Ed, Chuck, any luck?" asked Ed.

"Do we look like we have anything to report?" responded Walter, as he flicked away a tiny piece of tree bark that had fallen on his knee.

Pulling his soiled baseball cap off, Chuck Trainor ran his fingers through his sweat soaked hair.

"We looked everywhere," said Chuck.

"Looks like you didn't do any better," said Walter.

"I'm not done yet. I still have a couple of motels on the north end to check out," said Ed.

"It don't look good, Ed. What are we gonna do now?" asked Ed Foley as he stood up from the bench and stretched his lower back.

"We look again is what we do. If the two of them are moving around, we might have just missed them," answered Ed.

"Say, Ed, maybe they're camping out somewhere. There are plenty of empty deer camps they could be hiding in," said Walter.

"You're right," said Ed. "Walter, I want you to round up a dozen or so church members. Send them out to all the campsites we know of. Tell them to be real careful not to spook Powell, and the woman. All we want is to locate them for now."

Chuck spoke up and said, "What about us?"

"You guys keep checking stores, restaurants, businesses, that sort of thing. We'll meet back here at 5 o'clock. Let's go."

Walter took off immediately. His new assignment invigorated him. Ed Foley and Chucky were less enthusiastic.

"Samuel sure ripped into you this morning. It must have pissed you off," said Trainor.

Ed Townsend refused to react. Instead, he turned away, and headed to his car.

Deep inside, Ed Townsend was seething with anger. He climbed into his car and drove away at a normal speed. The only sign of a reaction was his hands, which were gripping his steering wheel with such force, his knuckles were turning white.

"Why did you go and say that for? Are you trying to start something?" demanded Ed Foley.

"I was just trying to get a rise out of him. You know how he's such a tight ass, never showing any emotion."

"Yeah, well I don't particularly care for him myself, but that don't give us the right to insult the man. Without him, I don't think we'd be as close as we are to Powell."

"Shit Ed, you're becoming a tight ass, too," said Chuck as he strolled towards his car.

"You'd better not cross him Chuck, that's all I'm saying."

"Yeah, yeah, I hear you."

The two coven members each drove away in their respective vehicles. Neither had any expectations they would catch the proverbial brass ring, and find Powell. Nevertheless, they dutifully resumed their search.

***

The smell of spent gunpowder lingered in the air.

Korie ran up to Aaron. She turned him away from the sight of the dead boy and Miss Beacon. Aaron dropped the piece of blood stained wood he had been holding. Korie held him tightly. Her eyes were welling up with tears, but she held them back. She wanted to be strong for Aaron.

Aaron was surprised by his own reaction. He felt neither remorse nor guilt. He was busily taking inventory of his senses.

"Well, are either of you going to help me up?" asked Miss Beacon.

Aaron and Korie both turned and looked at Miss Beacon who was now sitting up.

The look on their faces clearly conveyed their shock. Both had assumed that the boy had killed her.

"You're okay?" said an excited Korie.

"Of course," said Miss Beacon as she reached up for a hand from Korie and Aaron. They each took a hand and pulled her to her feet. She brushed off her dress.

"I can't believe he missed," said Aaron.

"Well, he put a nice hole in my dress. Will that do?" answered Miss Beacon.

She pointed to a hole that was located about five inches down from her left shoulder. Korie stepped to the side and looked at the back of Miss Beacon's dress, and there was another hole located about three inches from the top of her left shoulder. There was no sign of blood anywhere.

"But that hole, there's...no blood," said Korie.

"I'm an Angel, or have you forgotten?"

"Amazing," said Korie.

"We can't stand here all day discussing this. We've got to go," said Miss Beacon.

"But what about the boy's body?" asked Aaron.

"What do you want to do with it?" asked Miss Beacon as she furrowed her eyebrows.

"I'm not sure, I uh...I want."

"What?" asked Korie

Suddenly, without warning, Aaron bent down and picked up the limp body of the dead boy. Carrying him, Aaron headed towards the altar. He placed the boy on the altar, and then ran back to where the two women stood. He picked up the pieces of wood that had once been his weapon of necessity, and raced back to the altar. Korie and Miss Beacon followed him to the altar.

Aaron used the two pieces of wood to form a crude cross, which he placed across the boy's chest. Aaron folded the boy's arms over the cross shape.

"Interesting," said Miss Beacon.

"We can go now," said Aaron.

At that very moment, a loud crackling sound was heard at the same instant a bright blinding flash was seen directly across the clearing. It was a bolt of lightning. It had struck a tree next to the cemetery. The top half of the tree exploded. Directly overhead, a solo, dark, menacing summer storm cloud hovered less than five hundred feet over the mountain top. An earth-shaking rumble of thunder pounded the ground.

All three took off and raced back to the Land Rover. A heavy stinging rain started to fall soon after the initial lightning strike. They were drenched to the skin by the time they reached the Land Rover.

They climbed inside of the vehicle and Miss Beacon wasted no time starting the engine.

"Aaron." said Miss Beacon.

"Yes."

"Killing that boy back there was righteous. I want you to know that."

"Thanks."

Korie was still somewhat out of breath, when she asked "Why did you put the boy on that altar like that?"

"Because I want them to know I was there," said Aaron.

"Oh, they know Aaron, believe me they know," said Miss Beacon, as she put the Rover in gear and began to inch her way back down the mountain.

The ride down the mountain was bumpy and dangerous. Miss Beacon seemed bent on taking the most direct route possible, regardless of how dense the forest, or how steep the slope. Several times it seemed the vehicle would tip over while Miss Beacon fought with the steering wheel to keep the Land Rover upright. Finally, they drove through some thick brush and into a small clearing. They were next to a small abandoned orchard. Zigging and zagging, Miss Beacon managed to drive through the orchard, and at the opposite end she located a dirt road. Moments later, they were back on a paved road heading to Miss Beacon's place.

"I think you ought to climb back under that blanket back there. We don't want you discovered quite yet," said Miss Beacon.

Aaron and Korie did as she requested. It was stifling hot under the blanket. The windows were rolled down, which did allow some movement of air, tempering the oppressive heat.

Miss Beacon pulled the Land Rover into her driveway. She wheeled it around back, hitting the brakes a bit hard as the vehicle lurched to a stop.

"Stay down. Someone's coming. Don't move a muscle," commanded Miss Beacon.

Aaron and Korie heard the front seat creak as Miss Beacon climbed out. The next sound they heard was the slamming of the driver's side door.

There was a pause, and then they heard the crunching sound of another vehicle's tires rolling in their direction. That vehicle came to a stop and the driver turned off the car engine. A car door opened and closed.

"Good afternoon, Miss Beacon," said an obviously male voice.

"Well if it isn't Ed 'Mr. FBI' Townsend," said Miss Beacon with a slight chuckle in her voice.

"It sure is a hot one," said Ed.

"Now that is stating the obvious."

"Yeah, I guess you're right."

"So, what brings you to Mother Nature's? It sure can't be for small talk about the weather."

"No, no, you're right. Let me get right to it. I'm doing a little job for an insurance company trying to track down a fella they think is in the area. I was wondering, have you had any overnight guests in the past couple of days?"

"Now Ed, you know what it is like this time of year around here. My last overnighter was, let me think...oh...it must have been close to Memorial Day weekend."

"I see. Well, maybe someone might have stopped in to your store or stopped to ask for directions. This fellow is also traveling with a young woman; I believe they're from Massachusetts."

"What do they look like? Do you have a photo or something I could look at?'

"No. . . I don't have a photo, but I can give you a general description."

While Ed provided a description, Aaron and Korie were struggling with the challenge of remaining still and quiet in the rear of the Land Rover. Now that the Rover wasn't moving, there was no fresh air swirling around inside. The Rover was parked in the sun, and even with the windows down, the heat was rapidly building up inside. Under the blanket it was worse. The musty smell of the blanket was almost overpowering. Beads of sweat rolled across every inch of their cramping bodies.

"Well, from what you describe, I can safely say that I don't believe I've seen anyone fitting that description."

"Really," said Ed with a touch of disbelief in his voice. He was looking down at the tires of Miss Beacon's vehicle, and the heavily soiled wheel well. Clumps of grass and a thick crust of dirt covered the lower half of her vehicle.

"Been out driving in the woods, have we?" asked Ed.

"Why, Ed, you are the inquisitive one. As a matter of fact I have. I drove up to my secret blackberry patch to pick a few quarts. I'm going to make some of my very special preserves with them. My winter guests really like having homemade preserves at their breakfast table. I even sell some on the side. You know, a little extra always comes in handy."

"Yeah, I understand," said Ed who still seemed curious about the soiled condition of her Rover.

"Would you be so kind as to give me a hand with the berries? I might manage to find a jar of last year's preserves for you."

"Sure."

Underneath the blanket, Aaron and Korie wondered what she was up to. Neither had seen any berries in the back of the vehicle. They both kept perfectly still as they heard the opening sound of the rear door latch. They were now drenched in sweat.

"Here they are. Now you take that large basket right there. Yes, that one. I'll take these two smaller ones. Good."

Somehow he didn't notice the two shapes beneath the old blanket.

Aaron and Korie felt the rear door slam shut and heard the sound of feet walking down the gravel driveway.

"What do we do now?" asked Korie.

"Where did those berries come from?" asked Aaron.

"Who cares? I'm about to pass out from heat exhaustion here."

"Okay. Wait a second," said Aaron as he slowly pulled the blanket off his head. He carefully raised his head up and looked out the side window. He could see the back door to Miss Beacon's store swing close.

"Can't we get out of here while she has him distracted?" pleaded Korie.

"I don't know. Maybe we shouldn't take a chance. Oh, shit, they're coming back," said Aaron as he ducked down under the blanket.

"Thanks again for the preserves."

"Don't mention it."

"Listen, if you . . ."

"I know, if I see these two young people I'm to give you a call."

"That's right!"

"Oh, I'll be sure to let you know. I can tell you're anxious to locate these people. I have a feeling they'll turn up before you know it. After all, Sutton is a small town."

"Small towns still have plenty of hiding places."

"And I bet that 'Mr. FBI' knows where all the hiding places are in Sutton."

"Maybe I do," said Ed with a slight smirk.

He climbed back into his car and started it up. He put it in gear. He watched Miss Beacon give him a wave, which he politely returned. She turned and started for the backdoor of her store. With that, Ed backed his car up and left Mother Nature's.

Aaron and Korie both received a loud mental message from Miss Beacon.

Stay where you are and don't try peaking out the window, said the voice of Miss Beacon inside their heads.

They did as they were told.

Ed turned out onto the highway and slowly drove away.

Now I know where they are, thought Ed.

Several minutes passed before the driver's side door opened to the Land Rover.

"Relax, it's just me. I'm going to pull closer to the building. I'll tell you when you can get up."

She pulled the land Rover forward and then turned a half circle before it came to a stop in the shadow of the store.

"Okay, you can come out now," said Miss Beacon.

Without waiting for another signal Aaron and Korie threw off the blanket. Their clothes clung to their bodies from the heavy perspiration.

Korie wiped her face with the back of her right hand.

"Do you think you fooled him?" asked Korie.

"Not for one instant," was her reply.

"Then why didn't he say or do something?" asked Aaron.

"Because now is not the time."

"What do we do now?" asked Aaron.

"You two can take a shower upstairs. I'll make some ice tea. Then Aaron, I want you to finish reading the last twenty or so pages of your family diary."

Aaron and Korie climbed out of the Land Rover. After a brief stretch they went up the back steps heading inside to the coolness of Mother Nature's store.

"Miss Beacon, I don't remember seeing any blackberries in the back of the Rover. Where did they come from?" asked Korie.

"I'm an angel, remember?"

***

Ed Townsend delivered the news in person.

Samuel's reaction was quite restrained.

Ed leaned against his car and waited for Samuel to move to the question, what now?

"Ed, I want you to go and pick up Judy for me and bring her here."

"Anything else?"

"Yes. Can you get a message to either Bob or Walter?"

"Bob's in town searching stores. I sent Walter up in the mountains to search hunting camps. I can reach them both with the portable radios I gave them. What do you have in mind?"

"Have Bob set up near Mother Nature's to keep an eye on the place. I want to know the minute anyone comes or goes."

"No problem. I'll get right on it. I'll be back in a few minutes with Judy."

Ed climbed back into his car and quickly pulled away leaving Samuel standing alone on the sidewalk in front of his house.

***

Judge Fairchild and Reverend Mitchell were as yet unaware of Ed Townsend having pinpointed the whereabouts of the Powell descendant. After leaving the meeting earlier in the day, they moved to the Reverend's office to discuss their plans.

"You know, Arthur, I feel certain Ed Townsend would come over to our side."

"I'm not quite as confident as you. I know Ed has had to put up with Samuel's overbearing and insulting behavior, but that is a far cry from choosing to turn against him."

I agree, but I am convinced the look he gave me before he closed the door at this morning's meeting was meant to convey something. Perhaps it was meant to . . ."

The conversation between the Judge and the Reverend continued.

***

Meanwhile Ed had picked up Judy and was taking her back to see Samuel. She had been dressed and waiting at the door. She was wearing a hot pink spandex t-top with matching hot pink spandex tights. She also had on white ankle socks and brand new Reebok cross trainer shoes with pink shoe laces. Her hair was pulled into a ponytail held tight by a pink and white scrunchy.

She had applied a liberal amount of perfume and her makeup was just perfect.

"Damn Judy, you overdid it with that perfume," said Ed as he rolled his window down.

"Stop complaining. I know what I'm doing."

"Haven't you thought that the man might have allergies or just doesn't like strong perfume?"

"Honey, it's all part of the package," she said as she pushed her breasts upward so there was now additional cleavage showing at the top of her spandex t-top.

Ed pulled the car over to the curb in front of Samuel's house. He was about to blow the horn when Samuel came running out of his house and up to the car. He gestured for the two to stay in the car.

Judy rolled down her window. Ed kept the car running.

Samuel looked Judy over and nodded his approval.

"Judy, you're going to get your chance just like you asked this morning."

"Good. I'm ready."

"Ed, take her over to Bob and leave her with him. Judy you can make your move anytime, the sooner the better of course. Remember Judy, we need information and we need Powell to join our coven, nothing more."

"You can count on me, Samuel," she said with her usual sultry smirk.

"All right, we're off," said Ed as he put the car in gear.

Samuel watched as Ed and Judy left. He had much to do and little time to do it in. He would call the others. He would notify Shirley and Phyllis to be ready to approach the woman traveling with Powell. After putting things in motion he would call to Moloch and share the news with him.

Samuel knew things were going smoothly now, but he knew he would have to be on his guard. Moloch was counting on him and Samuel wasn't about to let him down. This coven had waited for over 160 years, and had been once so very close to completing that first critical step towards Armageddon. Samuel felt this would be their last, best chance. Even though Samuel was only fourteen, he had been imbued with extensive knowledge of Satan's long struggle. He was well aware of his fate, and the fate of the others should they fail. Satan was patient but unforgiving.

Twenty-three covens since the beginning of human history have tried and failed to complete the fateful ceremony. Their failure left their souls suffering and tormented in Hell. They were abandoned by God, and were now despised by Lucifer. Each individual coven member was consigned to suffer one human pain, to the extreme, for all of time.

***

Ed pulled up behind Bob's tow truck. Judy and Ed got out of Ed's car. They approached the tow truck on the passenger side. The truck shielded them from view by anyone in Mother Nature's.

Ed opened the passenger side door of Bob's truck for Judy, who hopped up inside the cab.

"Any sign of him?" asked Ed.

"Nope. I've only been here a few minutes though. I've been checking the place out with these," he said tapping a pair of binoculars sitting on the dash.

"Good. Listen I've got some work to do so I'm going to leave you two for now. I wouldn't try to get any closer than you already are Bob, okay?"

"Sure."

Ed closed the truck door and headed back to his car. Bob had parked the truck about four hundred feet to the north of Mother Nature's. Ed backed his car up just a bit and then did a U-turn in the street and headed back into town. He was heading over to Reverend Mitchell's place. He had a hunch he wanted to follow up on and now was the perfect time.

***

Inside Mother Nature's Aaron was sitting in his room on the bed, reading the last twenty pages of his family's diary while Korie showered.

His mother had written all of the last twenty pages. She wrote of close encounters with coven members pursuing her. She wrote about car chases, tapped phone lines, and opened mail. She wrote about elaborate disguises and constant moving. She also wrote about her fears for her son, who doesn't even know she is his mother.

In the last couple of pages Aaron read about her hopes for him. She is clearly expecting Aaron to be the one Powell who will ultimately face the coven straight on.

It will be my Aaron, who will be called on to do battle with Moloch. Of this I am now certain. Oh, how I wish I could be the one, and take his place. I can only pray he will be graced with all the powers of our family. Dear God, grant him the power of second sight, so that he can truly see evil in all of its forms. Grant him the four powers of earth, wind, water and fire. Oh merciful God, please bestow on Aaron the power to heal. Also, extend to him the great power to condemn. I beseech you Lord, to protect him until he is called upon to do battle. May his Guardian Angel be ever vigilant.

These prayerful words seemed to hang in the air for Aaron. He closed the diary and set it on the bed.

At that moment Aaron sensed the need to look outside. He rose from the bed and headed over to the window. Parting the curtain only slightly, he looked outside. Nothing unusual stood out to him. Then his eyes closed in on the truck, as if he were looking out the window with a high powered telescope. He could plainly see two people sitting in the truck. The driver, a man, was looking at Mother Nature's with a pair of binoculars. The other person was a woman who was busy applying some lipstick.

Aaron let the curtain gently fall back into place.

Without knowing how, he knew they were coven members sent to watch the place.

The sound of the shower stopped. Aaron picked up the diary and placed it in the bottom drawer of the dresser. He felt strange.

Aaron turned to look at himself in the dresser mirror. He didn't notice anything unusual, yet the feeling was unmistakable.

"Your turn honey," said Korie as she padded into the room.

He stepped closer and pulled her to him. He kissed her hard. She winced a bit at first but soon succumbed to his passion. The touch of his lips felt as if they were on fire.

After a breathless moment, their lips parted and Korie said "Wow, that was some kiss. So what do you have in mind now, big fella?"

"I just had to kiss you," he said with a playful wink.

He pulled away from her and headed into the bathroom to take his own shower.

Downstairs, Miss Beacon had also looked out her own window and noticed the truck parked down the street. The coven was wasting no time. They undoubtedly had a plan to contact Aaron, and try to lure him into the coven of his own free will. That would make everything easier. Failing that, she knew the coven would willingly resort to force. They were not going to let this Powell slip away.

She had told Aaron to read the rest of his family's diary. What he didn't know, was that the last words were the most powerful of all. These words, when read by Aaron would complete a transfer of all of the powers each of his ancestors had at one time possessed, and were now conferred upon Aaron. He would need these gifts to be able to meet the challenges that lay ahead.

She heard the shower starting up for the second time.

***

Ed Townsend knocked on the door yet again. After a moment the door opened just a crack and one human eye looked through this crack at Ed. Suddenly the door swung wide open. In the foyer stood Reverend Mitchell. He was grinning from ear to ear. He seemed excited to see Ed.

"May I come in?"

"Why of course," said the Reverend.

"The Judge and I were just conferring on the current situation with our Powell. He's in my study. Would you care to join us?"

"Interesting choice of words, Reverend."

The Reverend was knocked off guard by Ed's mocking of his invitation. He suddenly felt uneasy.

Ed walked past the Reverend and headed straight to the study. The Reverend followed closely behind.

"Could I get you something to drink? Ice tea perhaps?"

"That would be perfect, thanks."

"Judge, it's good to see you," said Ed as he boldly strolled over to the Judge who had not risen with Ed's arrival. The two men shook hands.

In a moment, the Reverend arrived with a tall glass of ice tea. He handed it to Ed and then he too sat down. Ed took a long swallow. The judge and the Reverend exchanged sideways glances.

"Ah, that's good. A real thirst quencher."

"So, do you have any news about our Powell?" asked the Reverend.

"Indeed, I do."

The Judge sat forward in his chair and said "Tell us, is he still here in Sutton?"

"Oh, yeah. He's staying over at Mother Nature's Bed and Breakfast. Bob Senecal is keeping an eye on the place for us."

"Does Samuel know?"

"Oh, he knows, all right. He had me pick up Judy and run her over there to sit with Bob. She dressed up like a teenybopper and we all know how far she is from one of those. She's wearing a pink spandex two piece suit the color of penny bubble gum."

"I see. So Judy gets to play vixen for this Powell. Think he'll go for it?" asked the Judge.

Ed took another drink of his ice tea, finishing the rest.

"We'll have to wait and see. It's Samuel's plan. I just take my orders."

The three men looked at each other wearily.

"I see," said the Reverend.

"And what do you think about this plan?" asked the Judge. He studied Ed closely. It was an opening gambit.

Ed sat back in his chair and closed his eyes for a moment.

He then sat back up and looked at both men, as he cleared his throat.

"Maybe it will work, maybe it won't. My guess is that it won't work."

"Then what?" asked the Judge.

"Okay, look. Let me put my cards on the table here. I believe you two might be forming a backup plan. Am I right?"

"What do you mean?" asked the Reverend in mild protest.

"Look, Reverend. This is not the time to bullshit me. Look me straight in the eye and tell me you're not planning something," said Ed.

"Ed, surely you understand . . ." said the Reverend.

"Okay, you two, I'm out of here," said Ed rising from his chair.

"Sit down, Ed," said the Judge.

"Why should I?"

"Because we need your help," said the Judge.

"And what sort of help do you have in mind?"

"If I may quote you, let me put the cards on the table. The good Reverend and I believe Samuel is being swayed by Moloch to not help pave the way for the Great Dark One. Rather, we believe Moloch, at the least, is deceiving Samuel, or at the worst, Samuel is in league with Moloch. In short, Moloch may be using us all to serve his own ends."

"That's fucking incredible," said Ed.

"We think so," said the Reverend.

***

Bob Senecal looked over at Judy in her pink spandex outfit.

"Damn, Judy, aren't you overdoing it a bit?"

"Now Bob, don't give me any shit. Samuel approved of this personally and I just know that he would be pissed if anyone tried to bail out on him. So you just watch yourself."

Bitch, thought Bob.

Judy reached over and turned the air conditioner fan up another notch.

"I'll sure be glad when that cold front comes through later today," said Judy.

Bob Senecal passed on the chance to continue making small talk with Judy.

***

Korie and Aaron came downstairs and entered the air conditioned kitchen.

Miss Beacon was standing at the window looking through the parted curtains.

"Are you checking out that truck down the street?" asked Aaron.

"What truck?" asked Korie.

Turning from the window, Miss Beacon said, "It's Bob Senecal's tow truck that's parked down the street. He's a member of the coven. This means the coven has concluded that you're here. He's been assigned to watch us and to report on our movements."

"He's not alone," said Aaron.

"I know," said Miss Beacon.

"Know what? Will somebody tell me what's going on?" demanded an exasperated Korie.

"Aaron, they are probably going to try and make contact with you directly. They will also try and make contact with you too, Korie."

"What about you?" asked Korie. "Do you think they know about you?"

"I don't think so, but time will tell."

"So what do we do?" asked Aaron.

26

Walter pulled his Jeep to a stop. He put the emergency brake on. He had a hunch he wanted to check out.

Walter walked over to the barn and checked the lock. It was engaged and showed no visible signs of tampering. He walked around the barn perimeter. There were no outward signs of anyone having been snooping around. He stood at the southeast corner of the barn and scratched his head. He was missing something, he was sure of it. He refocused his eyes and surveyed the perimeter again, this time at a greater distance.

There it was. He had missed it the first time around because he was looking only around the immediate perimeter. Now that he had searched the grass and woods around a hundred feet away from the barn, he had discovered a trail. More specifically, three trails of recently tramped down wet grass were evident, where at least three people had passed, heading away from the nearby barn. Now he returned to the barn and using a key that was among several chained to his belt, he unlocked the barn door.

He swung the door wide open. Stepping inside, he quickly surveyed the interior. Nothing seemed out of place, although he couldn't be absolutely sure without a complete inventory. He still felt uneasy about this.

Who was here? What do they know? he thought.

He quickly left the barn locking the front door.

He decided he needed to check on the young boy who was guarding the altar. He jumped into the jeep and after releasing the emergency brake, he drove off towards the altar.

After a brief moment, he pulled his jeep over next to the lower edge to the field his coven and church members so often worshipped in. He turned the engine off and reapplied the emergency brake.

Stepping out of the jeep he hollered, "Danny…"

Only a faint echo of his own voice came back to him.

He shouted louder this time, "Danny, answer me, boy."

Still only silence.

Something's wrong, he thought.

Walter turned and headed up across the field towards the altar. He had traveled about half way across when he noticed there was something on the altar. He broke into a half run and quickly closed the distance to the altar.

Walter stopped next to the altar and blurted out, "Shit, this is bad, real bad!"

He pulled the portable radio from its belt holster. He flipped the "on" switch. Static crackled noisily from the radio.

"Base, this is Walter, over."

The radio hissed, "Walter this is Charlie, over."

"Find Ed Townsend for me will you, Charlie? It's urgent. Have him call me on channel 23, over."

"Roger, Walter."

The radio went silent. Walter turned his channel switch to channel 23. He set the radio to monitor the selected channel. Now he would wait. He wouldn't attempt to move the boy's body without Ed's approval. He sat down in the grass and waited.

Gases had begun earlier to build inside the dead boy's body, hastened by the exposure to the hot afternoon sun. His body's belly had begun to swell.

A swarm of small flies hovered over the body, with several of the shiny insects landing on the boy's head wound. They scampered over the now dried blood, with some of them exploring the crevices of torn flesh. After these brief landings, the flies rose up and hovered again while others landed and repeated this gruesome ritual.

Walter watched several of these landings and takeoffs when his radio suddenly crackled.

"Walter, this is Ed, over."

"Ed, I'm up here on the mountain at the altar, over."

"Yeah, and what's the situation?"

"Ed, someone killed Danny Almore."

They had both dropped the radio formalities.

"Dead, how?"

"Looks like he was slugged from behind by a large piece of oak. His head's split wide open. The piece of wood that hit him appears to have broken in two."

"What else?"

"The killers put his body up here on the altar, Ed. They even put the broken piece of wood here, too. They laid it across his body in the shape of a cross."

There was no response from Ed.

"Ed, did you catch what I just said?"

"Yeah, Walter, I did."

"Walter, a moment ago you said killers. How do you figure there's more than one?"

Walter then reported to Ed what he had seen earlier at the barn.

"I think you may be right, Walter."

"You gonna tell Samuel?"

"Yeah, I will."

What do you want me to do with the Almore boy's body?"

Bring it down to Ed Foley. He'll take care of it. I'll get word to him to expect you."

"Okay."

"Later," said Ed.

"Yeah, later," said Walter

Walter set the channel on his radio back to 19 and the radio back to its monitor mode. He put the radio back into its holster. He walked down the hillside to get his jeep. He would load the boy's dead body into the back.

***

"Aaron you've got to leave here, alone. We have to continue to act as if we don't know anything, for as long as we can get away with it. When you leave they will try to make contact with you, maybe even try to trick you or test you somehow. You're going to have to have your wits about you. They'll try anything," said Miss Beacon.

They had been debating what to do next for the past half-hour. Miss Beacon was insistent that Aaron was ready to handle direct contact with coven members. Korie and Aaron both were reticent to accept the prospect of Aaron being alone with one or more coven members. Miss Beacon knew the risks, yet she felt confident that Aaron, at this point, was as prepared as he could be.

"Look, time is ticking here. It won't matter what we do if we just wait. Sooner or later they'll just come in here and take Aaron, drag him kicking and screaming to their sacrificial altar and the calling ceremony. At least this way we might learn something that could be useful later. You can do this, Aaron. I just know it," said Miss Beacon.

"Maybe she's right, Aaron. After all, she is your guardian angel," said Korie.

"Okay, for my family, and for you two," said a reluctant Aaron.

"Good," said Miss Beacon, "now what I think you should do is take the Land Rover into town, and go to the grocery store. Buy some bread or something. I'm sure they'll try and make contact. Go along with them. When you think you might be getting into some danger, just use that Powell instinct of yours and get out. Don't even hesitate," said Miss Beacon.

"Okay, I will. I promise," said Aaron.

He reached out and hugged Korie and gave her a warm lingering kiss goodbye. He then hugged Miss Beacon. He turned and headed out the door.

"Whew . . .I don't know about this. Maybe we should follow him," said Korie, obviously concerned for Aaron's safety.

"No, we have something important to do," said Miss Beacon.

"What's that?" asked Korie.

"We have to save a girl's life. "

***

Bob sat up like a shot. He reached for the binoculars. In a moment he was letting out a whistle.

"What is it?" asked Judy.

"It's the Powell fella. Looks like he's about to leave the place, alone."

"Does it look like he's going to drive down towards us?"

"Can't be sure, maybe."

"That's good enough for me," said Judy as she bounded out of the truck. She quickly ran to the rear of the truck. She glanced up the road towards Mother Nature's and then she ran across the road. She stopped by the side of the road and fluffed her hair before setting out on a slow jog heading away from town.

Bob looked at her from the driver's side mirror of his truck.

"She's...good."

Meanwhile, Bob noticed that Mother Nature's Land Rover had pulled out onto the road, turned and was headed in Bob's direction. Bob slouched down in his seat so the driver of the Rover would not see anyone sitting inside of the truck.

The Land Rover drove slowly past Bob's truck.

Aaron glanced only briefly at the truck and seeing no one inside, continued along the road heading away from the center of town.

After turning past a short curve he noticed up ahead, on his side of the road, a woman jogger stumble and fall to the ground. She immediately sat up and clutched her right ankle.

As he pulled closer to the injured jogger he noticed her bright pink spandex outfit. Earlier, when he had looked out his bedroom window he noticed there were two people sitting in the tow truck he had just driven past. One of the two people was a woman.

He wondered, *Could she be the woman? Was she a member of the coven?*

He decided to pull over and find out.

He pulled the Rover to the side of the road just ahead of the woman. He climbed out of the vehicle and walked over to the woman.

"Are you okay?" he asked.

With moist eyes she looked up at him and said, "I don't think so. I think I broke my ankle. It really hurts. Owww."

"Let me check it out for you."

"Are you a doctor?" she pouted.

"No, I'm actually a teacher. Look, I'm going to touch it. I'll be gentle. I promise."

His eyes were soaking up her incredible beauty. She looked like a Hollywood starlet.

Aaron knelt down next to her feet and gently reached out and touched her ankle, probing for any sign of swelling. When he touched her ankle sock he felt a cold chill rush through his own body.

"Does this hurt?"

"Uh-huh," she said with a wince.

"How about when I touch here?"

"Oh, yeah, that hurts, too," she said. "Is it broken?" she asked.

"I don't think so. It's probably just a bad sprain. Would you like me to give you a lift home? We seem to be traveling in the same direction anyway."

"That would be wonderful."

"All right," said Aaron standing up. "Here, take my hand and put all of your weight on your left foot. I'll pull you up."

She reached out and put her hands into his. There was no cold chill this time. *She seems nice, maybe she's not one of them,* he thought.

With a gentle but firm tug he pulled her to her feet. Her momentum however, caused her to fall forward into his arms. He had to hold her up as her body collided with his.

Aaron looked down into her sparkling blue eyes. She gave him a warm friendly smile. Her teeth were a perfect white. Her lips were smooth and full.

"Sorry. I guess I don't know my own strength," said Aaron.

"Oh, I don't mind. By the way, my name is Judy. What's your name?"

"Aaron Powell."

"Well, Mr. Powell. I don't know what I would have done if you hadn't come along to rescue me," she purred as she leaned into him.

"Please, call me Aaron."

"All right, Aaron."

He found the scent of her perfume to be very sensual. She continued to lean into him. He could feel her trim but soft body pressing against him.

"Here, let me get you to the Land Rover. Now put your arm like this," said Aaron as he tried to walk her on her one good foot.

"I don't think I can."

"Try."

They went one step and she lost her balance tipping into to him in the process.

"Well, I guess I'll just have to carry you. If that's okay?"

"It's okay, I'm sure you'll be gentle with me."

He lifted her up into his arms. She felt feather light. She wrapped her arms around his neck. He couldn't help but notice the swells of her breasts pushing at the scoop neck line of her spandex top. The sensual smell of her perfume enveloped him.

He carried her over to the passenger side door. Aaron was able to reach out and open the door. He carefully placed her on the front seat. As he closed the door, he noticed how ample and firm her breasts were from the sideways profile set out before him. He even noticed that her nipples were erect.

"Thanks," she said.

"No problem. Now buckle up. We can't have any more accidents."

"Okay."

As Aaron went around to the driver's side to climb in he thought *Bazooka Gum, that's the color of her outfit.* That mental recognition brought a smile to his face.

He started up the Land Rover and after checking his side mirror, he pulled back onto the road.

"You're going to have to direct me to your place. I'm not from around here and I don't know my way around."

"I thought so. I know most everyone around here and I sure didn't recognize you," she said while she looked him over from head to toe.

They drove along for a moment.

"Directions?"

"Oh, I almost forgot. Sure, uh... you will have to turn around on this road and head towards the town center until it intersects with Route 7, and then turn right and my place is about a half a mile up, on Route 7. You can't miss it. I own a motel called Grand View Motel. I hope that it's not taking you out of your way."

"Trust me, it isn't a problem. So are you very busy this time of year?"

"Not really. This time of year I mostly get traveling salesmen. Fall foliage time and winter ski season are my busiest times."

"Owned it long?" asked Aaron, continuing to make small talk.

"It seems like forever," she sighed.

***

"Miss Beacon, how is it that this coven doesn't know exactly what we are doing? Don't they have special powers like the ability to read minds?"

"They have powers, yes. As to the ability to read minds, well that's a different matter. They all have special powers. Most have changeling powers, you know, to change shapes. They sometimes can read one's mind, if that person is weak and lets them in."

"But, what about their master, can't he read everyone's mind? He must be able to tell them what is going to happen?"

"No, dear. Their master, Moloch, can only know what is happening on this earth through the senses of his minions. He too can't read just anybody's mind. He has to be invited in first."

"Then it should be easy. All we have to do is just not let him or his followers into our minds."

"I wish it were that simple. Moloch is very powerful. The coven member's devil partners are, too. They all use tricks and deceptions to try to knock you off guard. Then, when you are distracted or confused, they will try to get you to invite them in. They can disguise themselves as one of your friends, a relative, a pet, or someone you might trust. They will tempt you until you give in. They are relentless."

"Then how can Aaron possible succeed against Moloch's powers?"

"He is a Powell, with his own special powers passed down to him by his ancestors. What he must now contribute is free will and courage. I believe he is strong enough on both fronts. It will remain to be seen whether he uses them wisely."

"I'm afraid for him."

"Korie, don't be afraid for him, just be strong for him."

"You're his guardian angel. Why can't you go with him and protect him?"

"Because, as his ancestors before him, and the other families throughout human history who have faced this challenge, he too, must battle alone. He will soon have to make a choice between good and evil. God imbued humankind with free will. So it is that Aaron will be called upon to freely choose. Only he can make that choice. While it is true that I have journeyed alongside him and his family for many years, for this, it is God's will the chosen one must stand alone."

"I hope we're all ready for this."

"I agree, child."

"Now we wait for darkness, then as I said earlier, we have to save a young girl from the clutches of those evil parasites."

"Will Aaron be back by then?" asked Korie.

"Maybe he will, maybe he won't. It's in his hands Korie. We're just going to have to trust him."

Swallowing hard Korie said, "I hope that you're right about all of this."

"Hope and pray, child, hope and pray to God Almighty that we defeat Lucifer and Moloch and all the coven members here in Sutton."

"I will."

"Shhhhhh!" said Miss Beacon as she put her right index finger up to her lips to signal for silence.

"Someone's here!" said Miss Beacon.

Miss Beacon quickly moved to the kitchen window, looking north along the road that passed her property. Bob Senecal's tow truck was making a U-turn in the road. It left her place, heading north away from town.

Miss Beacon half ran down the hallway towards the front door. She turned and in a whispered voice said, "Stay in the kitchen."

Korie moved to the hallway entrance to the kitchen, and took up a position so she could listen to whatever was about to take place.

Miss Beacon waited at the front door. There was a single knock, then a pause followed by a succession of heavier knocks.

Miss Beacon waited a moment before she opened the door. She placed herself squarely in the doorway entrance. She made no effort to open the screen door. However, whoever was standing there on the porch side pulled the screen door open.

"Afternoon, Miss Beacon. I'm sure you remember me. I'm Phyllis Atkins. I'm a local realtor, and this is..."

"Shirley Carter, yes, hello," said Miss Beacon as she extended her hand and shook hands with the two women.

"To what do I owe the pleasure of your visit ladies?"

"Well, Miss Beacon, I do appreciate that you are a business woman, and as such, you are most correct to ask us to get to the point of our little visit," said Phyllis.

"And that point is?" asked Miss Beacon.

"We're heading up a committee of local business leaders, looking into the possibility of starting up some sort of welcoming service for any newcomers to our quaint little Vermont community. Don't you think that it is a good idea?" asked Phyllis.

Miss Beacon noticed that Shirley's eyes were roaming about, as she not too subtly scanned for some sign of anyone else inside.

"It might be a good idea. Look I really don't have the time right now to discuss this, perhaps another time," said Miss Beacon, as she tried to pull the screen door closed.

Phyllis held firmly to the screen door outside handle. She had a cold stare, which she fixed squarely on Miss Beacon, searching for some sign of weakness, some area that could be exploited to perhaps get her to invite her and Shirley Carter inside.

"But we were hoping you could join us weren't we, Shirley?"

"Why yes, Miss Beacon, you would fit right in."

"No thanks. Look I have some work to do. I was in the middle of sorting out some curios that just arrived from downstate and really must. . ."

"It's so hot Miss Beacon. Could you perhaps spare us girls a cold glass of ice water or perhaps some tea?" said Phyllis Atkins.

"I would like to but I ah...ah...ah," Miss Beacon's eyes squeezed shut as she lets loose with a powerful sneeze that managed to spray spittle upon the two women standing in her doorway.

"Oh, I'm so sorry, really, I think I'm coming down with one of those nasty summer colds. I'm sure I could make some fresh ice tea for you ladies, ah...ah...ah choo," sneezed Miss Beacon once more.

This time however, the two women managed to have backed themselves up in time, to avoid the brunt of the spray of spittle. Shirley Carter put her hands up to her face to cover her mouth. Phyllis Atkins covered her own mouth with the back of her left hand.

"You do seem a bit pale, Miss Beacon. Perhaps we could come back again, when you are feeling better," said Phyllis.

"You're probably right. I am feeling a little weak. Later then."

Phyllis released her grip on the screen door handle as she and Shirley turned and walked down the front steps to Phyllis' car.

"I hope you feel better real soon," said Shirley as she gave a wave to Miss Beacon, before she settled into the passenger side of the car.

Miss Beacon waved back from behind the closed screen door.

Phyllis Atkins started up the car and under her breath she said, "Fucking old maid. She's faking that cold. There's no doubt she's hiding something. I'd like to rip her fucking heart out with my bare hands," she said from behind clenched teeth, as she pulled the car out of the driveway.

"Well?" asked Shirley.

"Well, what?"

"Aren't you going to ask me if I noticed anything, or are you too busy planning to rip out the old lady's heart?"

"Well, did you?" asked an exasperated Phyllis.

"Didn't see anything, but I sure smelled something," said Shirley tapping the side of her nose.

"Yeah, what?"

"There's another woman in there with her. She's young and she's afraid," said Shirley with a wide smile.

"Afraid? What else?"

"Well, once my trusty nose sniffed her out, I was able to mentally search her out. I tell you she's got a strong mind, that's for sure. She was hiding and listening to us, and she suspects we're members of the coven."

"Well, it looks like we're on to something here. We should go report to Samuel and see if he wants us to try again."

The two coven members drove down the road feeling pretty proud of themselves.

Meanwhile, back at Mother Nature's, Miss Beacon watched the car drive away until it was out of sight. Then she closed and locked the front door.

***

Aaron pulled the Land Rover to a stop. He parked in front of the large white house with a wrap around, open porch. The house was set on top of the small hill behind two rows of single story motel units which Judy Perillo owned. There were forty motel rooms in the two rows. At the end of the first row was the motel office with a sign in the front window indicating the motel was closed until September first.

Aaron got out of the Land Rover and quickly moved over to the passenger side door. Judy had already opened the door before he arrived. She sat on the edge of the front seat, extending her arms out to Aaron.

She held onto his neck as he held onto her. He used his hip to close the Land Rover door. Aaron went up the front steps and moved to the front door.

"It's unlocked," said Judy.

"Really?" said Aaron.

"Look," said Judy as she reached down with her right arm and turned the door handle, opening the door. She pushed it wide open.

Aaron carried her inside.

"In there," she said pointing to the living room. She used her left hand to close the front door.

Aaron carried her into the living room and gently lowered her unto the camel-backed couch.

Judy managed to hold onto Aaron for an extra moment. Her hands caressed his neck. He looked down at her. Judy's eyes locked onto Aaron's.

He stood up.

"Well, I guess you'll be okay now that you're home."

"How can I possibly thank you for all you've done?" said Judy, as she reached out and took his right hand with both of hers.

"No thanks are necessary, really," said Aaron. Standing over her gave him a good viewing angle for her ample breasts. He could see deep into her spandex top, past the swells of her breasts. He felt himself blushing.

"You've done so much for me already, I hate to have to ask you for another favor," she said with a pouting expression.

"Ask away."

"Well, could you be a dear, and get my mail for me? It's in the mailbox down next to the road. I forgot to ask you to stop when we arrived."

"Sure, I'll be right back."

Aaron turned and headed outside to get the mail. When he stepped outside he noticed he had an erection. She was an incredible looking woman. Certainly more attractive than any woman he had ever met. He stopped in front of the mailbox, removed several envelopes, closed the mailbox door, and headed back up to the house. As he walked back to the house, Bob Senecal drove past in his tow truck. He spotted Aaron immediately. He picked up the CB microphone from its hook on the dash and flipped on the CB radio. He would radio in and report Judy was successful in connecting with the Powell male.

When Aaron reentered the house, he headed back into the living room to find Judy standing up with a tray in her hands. The tray had a pitcher of lemonade and two glasses. Judy seemed to be favoring her injured foot.

"You caught me," said Judy with a surprised tone in her voice. "I wanted to offer you some hospitality. Are you angry with me? Maybe I'm being too…oh, I don't know."

"Presumptive?" said Aaron in an effort to finish her sentence.

"That sounds better than pushy," said Judy giggling in a little girl sort of way. "Please stay for some lemonade!"

"Okay, I'll have just one glass!"

"Good."

He sat down on the couch.

Judy bent over and put the tray down on the coffee table directly in front of him. He got another look at her ample breasts.

Shit, they seem bigger, he thought.

Judy hobbled over to the couch, and sat down next to Aaron, on his right side. She put her left hand half way up his right thigh, as she reached for the pitcher of lemonade. She managed to give his thigh, a gentle squeeze.

Aaron now experienced a full fledge erection.

Judy poured two glasses and handed one to Aaron. She offered her glass up and they clicked them together.

"To fate it is," said Aaron.

Aaron drank some of the lemonade. The flavor exploded inside of his mouth. It was undoubtedly the best tasting lemonade he had ever experienced.

"I can't help but noticing, you're not wearing a wedding ring," said Judy as she swept her blond hair from her eyes.

"That's right. I'm not married."

"Seeing someone?" said Judy smiling.

A strong whiff of her perfume suddenly breezed past his face, igniting his olfactory senses. His erection seemed to grow, if that is possible.

"Uh. . .Yeah.. I have a good friend. She and I...are..."

Judy reached up and touched his lips with her right index finger.

"Sh...sh, say no more. I understand. I'm not a home wrecker."

Her finger felt hot against his lips. Sexy hot. Before he realized what he was doing, he kissed her finger.

Judy pulled her finger away and then, after putting her glass on the coffee table, she tried to stand up. She again put her left hand on his right thigh as she pushed herself to her feet. She wobbled for a moment, and then fell back down, right into Aaron's lap.

He recognized she was about to fall and held his arms apart, trying not to spill any of the lemonade in his glass on her beautiful couch.

When her body landed on his, it seemed to him she was burning up with fever. He could feel heat radiating from her body. She turned towards him and looked down into his eyes. He saw in her eyes an unmistakable look of lust. He tried to look away. His eyes looked downward and there, just less than an inch from his chin, were her breasts. Her nipples were all too obviously hard as they strained against the spandex.

She reached over and took his glass away, and put it with her own on the coffee table. As she reached towards the coffee table with her back to him, her buttocks settled down into his lap, firmly against his now highly aroused body.

She again turned to face him. She was smiling at him. He sheepishly smiled back.

She took his head with her two hands and pulled him towards her, as she passionately kissed him. Her lips ignited his own. Her tongue probed his waiting mouth. He responded in kind. He seemed to feel as if his breath was being sucked from his body, it was both pleasure and pain.

She pulled away from him and smiled down at him once again.

He leaned forward and kissed her breasts repeatedly, through the tightly stretched spandex. After a moment he paused. Her spandex top was now stained from his moist kisses.

Judy now maneuvered herself so she could kneel on the couch, straddling and facing him. She reached down and pulled at her spandex top and in slow teasing movements she removed it. She tossed her top on the floor. Next she caressed her breasts with slow, teasing movement of her hands.

Aaron watched this, transfixed by her enormous beauty.

She reached down for his hands, and then, she placed them on her breasts, encouraging Aaron to continue the massage. Her breasts felt firm to the touch. He gently stroked her.

She pulled herself closer to him, offering her breasts to his lips. He responded with ever increasing lust filling him.

Judy moaned softly as Aaron's breathing began to grow more rapid.

She pressed her breasts against his face. She leaned close to his right ear, and whispered, "Carry me to the bedroom, please."

He responded immediately, by wrapping his arms around her body, and after a momentary struggle, he gained his feet. She pointed to the bedroom down the end of a hallway. As he carried her towards the bedroom, she began to unbutton his short sleeve shirt. The aroma of her perfume was intoxicating. Aaron felt drawn to her, by a powerful, consuming lust.

He laid her down on her king-size bed. He stood next to the bed, looking down at her.

"Take off my socks and shoes," she commanded in a gentle whisper.

He moved to her feet and began to gently remove her socks and shoes.

"Now, take off your shirt."

Aaron did as he was asked.

"And take off those pants too."

Aaron kicked off his shoes and quickly pulled his own socks off. Next he unbuckled his pants, unzipped them, and let them fall to the floor.

He stood there in his designer under shorts, with an enormous bulge, lurking just beneath the surface.

"Don't be bashful, take those off, too," said Judy as she reached for his under shorts with her left foot, tugging at the bottom edge with her toes.

Aaron did as he was told.

"Oh, my," sighed Judy, with a lustful smile.

Now it was Judy's turn. She slowly began to peel the spandex bottom off. She swung her hips in such a way that Aaron's state of arousal began to transform from a human level to an almost animal like level.

His mind's eye noticed in the designer bedspread covering her bed, a pattern, one that seemed faintly recognizable. Now, a swiftly building struggle inside Aaron's subconscious began. The bedspread pattern showed a puritan style dressed woman with her back to the viewer, or turned sideways, depending on the fabric's pattern. The woman had obviously been picking flowers from a small patch at her feet.

One of the images of the tiny woman turned and looked at Aaron. He recognized the woman immediately, it was Miss Beacon.

The woman seemed to be trying to shout something to Aaron.

His eyes flickered back and forth between the now nearly naked Judy Perillo, and his guardian angel, Miss Beacon.

Much of him wanted Judy Perillo. He wanted to make love to this goddess like body with every ounce of his sexuality. Yet another part of him knew he needed to hear what Miss Beacon was trying to say. His mind focused in on the small figure shouting out to him from the bed.

"Aaron, use your eyes, look at her, really took at her, for God's sake!"

In a flash, the figure faded back into the bedspread's fabric.

Aaron now turned his full attention to Judy. He looked at her, only this time, his mind was taking control.

Judy had removed her spandex bottom. She knelt up on the bed and reached out to Aaron.

"Come here, come to me," she teased.

He began to reach out for her when his eyes, still straining at the sight of her enormous breasts, now noticed that the left breast was bleeding from the nipple. A trickle of blood streaked down her breast, underneath and out of view. The other breast was also leaking blood. He hesitated.

"I want you," she said licking her tongue against her full lips.

Her teeth now seemed slightly yellow. In fact, he noticed her lips were cracked, and caked with black scabs of blood. His eyes began to take frantic inventory.

"Aaron, I'm going to make love with you. I want you, now," she demanded.

She reached out to him, and her hand felt icy cold to the skin on his chest. He looked down at her hand and it was wrinkled, covered with dark welts, and occasional long white strands of hair.

314

He looked back up at her, and her blond hair was gone, her head was deteriorating as well. Her breasts, once firm and bountiful, now hung against her body like a pair of deflated, cheap balloons. Her chest and arms were covered with sores that oozed a yellowish colored puss.

He tried to step back. She reached for him, trying to clasp his now former erection. He stumbled backward.

"What's the matter? Are you shy? I can fix that," she said. As she pronounced the word "that" a couple of her, now deeply yellowed, teeth tumbled onto the bed.

"No, I. . . uh. . . just can't do this. I . . ." said Aaron as he quickly bent down and began to pick up his clothes.

"You seemed ready, just a moment ago. What changed?"

Aaron picked up his clothes and began to back out of the bedroom. Judy Perillo's body was now reduced to a sickly, emaciated shell. Her skin clung loosely to her body. The room smelled of rotting flesh. Aaron heard the buzzing of flies. He didn't see them, but could clearly hear them. He turned and ran from the room. He ran out of the house, closing the front door behind him.

Naked and in a full panic, he ran down the front steps and climbed into the Land Rover. He locked the doors. He got dressed as fast as he could. He wanted to get away from her as quickly as possible.

He was buckling his belt when he looked back up at the house. Judy was standing on the front porch. She was totally naked. A swarm of flies buzzed around her. She casually swatted at them.

"Listen, if you change your mind, I'll be waiting."

As he looked at her, her body began to transform itself again, this time it quickly evolved into what seemed to be, a totally different person. This person, also naked, was incredibly beautiful. Her hair was as black as night. Then he noticed the horns, two small horns at the top of her forehead. This new image now flashed back to the form of the Judy Perillo that Aaron had seen and felt on the couch. The image seemed to flip back and forth between the dark haired creature, and the blond statuesque woman that had tempted him earlier. The flipping images flickered like the flicking of an image on a television set. First the rotting, decayed old woman, then the horned woman, then the blond temptress and back again to the old woman, and so on.

Aaron put the key into the ignition and backed the Land Rover up. He turned around and began to drive away. In his rearview mirror he could still see her standing on the porch. The image had stabilized into the Judy Perillo he had first encountered. He kept driving.

***

"Shouldn't we wait for Aaron to return?" asked Korie.

"No dear, we can't wait. Look, the coven is mostly focused upon him right now, and we need to take this opportunity to save a young girl from a certain death and eternity in hell."

"So, what do I have to do?" inquired Korie.

"When we get there you can watch my back," said Miss Beacon.

"That sounds easy."

Miss Beacon handed her a small, chromed revolver.

***

Aaron pulled the Land Rover to a stop in one of the parking spaces next to the park in the center of town. He turned the engine off. His hands were shaking. His stomach felt all twisted, and his head pounded with each breath that he took.

He had almost been unfaithful to the love of his life, Korie. He had almost betrayed his family, God and the whole human race. If ever a man felt shame, it was Aaron. He sobbed and sobbed as he sat in the stillness of the Land Rover.

It was sweltering in the vehicle, and Aaron was soon drenched in perspiration. He couldn't face Korie or Miss Beacon right now. Miss Beacon, after all, had to warn him by sending him that apparition.

Shit, she must have seen me standing there, he thought.

27

Aaron had been sitting in the Land Rover for just a few minutes. He was feeling ashamed and angry. He slammed his right hand on the dashboard.

How could I have been so stupid? he thought.

He put his head down onto the backs of his hands, which were now gripping the steering wheel. He needed time to think and to clear his head.

A loud "click, click" sound startled him. Aaron sat up in a start. He looked out the driver's side window into the face of a teenage boy. The somewhat steamed up window clouded the image. Nevertheless, Aaron could plainly see the concerned expression on the boy's face.

Aaron opened the driver's door and stepped out of the Rover. He wiped a tear from his right eye with the back of his left hand.

"Hey man, are you okay?" asked the boy.

"Yeah, I'm okay."

"I wasn't sure, you know. I thought maybe you were sick or something. You know, maybe needed some help."

"That's really nice of you to be so concerned. Thanks, I'm really fine."

"Don't look fine to me. Is it woman trouble?"

"Maybe, yeah."

"You're not from around here are you?"

"No I'm not. I'm just visiting the area for awhile."

The boy was standing on a skateboard. He stepped off of it. Looking down, he stepped on the skateboard's tail and flipped the board upward. He caught the front end of the board with his left hand. He was wearing oversized jeans and a black colored tee shirt, which had a slogan silk screened on it in bright yellow. The slogan said "Fear No One." His sneakers were well worn. His light brown hair was slicked back. He stood about six feet tall.

"Nice board," said Aaron.

"Thanks."

"My name is Aaron, what's yours?"

"Curt, but my friends call me Hondo."

Just then raindrops began to fall. These drops were large. The wind began to pick up as well.

"Well, I've got to go," said the boy as he put his skateboard down. Stepping aboard with his left foot he pushed off with his right.

Aaron turned to head back to the Rover when he heard the skateboard skid to a halt.

"Say, Aaron," said the boy.

Turning around Aaron looked over at the boy.

"You be careful around here. There are some really freaky people in this town, and they especially don't like strangers."

"Thanks, I will."

"Like that one over there. He's been watching us."

"Where?"

"He's sitting in that station wagon on the other side of your Rover."

Aaron slowly turned and looked through the front side windows of the Land Rover. He could see the outline of the station wagon and its driver.

Aaron turned back to speak to the boy, but he had already moved on down the street. The rain began to fall at a much heavier rate. In the distance came the low rumble of thunder. Aaron's shirt was quickly soaked from the heavy rain. He climbed back inside the Rover, started up the engine and turned on the air conditioner to clear up the fog on the windows. As the windows slowly cleared, Aaron looked over at the station wagon. Its driver boldly stared back.

***

"We've got to go," said Miss Beacon.

"But it looks like its starting to rain."

"All the better. Now remember to keep the gun ready that I gave you earlier."

"You really think that we'll need a gun?" said Korie.

"Yes, where we're going we might need it."

"Are you expecting trouble?"

"I expect everything."

"Well, I checked and this gun only has six bullets."

"It'll be enough."

"How can you be so sure?"

"A guardian angel just knows things!"

Miss Beacon picked up the small bag she had been packing and headed for the back door. She opened it slowly and looked around outside. She motioned for Korie to follow. Korie pulled the back door closed. There was a "click" as the door lock engaged.

The rain had just begun to fall. The two women headed over to the barn, which also served as a garage. They entered the front side door. The sound of the rain falling against the tin roof could be heard from inside of the building. Moving swiftly in the semi-darkness Miss Beacon led Korie to the rear. With a tug, Miss Beacon pulled open the rear door and headed out the back. Korie tagged along behind her after closing the door. They headed into the woods. The rain was falling more heavily now. Inside the woods the full effect of the rainstorm was less noticeable, due to the canopy effect of the pine, maple and oak trees. Other than the sound of rain and their footsteps, it was quiet here in the woods.

Miss Beacon stopped for a moment.

"Look its going to be dark soon. Stay close to me and keep low to the ground. These low branches can take an eye out before you know it. We'll be cutting around a few streets and through back yards. It'll take at least an hour to get there."

"Okay, but we're going to get soaked."

Ignoring Korie's remark, Miss Beacon turned and moved along in a sort of semi-crouch position.

Korie stayed close behind.

In the distance they heard a dog bark.

It barked again.

Darkness closed in quickly in the woods. Now the heavy rain was making its way completely through the canopy of the woods. Both women were soon drenched from the cool summer rain.

The dank odor of the wet forest floor filled the air. It was a blend of pine, sumac, oak and maple fragrances. These were the decaying odors rising up from the moist compost of forest droppings, which covered the ground.

Miss Beacon stopped.

She reached back and touched Korie with her left hand. Korie stopped, too.

In the darkness ahead was something or someone, which had caught the attention of Miss Beacon.

Korie could hear her own breathing and Miss Beacon's as well. The only other sound she could detect was the sounds of the forest and the rainfall. The two women stood still. Korie's heart was beginning to pound inside of her chest. This waiting in the dark made her nervous. She slowly wiped raindrops from her eyebrows. A mosquito landed on her left arm and proceeded to extract a full meal of fresh blood. Korie couldn't see the insect, but could feel it. She wanted to slap at it and kill it, but wasn't sure if she should, while they waited in the darkness.

Miss Beacon pulled at Korie's left arm in a gesture to follow along. The two women moved cautiously forward. After a few feet Miss Beacon stopped again.

Directly in front of her came a low "growl."

That sound gripped Korie.

The growling came closer. Korie reached for the gun she had slipped into her waistband. Miss Beacon knelt down on one knee.

***

Judge Fairchild stood outside at the curb looking skyward. The sky was filled with dark, swiftly moving clouds. The wind, which had picked up, carried cooler air. In the distance, a rumble of thunder could be heard. A nearby silver maple tree twisted about in the wind, with leaves turned upside down, a sure sign of an approaching storm.

The front door to the Reverend's house opened and Chuck poked his head out.

"You coming, Judge? Everyone's inside waiting for you so we can begin."

"Yeah, I'm coming."

Rain had just begun to fall. Large raindrops pelted the Judge as he half jogged towards the front door. As he stepped onto the front step a crackling sound was heard coming from somewhere to the Judge's right. It was accompanied by a huge burst of pulsating light. In a half second, a pounding explosion of thunder shook the ground.

"You just made it, Judge," said Chuck as held open the door. "Looks like that lightning strike was meant for you," he continued nodding in the direction behind the Judge.

The Judge looked back out onto the front yard. Where he had been standing just seconds before lay a huge smoldering branch from the nearby silver maple tree. The branch had to be close to a foot in diameter.

"That sure would have done some damage, right Judge?"

"Yeah, it would have killed me."

"Well, relax. It wasn't your time, at least not yet," laughed Chuck as he headed off in the direction of the Reverend's office.

There were now many flashes of lightning and rumbles of thunder, as the storm stationed itself over the valley.

The Judge walked into the office where everyone else was waiting.

Samuel was standing over by a large floor to ceiling window staring out at the storm. Cascades of rain shimmered down the panes of glass.

"We're all here, Samuel," said the Reverend.

"Go ahead, Reverend," said Samuel without turning around.

"If you insist," said the Reverend. Let's begin then with Shirley and Phyllis. What did you learn?"

The two women spoke for several minutes. They both embellished what they had seen or learned.

"So it seems that Miss Beacon is involved with Powell and his girlfriend. She shouldn't be much of a problem. We'll just have…"

Just then a loud clap of thunder rattled the walls. At that instant the power went out and three small lamps which had been on in the office went out.

"You got any candles?" asked Walter.

"Yes, there are a couple over on the book shelf, and another one sitting on the small table by the door."

Samuel still hadn't turned from the window. However, he raised his right hand upward in a gesture that resembled taking an oath. Suddenly, a small flicker of a flame danced from the end of his index finger. Its appearance caught everyone's attention. Now, pointing his right hand as if it were a weapon, the flame left the end of his finger and moved through the heavy air of the office. The flame moved to each of the candles lighting each. It then returned to the tip of Samuel's index finger.

"Continue," said Samuel without turning around.

Hellfire, thought the Reverend, as did most of the others in the room.

"Well, Judy, it's your turn," said the Reverend.

***

Aaron wanted to go over to the man in the station wagon and give him a piece of his mind.

You want a piece of me? Well come on, he thought.

He stared at the man who just simply stared back.

Aaron looked away for a moment to his left. The rain was coming down in sheets. The wind was rocking the Land Rover. Aaron turned again to his right to get another look at the man in the station wagon, when he was startled by the presence of his mother sitting next to him.

"Mom?"

"Yes, Aaron."

"What are you doing here?"

"Don't you think I should be asking you that question?"

"I don't understand."

She looked straight ahead at the rain beating down upon the windshield. She closed her eyes. Her chest heaved with a sigh.

Aaron wanted to touch her, to let her touch him. He so wanted her to hold him, as she once did many years ago. He didn't dare to however. He didn't want to break the spell that had brought her to him. He needed to be able to talk to her right now. He needed her help.

"Aaron, what happened earlier wasn't your fault. These devils are cunning and ruthless. You had to learn this for yourself."

"But, I feel so, so wrong. I felt like I let you and everyone else down. I should have been stronger."

She half turned and faced him. Over her shoulder Aaron could see the man in the station wagon took renewed interest in Aaron's

Land Rover. His mother noticed Aaron's eyes were shuttling between her and the man in the nearby car.

"He can't see me. Only you can see me."

"He sees something!"

"You must listen to me, Aaron. There isn't much time left. Tonight, the coven is meeting to plot its final move against you. For you to be able to defeat them, you will have to let them get very close to you. They are going to have to trust you. Whatever they do, you must not let them provoke you into losing your self-control with anger, pity or despair. You must remain strong and true. Do you understand me?"

"I do, mother, I do. I will be strong."

"No matter what happens?"

"No matter."

"They can't get to you through our family, but they have other ways Aaron. They have ways."

"I understand what is at stake here. I'm a Powell, descended from a long line of brave Powell's. It's has been our responsibility to defeat the devil and his followers, ever since that night in 1843. I can only promise to do my best."

She smiled at her son. Her smile warmed him. Her eyes seemed moist as if she were about to cry.

"We shall all pray for you my son."

"Mother?"

She had begun to fade from view. Just before she did, she blew him a kiss. At that moment, he felt a slight brush of warm air against his right cheek. He touched at it with his right hand. She was completely gone now.

The man in the nearby car had rolled his window down to get a better look. Something had caught his attention. He was still trying to see something inside Aaron's Rover.

Aaron looked over at the man. Their eyes met. Aaron smiled at the man, and gave him a slight wave. This gesture seemed to frustrate the man who now quickly rolled up his car window.

Aaron put the Rover in gear and backed out of his parking space.

***

Miss Beacon and Korie were frozen in place.

What the hell is that? thought Korie.

Miss Beacon moved forward.

A low guttural growl rumbled in their direction. The sound was much closer now. Because of the dense low brush, tree branches, and the onrushing darkness, the women couldn't see more than ten feet ahead.

Miss Beacon whispered, "It's a dog, a big dog."

"What does it want?" Korie whispered back.

Just then the dog bolted out of the darkness directly ahead. It was a German shepherd, it was very big and it seemed very angry. The dog lunged towards Miss Beacon, who was surprised by the suddenness of the dog's charge. She half stumbled backwards and bumped against Korie.

Korie was about to draw the pistol she was carrying when Miss Beacon stuck out her right hand, palm side facing the dog, fingers pointed upward.

The dog stopped in mid-charge, as if it had just slammed into a wall. It let out a small yelp. The dog backed up a couple of feet and baring its teeth, leaped directly at Miss Beacon. This time the dog stopped in mid-air and then fell to the ground. It quickly collected itself. The dog now crouched down facing the women, its ears laid back, teeth showing. This time the dog didn't charge at them.

Miss Beacon formed a fist with her right hand and held it out in front of her as she knelt down in front of the dog. The dog crept forward a couple of feet and sniffed at her hand. Its ears began to move slowly forward. Korie noticed its tail was moving slowly from side to side. The dog inched forward just a bit more and it playfully licked at Miss Beacon's hand. She opened her hand and reached over and scratched the dog's ears.

"That's incredible, just incredible," said Korie.

"No, it's not. It's just a matter of trust."

"All right, so now what?"

"We take him along," said Miss Beacon.

With that, Miss Beacon bent over and kissed the top of the dog's head. She then whispered something into the dog's ear. The dog licked her face once and stood up. He turned around and began to walk slowly ahead.

"Let's go," said Miss Beacon.

"What did you say to the dog?"

"I asked him to help us save the life of a young girl. Besides, he knows these woods better than either of us."

"Like I said, incredible."

The dog looked back at the two women. They were right behind him. He turned to his left, down what seemed to be a well traveled path. The women continued to follow the dog's lead. The path taken by the dog was smoother and easier to travel. They were making good time now.

The dog stopped in the path and sat down. Miss Beacon bent over and patted the dog.

"This is as far as he is going. If I'm not mistaken we will be coming out of the woods up ahead."

"So, where are we?" asked Korie.

"You'll see," said Miss Beacon.

The dog stood up, walked past the two women, and in a moment it disappeared into the woods.

Miss Beacon walked on and Korie followed right behind her. In a moment, they emerged from the woods. They were standing in what appeared to be, the back yard of someone's house. There were no lights on in the house.

Miss Beacon signaled they needed to be as quiet as possible. Korie nodded her agreement.

Slowly the two women crossed the backyard. They moved along the driveway until they were standing on the sidewalk at the end of a cul-de-sac. The overhead streetlight cast its eerie yellow haze over the glistening surface of the street. From where they stood, they could see clear up the street to the connecting road, at the end of the street. The rain had let up a bit but still fell as a steady drizzle.

Miss Beacon motioned for Korie to follow as she crossed the street. The two women walked side by side, along the sidewalk. In a few moments, they had reached the gravel drive leading to an old church. There was a ground based spotlight which illuminated the church, especially its steeple. The church windows were as black as the night sky.

The only sound Korie could hear was the sound of cars traveling along nearby Interstate 89. She had no idea where they were, but the unmistakable whine of tires speeding down a superhighway was quite recognizable to her. This neighborhood was completely silent. While some houses had lights on and their windows partially opened, strangely there were no sounds, emanating from any of the homes.

Miss Beacon moved carefully down the gravel drive to the rear of the church. Korie followed.

Miss Beacon stopped next to a bulkhead at the rear side of the church. It was locked with a padlock. She removed her backpack and set it down. She opened it and soon removed a small tool, which she used to work the lock. After a moment the lock opened and Miss Beacon pulled it off and set it on the ground. She stood up and with Korie's help they opened the bulkhead heavy doors. She took out a small flashlight, turned it on and shined it down the stairs, which led to the church cellar.

"Why didn't you just command the lock to open, instead of picking the lock? You must have powers to open locks and things."

"God only gave me the powers he believes I need. I'm on my own for the rest."

"But I would have thought."

"Don't dear, have faith, its stronger."

With that Miss Beacon descended the stairs.

Korie followed behind. Miss Beacon stopped at the bottom of the stairs. She picked the lock at the bottom of the stairs. She pushed it open and stepped into the blackness of the basement. Korie watched her disappear into the darkness. The flashlight beam cut through the darkness. From where she stood, Korie could see that there was an old cast iron furnace to the rear of the cellar. The light also revealed that, along the walls were wooden shelves filled with boxes of various sizes. There was also a pile of folding tables, along with two stacks of folding wooden chairs.

"Korie, come here."

Korie haltingly stepped inside of the basement and headed towards the area lit by Miss Beacon's flashlight.

"Here, hold this," said Miss Beacon as she handed the backpack to Korie. Korie took the backpack and slung it over her shoulder with the one she had brought with her.

Miss Beacon focused the flashlight beam on a door at the rear of the basement which was just beyond the large cast iron furnace.

She leaned against the door and listened with her left ear.

She gently knocked on the heavy wooden door.

"Kelley, Kelley, are you in there?" she whispered.

"Wait a minute. We came all the way here, through a soaking rain storm, breaking into a church and you're not sure if she's in there?"

Miss Beacon turned towards Korie as the glow of the flashlight illuminated her face. There was no mistaking the look on her face. It fully conveyed her annoyance.

Miss Beacon pulled a key out of her dress pocket. She inserted it into the lock and turned. The lock "clicked" open.

"Where did you get that key?"

Looking back at Korie she said, "You ask too many questions, but if you must know I used to attend this church. As for the key, let's just say it came into my possession one day."

Miss Beacon pulled the door open and shinned the flashlight inside the darkened room beyond. She suddenly put her right hand up to her mouth and gasped.

"Oh, dear. Oh, dear God, what have they done to you?"

Miss Beacon rushed inside the room. Korie was reluctant to follow her inside, but soon had no choice in the matter, as Miss Beacon called for her help.

"Korie, you've got to help me. Hurry!"

When Korie stepped inside the small room she wasn't prepared for what she saw.

Chained to the wall was a teenage girl who hung limply against the wall. Her entire body seemed to be covered in thick spider webs. Large, thick-legged spiders scampered everywhere. The room reeked with the smell of urine. Miss Beacon, while holding the flashlight with one hand, pulled away large bats of spider webbing. As the webbing was brushed away, the girl's skin was revealed. Her arms, face, neck, the exposed areas of her body, were covered in large reddened welts from the hundreds of spider bites that she had endured.

"Hold her up for me while I work on these locks," commanded Miss Beacon.

Korie reached out and tried to hold the girl's body up. She didn't have much success. The girl's limp body was too heavy.

"You're going to have to put your arms around her and under her arms."

"Okay, okay."

Korie reached around the girl and clasped her hands together and lifted. She managed to hold the girl up enough for Miss Beacon to start working on the locks. Korie could see from the flashlight glow that the girl's eyes were completely closed. She noticed the girl was breathing, ever so faintly. She also noticed one more thing. Spiders were beginning to crawl along her arms, and they were biting into her own skin. She could feel the light touch of their legs as several of them scampered along her arms.

"Hurry up," said Korie.

"I am."

"Hurrieeee!"

"I said I am. What's wrong?"

"The spiders are biting meeeeeee!" said a panicked Korie. "I hate fucking spiders."

"There, I've got this one off. Hold still while I try this one," said Miss Beacon as she went from unlocking one of the wrist manacles to trying to unlock the leg shackles. In a moment all the locks were opened, the girl was now free.

"Carry her into the cellar," said Miss Beacon.

Korie half-carried and half-dragged the girl into the cellar. Miss Beacon followed right behind. Once inside the cellar Miss Beacon took one of the old wooden folding chairs and opened it up. Miss Beacon helped Korie set the girl into the chair.

"Turn around," said Miss Beacon.

As she did Miss Beacon began to rummage around inside the backpack Korie had been carrying. Korie kept her hands on the girl to hold her up in the chair.

In a moment, Miss Beacon turned Korie around and handed her the flashlight. She opened a bottle of what appeared to be some kind of medicine. Miss Beacon held the girl's head back, and slipping an index finger into the girl's mouth, she was able to get her to slightly open her mouth. Miss Beacon poured a couple of ounces of the bottle's liquid contents into her mouth.

"Benadryl," said Miss Beacon. "It will help with the spider bites."

Miss Beacon poured another couple of ounces into the girl's

mouth. She recapped the bottle and put it back into the backpack. Miss Beacon next removed a water bottle from the backpack. She pulled its squirt top open and proceeded to pour some water into the girl's mouth.

"She seems unconscious," said Korie.

"Not exactly, it's more of a cationic-like state. It's a sort of a defense mechanism, like a trance."

"Will she come to? You know, be alert. We can't possibly carry her back to your place."

"I know."

Miss Beacon knelt next to the girl and whispered softly into her ear. She whispered again. Korie couldn't hear what Miss Beacon was saying but it seemed to work. The girl's eyelids began to flutter.

"Who is she?"

"Her name is Kelley. Her brother, Samuel, is new leader of the coven."

"Is he responsible for this—his own sister chained up in a cellar hole left to die? Left with all those damn spiders."

"Not left to die. No, rather you could say, she was being stored for use later on. Samuel needs her for the welcoming ceremony. She was going to be offered up to either Moloch or Lucifer."

"Uh, uh, I ah," said Kelley as her eyelids fluttered.

"She's regaining consciousness?" asked Korie.

"Maybe. Kelley, Kelley, listen to me. We're here to help you. Do you think you can stand? Can you walk?"

"He's dead. He was my friend. He…"

"Who's dead?" asked Miss Beacon.

Just then Korie and Miss Beacon heard a car door slam shut.

Miss Beacon turned off the flashlight. She held onto Kelley who was beginning to slump down off the chair.

Now they heard a second car door slam shut. Outside the cellar there were voices, men's voices and they sounded angry.

Miss Beacon whispered to Korie to move over against the wall next to the cellar doorway.

"Get that gun ready. It looks like trouble is heading our way."

Korie didn't answer Miss Beacon. She wasn't sure Korie had the courage to follow through. She could only hope that the confidence she had in her would prove to be correct.

The men had spotted the open cellar door

"I'll go first," said one man's voice, "and you cover me."

"I'm right behind you," said the other man.

The men slowly and carefully went down the cellar stairs. When the first man reached the bottom stair he quickly reached around to the right side cellar wall with his left hand, and flicked on the overhead lights. Miss Beacon caught a glimpse of his arm retreating back behind the cellar door.

In the light Miss Beacon could see Korie, who had managed to position herself directly behind the cellar door. She had removed the pistol from her waistband, and now held it firmly with both hands in a classic shooter's grip. She held the gun pointing upward, her hands next to her left cheek.

Miss Beacon knew she had to provide a diversion to give Korie time to get the drop on both men.

The first man pointed his gun around the edge of the open door. After a moment he poked his head around the edge of the door for just a brief moment to check out the cellar area.

"Don't shoot. Please don't shoot. I'm unarmed," said Miss Beacon in her best pleading voice.

The first man now peeked around the edge of the door and looked straight in the direction of Miss Beacon's voice.

"Please help me. She's very sick. I was sent here by Samuel to give her some medicine and when I found her she was having a seizure. I think she may be dying."

Miss Beacon was gambling these men might be thrown off balance by her referral to Samuel. She also was gambling that Kelley wouldn't speak out and tip off these men to her ruse.

The first man stepped out from behind the door. He held his pistol down at his side. Miss Beacon recognized him as Junior Fecteau, a low ranking member of the church and a coven wannabe.

"Why if it ain't Miss Beacon? I didn't know Samuel had sent anybody else."

Miss Beacon had to hold his attention until the other man entered the cellar.

"Could you give me a hand so I can give her some medicine? I'm afraid I can't do it alone."

"Sure. Bobby, get your ass in here, man," said Junior as he started to walk towards Miss Beacon.

Just then Kelley let out an eerie screeching sound. That sound riveted Junior's full attention on her. His younger brother Bobby now stepped out from behind the door. He was obviously very nervous. He was holding a pistol in his left hand, pointing only slightly downward. His hand was shaking.

As Bobby stepped completely into the cellar his nervous eyes glanced sideways. He half noticed Korie. Because his brother had said to come on in, he allowed himself to let his guard down, just a bit. It was enough.

Korie stepped towards Bobby and put the end of the barrel of her own pistol just inches from the side of his head.

"Freeze right there, you bastards," she shouted.

Junior spun around bringing his gun up, ready to fire, when he spotted Korie's gun against the temple of his younger brother.

"Don't even think of it," said a very tense Korie.

"Now Junior, you don't want that nice young girl to shoot your brother do you?" asked Miss Beacon.

"Shut up!" he shouted back.

"Junior, she's got a fucking gun pointed at me."

"I know, I know."

Korie cocked the hammer. "If you don't both put your guns down now, my finger might just slip on this trigger."

"I'd get you next," said Junior through clenched teeth.

"Maybe you will and then again maybe not. You see, Junior, when you came in here I noticed you hadn't flipped the safety off. Your gun's locked, Junior."

Junior Fecteau wanted so badly to take this bitch out but he couldn't remember if he had flipped off the safety.

He decided in an instant to glance down at the gun in his right hand. At that moment Korie used her left hand to push Bobby towards his brother.

Junior noticed immediately that the safety was off. He began to raise his gun when his younger brother stumbled into him. In the momentary confusion Junior made a deadly decision. He stepped sideways to get a shot off.

Korie now stepped to her right in a circling move while at the same time crouching lower to the floor. Her gun was poised to shoot.

Miss Beacon tipped over the chair with Kelley in it. Miss Beacon half caught her as the two women fell to the floor.

Junior got off a shot. It missed wide. Korie returned fire with two quick shots. Both bullets hit their target. Junior fell to his knees. He was hit in the right shoulder and also in the right side. He tried to fire his gun. As he raised it, Korie fired again. This time he was hit in the chin area of his face, as the bullet's slightly upward trajectory led to a complete severing of his brain stem. In a single violent reaction, he flipped backwards onto his back from his kneeling position. His legs remained bent at the knees as his lower legs remained twisted under his now lifeless body.

Bobby was facing his brother during this split second shootout. He watched in horror as his older brother, whom he loved and admired was shot to death.

"Listen. Put your gun down. Don't make me shoot you, too."

Bobby looked at his own gun. Its safety was off. He had no

choice. He knew it. He turned, firing away as he did.

Korie couldn't take a chance. She took aim and pulled the trigger twice. Both shots hit him in the chest in vital locations. The first shot hit him in the heart, it caused his body to twist, and the second hit him in the lower spine, shattering it, and shredding his spinal column at the same time. His dead body convulsed backwards. He fell, tumbling over Miss Beacon and Kelley in the process.

The quick succession of shots that had exploded in the closed cellar rang in Korie's and Miss Beacon's ears. The acrid smell of spent gunpowder filled the now smoky cellar.

In a moment, the room was about to be inundated by the smell of the dead men's bladders and lower intestines, as their bodies could no longer control their normal functions.

Miss Beacon pushed at Bobby's Fecteau's dead body, rolling it off of her own.

"Where did you learn to shoot like that?" asked Miss Beacon.

"A few years ago I took a self defense course. I got a chance to target practice at the police station firing range. I guess I was pretty good." Looking down at the floor she continued, "Afterward, I signed up for a month's worth of lessons at a local gun club."

"Well, it sure came in handy."

"Right," said an obviously stressed out Korie. Tears were running down her cheeks.

Miss Beacon went to her and gave her a big hug.

"You saved Kelley's life. Look, we still have a chance to stop this madness thanks to you. I know Aaron will be proud of you."

"What now?" Korie said wiping away a tear with the back of her hand.

"Well."

Just then, they both heard a low moan. They turned to see Kelley trying to sit up.

"Now, we get her out of here," said Miss Beacon.

28

Aaron returned to Miss Beacon's place. He parked the Land Rover outside of the sometimes barn, sometimes garage. There was no one home, so he decided to sit and wait in the kitchen. He turned off the table radio, which had been left on. He sat in the dark listening to the steady rain. There were occasional flashes of lightning, along with the rumble of accompanying thunder. Sitting at the kitchen table, he could see out the side window, which overlooked the road, that passed by the front of Miss Beacon's place.

His mind was swimming with images. He put his hands to the sides of his head, in a gesture to try and control the crosscurrents of his mind. He hoped Korie and Miss Beacon would return soon. He needed someone to talk to.

At that moment, he noticed the light from an approaching vehicle shining on the road below. He stood up from the kitchen table and stepped over to stand to the side of the window. The vehicle was moving along the road at a very slow pace.

Aaron quickly slipped to the front room and looked out the front window at the road below. A station wagon rolled into view. It never quite stopped but moved at less than a walking pace. From the faint light provided by the street light, Aaron thought he could only see one person in the car.

Once past the front of Miss Beacon's place, the station wagon quickened in pace and pulled out of sight down the road.

Just as the car rear taillights disappeared from view, the telephone rang.

Its loud ring startled Aaron.

It rang again and again. Aaron didn't want to answer the phone. It kept ringing. After the nearly twentieth ring he decided to answer the phone.

"Hello."

"Hello," he repeated.

"Hello, Aaron. Do you recognize my voice?"

He knew who it was but chose not to answer.

"It's me, Judy. How are you, Aaron?"

"I'm fine."

"Really. You left today in quite a hurry. Was it something I said?"

"No."

"Well, it couldn't have been something I did because I never got to, you know, hold you close," she purred.

"Look, I'm not interested," he said getting ready to hang up on her.

"Aaron, there's someone here who wants to speak to you."

Aaron hesitated for a moment.

"Hello, Aaron. My name is Samuel. I would like to meet you. We have so much to talk about."

"I know," said a nervous Aaron.

"I could have someone pick you up in a few minutes. What do you say?"

"No, not tonight."

"Then when?"

"Tomorrow. I'll get in touch with you, tomorrow."

"Fine. Let me give you a telephone number."

"No need. I'll find you."

"Good. I'll be waiting."

Aaron hung up the phone. He was breathing rapidly, almost on the verge of hyperventilating. His hands were wet with perspiration. The voice of Samuel sounded young but deadly.

"Where are they?" said an exasperated Aaron referring to Miss Beacon and Korie.

Across town, in the office of Reverend Mitchell, the coven members were beside themselves. Their leader, Samuel had spoken with this Aaron Powell. To everyone's surprise Aaron had agreed to meet with Samuel tomorrow. It almost seemed too good to be true.

"I softened him up for you Samuel," said a beaming Judy.

"Bad choice of words," said Chucky breaking into a raucous laugh.

Everyone was in a celebratory mood, everyone that is, except the Reverend and the Judge. They acted pleased as punch but inside, they were fuming.

One by one they left until there was only the Reverend, the Judge, Samuel and Ed Townsend.

"Ed, I want you to check up on the Fecteau brothers for me. I sent them to guard my sister. I don't want any screw-ups now that we're this close. If everything goes well, we might have the calling ceremony tomorrow night."

"Why didn't you tell me you wanted her under guard? I would have called a couple of my men, reliable men. Those Fecteau brothers always manage to screw things up, somehow."

"I made the decision, Ed. They are completely loyal to the church and this coven. Anyway, how hard could it be? Are you questioning my judgment?"

Ed wanted to say something in retort but decided to hold his tongue. No need to piss off Samuel. Samuel was close to Moloch who is obviously close to Lucifer. Ed knew where he stood in the pecking order of things and right now Samuel was "the man."

"No, it's fine with me. You're right. How hard could it be? I'll head over there right now and check up on them. Anything else?"

"No."

Ed turned to leave. As he turned from Samuel he glanced over at the Judge who seemed to be studying him. The Judge nodded to Ed who managed a slight nod in return. Ed left the room.

"Well, Judge, Reverend, it seems that we shall be the ones who deliver on the promise made long ago. We are the true Keepers of the Agreement, our sacred Covenant. There will be much to do. I'll need both of you to help me organize our calling ceremony. I want to meet early tomorrow morning. Plan on coming over for breakfast at eight."

"Whatever you say," said the Reverend, as eagerly as he could.

"Do you need a ride home? It's still raining," asked the Judge.

"No, Bob's waiting for me outside."

"Well then, tomorrow it is!" said the Judge.

With that, Samuel turned and left. He exited with a spring in his step.

The room was silent for the moment.

"Whew," said the Reverend as he slumped into his office chair.

***

"Why don't we take the car?" asked Korie. The Fecteau brother's car sat silent in the church's driveway.

"No. We could be stopped. It's too risky. We'll take her back through the woods."

"The woods, are you kidding? She's not strong enough and we sure can't carry her."

"Oh, I believe she's strong enough. You'll see."

They went back down the bulkhead stairs. Korie helped Kelley to her feet. At first Kelley rocked a bit on her feet, and then steadied herself by grabbing onto Korie's arm.

Korie shot a look at Miss Beacon's that seemed to say, "Look at her, she has trouble standing."

"Let's go. We can't stay here any longer."

Korie, holding onto Kelley, led her to the stairs. After a slight struggle Kelley made it to the top of the stairs. The three women were now standing in the gravel driveway of the church. The rain had slowed down a bit but was still steadily misting.

With Miss Beacon leading the way the women headed down the driveway turned left and headed down to the end of the cul-de-sac. In a few moments they entered the woods. After going just a few feet into the woods, Miss Beacon stopped.

She bent over and said, "Good boy, I knew you'd be waiting."

"Is that the dog?" asked Korie, somewhat amazed the dog had waited for them.

"Yes, it is. He's going to lead the way for us, aren't you boy?"

Korie and Kelley could hear the dog panting.

Korie slapped at her arm. It was a mosquito on a mission.

"Let's get going before the bugs eat us alive," said Korie.

"Oops, I'm sorry Kelley," said Korie.

Kelley nodded and said "It's okay. You guys saved me, thanks."

"Are you two ready?" said Miss Beacon.

"Yeah," said Kelley.

"Yeah, we're ready," said Korie.

Miss Beacon tied her dress cloth belt around the dog's neck in a sort of collar and leash.

"Well then, let's go."

The three women headed deeper into the woods, led by the dog, which earlier in the evening was prepared to take a bite out of one, if not both of them.

As they moved deeper into the dark and wet woods, the rain and fresh air seemed to refresh Kelley. She soon walked along without having to hold onto Korie.

Minutes later a car slowly pulled into the church driveway. It pulled to a stop behind the Fecteau brother's car.

Ed Townsend got out of the car. He walked completely around the Fecteau car. He noticed the car keys were still in the ignition. Looking over at the church, he noticed the church cellar lights were on and the bulkhead doors were wide open.

This isn't looking too good, thought Ed.

He drew his service revolver from his shoulder holster and holding it in the ready position, he slowly approached the bulkhead. In a quick, but highly trained move, he stepped in front of the bulkhead doors, and pointed his gun down the stairwell, ready to fire.

Nothing threatened him from the cellar. It was eerily quiet, except for the sound of falling rain.

He slowly descended the stairs. As he approached the bottom he noticed the all too distinct odors of gunpowder and human excrement. He had a good idea of what he was about to encounter. Still, he had to be very careful. Someone could still be lurking in the cellar, ready to take him on. He almost wished there was someone hiding in the cellar. He hadn't plugged a perpetrator in quite a while.

He leaned against the left side of the bulkhead wall. He took a deep breath and then launched himself into the cellar rolling on the floor, gun pointed hand sweeping the cellar. His FBI training had taught him that in situations like this when you're alone and facing an armed assailant, you have to present the smallest target possible. And most important of all, identify the target, confirm it as hostile, and shoot first!

His eyes quickly scanned the scene in the cellar and in a moment he realized no one else was in the main cellar that could pose any immediate threat. He spotted the Fecteau brothers and concluded they were dead. He sprang to his feet and ran to the back wall. He quickly stood up against the back wall, still with his gun held ready. He moved along the wall and stopped, next to the opened door, which led to the back room chamber where Samuel's sister had been held. His ears couldn't pick out any unusual sounds. He moved quickly across the open entrance, pointed his gun inside, ready to fire in an instant. It was obvious the chamber was empty.

Ed holstered his gun. He turned and surveyed the "scene," as he would call it.

Two dead men, both shot with a large caliber weapon. He examined the bodies. One shot three times the other shot twice. Both men got off shots of their own, but had apparently not hit anyone. At least there was no evidence of anyone being wounded in this gunfight. There was a folding chair sitting in the middle of the room.

What significance did it hold? How many were there? One or more of them had to have been good shots, he thought. He surmised where he thought the shooter, or shooters stood, and checked the floor for any sign that might give him some information he could use.

Whoever they are, they weren't just lucky. No sir they were smart. They had to have used some kind of distraction in order to get the drop on the Fecteau brothers. Clever bastards, he thought, as his highly trained mind raced along in its typical analytical fashion.

Two men dead and Samuel's sister missing. Samuel isn't going to like this news.

Cocky little bastard is going to be pissed off, thought Ed. *I can't wait to break the news to that little know it all freak.*

Ed turned out the church cellar lights and exited from the bulkhead. He closed and locked the bulkhead doors. Ed also removed the car keys from the Fecteau brother's car. He tossed them into his jacket pocket. Ed had a smile on his face as he pulled his own car out of the church driveway. He turned right at the end of the driveway and headed towards Samuel's house.

Ed was thinking about how he was going to break the news to Samuel. It had to be done just right. It had to be done with style. It had to say, "I told you so" without coming right out and saying it.

No need in going too far with that little bastard. No telling what he might do, thought Ed.

Suddenly, Ed turned his car down a street that took him away from Samuel's house. On a hunch, he decided to first stop in over at the Reverend's place. He stepped on the accelerator.

In a few minutes he arrived at the Reverend's place. He quickly jumped from his car and ran up to the front door. He knocked loudly on the door and rang the doorbell.

The door opened. The Reverend seemed surprised to see Ed.

"Ed, what brings you back here?"

"Reverend, you're not going to believe this. Samuel's sister is missing and the Fecteau brother's are dead. They were both shot to death."

"Come in. The Judge is here and I'm sure he would like to hear what you have to say," said the Reverend as he swung open the door.

Ed rushed in and headed straight for the Reverend's office.

"Hello, Judge!"

"Ed."

"Judge, it appears Ed has some rather disturbing news."

"Do tell."

"Yeah. I was just over at the Church. When I got there, I noticed right away that things didn't seem right. Anyway, I'll cut to the chase. I went down in the cellar and found the Fecteau brothers both shot dead. They got off some shots of their own, but hadn't hit anything that I could tell. Then I checked on Samuel's sister, Kelley, and found she was gone."

The Judge leaned forward and looked Ed squarely in the eyes.

"And, have you told Samuel?"

"No, I haven't, not yet.

"Why did you come here first?"

"I've been thinking about things, you know. Look, its no secret I can't stand that little bastard. I'll tell you what I think. I think he's going to find a way to screw this up for us. I also think it's a mistake to have him in charge. We should have just grabbed this Powell and made him cooperate. There are ways you know. Instead we're told to just let Powell run around town. Keep an eye on him, he says. Shit!"

The Judge leaned back in his chair and folded his fingers together as he studied Ed.

"Judge, don't you think Ed's right?" said the Reverend in an attempt to lead the Judge.

"Perhaps. Listen, Ed, suppose we agree with you on this. What are you prepared to do? What are you prepared to risk?"

Ed looked at both men. He was about to step across the line. He knew it.

"Look, I'll tell you what. I'm prepared to help replace him. And if that means killing him, I'm prepared for that, too. What am I prepared to risk? I'm prepared to put my life on the line here. If you want, I'll pull the fucking trigger myself."

There was silence in the room. No one spoke for over one minute. The only sounds to be heard, was the sound of light rain still falling against the window, on the westerly side of the room, and the sound of the bookcase clock.

"You have presented us with an attractive proposal. As you might have surmised we too are, shall we say, disappointed with Moloch's choice of Samuel as the coven leader. However before we go much further, I suggest you proceed to inform Samuel of what you found at the church."

"Yes, Ed, remember he sent you to check on things. He knows how long it takes to get to the church. He'll wonder why it has taken you so long to inform him. He'll be suspicious."

"Indeed. Ed, go inform Samuel. You can come back here afterwards. We'll be here waiting for you. We can discuss our options when you return."

"I understand. Okay, I'll head over to his place right now. I'll tell him what happened. He might want to send me off to do something, I don't know. If he does, I'll give you a call and let you guys know what's happening."

With that, Ed stood up and quickly left the room. In a moment, they heard the front door close, followed by the sound of Ed's car starting up.

"Well, Judge, it seems we now have a powerful and committed ally."

"Perhaps an ally or perhaps a decoy. We shall see, won't we? The end game is so very important Reverend, very important."

***

Samuel was standing in his room looking out his window into the blackness of the night.

He had much to think about. Tomorrow was the day, the day of the Covenant. It was the day hoped for long ago, denied all these years and now about to be fulfilled.

He also knew there was treachery somewhere in his coven. Who the traitors were, what they might be planning, and when they planned to spring their dark plan, intrigued Samuel. He looked forward to assisting Moloch in punishing the offenders. Their punishment would have to be great, certainly as great as the treachery they perpetrated.

Samuel heard a commotion coming from downstairs.

Then he heard someone bounding loudly up the stairs. Suddenly his bedroom door burst open. He turned to face whoever it was, that was in such a rush to see him.

"Samuel," said Ed slightly out of breath.

"Yes, Ed. What is it?"

"Kelley's gone, and the Fecteau brothers are both dead. They were shot to death."

Samuel's eyes opened about as wide as humanly possible. He looked clearly angry.

"What happened?"

"I just told you. Those assholes you sent over there must have walked into an ambush," said Ed savoring the moment.

"I don't understand."

"What part don't you understand?"

"Besides our people, who else knew she was there? I'll tell you, no one. I personally saw her locked up. She certainly didn't escape on her own. This Aaron Powell is too weak to have done this. His woman friend is weak like him. The only other person is their friend, Miss Beacon. She is an old hag. No, no, no," said Samuel as he began to pace, "there has to be someone else, someone we have overlooked. Ed, I want you to return to the church. Get rid of the bodies. Get Foley and Yandow to help you. Check the church and the area thoroughly. See if there is anything, anything at all, that might give us a clue as to who is secretly helping this Powell."

"You're the boss!" said Ed as he turned and headed for the door.

"And Ed?"

"Yeah," he said turning back.

"If you get a lead on who our traitor is, remember come to me first. I want them alive. Moloch and I will deal with them."

"Sure," said Ed as he left the room.

"Moloch and I, Moloch and I," repeated Ed under his breath as he went down the stairs.

***

Aaron had been sitting in the darkened living room ever since the phone conversation with Samuel. He felt he needed to get this thing over with before he lost his mind. He hated being alone.

Miss Beacon, Korie and Kelley, along with the dog, arrived at the rear of Miss Beacon's barn. Everyone was soaked to the bone. Overly aggressive mosquitoes had been attacking them steadily, ever since they had entered the woods.

Miss Beacon knelt down on one leg, and scratched the ears of the German shepherd that had so reliably led them though the dark wet woods.

"Nice boy, yeah, nice boy. I've got a treat for you. Korie, in your backpack is a dog chew bone. Will you get it for me?"

"How did you know? Oh, never mind," said Korie.

"What do you mean?" asked Kelley.

Korie removed the backpack and opened up the top flap.

"I mean, how did she know ahead of time, that we would meet up with a dog, who would lead us back and forth through these woods? I'll tell you how, she's a..."

"Now Korie, don't you go and spoil our surprise."

"What surprise?" asked Kelley as Korie handed the chew bone to Miss Beacon.

Miss Beacon handed the chew bone to the dog, which took it in its mouth, turned and padded back into the dark woods.

"You'll just have to wait a bit."

"Come on. We're almost there," said Miss Beacon as she opened the barn door. "Kelley, take my hand and also hold Korie's hand, too. Good, now follow me."

The three women entered the barn. Korie closed the rear door. Once inside, it was hard to see because it was completely dark except for the soft glow that entered the south side barn windows. That was the side of the barn that faced the road, which passed by the front of Miss Beacon's property. The glow came from the two nearby streetlights, which lined the road.

With Miss Beacon leading the way, they quickly moved through the barn. Miss Beacon stopped at the front side door. She slowly opened it and looked out.

In a moment she said "Good. It's all clear. Let's go."

The women left the barn in quite a hurry. Korie barely had time enough to close the door. They half ran across the back yard driveway and scampered up onto the back porch. A flash of lightning lit up the back porch. The storm was beginning to wind down.

The three women stepped off the porch and entered the kitchen. There were no lights on.

"Where's Aaron?" asked Korie.

"I'm sure he's here," said Miss Beacon.

Just then Kelley looked past Miss Beacon. From the soft glow of the street light filtering in from the windows, she noticed the silhouette of a man coming through the doorway. The figure seemed overly large and menacing. She felt a rush of panic. She let loose a scream.

The scream startled the other women.

"Miss Beacon, look out," shouted Kelley.

At the sound of their screams, Aaron reached out to the wall, and flipped on the overhead light. Standing in front of him was Miss Beacon with her arm around a teenage girl. Stepping out from behind these two, was his girlfriend Korie, with a gun raised up and pointed directly at him. The three of them were soaked and dripping water on the floor.

As a reflex action he raised his two arms into the air.

"Shit, Aaron, you scared the hell out of us," said Korie as she lowered the gun to her side.

"Indeed," said Miss Beacon.

"Who's he?" asked Kelley.

"He's the man who's going to defeat Samuel," said Miss Beacon.

"Oh," said Kelley as she fell from Miss Beacon's arms onto the kitchen floor. She had fainted.

"Take her into the bathroom please," said Miss Beacon.

Korie put the gun back into her waistband, and with Aaron's help, managed to carry Kelley into the bathroom.

"Hold her," commanded Miss Beacon as she turned on the overhead light. Miss Beacon then opened the medicine cabinet and reached for a small bottle. She opened it and removed a small vial. She broke the vial and held it up to Kelley's nose. It was smelling salts. The odor immediately caused Kelley's head to snap backwards as she regained consciousness.

"There now, sit right here," said Miss Beacon as guided Kelley to sit on the closed toilet seat.

"I'll help her take a warm shower as soon as she feels alert enough."

"She looks like she could use one," said Korie.

"I'm sure, now Korie you should go and take a shower. Aaron, please stay with Kelley while I go get her some dry clothes to change into, for after her shower."

Korie left and headed upstairs to take a shower.

Miss Beacon left as well.

Aaron knelt down next to the girl. He could easily see her skin was marked with dozens of dark red spots. A purple colored bruise surrounded each spot.

"Her name is Kelley," shouted Miss Beacon from another room at the back of the house. "She's Samuel's sister."

Aaron froze.

Miss Beacon returned to the bathroom with a large bath towel and some clothes.

"What happened to her?" asked Aaron.

"It seems, she has been chained up in a cellar back room for a couple of days. Those marks were caused by dozens of spider bites."

"Did Samuel do this?"

Kelley moaned softly. She was still a little light headed.

"Yes, now get out of here while I help her out of her soiled clothes."

Aaron left the room and headed upstairs to the bedroom he and Korie shared.

After he left, Miss Beacon began to undress Kelley and change her out of her wet clothes.

Korie was already in the bathroom.

Aaron could hear the shower running. He sat at the foot of the bed and then fell back onto the bed.

How can I tell her? What will she say? thought Aaron as he pondered how to tell Korie about what had happened to him today.

What had happened to Korie, Miss Beacon and this young girl, Samuel's sister, Kelley? he thought as his mind raced along. *What about tomorrow? I still have no idea what to do.*

His mind began to freely drift along. He was tired, stressed out and deeply in need of a good night's rest. He quickly dropped off to sleep.

***

Samuel stood at the foot of his bed. He closed his eyes and extended his arms in front of him. He held his hands out, palm side up.

"Moloch, our counsel and leader, I call for you to appear. Our coven needs your help. I need your help. Moloch hear my words and answer my call," said Samuel.

The room temperature began to immediately rise, as if the thermostat had been cranked up to its maximum. The carpet that covered the pentagram painted on the floor, slid across the room. A twirling mass of pulsating lights formed in the air above the pentagram. The lights spun at ever increasing speed. The air in the room felt heavy. The light from the overhead light, and the light on the nightstand seemed to be literally sucked into this spinning vortex.

Samuel continued to stand as he did before. The hair on his head was pushed back, as if he were standing in front of an oversized fan.

The lights now stretched from the floor to the ceiling. The pulsating lights began to take on a shape. They formed an outline of a large figure. The figure was human like in shape but not in proportions. The figure itself was not spinning. This dark figure appeared at first without any detail. In a few moments distinct details began to appear.

A large head appeared first. The head had no hair but had two horns. Its skin seemed to move, as if there was something beneath, trying to find a way to break through and escape. Details now began to take form throughout the rest of the shape. The figure stood nearly seven feet tall. Its unclothed body was covered mostly with a scaly skin, whose color seemed to change from green, to brown, then black, and then back to green. This shape had two massive and powerful looking legs. In place of feet were two cloven hooves. The shape had a snake like tail that twisted constantly. Its hands were very large, with long fingers, and long misshapen nails.

The shape opened its eyes, revealing two deeply set red colored orbs that now looked about the room.

The swirling lights began to fade away. The shape had transformed itself into Moloch. Moloch took a deep breath, his chest swelling from the effort.

Moloch let Samuel remain in his trance-like state for a while. Meanwhile, Moloch walked around Samuel's room, his hooves clicking against the hardwood floor. He wanted to look out the window. The window was closed because of the passing summer storm. Moloch extended his right hand, and in a flash the entire window, casing and all blew off, crashing on the ground below. The nighttime air was still humid despite the effects of the storm. Clearer, drier air was expected to arrive on the backside of this storm. Its arrival was a couple of hours away. After drawing a breath at the window, Moloch returned to stand in front of Samuel.

Soon I will walk this place in human form along side of Lucifer. Our legions will march before us. We will have our Armageddon, thought Moloch.

Turning around he spoke, "I have come," in his deep and menacing voice.

Samuel's eyelids flickered for a moment before they completely opened. Samuel lowered his arms, which had become weary from having been held up for several minutes.

"Moloch, welcome, I have some news and I need your advice."

"Go on."

"I spoke with Powell tonight. He has agreed to meet me tomorrow. I don't think we should wait any longer. I will try to persuade him to join the coven, but if he should refuse, I believe we should be prepared to force his cooperation. I suggest we hold the ceremony tomorrow night, with or without his willing cooperation."

"I understand and I agree."

"On another matter, I must report that my sister Kelley escaped tonight. Two of our men were ambushed and shot to death."

"I know, I greeted their souls just moments ago. It seems two women set a trap for them."

"Two women?"

"Yes. An old woman and a younger one who did the shooting. You know who these women are don't you, Samuel?"

"I think I do."

"Good. You must also know where your sister is now."

"I think so."

Leaning into Samuel, so their faces were a mere couple of inches apart, Moloch furrowed his eyebrows and said, "Then make sure your sister is present at the ceremony along with these two women. Do what you have to do Samuel, you don't want to disappoint the Prince of Darkness, not when you are this close."

Samuel could see the twisted misshapen teeth and smell Moloch's breath. It reeked with an odor that reminded Samuel of rotting leaves.

"I understand," said Samuel. "But what about the traitors in the coven?"

"They will show their hand. Of that you can be sure. Only then, will you settle with them."

"But, I need to know who they are?"

"When you need to know, you will know."

"Moloch, I haven't asked this before, but I was wondering..."

Stepping back from Samuel, Moloch stood up straight saying, "Speak no more. Lucifer will show you his eternal gratitude for what you have done. As you know, many have tried before and many have failed. I can not say any more."

Moloch suddenly was surrounded by a swirl of pulsating light. He stood still and closed his eyes. The swirling lights spun faster and faster. Moloch's form began to appear as if it had turned into a sort of liquid state. It lost its human shape, and began to shrink down into a small dark mass. Suddenly, there was a flash of light as the shape, and swirling lights disappeared. Lingering about in the room was a strong odor of burnt sulfur. The temperature in the room had to be nearly a hundred degrees. Samuel was drenched in sweat. The temperature in his bedroom began to slowly drop.

He felt a slight breeze. He turned, and noticed his window had been blown away.

***

Korie was lathering up her body as she stood underneath the warm spray of water coming out of the showerhead. She applied a generous amount of soap. She rinsed herself off. Next she poured some shampoo out of the bottle into her left hand. She placed the shampoo bottle on the shower shelf and applied the shampoo to her hair.

She heard a "click" sound. It startled her. She was still jumpy from all that had happened earlier.

"Aaron, is that you?"

There was no answer.

She pulled back the shower curtain and looked around the bathroom. The air in the room was already fogging up from her shower. There was no sign of Aaron. She quickly surveyed the room and didn't notice anything out of place.

Korie returned to washing her hair.

Suddenly, she felt as if someone was watching her. The feeling was very strong. She slowly turned to look at the shower curtain. She was looking to see if there was a shadow of someone in the room. She saw nothing. She decided to pull the shower curtain partially back, in a sudden move, to surprise whoever had come into the bathroom.

She snapped the curtain partially back.

No one was there.

"Damn," she said.

She looked over at the pistol she had left on the toilet tank shelf. She could reach it, but she would have to leave the shower to do so. In the back of her mind she had an odd feeling about the gun. She couldn't quite settle on the reason. She looked at the gun again, and then she noticed that it was not lying in the same position she had placed it. She had put it down, with the handle lying away from the shower. Now it was sitting there, with its handle pointing towards the shower. Someone had moved it. She was sure of it.

She surveyed the room again.

Where could someone hide? she thought.

She considered calling out to Aaron but decided against it. She didn't want him thinking she was loosing it. Not after coming this close to settling this long standing Powell family fight, against these minions of the devil.

She finally decided it must be her mind playing tricks on her. After all, she had been through a great deal too, and she was very tired. She and Aaron would exchange stories tomorrow morning about their individual adventures. Tonight everyone needed to just get whatever sleep they could.

***

Miss Beacon applied a cold compress to Kelley's forehead. She was still running a slight temperature, perhaps as a reaction to the spider bites. Nevertheless, Kelley was responding well. After her shower, she had briefly laid down on the couch in the living room. She just sat up, sipping some lemonade that Miss Beacon had brought her.

"Would you like something to eat, dear?"

"Sure, that would be fine."

"Good, then come with me," said Miss Beacon.

The two women headed into the kitchen. Kelley sat down at the table. Miss Beacon took a large bowl out of the refrigerator and began to scoop out fresh cut fruit into a bowl. Then she put the large bowl back in the refrigerator and removed a can of whipped cream. She shook the can and applied a generous amount on top of the fruit.

Miss Beacon put the bowl down on the table in front of Kelley. From a large mug on the table she removed a teaspoon and handed it to Kelley.

Kelley began to sample the delicious cream covered fruit.

"Do you have any idea what is about to happen here in Sutton?" asked Miss Beacon.

"I think I do. That's why I was trying to run away."

"I see."

"I thought about that again tonight as we walked through the woods. I guess there really isn't any safe place to run away to if Samuel wins, right?"

"That's right."

"Why my bother?"

"He was chosen."

"By who?"

"The devil himself."

"Then this isn't really his fault."

"I'm afraid he's responsible for his share. He still has a free will."

"But he's changed," said Kelley as a tear ran down her cheek.

"I know dear, I know."

They both heard a stumbling like sound coming from the floor above them.

It caused just a momentary distraction.

"Kelley, tomorrow, the young man you saw in this kitchen earlier will be faced with the challenge of stopping your brother. His girlfriend, Korie who helped both of us tonight, and I, will be by his side. We will join him in this battle. And make no mistake about it Kelley, it will be a life and death battle. It is one that we must win, or Lucifer, the most evil one, will have his way and the entire human race will face Armageddon."

***

Korie was finishing up with her shower when she spotted a spider climbing up the shower wall. She killed it with a slap of her right hand. She watched it fall into the swirling shower water at her feet and disappear down the drain. Her gazed fixed upon the shower drain and then she noticed three spiders just like the last one scamper out of the drain.

How is that possible? she thought.

She tried stepping on them but they were too quick. Then, she noticed dozens of spiders pouring up from out of the drain. She stumbled out of the shower, tearing the shower curtain from its hanger, as she fell onto the tiled floor. The shower was still on. The entire shower wall was now crawling with spiders. She stood up and reached for her towel, which she quickly wrapped around her.

She began to back away from the tub, her wet feet slipping under her as she tried to steady herself. She spotted the pistol and grabbed it out of instinct. Suddenly, she felt something crawling up her left leg. She looked down and was horrified to see several spiders making their way up her leg. There were dozens more crawling out of the shower, which were now also heading in her direction. She frantically slapped away at these determined insects.

She despised spiders. She loathed spiders. She was completely terrorized by spiders.

She felt something moving in her hair. She swatted at her hair and then noticed a spider clinging to the back of her hand. Korie clutched her towel. She wanted to scream.

She looked up and froze. Looking into the steamed haze of the bathroom mirror she could see someone standing directly behind her. It was a man. And then again it wasn't human. The eyes were glowing, a deep yellow-red. It was as if the eyes were embers from a campfire. The reflected image smiled at her. It was a look of lust and evil all rolled into one.

Korie remembered she still had one bullet left in her gun. She was prepared to use it. She turned around and fired at point blank range. The sound of the gun going off was deafening in the closed confines of the bathroom. Korie, more out of panic than anything else, pulled the trigger a total of three times, in rapid succession. To her great surprise, the gun fired each time. To her greater surprise there was no one behind her. She spun around and looked for the spiders. They were gone. The shower curtain was still on the floor where it fell when she tumbled out of the shower. Otherwise everything looked normal.

She suddenly felt weak. She let the gun fall from her hand. It landed on the tile floor with a loud "thunking" sound. She let her towel fall next. Her mind, once filled with the terror of the spiders, then the mysterious stranger, was now totally blank.

***

Aaron had entered deep sleep. He was drifting off in a dream about a time when he was a small boy and his mother, who he believed then to be his aunt, had taken him to a long sandy ocean beach somewhere in Maine. He was standing in the shallows where the waves washed up on the beach. The water was cold. His teeth were chattering. He turned to look back at the beach. He saw his aunt frantically waving to him and shouting something that he couldn't quite hear.

Bang, bang, bang.

The thunderous sounds exploded in his dream. In a reflex action Aaron bolted awake, rolled off the bed and fell to the floor.

***

Kelley jumped out of her seat. Miss Beacon did the same.

"What was that?" demanded Kelley.

"It was gun shots! They came from upstairs."

Without waiting for more conversation, Miss Beacon turned around and scampered towards the stairs. Kelley was right on her heels. The two of them reached Aaron and Korie's room. They looked in and saw Aaron lying on the floor against the foot of the bed. He gestured towards the adjacent bathroom.

Miss Beacon nodded.

"Korie, it's me," said Miss Beacon. "Are you all right?"

There was no answer.

Miss Beacon gestured to Aaron to call her.

"Korie, please answer us. Are you okay?"

Still there was no answer. Everyone could hear the shower running. Nevertheless there was no other sound coming from the bathroom.

Miss Beacon slowly and carefully looked around the door jam towards the bathroom. The door was closed, and there were three holes in the upper middle of the door. Streaks of lights shone into the bedroom from these holes.

Miss Beacon stood up and walked to the bathroom door and slowly tried to open the door. It was locked from inside.

"Korie dear, please unlock the door for me?"

Silence.

Miss Beacon stood up on the tips of her toes, and removed a key from the top of the door. She put it into the lock and opened the door.

As the door swung open, she found herself looking straight ahead at Korie, who was standing before her totally naked. Her towel had fallen away after the gun shots. Korie had a blank expression on her face. She looked lost.

Miss Beacon picked up the towel, and wrapped it around her. She picked up the gun and led Korie out of the bathroom.

"Kelley, please be a dear and turn the shower off for me."

Kelley moved past her into the bathroom.

"Here, hold this for me," said Miss Beacon as she handed the pistol to Aaron.

He took it by the handle. He turned it around and rotating the cylinder he noticed that the six shot cylinder appeared full.

29

The bodies of the Fecteau brothers were removed from the church just as Samuel had directed. Ed Townsend remained at the church after the bodies had been removed. He was now doing some investigating on his own. He was looking for the bullets that had passed through the Fecteau brother's bodies during the shootout. He had no trouble locating the bullets or their fragments, which came from the Fecteau brother's own guns.

He spent the better part of an hour looking. He found nothing. It puzzled him. Finally he left the church after turning out the lights and locking up.

As he walked over to his car, he noticed the early morning sun was beginning to light up the sky to the east. The sky radiated a soft pink. There were only the faintest traces of clouds. Birds were already awake and chirping. There was also a cool dry breeze blowing in from the northwest.

He climbed into his car. He started it up, rolled down the front windows, and then turned around and drove out of the driveway. He didn't feel like getting any sleep. He decided that what he needed was some coffee. He headed into town.

***

Aaron, Korie, Kelley and Miss Beacon had stayed up all night. Nobody wanted to go to sleep. They had decided to share information. Aaron and Korie told their story and then Kelley told hers. Miss Beacon, with a nod to Aaron and Korie, withheld the important detail of who she was. Nevertheless, she was able to add much to the unfolding story, by relating things she had learned about the coven during her time in Sutton.

"I am frightened," said Kelley. "I told you what they did to my friend. Their power is awesome. How can we stop them?"

"We can't, remember I told you, only Aaron can," said Miss Beacon.

Kelley looked at Aaron and said, "Do you think you can?"

"I don't know. All I do know is that I'm going to try."

"Can't your mother and your ancestors, you know those ghosts or whatever help? They must be able to do something," said Kelley.

"I don't think so. I guess this struggle with Lucifer over his plans for Armageddon has always been between him and just one human being."

"It's not fair. He's got the coven, he's got Moloch and he's got all his other devils. What have you got?" Kelley said with exasperation in her voice.

"Now, now, Kelley. Aaron's got more than you might think. You must have faith," said Miss Beacon.

Korie sat quietly throughout this exchange. She sipped at her coffee. Her eyes looked away, towards the kitchen counter at the gun Miss Beacon had given her. She pushed herself away from the table, and went to the counter, and poured what was left of her coffee into the sink. She poured herself a fresh cup of coffee. While she was doing this she looked again at the gun. It seemed to be fully loaded. At least she could see five bullets in the cylinder.

She turned around and rejoined the others.

Early morning sunlight was beginning to fill the sky. Outside birds were chirping. A slight breeze blew into the kitchen through the open windows. The morning air felt cool and dry. The lace curtains swayed in the breeze.

"We should have something to eat. Would you like some waffles or eggs and bacon?" asked Miss Beacon.

Everyone opted for waffles.

Miss Beacon went over to the kitchen counter, and began to busy herself making waffles.

A cicada bug buzzed somewhere off in the distance.

"Aaron, can I ask you something?" asked Kelley.

"Sure!"

"Do you know what you're going to do, you know, do you have a plan?"

"Not yet."

Kelley looked down at the table for a moment then she looked up at Aaron. Her eyes were all watery as if she was about to cry.

"I want to help. I want to be there with you," she said.

"But it will be very dangerous," answered Aaron.

"I know, but I just can't run away from this, not now."

"I understand," said Aaron.

Korie spoke up for the first time in awhile "What do you think Miss Beacon?"

Miss Beacon turned towards them while still mixing the waffle batter in a large blue bowl "I think God will be pleased. It is certainly her choice to make. Choosing to fight evil is the righteous thing to do."

"So how do we do this? You must have some ideas. Don't you have some knowledge of how the others defeated Lucifer in the past? Can't you share some of that information with us?" asked Korie.

"Each time was unique."

"I can't buy that."

"Korie ease up a little. We both know Miss Beacon can't help me in this. Her role, if any, must be limited and that's just the way it is. Now look, I promised Samuel I would meet him today. Any suggestions people?" said Aaron.

"Only one," said Miss Beacon. I recommend you meet him at the ceremony and not before. The less chance he has to size you up the better."

"I agree," said Korie.

"Me, too," said Kelley.

"Then it's settled. I'll call him and tell him I'll meet him at the ceremony and not before."

"But he's going to want to know if you're going to join the coven and help bring Moloch to human form. What are you going to tell him?" said Kelley.

"She's right," said Korie.

"I don't know," said Aaron.

"Come on, Aaron. Think, think! Of course you're going to tell him you will join the coven," said Miss Beacon. "To defeat him you're going to have to get close to him. You can't do that unless he believes that you're with him."

"You're right," said Aaron.

***

Judge Fairchild had just picked up the Reverend. The two were heading out for breakfast, before the meeting of the coven Samuel had called for later in the morning.

The Judge pulled his car to a stop in the parking lot next to the Green Mountain Diner. The restaurant was a throw back to the diners once popular across the country. This diner had been in business since the Great Depression. Its chrome trim counter top and chrome tube chairs had been polished thousands of times over the years. It served the best breakfast in the area. The lunch and dinner cuisine was basic, generous, and reliably excellent. Everything was made from scratch. The owner and head cook, Nick Karagiotas, would tolerate nothing less.

The two men entered the diner and moved to a booth at the far end. Sitting at the counter across from the booth was Ed Townsend. He was reading a newspaper. The waitress refilled his cup of coffee.

"Thanks, Angela," said Ed.

"Morning, Ed!" said the Judge. The Reverend said the same.

"Morning, Judge, Reverend,"

"So, what's in the news?" asked the Judge.

"Not much, Judge, not much."

"Why don't you join us?" said the Judge.

"Thanks," said Ed as he put the newspaper down and moved his coffee cup and saucer to their table. He slid in next to the Reverend.

"Today is our day," said the Reverend.

"Indeed it is," said the Judge.

"Obviously, you guys haven't heard the latest," said Ed.

"What do mean?" asked the Reverend.

"As I told you last night, the Fecteau brothers are both dead. Shot last night over at the church."

"Yes, we know, but you reported all this to Samuel. What did he say, what did he do?" said the Reverend.

"It's simple. Our 'know it all' leader continues to screw up. First, he sends a couple of fuck-ups to guard his sister. Did he warn them to be alert for intruders? No, of course not. Has he made a move on this Powell character, you know, pick him up, and see what's ticking? No way! Samuel keeps saying everything is under control. It's not, thanks to this boneheaded, stubborn asshole. This whole thing just pisses me off. The little wise ass is going to screw it up for all of us. Mark my words gentlemen, he's totally incompetent."

The look on his face spoke to his seriousness.

"Well, Ed, it seems you have laid out a strong case that Samuel must be removed, wouldn't you agree, Reverend?" said the Judge.

"Why, yes, of course. Ed is a man of great loyalty to our cause. He's proven it beyond reproach. I think he's made an excellent point," said the Reverend in a hushed tone as his eyes darted back and forth.

"Would you gentlemen care to order?" asked the waitress. She had just arrived at their table and stood ready with a small note pad and pencil in hand.

"Reverend, why don't you order first," said the Judge.

"Thanks. Well, let's see, I'll have a large cup of coffee, and a small glass of orange juice, two eggs scrambled, wheat toast and hash browns.

"And you, Judge?"

"I'll have a small cup of coffee and a three egg vegetarian omelet. Ed, will you have breakfast with us? It'll be my treat."

"No thanks, Judge. I'm not in the mood for food right now."

The waitress left to take care of their orders. In a moment she returned with the two coffees and the orange juice.

"Have you formed any ideas about how one goes about removing Samuel?" asked the Judge.

"No, not really."

"Well perhaps we can be of some assistance in that matter."

"Go on."

"Well, first of all, I don't think any other members of our coven could be relied upon to join in, or support a coup. On the other hand, I likewise don't expect they would interfere either."

"Okay, then if that's so, it should make it easier."

"Perhaps. But Ed, timing is going to be very important in this affair."

"Timing and the element of surprise."

"Yes."

"How about at the coven meeting this morning?" asked the Reverend.

"Too soon," answered Ed. "We need more time to plan this. I think we should look to taking him out just before or during the calling ceremony. His entire focus will be on the ceremony."

"I agree with Ed," said the Judge.

"How about we get together after the coven meeting this morning and think this through?" asked Ed.

"Sounds good to me. Let's meet then," said the Judge.

"Wait," said the Reverend. What about the saboteurs that killed the Fecteau brothers and now have Kelley?"

"Yeah, you're right," said Ed.

"I am sure that when the coven meets this morning, we will decide what to do about those matters. If there is to be an assignment to either of us to address this, then we shall postpone our business meeting until after. I feel confident we shall have enough time to set our plans in order," said the Judge.

"I agree. Look, I've got to get going. I need a shower and shave. I'll see you over at the meeting," said Ed as he slipped out of this seat.

Just as he left their waitress arrived with their breakfast orders.

They both enjoyed their breakfast.

***

Kelley decided she was tired and needed to take a mid-morning nap. She went up to Miss Beacon's room to lie down. Aaron decided he needed to shower and shave. He left the kitchen, and headed up to the bathroom.

Korie and Miss Beacon were now alone in the kitchen. Miss Beacon started to wash the breakfast dishes, and Korie picked up a dishtowel and began to dry.

"Can I ask you a question?" asked Korie.

"Now dear, with everything we've been through you should know you can ask me anything you like."

"The pistol you gave me to use last night."

"Yes."

"You said that it once belonged to Aaron's mother."

"Did I say that?"

"Yes, you did."

"Yes, it did belong to her."

"How did you get it?"

"She gave it to me."

"Why?"

"Why is this so important to you?"

"Just answer my question, why did she give it to you?"

"She knew I was Aaron's guardian angel. I was known at that time as old Mr. George Garrity, Aaron's neighbor. Aaron used to mow my lawn for me, do small chores and sometimes run to the store for me."

"So, how did she spot you as Aaron's guardian angel?"

"Because her own guardian angel told her about me, in fact, she introduced us to each other."

"She?"

"Yes, her guardian angel back then was a pretty young thing. She was an aerobics instructor at the gym where Aaron's mother was a member. Aaron's mom was a big believer in fitness. Worked out almost every day. Her guardian angel's name was Bethany Hunter."

"So why did she give you the gun?"

"She had a premonition about Aaron. She said she believed Aaron was going to receive help from the woman he loved and without that help he might not succeed. She said she had been given this gun by her own mother and she somehow knew it had to be given to the woman that Aaron loved.

"That's it?"

"I believe so. What is it dear?" said Miss Beacon as she started to drain the water from the sink.

"Last night, at the church, I shot the gun five times. I'm certain of that. Later when I was in the bathroom, I shot the gun three times, yet, I hadn't reloaded it. I am sure of that. Now the gun is fully loaded. Look for yourself. Now how could that be?

"And your point is?" asked Miss Beacon unsure of what Korie was getting to.

"Look," said Korie as she picked up the gun. "I told you its fully loaded. It only holds six bullets. How did it get reloaded? Did you do that?"

"No, I didn't.'

"Then explain to me how it keeps reloading?"

"I see your point."

"What's going here?"

"Let me be as candid as I can be. I really and truly don't know. Remember, I only have the powers and knowledge God gives me. I just don't have an answer for you on this."

"There's got to be a reason, a purpose, something I'm supposed to understand. I wish I knew what it was. I have a feeling it's very important," said Korie as she looked over the gun from end to end.

"If you're right, I hope you figure it out soon. We're running out of time here and we can't afford to miss a thing."

Korie didn't say another word. She slipped the gun into the waistband of her jeans and pulled her tee shirt over the gun concealing its presence.

***

The coven members had all arrived at Phyllis Atkins' real estate office.

Samuel sat down at the conference table and the others took that as a sign that their meeting was to begin.

"Has Powell contacted you yet today?" asked Walter Yandow.

"No," answered Samuel.

"Shouldn't you try to contact him?" asked Josephine Lawless.

"No! He said he would contact me and I fully expect him to. We know where he is. In case he changes his mind and tries to leave town, Ed's arranged for some people to keep track of him."

"Reverend?"

"Yes, Samuel. I want you to head up to the mountain right after this meeting and get the altar ready as required by the covenant. Bob, I want you, Chucky, and Ed Foley to go along and help the Reverend. I also want two crosses set up, one on each side of the altar."

The Reverend shot a sideways glance at the Judge then asked, "How big are these crosses supposed to be?"

"Big enough to hold a man."

The Reverend swallowed slowly as he heard those words.

"Chucky, make sure we have enough wood for several bonfires."

"About the same as always?" asked Chucky.

"No, make it twice as much."

"Will do!"

"Shirley, it will be your job to bring the sacred cup and knife."

She nodded her agreement.

"What about your sister?" asked the Judge.

Everyone in the room immediately tensed up upon hearing this question. Now all eyes were squarely fixed upon Samuel.

"Judge, I want to thank you for bringing her up. I believe she, too, will show up at the calling. We know she's with Powell, right?"

"Yeah, we're pretty certain she's hiding out at Miss Beacon's place," answered Ed Townsend.

"If Powell comes to the meeting without her, we will know it's because we're watching Miss Beacon's place. Once he leaves there, we will go in, grab her and bring her to the calling."

"Very well," said the Judge.

"Does she still belong to Moloch?" asked Judy.

"Yes."

The meeting continued on for several more minutes as coven members conferred with each other on their roles.

Finally Samuel spoke again, "Chucky, make sure you get the announcement out on the radio this morning. I want all of our faithful to be aware of tonight's long awaited calling ceremony. The word must be spread to all to join us in the greatest celebration of our time. Our efforts have prepared the way. Tonight begins a time of reward for our loyalty."

Instead of his usual wise cracking rhetoric, Chucky answered with a sense of seriousness, "I am honored and grateful to have this privilege."

"Thank you. Now go and do your jobs well. Remember, Moloch is counting on all of us."

The coven members all rose from the table and headed for the exit. Samuel stayed behind, still seated at the table. He seemed deep in thought. Phyllis Atkins was about to turn the lights out when she noticed Samuel was still sitting at the table.

"Samuel, is something wrong?"

"No."

"Do you need a ride somewhere?"

"No, thank you. I just want to stay here for awhile, if it's okay," he said in a tone that was more like the young boy that he was.

"Sure."

"Please turn out the lights."

Phyllis did as she was asked. She closed the door to the conference room leaving Samuel alone in the semi-darkness.

Outside the offices, on the sidewalk, Ed Townsend was speaking in a hushed tone with the Judge. The two men nodded and then separated. The Judge went over to the Reverend and whispered something into his ear. The Reverend responded with his own whispered response. Now the two of them separated as well. The various coven members began heading for their vehicles.

From inside the real estate office Samuel watched intently through the slightly parted window blinds, the group dynamics of the coven members. He took notice of the small group meetings and whispered exchanges. He smiled at what he saw. He closed the blinds and left the conference room. Soon he left the building. All the other coven members had already left. Now alone, he turned onto the sidewalk and headed home.

Moments later the local radio station interrupted its regular programming for a public service announcement.

"The Church of Everlasting Faith of Sutton has scheduled its homecoming barbecue for tonight. All members are invited to attend. Again, that's the Church of Everlasting Faith of Sutton has scheduled its homecoming barbecue for tonight. All members are invited to attend," said the radio announcer. "Now, back to our regular programming. Today's farm report is brought to you by Valley Hardware."

As the radio announcer continued his presentation he gave a wave to Chucky Trainor, his station colleague, who was standing just outside the broadcast booth. Chucky acknowledged his gesture with his own thumbs up signal.

The radio announcer noted that the announcement bulletin indicated the public service message needed to be read six more times throughout the late morning show. He stuck it up on the broadcast announcement board and checked his watch.

***

As Samuel walked down the sidewalk he noticed the tall, slender boy with oversized baggy pants skateboarding towards him on the sidewalk. He recognized the boy. The skateboarder pushed off with his right foot to maintain speed. The two boy's eyes met only briefly as they passed each other on the sidewalk. Samuel never yielded any space. The skateboarder deftly avoided contact as he skated past Samuel. It was the same young boy who had met Aaron Powell the day before.

***

Kelley was lying on the bed. She needed the rest. She had drifted off to sleep tossing and turning on the bed. She kept rubbing her arms, and running her hands through her hair, as if to rid herself of the spiders that had tortured her in the church basement.

After awhile, calmness seemed to settle in. Her sleep became deeper, more relaxed. Her breathing was now more rhythmic and slower.

She had drifted off into a dream state. In her dream, she noticed she was wearing a wedding dress, a black wedding dress. The veil was black and she was carrying a bouquet of black, half-dead roses. She glanced up and saw that she was standing at the back of a large gathering. There was a path through this gathering, which led directly to the stone altar, which she recognized.

Many faces were turned towards her. She recognized these faces as fellow church members. The people were smiling and speaking, though she could not hear what they might be saying.

Interspersed in the crowd were faces she didn't recognize at first. These faces were hideous and disfigured. Blood and mucous draining sores seemed to dominate these faces. Their hair was matted, or missing, and teeth, where present, were stained green, or black with rot. Kelley could barely stand to look at these monstrous faces. Gradually some of the grotesque figures changed into those of regular church members, while some regular church members took on their own hideous characteristics.

Kelley felt someone pulling on her left arm. Startled she looked to her left and recognized her own father smiling down.

"Kelley, this is the proudest day of my life. Your mother and I want you to know you have always been special to us, and we love you very much."

He was wearing a black tuxedo with a black carnation in his lapel.

"Daddy, I don't want to do this. How could you and mom let Samuel do this to me?"

"Don't be so ungrateful," he said with a slight expression of anger in his tone.

As Kelley looked at her father, his face began to change. His lips turned black and blue in color. They appeared cracked and withered. His skin sagged and turned gray. Lumps appeared under this skin and seemed to move about on his face. Dark purple veins tracked across the top of his head, as his hair seemed to disappear.

Kelley couldn't let herself continue to look at him. She looked away. Her eyes dropped down, and it was then, she noticed his hand, which gripped her arm. It was greenish black in color, and scaly, too. She tried to pull away from his grip but he was too strong. He took a step forward pulling at her arm as he did so. She immediately spotted his cloven feet. She let out a scream. Only in her dream, this scream was silent. No one could hear her.

The more she struggled the tighter his grip seemed to get.

"Kelley, it's time," said her father.

"No, no," she protested.

He pulled her along the aisle towards the altar.

She looked up and saw her brother, Samuel, standing in front of the altar. He was smiling. Standing to his left was a very tall creature. It seemed to stand seven feet tall. Its skin was a scaly dark green and black. There were pulsating red veins bulging everywhere beneath the surface of his monstrous skin. He stood on two cloven feet. On top of his head were two horns. His widely set eyes looked at her with a power that seemed to burn right through her. The eyes were bright yellow in color with black, snake-like, irises. Large stained teeth could be seen as the creature smiled down on her. Beneath his arms, she could make out large folds of skin, membrane-like, which seemed connected from his wrists to his underarms and along his sides. They were wings. A snake like tail swished back and forth behind him.

She knew who it was. It was Moloch.

She tried to look away for someone to help her. Then she noticed the two blackened crosses, one on each side of the altar. Hanging on these crosses, were the charred remains of two people who had been burned to death. The sickly, sweet smell of burnt human flesh still hung in the air. She felt a strong urge to heave.

"Won't somebody help me, please?" she pleaded.

Samuel reached out and took her left wrist firmly in his grip.

"Welcome, Kelley. Moloch and I have been waiting for you. Now the ceremony can begin."

"Samuel, please, for God's sake, I'm your sister. Please don't do this."

She sobbed uncontrollably as she thrashed about, trying to break free from his grip.

"Help me!" she pleaded.

"Kelley, Kelley, wake up. You're having a bad dream. Wake up" said the somewhat familiar voice.

Through the deep fog of her dream, Samuel began to loose his grip on her. Everything began to quickly fade, and in another instant she sat up, fully awake.

Miss Beacon was sitting on the side of the bed. She was holding Kelley's left wrist.

"Everything's fine now," said Miss Beacon.

Kelley looked at her through tear filled eyes and said, "I was there, Miss Beacon. My father and Samuel, they were, offering me to Moloch. I was going to be his bride."

Kelley started to cry. Miss Beacon handed her a tissue from the nearby nightstand.

"There, there, child."

"Miss Beacon. I saw something else," she said sniffling as she did.

"There were two crosses with two burnt bodies on them. What does this all mean?"

***

Korie found Aaron sitting in the wing backed chair in their room. He had been leafing through the Powell family diary. When she came into the room, he closed the dairy and put it down on the floor.

Korie sat down on the bed and folded her legs underneath her.

"Aaron, when are you going to contact this Samuel character?"

"In a little while, I guess."

"Have you been able to think of something we can do to stop this madness?"

"No, but you know what?"

Korie slipped off the bed and came over and sat on his lap.

"What?" she said.

"I have been thinking, perhaps the best thing is to just have faith."

She looked down into his eyes. She ran her fingers through his hair, and then, leaned over and kissed him on top of his head.

"He's right," said Miss Beacon from the doorway.

Miss Beacon and Kelley were standing there together. Kelley looked pale. Her eyes were swollen and red as if she had just been crying.

"I want you both to hear this," said Miss Beacon as she ushered Kelley into the room.

Kelley and Miss Beacon sat on the foot of the bed.

"Go on, Kelley, tell them about your dream."

Kelley's lower lip was quivering slightly as she began.

30

Throughout the town of Sutton, among the members of the Church of Everlasting Faith, there was a buzz of excitement that was reaching a feverish pitch. Men and women received calls at work from family members still at home. Their faces lit up with joy when they heard the news. The message had been announced on the local radio station and word was spreading. They made up excuses and left work to hurry back home. Some members closed their businesses and sent their employees home, with the rest of the day off.

Soon families were together discussing their plans for tonight's calling ceremony.

Other people in town generally took little notice of the scurrying about by the excited Church members.

Bob Senecal closed his garage, and sent one of his employees home for the rest of the day. The other fellow was a Church member, who had also left, to get ready with the rest of his family.

Ed Foley hung a closed sign up on his front office door. He wouldn't be treating anymore animals today. He and his daughter danced in their living room with joy.

"I can't wait," she shouted.

"Me, either," said Ed.

Phyllis Atkins closed her real estate office.

Josephine Lawless called into the Governor's Office. She left a message with the Governor's Chief of Staff saying she had to take care of some unexpected business today.

Judy Perrillo put out a closed sign on the front door of her motel office. She went to her house and into her bedroom. She spent the next hour giving pleasure to herself. Then she began primping for the evening's calling ceremony.

By now it was getting late in the afternoon.

The Reverend drove his car around back, behind the town library. He slowly pulled behind the building looking around to see who might be there. He was alone. He got out of the car and walked across the back parking lot. He walked a short distance across the adjoining field, and entered the town cemetery.

He spotted two men standing together, at the back edge of the cemetery, near the woods alongside the railroad tracks. It was Ed Townsend and Judge Fairchild. The Reverend walked quickly in their direction.

"Anybody follow you?" asked Ed.

"I don't think so," said the Reverend.

"You don't think so?" said Ed.

"No, no, I'm sure I wasn't followed," said a very nervous Reverend.

"He said he wasn't followed, now let's finish this. We can't be wasting time here," said the Judge. "Now Ed, let's hear your plan."

"All right. Tonight, when we're all standing next to the altar and Samuel is reading from the Covenant, I'm going to shoot him. I need another one of you to also have a gun and be ready to fire in case something goes wrong. Think of it as insurance. I figure that would be you, Judge. I brought this forty-five with an ankle holster. Reverend, we'll need you to start a diversion, just before I whack him. I need to have his concentration broken for just a split second."

"What kind of diversion?"

"I don't know, fake a heart attack or something, shit!"

"A heart attack?" stammered the Reverend who was still nervous.

"I like this plan," said the Judge. "If we each do our part, then it should work. The key is going to be the Reverend. His heart attack has to be convincing." Turning to the Reverend he asked, "Do you think you can do this?"

"Sure, I uh, yeah, I can do it."

"All right, then I'll give you two guys a signal when we start this thing. I'll fold my arms like this," which he demonstrated.

"One more thing. We must be very careful from here on. We can't do anything out of the ordinary which will draw attention to ourselves. We don't want to arouse any suspicion on Samuel's part," said the Judge.

"Then it's done," said Ed as he extended his hand to the Judge.

Each man exchanged handshakes and parted in different directions.

The Reverend returned to his car and drove home.

As Ed left the cemetery he mumbled, "If those fuckers loose their cool I'll just have to whack them, too."

***

Samuel sat in his bedroom waiting. It was getting late in the day and he still hadn't heard back from Powell. He was almost ready to set his backup plan into motion when the phone rang. He heard it ring for a second time and then he heard his mother's voice as she answered the phone.

In a moment she yelled upstairs, "Samuel, it's for you."

He quickly ran out of his room and hurried down the stairs. He took the phone from his mother and waived her away. He put the receiver to his ear.

"Yes."

"It's me, Aaron Powell. I just wanted to let you know that I've thought about it, and I've decided to join in."

"Good. And what do you wish to get out of this?"

"Not much. I want to be able to live forever like the rest of you, including my girlfriend. And I want to be a great bass and harp blues player."

"That's it?"

"Yeah."

"Then consider it done. Let me come over and take you to the calling ceremony. I'll introduce you around. After all, we need to initiate you into our little group first."

"I don't need initiation. My mother told me in her diary that our family bloodline still contains the vestiges of our ancestors. You and the others have known that the Powell family has always been a part of the coven. I'll meet you there. I presume the ceremony will be held at the stone altar on the mountain top."

"So, you know where it is?"

"Yes, it's next to the cemetery, where the original coven members buried my family."

This comment caught Samuel by surprise.

"What time is the ceremony?" asked Aaron.

There was no answer.

"I said...,"

"I heard you. The ceremony begins at nine o'clock and Aaron, don't be late."

"I won't be. Oh, and by the way, I'll be bringing your sister along. I hope you aren't uncomfortable with that."

Trying to sound confident he answered "Of course not. Why should I? We are all looking forward to seeing her again."

"Click," was the sound Samuel heard as Aaron hung up the phone.

His parents watched him from the hallway. His father had come home early when his mother called to say the radio had announced that the calling ceremony was to take place tonight. They watched as he hung up the phone and went back upstairs.

"I'm so proud of Samuel. I just knew that if anyone could bring forth Moloch and then Lucifer to complete our covenant, it would be our son," said Samuel's mother.

Samuel's father wasn't quite as excited as his wife. He still feared Samuel.

Meanwhile Samuel went into his room, closed the door and called forth Moloch. They had some business to discuss.

***

Aaron hung up the phone. He looked relieved that the call was over.

Everyone waited to hear what he had to say. He looked at Korie, then Kelley, and finally at Miss Beacon.

"You heard what I said to him. I guess we're all in this to the end."

"We're with you," said Korie.

"Aaron, you have got to stop Samuel and Moloch. I can't be Moloch's bride or whatever he wants of me. I'd rather be dead. I wish you people would shoot me right now," said Kelley. She was filled with despair.

Aaron reached over and took her hand and said, "All of my ancestors, going back to the family that's buried up on that mountain, have lived and died in their struggle against the Devil. I won't let them down. Look at me, Kelley!" he said lifting her chin. "I won't let any of you down. I will fight this thing with every ounce of strength I have. My ancestors will be with me. Each of you will be with me and together we will win. We will find a way. I just know it."

"Kelley, he's right," said Korie. "It's his destiny to face this challenge. None of us can predict the future, but we know what is in our hearts and there is no room for this evilness."

Miss Beacon watched this exchange and smiled. However, deep inside, she knew what sort of trouble they were going to face. It certainly was going to get much worse before it got any better.

***

As it had been a picture perfect day, the evening promised to be just as beautiful. The air was dry and cool. The sky was cloudless. As twilight began to descend on the valley that held the town of Sutton, certain people began to take to the streets and back roads as they headed out to the mountain site for the calling ceremony. Many members of the Church of Everlasting Faith wanted to be there early. No one wanted to miss a thing.

One by one the cars pulled to a stop and parked along side the narrow, rutted, dirt road next to Walter Yandow's Game Warden and Fire Marshall Lodge. The nearly mile long trail leading up to the altar was soon filled with people streaming up to the site. Conversation along the trail was buzzing with excitement.

As everyone reached the clearing leading up to the altar, they immediately noticed the two large crosses that were set in place to either side of the altar. Next to the crosses were large piles of seasoned, split, dry wood. Several torches were set in place around the perimeter of the clearing. A couple of them were already burning. The night sky was getting darker as the first stars began to twinkle.

Several of the coven members were already there. They mingled about accepting congratulations from the faithful.

Ed Townsend arrived. He had walked most of the path alone. He now crossed the clearing, taking long purposeful strides as he headed straight for the altar. He quickly looked things over. He noticed that off to the edge of the clearing, next to the changing tent, were several red cans clearly marked "gasoline."

"Hello, Ed," was spoken in an intimate tone. A hand gently caressed his left arm.

He turned to his left. It was Judy Perrillo. She seemed so aroused by the moment that she practically purred with sexuality.

"Isn't this so wonderful?"

"Yeah, sure."

"I almost can't wait. Soon, I'm going to be able to have as many men as I want, anytime I want."

"That's nice."

"I don't know where to begin," she said as she looked around at the growing crowd.

"I'm sure you'll figure something out."

"How about you and I, Ed?" she said as she licked her lips with the end of her long and slender tongue.

"Don't you think it would be nice to, uh, celebrate a little?"

"I don't think so," he said as he tried to pull away.

"Ed, it would be incredible!"

"No thanks, Judy," he said as he pulled himself away.

Judy seemed momentarily disappointed. She turned to her right and spotted Chucky Trainor just arriving.

"Chucky, Chucky, I need to speak to you," she said as she half jogged towards him. She made sure her enhanced figure got full notice, long before her arrival.

Chucky was smiling at her as she arrived.

Ed moved off to stand next to the changing tent. No one else was there and that suited him just fine.

The Reverend arrived next. There was a small crowd of people with him. They all seemed to enjoy listening to the Reverend, whose conversation appeared to be punctuated with several animated gestures. He clearly appeared to be in good spirits.

Next to arrive, came the tall gangly figure of the Judge. He walked with his head held high. Two older women from the Church accompanied him. One was doing all the talking and the other woman and he were doing all the listening.

The Judge looked around and spotted the Reverend. He then looked for Ed Townsend. After a moment, he located him at the far edge of the clearing next to the changing tent. Once the Judge and Ed's eyes locked into each other, they both looked away.

There suddenly, was a rise in volume from the assembled as several of them spotted Samuel and his parents arriving. Many rushed forward to greet the coven leader. Samuel smiled at them and raised his arms in recognition. Ed Townsend watched him from his distant vantage point.

Samuel moved through the crowd. As he did so, he reached out for some people and touched them on their arm, then he would touch the top of their heads. Ed watched this curious behavior for a moment, focusing upon the people Samuel was choosing to touch in this special way.

Ed noticed these people had been changed after Samuel's touch. These people seemed suddenly more subdued. Their faces were almost expressionless. They still moved and spoke but with far less spontaneity than before.

"The little bastard is changing them," he said in a hushed whisper. "He's invited a devil to share their bodies and they don't even know it. Clever son of a bitch."

Ed's cell phone buzzed inside his sport coat. He removed it, flipped it open, and spoke.

"Yeah."

"They're leaving. Miss Beacon, Samuel's sister, and a man and woman got into an old Land Rover and appeared to be heading your way."

"Thanks."

Ed closed his phone and returned it to his pocket. He continued to watch Samuel.

Samuel stopped briefly and turned around and said something to his father. His father and mother had planned to move away to be with some friends. They wanted to let Samuel be free to do what he needed to do.

His father broke away from Samuel's mother and the others. He stopped in front of his son, Samuel.

Samuel spoke briefly to him, then he placed his hand on his father's arm, after which he put his hand on his father's head.

Samuel spoke again to his father who nodded twice. Now his father turned around and returned to Samuel's mother.

Ed whispered, "Fuckin-A, he's slick."

Samuel continued to mingle with folks.

Ed's phone buzzed again.

"Yeah."

"The Land Rover, it just moved past me. They turned onto Old River Road. They're coming, shit, they're really coming."

"That's good."

Ed put the phone back into his pocket.

He decided to tell Samuel the good news.

Ed drifted past the altar which now had a black silk cover draped over it. He slowly headed towards Samuel.

Samuel saw him coming and smiled. His smile was friendly.

Ed smiled back. He arrived next to Samuel and said, "My people have called to say they're on their way. It looks good, Samuel. It looks real good," he said for emphasis.

"That's great. Well, we should get ready then. I'll get the others together. Ed, we'll meet at the changing tent. Let me know as soon as you hear they're on the trail heading up here."

"I will."

Samuel moved away. He began to gather the coven members together.

Ed headed back to the changing tent. It was getting dark now. He directed a couple of the men to light more of the torches that were around the perimeter. Soon there were at least a dozen large torches lighting the area. A few people lit their own lanterns. The clearing was now illuminated and glowed from the yellowish low level light. The faces of the assembled took on a ghostly pallor.

The coven members were now gathered together at the changing tent. Their ceremonial robes were already laid out and waiting inside of the tent. The women went in first.

Ed, the Reverend, and the Judge had not spoken once this evening.

After a few moments the women exited the tent. They were wearing the long black robes that the first coven members had made over a hundred and sixty years ago.

Several of the men and Samuel went inside next.

Ed and the Judge waited outside.

"Come on, you two!" said Samuel.

"It's okay, I'm waiting for a call that Powell is on the trail heading up here, remember," said Ed.

"Go ahead, Samuel, it won't take me much time to change. I'll be right along," said the Judge.

"All right," said Samuel as he ducked inside of the tent.

"Is it a go?" asked the Judge.

"As far as I'm concerned, it is," said Ed out of the side of his mouth.

"Good, we shall be truly rewarded for keeping the true faith with the covenant."

"That's what I'm counting on."

Some of the men coven members began to leave the tent.

The Judge headed into the tent just as Samuel was exiting. The Judge smiled at Samuel who returned his smile.

Samuel walked over to Ed and asked him, "Any word yet?"

"No, not yet."

Samuel accepted the answer and walked away.

Judy Perrillo came over and stood next to Ed.

She leaned into him and whispered, "I'm not wearing anything under my robe."

"Judy, look I'm really not interested," he said. Ed had seen Judy in her altered state of being and it was not a pretty sight. The thought of sex with her repulsed him.

"Okay. Ed Townsend, just you remember when I'm a big movie star, don't you come running to me looking for a piece," she said as she stormed off.

"These people are fucking delusional. They have no idea what Armageddon is going to be like. I'll bet they have never even read the *Bible*."

Samuel looked over at Ed who gestured with his arms out and palms extended upward, that he hadn't yet heard from the last spotter down on the trail.

***

Kevin Culpepper was sitting in the tree stand that he had placed up in a pine tree, about fifteen feet off the ground. From this position, he could take in a 270 degree radius look at the lower end of the trail. He was getting anxious.

Miss Beacon had stopped the Land Rover next to the first car they came upon along the side of the dirt road. They were about a quarter of a mile from Yandow's place.

"We'll have to walk from here," said Miss Beacon.

Everyone climbed out of the Rover. Miss Beacon handed the keys to Aaron.

"You take them. I don't think I'm going to be in the mood to drive this thing, after this is over."

Aaron slipped the keys into his pants pocket.

Miss Beacon opened the back of the Land Rover and rummaged around for a moment, before she found what she was looking for.

"Aaron, think you know how to use this?" said Miss Beacon.

She held out a small reed like tube that was approximately two feet long.

Aaron took it from her.

"This goes with it," she said as she handed him a small tin. "It's a blow gun and the tin contains a couple of small tranquilizer darts."

"What am I supposed to do with this?" he asked.

"Up ahead on the trail road will be a lookout. I figure if you can use this to knock him out, it will give us a little edge. That way, when we arrive, it will be somewhat of a surprise."

"I like that," said Aaron.

"Well then, let's go."

"How will we know where this lookout is?" asked Kelley.

"I think I have a good idea where he might be. After all, I've learned a thing or two since I've been in this twisted little town."

The four headed off up the trail road.

They walked past Yandow's cabin. After they had gone about another 150 yards Miss Beacon signaled for everyone to stop and be quiet.

Then she whispered, "Korie, you and Kelley stay here for a few minutes. Aaron and I have to leave the trail and sneak up behind the spotter. I think he's somewhere in a tree stand, up there on the left, at the turn before the small bridge over the brook."

"I don't like the idea of being left here," said Kelley.

"Don't worry, Korie's pretty tough. I think she can handle any surprises. And I don't think there will be any. These people want us to get there. They sure don't want to stop us. Ready?"

At that, Miss Beacon led Aaron off the trail into the woods. They quietly slipped into the thick woods and soon disappeared.

Kelley and Korie waited in silence.

Meanwhile, Miss Beacon walked carefully through the woods. Aaron tried to mimic her every step. Some ten minutes later she stopped and gestured to a tree about thirty feet ahead. She pointed to a spot about fifteen feet up into the tree. At first, he didn't see anything, and then he spotted what she had seen. On either side of the tree trunk were a man's legs covered in green pants and wearing hiking boots. He was sitting on a tree stand on the other side of the tree. From where he was he couldn't see them unless he stood up and looked around the back of the tree.

Whispering she said, "You're going to have to move up closer to the tree. See that blue spruce over to the right. It should provide you with enough cover. Start heading over there. I'll try and divert his attention. When he looks away you make a move to the spruce and set up. You should be able to get a good look at him from there. Try and get him in the neck. The medicine will work faster that way. All you need to do is to hit him with one. Now go!"

Aaron nodded his acknowledgement and headed forward, careful to keep the spotter's back to him.

When Aaron was about twenty feet away from the spotter's tree and about ten feet away from the blue spruce, he crouched down and examined the exact route his steps would need to take him to quietly reach the spruce.

He turned to signal Miss Beacon he was ready. She wasn't there. She had disappeared. He turned around and looked up at the spotter and waited.

Just then, about thirty yards away from the spotter, in a small clearing, a large deer stepped forward from the nearby dense bushes. This was a very large buck. It had a huge rack of antlers. Aaron counted at least twelve points. It was a true trophy deer. The deer pawed at the ground. When it did so the noise reached the spotter who stirred a bit as he noticed the deer.

"Holy shit," whispered the spotter.

Aaron could clearly hear him. Then the spotter stood up slowly, to get a better look at this incredible deer. As he did so, Aaron moved as quietly as he could to set up next to the spruce tree.

"The things you see when you don't have a gun," whispered the spotter.

Just then, the deer looked up directly at the spotter and turned and scampered away into the woods. Its exit made a crashing sound as it quickly broke through low branches in a hasty retreat.

The spotter sat back down.

Aaron knelt and opened the small tin. There were three darts. He put one carefully into the end of the reed. It fit perfectly. He aimed it at the spotter. Inhaling a deep breath he blew into the end of the blowgun. The dart flew out and stuck into the tree just behind the spotter's head. It hardly made any noise.

Damn, he thought.

Aaron reloaded the blowgun and tried again. This time he held the blowgun as steady as he could and took aim. The dart missed the spotter completely and flew into the woods beyond.

Aaron closed his eyes and prayed for help. Then he reloaded the blowgun for one last try. He took aim and blew into the reed. The dart flew true this time and landed in the spotter's neck, just behind his ear. It stung him. He slapped at the stinging sensation. He felt something on his neck and removed it. It was a tiny, feathered dart. It was the last thing he saw as his mind shut down completely. His head slumped forward. If he hadn't buckled a safety line to the tree, he would have fallen out of the tree stand. As it was, he slumped forward so much that his forehead was now nearly touching his knees.

Aaron stood up.

There was a cracking sound coming from behind as a small branch broke underfoot.

Aaron turned suddenly and there was Miss Beacon again.

"It safe to make noise now. He's out cold. Should be out at least a few hours anyway. Let's go."

Aaron followed her through the woods where they soon exited the woods and were back on the trail road again. Looking back down the road, Miss Beacon got the attention of Korie and Kelley as she signaled for them to come along.

When Korie and Kelley arrived the four joined hands and headed up the trail road. In a few moments, they crossed over the wooden bridge that spanned the adjacent stream. It was nearly completely dark now. The woods themselves were completely quiet except for the crunching sound their shoes made on the hard exposed surface of the trail.

At this time they were about three-quarters of a mile from the clearing adjacent to the offering altar. The lower level of the night sky, in the general direction they were now heading, reflected a reddish, yellow hue from burning torches.

Each had a different idea of what lay ahead. But even their separate ideas had one thing in common. Each was certain they were about to face something that was monstrously evil.

***

The gathered faithful began to grumble as they checked their watches. It was a few minutes past nine and nothing had even begun.

"What's the hold up?" shouted someone from the back edge of the large group.

"Yeah, where's Moloch?" said another.

"Let's get started," shouted someone else.

Samuel heard these calls. He checked his own watch. He was growing angrier by the moment.

"Has your man seen anything?" Samuel asked of Ed Townsend.

"Look, why don't I go check?"

"No."

"Just give me a minute."

"All right, you've got exactly one minute."

Ed ran over to the changing tent and picked up his hand held radio, his backup communication device. He quickly checked with the other men he had set up at the various checkpoints along the way here. Each confirmed Powell had moved past their locations and they had not seen him backtrack. He quickly threw on his black robe and hurried back.

Ed ran to Samuel and said, "I am certain he's on his way. I'd bet my life on it."

"You have," said Samuel sternly. "You already have."

With that Samuel moved over to the altar. He stood behind it and raised his arms.

The crowd quickly became silent.

"Fellow members of the Church of Everlasting Faith, I now call for the members of our coven to join me at this, our offering altar."

One by one the coven members moved to stand with Samuel. They divided themselves so an equal number stood to either side of him.

Already set out on the altar was the Book of Final Covenants, a knife, and a cup.

"Please raise your hands with me as we now begin the greatest of ceremonies. Tonight, together, we will complete a journey begun by our ancestors long ago. Our ancestors, faithful disciples of Lucifer, entered into a solemn agreement. Their word, their bond, was to help bring Moloch, Lucifer's closest and most faithful of all his servants, to human form. Moloch, with their help, would prepare the way for Lucifer to walk upon the earth. Our ancestors were promised that in return, each would have eternal life and would enjoy the riches and pleasures of this world. Join me now as we fulfill that long ago covenant."

There were shouts of, "Amen, and Praise Samuel," and "Praise Lucifer."

Samuel closed his eyes and began to sway. The coven members looked at each other and the crowd before them. There was a nervous expectation in the air.

"We now call upon the great Moloch, Lucifer's most faithful servant, our counsel, our guide, to rise up before us."

The night air began to swirl up, in front of the altar.

"Oh, almighty Moloch, slayer of the enemies of Lucifer, we are prepared, this night, to fulfill our great covenant. We call for your presence."

The swirling air now contained sparking explosions of different colored lights.

"Moloch, show yourself before us now. Let the unfaithful fear you in life, as they should in death, and let we, your faithful, share in the promises once made."

Inside the swirling lights, a shape began to take form. This shape was dark and kept shifting inside the swirling lights.

The crowd continued to sway. Some people even murmured their own personal prayers. Young children sat or stood in silence, mesmerized by this metamorphic spectacle. Infants, held by their parents were completely silent.

The shape now began to take on a definite form. The air around the swirling lights became electric. Small lightning like charges of twisting, cracking light snapped in the surrounding air.

Just then Ed Townsend looked over at the Reverend and the Judge. According to their prearranged signal he folded his arms. As he did so, he reached inside his cloak and unlatched his pistol from his shoulder holster.

The Judge looked over at the Reverend and nodded.

The Reverend knew his time had come. It was now or never. His convictions were strong. He firmly believed he was about to do the right thing by Lucifer.

The Reverend suddenly clutched his upper left chest, and let out a huge moan, "OooooooH!"

So Samuel couldn't look into his eyes as he slumped forward onto the altar, he turned his face away.

Samuel took notice of what the Reverend was doing. He had expected something like this would happen.

Ed quickly pulled his pistol out and raised the weapon up with both his hands, and took aim.

The Judge hesitated.

Samuel turned at that moment and in a flash held out his right hand palm side facing towards Ed.

Ed was suddenly frozen in place. Every muscle in his body was suddenly beyond his control. Only his mind was his own. He instantly knew he had failed. His only hope now was that the Judge would follow through while Samuel was occupied with him.

Samuel kept his arm extended towards Ed even as he returned his attention to the imminent arrival of Moloch.

The Reverend was still bent over the altar. There had been no shots fired. That could mean only one thing. Their planned coup had failed.

I'm still alive, must be a good sign, thought the Reverend. *Maybe Samuel hasn't connected me to the planned assassination. I've just got to keep faking this heart attack.*

The Judge was now frozen by his own hesitant choice. Somehow Samuel had anticipated Ed. *How?* thought the Judge. *What tipped him off?*

Moloch's shape was nearly complete. This shape began to reach and stretch, much like one does upon rising from an extended nap.

The swirling lights began to extinguish. Moloch was now fully formed.

"I am here!" he bellowed to the assembled.

Everyone opened their eyes and lowered their arms. Applause and cheering broke out.

"I am here to fulfill our great agreement. Tonight you shall be rewarded, but first we must deal with the traitors in our midst."

The crowd began to murmur. There was confusion and concern.

"Here Moloch, is a traitor," said Samuel.

Moloch turned and extended his long right arm, then his hand and finally his long gnarled index finger directly at Ed Townsend.

"Traitor, the lowest of fiends, you were planning to kill your coven leader, and then you planned to destroy me. By your deed you would have denied Lucifer his rightful place, here on earth."

"What is to become of this traitor?" asked Samuel sardonically.

Moloch turned to the crowd and gestured to them that it was their call to make.

"Destroy him," said some.

Others shouted, "Kill him."

Even the children joined in with this populous demand.

"Samuel, the faithful have spoken," said Moloch in a mocking tone.

With that, Samuel now faced Ed and extended his two arms towards him. Ed dropped his gun. Now his body begins to rise into the air. He moves through the air until he is hanging in front of the cross to Samuel's right.

"Tie him to the cross," commanded Samuel. Several men standing in the front run forward. Samuel reaches under the covered altar and tosses a bundle of rope towards them. Some of the men use their pocket knifes to cut the length of rope and then tie up Ed Townsend.

"Samuel, what of the other traitor?" asked Moloch.

Both the Judge and the Reverend froze upon hearing those ominous words.

"Yes, the other traitor," said Samuel as he turned and looked directly at the Judge. The Judge lowered his arms to his side. He looked back at Samuel and nods.

Samuel now raises his arms together, as he had done with Ed, just moments ago. Upon doing so the Judge's body stiffens from the paralysis induced by the Samuel's powers. His body rises and moves through the air until it hangs suspended, in front of the cross to Samuel's left. Samuel retrieves another length of rope from beneath the altar and tosses it towards the foot of the cross. The same men cut this rope and tie the Judge to the cross.

The Judge looks over at Ed. The Judge seems more resigned to his fate. Ed on the other hand is angry and defiant.

"What seems to be the trouble with our Reverend?" asked Moloch mockingly.

Upon hearing Moloch speak of him the Reverend lifts his head slightly and speaks in a faking sickly tone "I, I think I'm having a heart attack."

The other coven members don't know quite what to make of these events. They stand rigid in their positions, unsure of what is about to happen next.

"So you say you are having a heart attack. Tell us what it feels like," said Samuel.

"Uh, feels like I don't," spoke the Reverend when suddenly his heart felt like someone had just stabbed it with a jagged edged knife.

"Oh, God," said the Reverend as he grabs at his chest with both hands. His left arm tingles and aches.

"He dares to speak of God," bellowed Moloch. "God is not here Reverend. Does he care about you, a sinner?" hissed Moloch.

Moloch walks towards the Reverend who was now in excruciating pain.

The coven members step aside to let Moloch move closer to the Reverend.

Moloch lifts the Reverend's chin with his left index finger. His fingernail pierces the tender skin just beneath the Reverend's chin.

The Reverend's face on its right side begins to droop, as if he no longer has any muscle control over that part of his face. To add to the Reverend's humiliation, his bowels let go, as he soils himself.

With his one finger Moloch has now lifted the Reverend high over the altar.

"Please, Moloch?" pleads the Reverend in a whispered voice.

"He asks for mercy," shouted Moloch.

Samuel watches every move Moloch makes, much like a student might watch and study a master.

Moloch reaches out with his right hand and makes a gesture in front of the Reverend's chest like he had just grabbed something and was giving it a good twist.

The Reverend cries out in pain, "Moloch."

Then Moloch reaches directly into the chest of the Reverend. His powerful hand, long fingers, and razor sharp fingernails soon find what he seeks. He rips the still beating heart out of the Reverend's chest. Moloch holds it aloft for everyone to see. The Reverend's blood runs down his arm. The heart beats a few times then stops.

A loud cheer rises up from among the faithful. They clap and celebrate. Moloch deposits the heart into the cup on the altar.

It lands inside with a smacking sound.

Moloch tosses the Reverend's lifeless body down on the ground in front of the altar. Some people move to the body and spit on it or kick it.

Samuel raises his arms and beckons for attention.

The crowd quiets down.

Samuel then speaks, "Bring to these crosses, wood from those piles."

Many people quickly do as he requested.

Samuel turns to Walter and Chucky and says, "Take the gasoline from the cans near our changing tent and pour it on the wood, at the feet of the crosses. Do it quickly."

They move at nearly a full run to carry out his command.

When the wood had been put in place and covered with gasoline everyone moves away from the crosses.

"Hear me faithful," said Samuel. "Before the great Moloch, we must show our loyalty, and destroy the traitors who would stand in our way."

Samuel extends his own arms outward, palm sides up. In each palm appears a ball of fire.

"Hellfire," whispers Phyllis to Shirley. They both seem excited.

The balls of fire move up into the air and hover over the altar. They grow and grow. Soon, they each are the size of a medicine ball.

Judy grows exceedingly aroused by all of this. She begins to touch herself. Her body begins to sensually gyrate. The other women also find themselves becoming aroused. The men in the coven also begin to experience heightened arousal, as they notice the aroused state the women seem to be experiencing.

Moloch took notice of this behavior, and it pleased him.

The balls of fire suddenly fly towards the crosses and crash directly at the feet of the two coven members tied to the crosses.

The gasoline soaked wood explodes into flames. In a few seconds both men and their crosses are engulfed in a blazing consuming fire.

A loud cheer sweeps through the faithful. Some of the Coven and the faithful join hands and dance with one another.

Neither Ed nor the Judge is able to speak. Their face muscles, the only muscles on their body that they still control, convulse violently. Their mouths hang open in a silent agonizing effort to scream. Their clothes quickly burn away, exposing their flesh, which burns with a fierce consuming heat.

The burning bodies emit a searing sound, much like steak sizzling on an open fire. As the wooden pyres burn, embers are carried aloft by the draft of the fire, and then drift away into the nighttime sky.

The Judge's gun, still strapped to his now burning body, let loose a shot, as the bullet in the firing chamber explodes. The bullet grazes Ed Foley's shoulder.

Within a couple of seconds the remaining bullets stored in the magazine also explode. Bullets and pieces of the gun fly everywhere. The flying shrapnel explodes through the air, nicking several people.

Moloch laughs at the scene of the faithful momentarily scurrying for cover.

All three conspirators are now dead.

Ed whispers to Walter, "How did Samuel know?"

Samuel heard the remark. He turns to Ed and Walter and said with a sinister smile, "You know that each of us has our devil mate. Well, one of theirs was disloyal to them but faithful to Lucifer."

"Samuel, look," said a suddenly excited Ed Foley.

30

    Aaron, Korie, Kelley and Miss Beacon were within a couple hundred feet of the clearing, when they noticed the nighttime air over the clearing glowed ever brighter. They could hear people cheering and clapping. As they moved closer, they could see flickers of still burning embers drifting upward over the tops of trees.

    The sound of the first shot rang out, soon followed by the sound of the other bullets exploding. The four moved steadily forward undeterred by these sounds. A strange, foul odor reached them as they stepped from the trail and into the edge of the clearing.

    What Kelley saw seized her with an intense terror that caused her to stop. There, across the clearing, next to the offering altar, were two smoldering crosses with two charred figures hanging from them. It was the scene from her dream. It was the very scene, which she had foreseen. She spotted Moloch next to the altar and then she located her brother, Samuel, proudly standing next to the fiend from hell.

    Aaron looked around at the frenzy of the crowd. His eyes moved to the altar and it was there that he first set eyes upon his two main opponents, Moloch and the young boy that must surely be Samuel.

    Korie didn't pay much attention to the crowd. Instead she focused directly on the altar area. She spotted Moloch, a hideous, tall, powerfully built creature. She also noticed all the coven members in their robes, and right away, their state of sexual arousal. Their movements were all too obvious.

Korie also noticed the two burnt bodies on the crosses.

Shit, what have we gotten ourselves into? she silently asked herself.

Miss Beacon looked upon the entire scene and recognized the all too familiar pattern. She generally knew what was to follow, but she also knew that each previous attempt to bring forth Lucifer had its own set of surprises.

One of the coven members spotted them. He pointed at them. Samuel turned around and looked across the clearing. His eyes met his sister's. Samuel was now grinning from ear to ear.

"Silence," shouted Samuel.

The crowd immediately behaved as directed.

"Moloch, I present to you, Mr. Powell, his woman friend, our own Miss Beacon and of course you already know my sister, Kelley."

The crowd turned as one and faced them.

"Welcome, Powell. It has been a very long time. As you can see, we have been busy awaiting your arrival. Everything is now in order."

Samuel stepped around the altar and stood in front of it. The faithful moved apart, leaving a path, which led directly to the top of the clearing.

"Powell, come forward and join our coven, so the Final Covenant may be fulfilled," said Samuel as he beckoned Aaron to leave the others.

Aaron released Korie's and Miss Bacon's hands and walked toward Samuel. The faithful erupt into a loud cheer. Several members reach out and pat Aaron on the back. Aaron keeps his eyes on Samuel and Moloch. He struggles to keep his mind clear and his emotions in check.

"Miss Beacon and Powell's woman please come down front and join us," said Samuel.

Aaron moved to the backside of the altar opposite from the side where Moloch is.

Miss Beacon released Kelley's hand and pulled at Korie's hand. The two women walk slowly and cautiously forward. They stop and stand in front of the altar on the same side as Aaron.

Moloch watched their every move. His yellow colored eyes gaze down upon the women. His face is filled with a triumphant grin. He licks his lips with his serpent like tongue.

"And now, for my dear sister who once thought she could leave our church. To show you there are no hard feelings, we are prepared to offer you, to Moloch. Dad, will you please escort her to the front?"

It was her nightmare turned into nightmarish reality.

She started to turn to run when her left arm was seized. She turned and noticed it was her father. His eyes were glazed over as if they were in a trance. He was dressed in a black tuxedo, and was wearing a dead, black rose in his lapel. Kelley suddenly felt a swoosh-like wind. She then looked down at herself. She was now wearing a black wedding dress. She also had on black, arm length gloves and a black veil. In her right hand was a bouquet of dead, black roses.

Kelley started to cry.

"Daddy, please let me go."

Her father neither heard, nor even saw her. At this moment his mind and spirit were not his to command.

The crowd of the Church of Everlasting Faith cheered wildly. There were shouts of "yes," and "at last."

Kelley's father began to walk down the parted path created by the crowd. He had to pull Kelley along.

Moloch stood tall as he fixed his eager eyes upon the woman he was about to have, body and soul.

Kelley fell to her knees. She was sobbing.

Aaron looked at Korie and Miss Beacon for some sign, perhaps a signal of what to do. They offered him nothing. He closed his eyes even as he could hear Kelley's sobbing and desperate pleading.

"Daddy, momma, somebody, help me, please," she cried.

A man stepped from the crowd near her and helped her to her feet. For a moment she thought that maybe, at last someone was going to help her. Instead, now that she was once again on her feet he pushed her along.

"Miss Beacon, Korie you've got to help me. Make this stop!"

They both knew this was not the time to interfere.

"Aaron, please save me," cried Kelley.

Aaron opened his eyes and looked at her. He wanted so very much to help, but when, how?

Moloch reaches his arms up to the night sky. His entire scaly, green black body glistens as it reflects the nearby burning torches. He lets out a roar that shakes the ground. Even the altar shudders from the force of his bellow. It soon echoes back from across the valley.

Moloch clenches his hands into fists. His tail swishes back and forth.

The remaining coven members are being worked up into a highly excited state, everyone that is, except for Samuel and Aaron.

Aaron silently prays for help from his ancestors. He prays to hear his mother's voice. He feels powerless.

Kelley arrived with her father. They both are standing before Moloch. Kelley is no longer sobbing. She seems to have slipped into a trance. She is looking at the ground. Her mouth is half-open.

Moloch reaches down and takes her right hand into his own hands.

"Go," he says to Kelley's father.

Zombie like, Kelley's father walks back into the crowd. The crowd slowly moves closer.

Moloch picks up Kelley and lays her on the altar. He picks up the cup that still contains the Reverend's heart. He holds the cup high over his head. His lips move, as he speaks a silent chant.

There is rumbling from somewhere off in the distance.

Now Moloch sweeps his right hand through the air just a few inches above Kelley's body. As he does so her clothing disappears. She is now completely naked.

Coven members begin tearing their shrouds off. If they have any remaining clothes, they rip those off as well. Soon naked, they begin to dance and gyrate around the altar. Their bodies begin to transform into a combination of human and their own unique devil partner.

Aaron's mind is racing. Suddenly his mind takes him back to the time he spent in the barn, just a couple hundred yards from here. He remembers the hundreds of lost souls crying out for justice. Aaron's mind calls out to them. He begins speaking to them.

Moloch leans over Kelley's body. He licks her face with his long, snake like tongue.

Kelley's mind is frozen in terror.

She can smell Moloch's breath. It smells of death.

Moloch takes the Reverend's heart from the cup and drags its' bloody flesh across her chest as he traces the sign of the pentagram.

"Hear me now," roars Moloch. "O almighty Lucifer, Prince of Darkness, I, Moloch, your faithful servant will take this human unto me. We will be as one. As one, we shall then call you forth to join us this night, to join with your faithful servants so you may rule this earth."

Continuing, Moloch spoke, "The missing member of the coven we once had is with us now. His family once stood in the way long ago. Now returned, he is here to witness your arrival, to see the final covenant fulfilled and to be here at the birth of Armageddon."

Moloch tosses the Reverend's heart out into the crowd, which begins a small frenzy as people compete for a piece of the dead flesh.

Aaron looks at Korie and Miss Beacon who haven't dared to move. They aren't looking at him. They both seem riveted to the actions of Moloch.

Aaron's dialogue with the lost souls is nearly complete.

Moloch's body rises into the air, until he is hovering just above the altar. He then settles down, standing upon the altar. He kneels down facing Kelley. His body has developed hideous genitals. He lies completely upon her body. His immense size alone should crush her. Instead she feels no weight.

Kelley is now face to face with Moloch. His mouth is dripping a mucous like substance, which falls on her forehead. She wants desperately to scream, or better yet to die. Instead, all she is able to do is silently cry. Tears run down her cheeks and drip upon the altar.

The coven members are dancing around the altar, rubbing their naked bodies upon each other. Several members reach out and touch Moloch and Kelley. Judy moves over to Aaron and rubs her body against him.

Chucky moves over to the Miss Beacon and Korie and begins to do the same.

Moloch's body begins to press down upon Kelley. He has entered her. His body begins to pulsate between a black-green color to a red-green one. Then slowly his own, immense body begins to fade. Twirling lights begin to fill the air in place of where his form once was. The ground rumbles and shakes.

The crowd now chants "Moloch, Moloch, Moloch."

Kelley, once able to move, stretches her arms above her head.

Aaron is looking down at her. She opens her eyes and they are yellow as Moloch's eyes once were.

Her hands caress her body. She explores herself.

Aaron knows she is no longer Kelley, but a human vessel for Moloch.

Kelley sits up and then slides off the altar.

Samuel watches this transformation with keen interest. He was very proud of what he has been able to accomplish. He couldn't wait for Old Scratch's arrival so that Armageddon could begin. Samuel believes he will be called upon to play a prominent role in Satan's plans. His luck couldn't be better. His own devil partner, Upuaut, pushes to become manifested in Samuel's body. The transformation has begun.

Kelley walks towards Samuel. As she does, her skin's complexion begins to transform. It darkens, it becomes scaly. Her feet transform into hooves. Her body glistens and pulsates as the changing process continues.

"Dear Brother," said Kelley with a deep throaty hiss in her voice.

"Yes, Kelley, or Moloch or."

"You seem happy. Are you happy?"

"Oh, yes, yes."

"Are you two proud of yourselves?"

"Yes, we are. We were the only ones who could make this happen. Remember that many others had tried and failed. We were the only ones," they bragged.

"Then it seems you both should be rewarded," she hissed.

Kelley now had a serpent like tongue, which seemed to dart in and out of her mouth.

Kelley reaches out to her bother and his transforming body with her left hand. He reaches out for her. He was expecting an embrace.

She grabs Samuel by the throat. Her grip is powerful. It catches him by surprise. He gasps for air. None would be forthcoming.

With one powerful hand she lifts Samuel's body into the air. He begins kicking. His arms reach up and try to pry himself loose from his sister's grip. It is no use.

Kelley looks over at Aaron and smiles.

Aaron looks back at her and returns the smile.

"Put him down," says Aaron.

"You dare command me," answers Kelley.

"Yes."

"You pitiful human. You have nothing. You command nothing. You are too late to stop me."

"You're wrong. I am not alone, and I will stop you."

The coven members stop dancing. The crowd grows quiet. Korie and Miss Beacon watch Aaron intently.

Except for the "cracking" and "popping" sounds from the torches there is complete silence.

Samuel has by now turned blue. He has lost consciousness. He hangs limply from Kelley's outstretched arm.

Suddenly a wind picks up.

Kelley was not the cause of this wind. She turns her head to try to determine who or what was causing this.

Hundreds of distant voices are heard racing towards the clearing.

The crowd turns to look towards the trail road. Suddenly the specters of hundreds of souls appear. These souls appear in their original human form. It was the souls of all the people slain by the coven and other church members since that fateful night over a hundred and sixty years ago.

They're shouting. Their voices carried by the wind. It was unmistakable. They're here to demand justice.

Kelley drops her brother's body to the ground. His interrupted devolution into Upuaut was nearly complete. She runs to the altar and jumps up on it. She stands defiantly with her hands on her hips.

"How dare you come here to challenge me!"

"They aren't here to challenge you. They are here to defeat you," said Aaron.

"Grab him" commanded Kelley. The coven members began to move towards him.

Suddenly gunshots rang out. In rapid succession coven members fall to the ground, shot dead.

Kelley looks over and sees Korie with a smoking gun in her hand.

In a furious rage, Kelley extends her left hand at Korie and suddenly the gun flies from Korie's hand. Now on the ground, the gun turns white hot and melts away.

Kelley lifts her arm and Korie is lifted into the air.

Miss Beacon shouts at Kelley.

"Moloch, you are weak and a failure. How many times have you failed Lucifer?"

Angrily Kelley sweeps her right hand towards Miss Beacon who is suddenly picked up into the air and tossed backwards several feet. She lands on top of several church members, knocking them down in the process.

Aaron reaches out his own right hand. He is able to retrieve Korie as he lowers her back to the ground.

"I will destroy you," shouts Kelley.

"Your mission has failed." Gesturing to the souls he says, "They demand justice. They are here to bear witness to your failure."

"I will bring Lucifer," said Kelley.

"You will bring nothing. You are going to go back to hell where you belong. You will answer to Lucifer for your failure."

Kelley stretches out her two arms towards Aaron. A huge ball of hellfire flies towards him. He holds up his own hands and the fireball vaporizes.

Kelley jumps down from the altar and reaches her hands into the air above her head. She flings them towards Aaron. Lightning bolts crackle as they erratically fly from her hands towards Aaron.

Once again, he raises his own hands and these lightning bolts rebound off of him back towards Kelley. The lightning misses her and explodes into the ground.

The crowd begins to back away.

"To hell," shouted many of the souls "Send him back," shout others.

"Kelley, listen to my voice," said Aaron.

"You wish to speak to Kelley," bellows Moloch. "There is no Kelley."

"Yes, there is. Kelley together we can cast him out."

Kelley now rushes towards Aaron. It is clear her intent is to get her hands on him, to kill him.

He raises his right hand and signals the sign of the cross in the air in front of him.

Kelley stops, cringing at this gesture.

"I call upon all of the saints, the angels and archangels, God's faithful and the Holy Trinity. It is they who now command you to leave this woman."

Kelley throws up her arms as if to ward off his words.

"Get away from her. Leave her body and spirit now. We command you to go."

"I'm not leaving. She's mine. Together we will bring forth Lucifer," said Kelley with less conviction than before.

Aaron steps towards her. She backs away. He moves still closer. She continues to retreat. Suddenly he reaches out to her. He places his right hand on her head. A huge explosion of light bursts out from under his palm.

Moloch lets out a huge cry, "No!"

"By all the power of goodness, by all that is holy, we the faithful hereby call upon Christ our Savior, the Holy Spirit, and God the Creator, in their name we now command you to go. Leave this person, leave this place. Return to the eternity of damnation that is your place."

Kelley's body begins to shake. Her entire body flashes back and forth from that of a young woman to one possessed by Moloch.

The ground shakes.

Suddenly Kelley's mouth opens and a twirling series of lights swirl out of her into the air.

Her body falls limply to the ground. She begins to evolve back into human form. Meanwhile the twirling lights explode into the air. Now standing over Aaron and Kelley is the ever-menacing Moloch.

Aaron turns and steps between Moloch and Kelley.

Moloch glares at Aaron. His snake like tongue flicks the air.

The two stare at each other.

Aaron reaches up and joins his hands in a prayerful clasp. He then opens his hands, and faces his palms towards Moloch. From his palms moves a bluish light which spreads out in front of him. This light appears to be composed of hundreds of tiny hands, all facing Moloch palm side forward. As these hands reach Moloch, his figure suddenly implodes. Moloch is now vanquished.

Korie runs to Aaron and throws her arms around him. She kisses him several times.

Kelley stands up and is fully clothed, as she was when she first arrived. She also runs over and hugs Aaron and Korie.

"Miss Beacon!" said Aaron.

The three of them turn and search the crowd for her. She is nowhere to be seen.

Many in the crowd are walking around holding their heads.

"What happened" says one. "What are we doing up here?" said another.

Samuel's body twists and cavorts on the ground as his evil spirit struggles to extricate itself from his body. He moans softly.

Kelley and Korie both go to him.

Kneeling next to him Kelley strokes his hair.

"Are you okay?" she asks.

He reaches up and touches his throat. It's still very tender.

"Ouch," he says.

"Samuel, say something!" said Kelley.

"Don't call me Samuel. You know I hate that. Where are we anyway?"

Kelley looks at Korie and they both smile.

Aaron continues to look for Miss Beacon. It seems she has disappeared. Aaron noticed the souls, the source of his righteous power had also vanished as well.

People began to drift to the trail road to leave the mountain.

Aaron knew his work wasn't quite done. The members of the coven are collapsed on the ground. Their bodies are trapped in a half-transformed state. One by one he approaches each coven member, reaching out to them, as he had with Moloch just moments before. The same bluish light and tiny hands push out towards the coven members. Soon the member's bodies give up their fiendish hell mates. The coven member's clothes reappear as well. One by one they regain consciousness and stand up. Soon they also begin to leave the clearing.

He couldn't do anything for Ed, the Judge or the Reverend. Their fates were well beyond his reach.

Aaron walks over towards the woods next to the changing tent. Just beyond was the cemetery of his ancestors. He went and stood next to the wrought iron gate. Standing just inside the gate is Aaron's mother. Behind her is Aaron's grandmother and so on. They all approach the gate. One by one they reach across and hug him.

His mother hugs him last. She reaches up and caresses his head with her hands, then she pulls him to her and she kisses him on the forehead. When he raises his head up he notices that they are all gone.

Sadly he turns back towards the clearing.

Aaron heads over to Kelley, Korie and Sammy. Together they leave the clearing and head back down the mountain.

***

The front door to Mojo's is open. Aaron and Korie step inside. Aaron pays the attendant the required cover charge. In a moment, a young man comes up to them and escorts them to a table for two on the left side of the room. A house band is playing a Junior Wells blues classic called *Messin' with the Kid*.

Aaron and Korie sit down. In a moment a young woman comes by and asks, "Can I get you folks something to drink?"

"Sure, I'll have a Green Slime," said Aaron.

"I'll have Sex on the Beach," said Korie.

"Are you guys sure these are real drinks?" asked the woman.

"Trust us," said Korie.

"Okay," said the waitress as she turns and heads over to the bar.

"I like this place," said Aaron.

"Yeah, me too," said Korie. "I'm glad we decided to come back."

Just then someone slapped Aaron on the back.

"Hey man, how're doin?" asked a familiar voice.

Aaron turned around and recognized the club's owner, Ron.

"We're doing fine, just fine."

"That's cool. Say, you know the last time you two were here?"

"Yeah," said Aaron.

"Do you remember a crazy son of a bitch looking to get his hands on you?"

"Yeah."

"Mean bastard."

"You could say that."

"He tried messin' with me. I knew I couldn't stop him but I tried to slow him up for you guys."

"You did good."

"Really?"

"Yeah," said Aaron.

"Is he still after you?"

"No. Let's just say that he won't be bothering anyone anymore."

"I see!" said Ron.

"Everything's cool. Just Cool!" said Aaron.

The house band announced their next song. It was a song written by Bono, from the band U2, for B.B. King. The song's title is *When Love Comes to Town*.

The band began to play.

"You guys going to be staying in town for long?" asked Ron.

"Don't know yet," said Aaron.

"Well, you're always welcome. Would you like to see my new Fender Strat? It once belonged to Albert King."

Korie looked over at Aaron. She reached across the table and touched his hand and said, "You two go on. I'll be okay, really."

Aaron pushed himself away from the table and stood up. He and Ron began to head back stage. The waitress arrived with their drinks.

Aaron looked back at the table and spoke up, "Hey, Angel, put that table on my tab."

The waitress nodded as she put the two drinks down on the table.

"Did he just call you Angel?" asked Korie.

"Yeah" said the waitress. It's my name, see," she said as she showed her nametag to Korie.

Korie looked at the nametag and sure enough it said, "Angel."

"Today's my first day."

"Uh-huh," said Korie as she looked into the waitress' eyes.

For a brief moment they looked at each other.

Korie smiled and then Angel, the waitress, smiled as well.

"Well, Angel, good luck with the job."

"Thanks," she responded. "If it's okay, I'll come back in a little while, for your dinner order."

"Sure."

The waitress turned and left.

Korie watched her walk away.

Aaron and Ron were heading back to their table. Ron was carrying a guitar and Aaron was toting a bass guitar.

Korie smiled at the sight of those two bluesmen wannabees.

She turned and looked across the room and noticed that Angel was watching, too.

***

It was an extremely humid night in the jungle. The daytime temperature had been over one hundred degrees. While the nighttime temperature had fallen to below seventy-five degrees, the humidity still remained.

Under lamplight, a man was mixing certain 'over the counter' chemicals, along with number two fuel oil, in a large blue plastic thirty gallon barrel. He slowly stirred the mix. He was mixing homemade explosives for a bomb he was building.

Several other men were huddled nearby over a large map, which was unfolded over the hood of a beat up old Toyota pickup truck. They were busy discussing their plans.

These men were part of the Cinque Liberos, a so-called people's revolutionary army, seeking to overthrow the government of Columbia. Ever since the U.S. Government had aided in the Colombian Army's coup of their government, the new military government had been able to wage a successful campaign against the drug lords. The drug lords had been striking back with a fury.

Assassinations and bombings had been going on nearly non-stop for over a year.

The U.S. was sending its top law enforcement official, General Francis Templeton, Drug Czar, to Columbia to meet with the Colombian President, as a show of solidarity with the struggles of the new Columbian government. The terrorists had learned of this meeting and were planning to set off several bombs at the meeting site.

One of the men looking over the map said, "I would kiss the ass of the devil himself to be sure that our plans would succeed."

"Yeah, me, too," said another.

The other men nodded their agreement.

"Maybe I could be of some assistance," said the voice of a stranger who stepped out of the darkness.

In an instant, all the men drew their guns.

The man mixing the explosives didn't. He was too busy praying that bullets didn't start flying, not while he was standing next to the explosives.

"Who are you?" demanded one of the men.

"My name is Moloch."

Acknowledgments

I have received support and encouragement from so many people. Where does one begin? For me, it begins with my parents, Reginald and Rose Hatin, who encouraged me to read anything and everything. They instilled in me a willingness to dream, to take risks and to embrace a mantra that "nothing is impossible." My very best friend and wife, Anne, has always shared my passion for reading and writing and is always the first to read and critique my writing. She faithfully gives me a "readers" perspective.

My oldest son R. Joel Hatin is a talented computer expert who is responsible for the design of my website www.richardhatin.com. He will also serve as my expert on all things, "social media." My second son Aaron Hatin designs all the covers for my novels and is in his own right a gifted and talented computer and video artist. My youngest son Brady Hatin is a very creative and talented man who has introduced me to new things in art and literature which challenge and motivates me. Thanks guys!

I also need to thank Liz Thomas who has volunteered to read my material and has lent a critical eye when necessary.

I also need to thank the dozens of friends, family and neighbors who have volunteered their time to read drafts of my novels. Their feedback and encouragement has provided me with needed fuel, that I drawn upon, as I continue to write.

I also wish to thank Lisa Kimball, who got everything rolling for me by introducing me to her friend, Tim Packman, an accomplished and recognized writer of family friendly books. Tim listened to my story about struggling to get published and offered his own excellent advice and encouragement. He introduced me to Cathy Teets, President of Headline Books. Cathy listened to my "pitch" and took a chance on me by considering samples of my work. I owe a big thank you to Cathy and her staff for all that they have done on my behalf.